Dychweler erbyn y dyddiad olaf uchod
Please return by the last date shown

LLYFRGELLOEDD POWYS LIBRARIES

www.powys.gov.uk/llyfrgell
www.powys.gov.uk/library

THE SPARSHOLT AFFAIR

ALSO BY ALAN HOLLINGHURST

The Swimming-Pool Library

The Folding Star

The Spell

The Line of Beauty

The Stranger's Child

ALAN HOLLINGHURST

THE SPARSHOLT AFFAIR

PICADOR

First published 2017 by Picador
an imprint of Pan Macmillan
20 New Wharf Road, London N1 9RR
Associated companies throughout the world
www.panmacmillan.com

ISBN 978-1-4472-0821-1

1 3 5 7 9 8 6 4 2

A CIP catalogue record for this book is available from the British Library.

Typeset by Palimpsest Book Production Ltd, Falkirk, Stirlingshire
Printed and bound by CPI Group (UK) Ltd, Croydon, CR0 4YY

For Stephen Pickles

ONE

A New Man

1

The evening when we first heard Sparsholt's name seems the best place to start this little memoir. We were up in my rooms, talking about the Club. Peter Coyle, the painter, was there, and Charlie Farmonger, and Evert Dax. A sort of vote had taken place, and I had emerged as the secretary. I was the oldest by a year, and as I was exempt from service I did nothing but read. Evert said, 'Oh, Freddie reads two books a day,' which may have been true; I protested that my rate was slower if the books were in Italian, or Russian. That was my role, and I played it with the supercilious aplomb of a student actor. The whole purpose of the Club was getting well-known writers to come and speak to us, and read aloud from their latest work; we offered them a decent dinner, in those days a risky promise, and after dinner a panelled room packed full of keen young readers – a provision we were rather more certain of. When the bombing began people wanted to know what the writers were thinking.

Now Charlie suggested Orwell, and one or two names we had failed to net last year did the rounds again. Might Stephen Spender come, or Rebecca West? Nancy Kent was already lined up, to talk to us about Spain. Evert in his impractical way mentioned Auden, who was in New York, and unlikely to return while the War was on. ('Good riddance too,' said Charlie.) It was Peter who said, surely knowing how Evert was hoping he wouldn't, 'Well, why don't we get Dax to ask Victor?' The world knew Evert's father as A. V. Dax, but we claimed this vicarious intimacy.

Evert had already slipped away towards the window, and stood there peering into the quad. There was always some tension between him and Peter, who liked to provoke and even embarrass his friends. 'Oh, I'm not sure about that,' said Evert, over his shoulder. 'Things are rather difficult at present.'

'Well, so they are for everyone,' said Charlie.

Evert politely agreed with this, though his parents remained in London, where a bomb had brought down the church at the end of their street a few nights before. He said, rather wildly, 'I just worry that no one would turn up.'

'Oh, they'd turn up, all right,' said Charlie, with an odd smile.

Evert looked round, he appealed to me – 'I mean, what do you make of it, the new one?'

I had *The Gift of Hermes* face down on the arm of my chair, about halfway through, and though not exactly stuck I was already alternating it with something else. It was going to break my daily rhythm, and was indeed rather like tackling a book in a foreign language. Even on the wretched thin paper of the time it was a thick volume. I said, 'Well, I'm a great admirer, as you know.'

'Oh, well, me too,' said Peter, after a moment, but more warmly; he was a true fan of A. V. Dax's large symbolic novels, admiring their painterly qualities, their peculiar atmospheres and colours, and their complex psychology. 'I'm taking the new one slowly,' he admitted, 'but of course, it's a great book.'

'Any jokes in it?' said Charlie, with a hollow laugh.

'That's never quite the point,' I said, 'with a Dax novel.'

'Anyway, haven't you read it?' said Peter, going over to the window to see what Evert was looking at.

Poor Evert, as I knew, had never read more than the opening pages of any of his father's books. 'I just can't,' he said again now, 'I don't know why' – and seeing Peter join him he turned back into the room with a regretful look.

After a moment Peter said, 'Good grief . . . did you see this, Dax?'

'Oh . . . what's that . . . ?' said Evert, and I was slow to tell the new confusion from the other.

'Freddie, have you seen this man?'

'Who is it?' I went across. 'Oh, the exhibitionist, I suppose you mean,' I said.

'No, he's gone . . .' said Peter, still staring out. I stood at his shoulder and stared too. It was that brief time between sunset and the blackout when you could see into other people's rooms. Tall panes which had reflected the sky all day now glowed companionably here and there, and figures were revealed at work, or moving around behind the lit grid of the sashes. In the set directly opposite, old Sangster, the blind French don, was giving a tutorial to a young man so supine that he might have been asleep. And on the floor above, beneath the dark horizontal of the cornice and the broad pediment, a single window was alight, a lamp on the desk projecting a brilliant arc across the wall and ceiling.

'I spotted him the other day,' I said. 'He must be one of the new men.' Peter waited, with pretended patience; and Evert, frowning still, came back and looked out as well. Now a rhythmical shadow had started to leap and shrink across the distant ceiling.

'Oh, yes, him,' Evert said, as the source of the shadow moved slowly into view, a figure in a gleaming singlet, steadily lifting and lowering a pair of hand-weights. He did so with concentration though with no apparent effort – but of course it was hard to tell at this distance, from which he showed, in his square of light, as massive and abstracted, as if shaped from light himself. Peter put his hand on my arm.

'My dear,' he said, 'I seem to have found my new model.' At which Evert made a little gasp, and looked at him furiously for a second.

'Well, you'd better get a move on,' I said, since these days new men left as quickly and unnoticed as they came.

'Even you must admire that glorious head, like a Roman gladiator, Freddie,' said Peter, 'and those powerful shoulders, do you see the blue veins standing in the upper arms?'

'Not without my telescope,' I said.

I went to fill the kettle from the tap on the landing and found Jill Darrow coming up the stairs; she was late for the meeting at which she might have liked to vote herself. I was very glad to see her, but the atmosphere, which had taken on a hint of deviancy, rather changed when she came into the room. She hadn't had the benefit of ten years in a boys' boarding school, with all its ingrained depravities; I doubt she'd ever seen a naked man. Charlie said, 'Ah, Darrow,' and half stood up, then dropped back into his chair with an informality that might or might not have been flattering. 'We want Dax to ask his father,' he said, as she removed her coat, and took in who was there. I set about making the tea.

'Oh, I see,' said Jill. There was a natural uncertainty in Evert's presence as to what could be said about A. V. Dax.

At the window Evert himself seemed not to know she had come in. He and Peter stood staring up at the room opposite. Their backs were expressive, Peter smaller, hair thick and temperamental, in the patched tweed jacket which always gave off dim chemical odours of the studio; Evert neat and hesitant, a strictly raised boy in an unusually good suit who seemed to gaze at pleasure as at the far bank of a river. 'What are you two staring at?' Jill said.

'You mustn't look,' said Peter, turning and grinning at her. At which she went straight to the window, myself close behind. The gladiator was still in view, though now with his back turned, and doing something with a piece of rope. I was almost relieved to see that the scouts had started their rounds. At one window, and then the next, a small black-coated figure appeared, reached up to close the shutters, and removed all sign of life. Across the way the scout came into Sangster's room, half-hidden by the oblong screen he carried through into the bedroom, and after a minute reappeared, edged round the two occupants, and kneeling on the window seat gazed out for a curious few seconds before pulling the tall shutters to. By dinner time the great stone buildings would be lightless as ruins.

'Ah, Phil,' said Charlie – behind us my own scout had come in to do the same for us.

I said sternly, 'Do you know who this fellow is, Phil?'

Phil had fought at the Battle of Loos, and after that earlier war had spent fifteen years in the Oxford police. He was affable and devoted to the College, but seemed sometimes to regret that he'd ended up in an apron, dusting and washing dishes for young men he was powerless to discipline. 'What was it, sir?' He propped his screen against the wall, and came over eagerly, as if I'd spotted a miscreant. I noticed now that our own reflections were hanging very faintly between us and the view of other windows. I pointed upwards.

'This . . . ridiculous fellow,' I said.

'Oh, him, sir,' said Phil, a bit disappointed but trying for a moment to share our own interest in the luminous figure. 'I happen to know there was a bit of trouble there.'

'What sort of trouble?' said Peter.

'Well, the noise, sir. Dr Sangster's been complaining about it.'

'Oh . . . ?' said Evert. 'Noise . . . ?'

'Rhythmical creaking, apparently, sir,' said Phil, with a grim look.

'Oh, goodness . . .' said Evert.

'He's not one of ours, though, in fact,' said Phil.

'Ah,' I said.

'No, he's one of the Brasenose men,' said Phil. In the vast gloomy College, its staircases half-deserted since the start of the War, new members of requisitioned colleges had been slipped

7

in here and there, disoriented freshmen who found themselves also evacuees. Brasenose had been seized by a ministry of some kind, who according to my tutor were rather unsure what to do with it. 'If you could just excuse me, Mr Green?'

'Of course, Phil.'

'You don't happen to know his name?' said Jill.

'He's called Sparsholt, miss,' said Phil, with a small cough as he swung the shutters to and dropped the iron bar safely in its slot.

'*Spar . . . sholt*,' said Peter, weighing the word and smiling slyly at Evert. 'Sounds like part of an engine, or a gun.'

Phil looked at him blankly for a second or two. 'I dare say you're right, sir,' he said, and went through into the bedroom. I set out my best Meissen cups, which I hoped might please Jill, and in the new closeness of the panelled and shuttered room we settled down to have tea.

Jill stayed on, as my guest, for dinner in Hall, and afterwards I went down to the gate with her. 'I'll see you back,' I said. She was at St Hilda's, a fifteen-minute walk away, but in the black-out a bit more of a challenge.

'There's absolutely no need,' she said.

'No, no, take my arm' – which she did, touchingly enough. We set off – I held the taped-over torch which, with her elbow squeezed snugly against my side, we seemed to turn and point together. Even so, I sensed some reluctance in her. In a minute she freed herself to put on her gloves, and we went on like that past the tall railings of Merton, the great bulk of its chapel and tower sensed more than seen above us in the night. Jill glanced upwards. The darkness seemed to insinuate something between us, and though I think she was glad of my company it was awkwardly as though she had agreed to something. As I knew, it could be easier, once your eyes had adjusted, to walk without the startlements of the torch. Oddly, you moved with more confidence. All the same, we spoke nearly in whispers, as though we might be overheard. Often on those nights you did brush suddenly against other people passing or waiting entirely unseen.

Now the lane was a little black canyon, its gabled and chimneyed rim just visible to us against the deep charcoal of the sky. Clouds, in peacetime, carried and dispersed the colours of the lights below, but in the blackout an unmediated darkness reigned. I thought I knew this street I'd walked along a hundred times, but memory seemed not quite to match the dim evidence of doorways, windows, railings that we passed. I asked Jill about her work, and she at once grew less self-conscious. She was reading History, but her interests were in archaeology, and in the remarkable things revealed by the London Blitz. She explained how bombs that knocked down City churches sometimes cut through the layers below, Tudor, medieval, Roman, exposing them in ways no organized human effort could have done. The human aspects of the devastation, the loss of life and home, clearly struck her rather less. She spoke excitedly about coins, coffins, bricks, fragments of pottery. I said it must be frustrating for her that Oxford itself had barely been damaged, and watched, if one can watch in the dark, her recognition, and disposal, of a joke. From the start she'd been one of those who pass through student life with their eyes set firmly on the future: it was an urgent process, not a beautiful delay. Now the future for all of us had changed, the town pervaded by a mood of transience, and of near-readiness for action which it never saw. Did other friends share my feeling we might lose the War, and soon? – defeatist talk was rare, and censored itself as it began. Jill had made her choice, for the army, but her mind was on the great things she would do once the War was won.

At the gate of St Hilda's I stood half-illuminating our parting. 'Good night then,' I said, with a humorous tremor.

Jill seemed to look over my shoulder. 'I wonder if Peter will paint that man.'

I turned. 'Who's that?'

'The new man,' she said, 'Sparsholt.'

'Oh, him.' I laughed. 'Well, Peter generally gets what he wants.'

'A good subject, anyway, I'd have thought,' said Jill, and we shook hands. It wasn't what I'd hoped for, and as I walked alone across the bridge, and then once more down Merton Lane, I worried at my own timidity and planned more confident advances when we met next time. I turned her face to mine, and found beauty in its symmetry. She had grey eyes, the strong chin of a Wagnerian soprano, and small white teeth. She gave off, close to, a tantalizing scent. For the moment, this would have to do.

2

Evert wrote to his father, and came round a few days later to say that our invitation had been accepted: Victor Dax would be more than happy to address the Club. The great man's letter was short and virtually illegible; the notepaper was headed with a murky crest and the motto 'Montez Toujours'. 'We'll put him down for fifth week, shall we?' – I smiled confidently and started to feel nervous myself about whether people would come.

Evert was still in khaki, having spent the past hour or so being marched back and forth along the great stone terraces of Tom Quad by old Edmund Blunden. I mean Blunden seemed old to us, when he came in to teach drill or to take the reluctant volunteers out on map-reading courses, though in fact he was still in his forties, a small bird-like figure with shadowy reserves of knowledge. I almost envied them their forays out to Cumnor Hill or Newnham Courtenay, overlaid, as I saw them, on a spectral map of the earlier war he had witnessed and written about. But Evert hated it all, and looked wretched in uniform; he marched, on the couple of times I'd seen him training, with an air of slighted dignity, close to insubordination.

He sat down and picked up a book with a just perceptible awareness of becoming a regular guest in my rooms. We had known each other a little in his first year, and now that all the friends he'd made then had been called up he clearly felt lonely. No doubt he dreaded the fast-approaching moment when he would be called up himself. There was something unsettled about him, his pale, dark-eyed face under its tumbling forelock gave hints of feelings that he rarely expressed. To me he had all his own interest, and then the glamour, and the burden, of his short but famous name. It had always been a part of his appeal to me that he was A. V. Dax's son; just as it was a sign of our friendship that I half-forgot the fact. To him it was a knottier and more inescapable matter. He sighed and put the book down, and showed me another letter, from his mother – I gathered that his parents, though still together in their house in Chelsea, led semi-independent lives, but I didn't feel I could ask more. It wasn't clear how much Evert himself understood of the situation. His mother's letter described the terrors of the Blitz in a cheerfully carping way. She said that his father had laughed when she'd flung herself on to the ground as a bomb came down, and ruined a good coat; he himself refused to go into the shelters with the ordinary people.

Evert got up to go, and said, 'Oh, by the way, have you seen any more of . . . what was his name?'

'Who was that?' I said.

'*Sparsholt*, was it, the new man?' He went to look out but it was only three o'clock and the long row of top-floor windows was opaque. Neither of us was exactly sure now which window it had been, and this year many rooms were uninhabited and locked up.

'Well, I think I saw him in Hall,' I said cautiously.

'Oh, I know,' said Evert. 'He sits at the rowers' table. They've put all the Eights together. It's enough to make you take up rowing – not Sparsholt, I mean, but all the extra food they get.' He blushed but the subject was fairly clear between us; I saw him deciding to say more. It turned out that the moment in my rooms in first week had not been his first sighting of Sparsholt. He had seen him before, jogging back from the river in his rowing kit, he had seen him in Hall, and late one night he had failed to see him, colliding with him in near darkness at the corner of Kilcannon. But the vision from my window, of Sparsholt half-naked in his square of light, had been the turning point, when interest roused by these random sightings had thickened into an obsession. I struggled slightly to understand it. It was as if he had willed his own submission, which assumed, as the minutes passed, a luxurious inevitability. He knew nothing about this young man, but at that moment he had given himself up to him. Or, as he put it, he had fallen in love.

'And have you spoken to him?' I asked.

Evert was almost shocked. 'Well, when he bumped into me,' he said, 'but not since . . . no, no.'

Peter Coyle, as I expected, had been much bolder, and had at once written Sparsholt a letter, on the Slade School's paper, asking if he could draw his portrait. There had been no reply, though I felt, two nights later in Hall, when I took a place facing the rowers' table, that there was something subtly self-conscious about Sparsholt, a first uneasy suspicion, in his stern young face and his upright aloofness, that he might be being watched, or have turned already, in this place that was so new to him, into the subject of a rumour. Whether he noticed me, or Evert casting keen almost terrified glances in his direction, I rather doubt. He seemed to look at us as an undifferentiated and still alien mass. After Hall he quickly left his fellow diners, and I thought how easily I could have called out to him as we moved with our separate flashlights through the darkened quads.

It was perfectly easy to find out more about him. In the Lodge next day I saw from the Boat Club notices that his initials were D. D., and from a tutorial list that he was an Engineer. These first meagre scraps were somehow discouraging: scientists and rowers moved in their own severe routines, set apart from the rest of us. But the fact of Sparsholt's instant appeal to Peter and Evert invested him, even so, with a faint if puzzling glamour. To me there was something unyielding in his surname, a word like a machine part, as Peter said, or a small hard sample, perhaps, of some mineral ore; but now I was curious about the D. D.

As it happened I stole a march on my two friends. Each morning Phil came in about seven to open the shutters and clean up my sitting room, while I as a rule still lay in bed, drowsing and dreaming to the squeak of casters and the to-and-fro noise of the carpet sweeper next door. He would lay the fire, and take out the china and glass to be washed up. When that was all done he would knock and open my bedroom door in one swift movement, with a policeman's instinct for surprise. I would then emerge in my dressing gown on to a stage set exactly restored in the interval – 'The Same. The Following Morning'.

Today as I waited for the kettle to boil I gazed out gratefully into the quad. There was a heightened sense of relief then, even in Oxford, at having come through the night unscathed. The lights that showed palely again at the windows as the scouts went round were cheering signals of survival. I watched the figures who emerged, in overcoats and slippers, to make their way to distant bathrooms. There were fewer people now, of course, and most I knew only by sight, but we were joined together in a manner that we had not been when I first came up, before the War. I was about to turn away when I realized that the person leaving the first line of footsteps across the wet lawn below was Sparsholt himself, striding out in pyjamas, a blue dressing gown and brown walking shoes, with a towel slung round his neck like a scarf. He gave off a sense of military indifference to the chilly morning as he swiftly disappeared from view.

Normally I shaved after breakfast, when no one was around, but this morning I seemed barely to take the decision to follow him. I put on my coat and the Homburg hat I had lately affected, and trotted downstairs, thinking of what I would be able to tell Evert over our porridge and tea. It was the comedy of competition that tickled me, rather than any intrinsic interest in the man I had decided to speak to.

I generally avoided the big subterranean bathroom in the next quad, with its rows of washbasins and maze of cubicles, no locks on the doors. I remembered the uneasy sensation there of being naked and alone, in my steam-filled partition, knowing others were lying almost silently around me. Sometimes someone would ask who was there, and a conversation would start, as if on the telephone, and slightly constrained by the presence of the rest of us, closed more silently still in our own cubicles. When I first came up I'd been told by my half-brother Gerald that it was the best place in College for a long soak, by which I suspect he meant something more. It was taken over at certain times by the muddied and bloodied rugby team, the exhausted rowers, who recovered and stretched in tender self-inspection among densities of steam, a great naked mixing and gathering. They threatened no danger, I went quite unnoticed there, but I knew I was out of my element.

When I came in, Sparsholt had just started shaving, and glanced at me with a second's curiosity in the mirror. I confess I felt a jolt of excitement at being in his presence. He was wearing nothing but his pyjama bottoms and his walking shoes, the laces undone. Now I saw his muscular upper body close to, revealed with casual pride. I hung up my coat and hat and went to the basin two along. 'Good morning!' I said. He turned his head, razor raised, and said, 'Morning!' – more cheerfully than I'd expected: I could tell he was glad to be spoken to. There was a splosh or two from a nearby cubicle, but the cavernous room had a desolate air. He took a stripe of lather off his jaw, and then another, and while I drew hot water I watched discreetly as his face emerged. I felt I hardly knew what it would look like.

'I haven't seen you before,' he said – again more in welcome than suspicion, looking across and smiling for a moment. His good strong teeth showed yellow in the square of white foam round his mouth.

'Oh – I'm Freddie Green,' I said. He set down his razor on the edge of the basin and reached out a hand:

'David Sparsholt.'

'Sparsholt?' I said, absorbing the 'David', to me the most guileless and straightforward of all the Ds. I saw that he was very young, under the pale armour of his muscles. His wrist was streaked with wet hairs but his chest and stomach were quite smooth. 'It's an unusual name.'

He blinked as if sensing criticism. 'Well, we're from War-wickshire,' he said – and there was a mild regional colouring I would never have been skilled enough to place. I didn't press him further, and in a minute he splashed fresh water over his face and dried himself roughly. As I began to shave I peeped across in a friendly way. He pushed his head to left and right as he inspected his jaw in the mirror, with the businesslike vanity I had rather expected: he seemed pleased enough with what he saw. Was he good-looking? I hardly knew. To me a man is good-looking if he is well dressed; and since Sparsholt was hardly dressed at all I was rather at a loss. It was a broad face with a slightly curved nose and blue-grey eyes set deep under a strong brow. His hair was clipped short above the ears; short, but dark and curly, on top. It was his physique, of course, that was more remarkable, and I could see why Peter would want him as a model; quite what Evert hoped to do with him I didn't try to imagine. 'Which force are you signed up with?' he said.

I explained to him about my condition, and my permanent exemption from military service; and as I did so I saw a first puzzlement in his eyes.

'That's bad luck,' he said – but the condolence hid a murmur of mistrust. He looked narrowly at me, in my vest, and then perhaps took pity on me. He seemed to play, like other physically powerful men I've known, with a small, barely conscious, instinct to threaten, as well as to reassure and even to protect. 'What will you do?'

'Well, I'm doing the third year, history, you know, a full degree. Then we'll see. Which service are you?'

He had his towel round his neck again now, his hands on his hips, feet apart. There was a careless glimpse of his sex in the open slit of his pyjamas. 'Royal Air Force,' he said, 'yes, I'll be learning to fly.' His narrow smile was again slightly challenging.

'Wonderful,' I said. And sensing some further approval was due: 'I can see you do a lot of exercise' – not liking to say I'd watched him at it, and thinking even so I sounded rather eager; but he smiled acceptingly.

'Well, you've got to be ready, haven't you,' he said. It was clear that the morbid uncertainty about the future that permeated most of our lives throughout these years had no effect on him. He was looking forward to it. 'I'm eighteen in January – I'll be signing up then.' And he went through his plan for me, in the way that a person nagged by anxiety will, though in his case I saw only the purposeful alertness of the born soldier. I said I was surprised he'd bothered to come up to Oxford for just one term. But he'd got in, and after the War he would come back – he had that planned too. He would get a degree, and then he would go home again and set up a firm, an engineering business. 'Well, they'll always be in demand,' he said.

The door of the occupied cubicle opened, and Das, the one Indian man in College, came out, wrapped in a towel and holding his glasses, which he was quickly wiping clean with a discarded sock. He looked with a kind of baffled keenness at Sparsholt, who had evidently encountered him before, and who took the opportunity to pull on his dressing gown and leave. 'I hope I'll bump into you again,' I said, as I heard the thump of the door. Das, who had now got his glasses back on, looked almost accusingly at me.

'Is that young gentleman your friend, Green?' he said.

'Mm?' I said, but testing the new possibility, and my feelings about it.

'He is like a Greek god!'

'Oh, do you think . . . ?'

'But arrogant, very much so.'

I rinsed my razor under the tap. 'I rather imagine the Greek gods were too,' I said. I began to see that Sparsholt's effect might be larger than I'd thought.

3

When Evert came to my rooms a few days later he was in uniform again, but I had a feeling he was changing his mind about it. He drooped and sprawled mutinously as usual when muffled in the styleless khaki, but now and then he straightened up; he set his shoulders back when he stood in front of the fire, as if the soldier's role might just be worth playing after all. 'How's Jill?' he said.

'Jill's very well,' I said.

'You seem to be seeing quite a lot of her.'

In fact I hadn't seen her since our night-time walk over the bridge to St Hilda's, and my note in the college mail had got the cryptic reply 'Henry III!' – an essay crisis, I assumed. 'I think we like each other,' I said. Evert started to roam around. I'd left my diary open on my desk, and I saw it distract his attention for a moment as he spoke:

'By the way, I took your advice about the bathroom.'

'I don't know that it was advice,' I said.

He came and sat on the sofa. 'Actually I thought I'd missed him, though I trekked over at first light. You notice how well I've shaved.'

'I noticed a nick under your chin.'

'That marks the moment when he finally emerged – he must have been in the bath for hours. He was just in a towel.' Evert smiled painfully through his blush. He'd spoken to him, and it seemed they'd had a brief conversation. He said it had gone very well in fact, and sat rather solemnly picturing it all, before getting up again to glance out across the quad.

'I don't know,' I said, 'I hope Sparsholt won't grow suspicious about these bathroom encounters.'

'You mean, you feel it's all right for you to encounter him, but not for anyone else?' I saw this was actually my view about various matters. 'You're not interested in him anyway!' said Evert; and then, quite suspicious for a second, 'Or are you?'

I said, 'I've developed an interest in him purely as the focus of your interest. Yours and Peter's,' I added, and watched him scowl. 'I'm following the whole Sparsholt affair scientifically.'

'I'd hardly call it an affair,' Evert said; and then, 'Why, what's Coyle been up to?'

'No idea. I think no news from him is good news for you. We'll certainly hear all about it if anything happens.'

Poor Evert looked haggard at the thought of his rival spending whole hours alone with Sparsholt, with the licence to stare at him and move him around, to ponder at leisure the nakedness he had glimpsed for a mere second, and all the while, in the semi-abstracted way of the artist, to draw him out about his past, his thoughts and his feelings. I wondered though whether Peter's flamboyance would alarm him. It was all a test, in a way, of Sparsholt's innocence. Was he still, as a freshman from another college, glad of any friendly attention? Was he even aware that his hours with the weights and clubs had made him, to a certain kind of person, an object of desire? It was one of those questions of masculine vanity hard even to formulate and impossible to put directly to the man himself.

I said, 'I expect you'd like a glass of port.' As it happened an affair of a very different kind had just begun in my own life, though I wasn't able to speak of it yet, even to someone who showed such trust in me. The bottle of port was related to it.

'Where did you get it from?' Evert said, seeing how ancient and expensive it was.

'It was given to me by my aunt,' I said.

'I didn't know you had an aunt,' said Evert.

'Almost everyone has,' I said, 'if you look into it.' I scraped at the blackened seal with my penknife. 'She's just moved to Woodstock – I went to see her yesterday on the bus.' Evert didn't really take this in.

'I've got an aunt by marriage,' he said. 'She's stuck in The Hague now, poor old thing.' His family were a source of worry to him of a kind I was spared; my father, twice married, had died when I was ten, and my widowed mother dwelt in the depths of Devonshire; Woodstock I felt was a fairly safe spot for an aunt. I tugged out the cork and poured him a good glassful.

'To victory, Evert,' I said.

'Oh, yes . . .' he said, though there was something further, which he seemed reluctant to come round to. It emerged in a while, under the prompting of the port, and when it did it threw the most withering light on his whole situation. 'The thing is, there's a woman,' he said, not looking at me: perhaps he thought I would laugh, or say (what I said only to myself), 'Well, of course there is.'

'Have you seen her?'

'No, thank God, but she took up a lot of the conversation.'

'You talked quite a bit, then.'

'Well, I didn't want to let him go.'

'Who is she, did you gather?'

'The ghastly thing is that she's coming to Oxford. To live here, I mean.'

'I expect she wants to be near David,' I said.

Evert glared at me. 'She's going to be very near indeed. As near as she can be. They're engaged to be married.'

'That does sound a bit rash,' I said, more tactfully. 'He's very young. Anyway, I'm not sure that undergrads are allowed to get married, are they? I've never heard of it.'

'Of course I said to him, "What's the hurry?" and he said, "Well, you never know what's going to happen, these days, do you. I might be dead otherwise before I get the chance." I said, "By that thinking, there are quite a lot of things you ought to do now, while you can!" '

'And what did he say to that?'

Evert gave a nauseated smile. 'He said what he wanted most of all was to have a son.'

I had finished Victor Dax's novel at last, and wondered what passages from it he would choose to read to the Club. It impressed me, though it wasn't exactly enjoyable; my regard for it had its share of self-regard, at having got through it and grasped what it was doing. It was unshakeably serious, and I liked my prose to have at least a glimmer of humour. Dax's nearest approaches to jokes were quotations from Erasmus and occasional mockery of the working classes. Still, I had seen the solemn praise of the book in the latest *Horizon*, and read the long *TLS* 'middle' which compared it favourably to the *Wand of Light* trilogy, books I'd devoured in the sixth form as the height of modernity and sophistication. If Dax wasn't going off, I perhaps was going off him.

I thought I could talk to Peter Coyle about the novel and went over to the Ashmolean the next day. If I expected to find Sparsholt sprawled naked on a rostrum in front of him I was disappointed. Peter had just come out of a drawing class with Professor Schwabe, and was more than usually restless. He missed London, and the evacuation of the whole Slade School to Oxford had been a great frustration to him. Nor did he get on with Schwabe himself, who kept trying to suppress the strong vein of fantasy in Peter's work. It was an inevitable clash: the Professor was a painstakingly old-fashioned craftsman, expert in topographical drawings and prints, while Peter was romantic, extravagant, at times rather silly, and a reckless taker of short cuts.

He signed out in the ledger by the door, and we went into the street. I was curious about Sparsholt, but wary of bringing the subject up; these black moods were short-lived but keen while they lasted. Besides, I was conscious by now of seeing the situation from Evert's angle, and it was possible Peter himself attached little importance to it. In Beaumont Street an eternal Army convoy was rumbling past, the eight-second gap between lorries a subliminal rhythm of those years – Peter dashed across the road, though I, with my lifelong propensity to trip, or drop something, whenever physical speed was required, stood waiting for two minutes till the line and its busy wash of backed-up bicycles had passed. I found him in the Randolph, ordering tea.

He started talking about a play he'd been asked to design the sets for, and in a minute the annoyances of school were forgotten. It was called *The Triumph of Time*, an allegorical play of a kind I resisted, but which gave him exciting scope for some large-scale backdrops – I doubted if the Oxford Playhouse was really big enough for the visions he had of them. I was able in a while to say almost dismissively, 'You might get Sparsholt as one of your devils, can't you see him painted scarlet?' and Peter then said that he'd had a brief note from him – it was in his pocket now.

'Dear Mr Coyle,' Sparsholt had written, 'I was quite surprised to get your letter, and can't think how you have heard of me! I do think it would be interesting to have one's portrait painted, however I am extremely busy at present, and you may prefer to find other models for your work. Thursday evenings are possible for me, if not too late for you. Hoping to hear from you, D. D. Sparsholt.' The letter was a diagram of divided feelings, written in a stiff schoolboy hand that yielded here and there to wide grown-up flourishes.

'So he's too busy,' said Peter. I was surprised by my own alarm that he might be going to drop the whole thing.

'Well, he has a lot on,' I said, and I filled him in on Sparsholt's various commitments – his rowing and his PT, and of course the long hours in the labs.

Peter shrugged, and peered round at the few other people taking tea beneath the dingy Gothic vault of the lounge. I filled up the pot from the scalding hot-water jug and gave it a stir. 'I've been drawing a young gardener at Corpus,' he said, a clear but mysterious emphasis on the word 'drawing'.

'Nude?' I said.

'I find it easier,' Peter said, and gave a smile that seemed to count on my admiration and perhaps to take pleasure in shocking me a little. I saw that to him it was an advantage to be free of the traps of college life. In his digs at the far end of Walton

Street he had no chance of meeting David Sparsholt in the bathroom. There was none of the deadliness of waiting and spying
or the fateful flutter of a chance encounter in the quad. I said,

'And you know he has his fiancée to take care of.'

Peter snuffled slightly, as if trusting this was a joke. 'Sparsholt, you mean?'

'Oh, yes,' I said, with a shake of the head. 'He told me all
about it.'

He reflected for a moment. 'It's rather sweet,' he said, 'in its
way. But it won't last.'

'They mean to get married quite soon,' I said.

He glanced again at the letter, and then tucked it away in his
big tweed jacket, the pocket thick with what looked like other
letters. 'I've got a pretty good hunch that she doesn't understand his true nature.'

'Well, you may be right,' I said.

'What's her name, anyway?'

'That I don't know,' I said, 'but I've told him I'd like to
meet her.'

'Have you?' said Peter, more distracted than resentful. The
fact that I'd told a lie intrigued me and should perhaps have
alarmed me. I'd conceived a blurred involuntary image of the
fiancée, as one does of anyone spoken of but unknown. There
was still everything to find out. Peter had the pride as well as
the charm of a rake, and with it the rake's ability to dismiss with
contempt anyone who resisted him. I wasn't sure now if I'd
sharpened his interest in David, or unwittingly encouraged him
to write him off.

4

Evert's rooms were on the far side of College, and unlike mine looked outwards – not exactly at the world, but at the Meadow, with its grazing cows and misty distances. On the gravel walk below his window cadets were drilled and couples strolled, and up the long lime avenue beyond, the rowing eights of half the university would trail home from the river in the dusk. In those days the building he lived in was thought a Victorian eyesore; for me the stone stairs and Gothic windows stirred chilly memories of being at school. To put his mark on his rooms, Evert was already buying pictures, a colour print of a Whistler nocturne, a drawing of Windsor Castle, apparently on fire, by Peter Coyle, a little Sickert drawing and a few other things from home. Victor Dax was a collector, and had what Evert said were important paintings by Derain and Chagall. He had given Evert an etching of a large-bosomed nude by Anders Zorn, which drew odd chuckles from his scout. I felt myself it was a funny thing for a father to have given his son, but I saw there was a certain contempt for convention in much of Victor's behaviour, and in this case perhaps a touch of wishful thinking.

'Come and have a Camp,' Evert said, as we jostled together on our way out of Hall a few days later. 'I haven't seen you for quite some time' – with an odd smile: I don't know if he thought I'd been seeing Sparsholt again. I said,

'I've been stopping in Woodstock for a night or two – helping the old aunt I told you about to get settled in.' I noticed again that my aunt meant little to him, and after a glance at him I thought I would say no more about her. As a fiction she was almost too successful – she escaped detection entirely. We made our way out into the quad, by the twitching light of his taped-over torch, which picked disorienting doorways and steps out of the near-dark. The narrow space behind his building, black-walled and cobbled like a stable yard, reached upward to gables barely darker than the sky.

His sitting room was doubly gloomy in the blackout, with stifling curtains of some heavy, crudely dyed material that stained your hands if you closed them yourself; they gave off a dim odour of tennis nets, at first pleasant, but over time oppressive. This evening, as I knew but Evert didn't, Sparsholt was having his first sitting with Peter – I'd noticed his preoccupied look, as we left Hall. The meeting was to happen in Sparsholt's rooms, behind those tight-closed shutters, and no doubt behind a sported oak. It had the secrecy of an assignation, and I couldn't help wondering, as Evert doled out drops of Essence into our two cups, just how far it would go. A head and shoulders only, surely, in this first session, which would after all be the first time they had met. Would Peter be patient enough for the long game? I took it from the start that his aim was seduction, and found myself incoherently believing he might pull it off, where poor Evert surely had no chance.

Evert, it turned out, had made his own small advances. He'd gone down to the river, and trailed along the towpath in the drizzle as the Brasenose Eight streaked past in one direction and then streaked back again. He had managed to be just by the College barge when the boat came in to the landing deck, but he'd fluffed things; his attempt at a surprised greeting over the heads of the crew had gone completely unnoticed. I said why didn't he do something more straightforward, ask Sparsholt out for a pint at the Bear one evening, or one of the little pubs in St Ebbe's if he wanted to be more private? It seemed this was a bit too straightforward for him as yet. He said he didn't know whether Sparsholt drank.

'Ah, you've got a new picture,' I said, and got up to look at it. 'Hmmm . . .' It hung over his desk, a small oil painting in a dark frame – I guessed it was an abstract work, though I saw it as a landscape, simplified to stripes of white, green and grey. 'What is it, exactly?'

Evert half-warmed to the subject – I thought he said at first Peter had painted it. 'Not Coyle, Goyle,' he said: 'Stanley Goyle. The names are more alike than their work.'

'Well, I thought . . .' I said hastily. 'He's someone you've discovered?'

Evert clearly liked the idea of this, but said, 'Oh, he's quite well known.' He'd found a man in Summertown who sold pictures – he had several of Stanley Goyle's, and hoped, when his father's allowance came through next month, to buy a second one off him. He said he'd paid twenty-five pounds for it, which seemed a lot to me. 'It's a Pembrokeshire scene, of course.' We examined it together, but I saw that he couldn't be distracted by it, or the pleasure it brought, for more than a minute.

His thoughts now were focused on the weekend after next, and on the fire-watching duties we all had to do. These entailed staying up all night with a colleague in the Bell Tower, taking it in turns to stand around on the roof, looking out for incendiary devices or other activity. We all had the roster two weeks in advance, and the pairings were deliberately mixed. As it happened, I was due to be doing it on the Friday with Barrett, another Brasenose man, whom I barely knew. Evert was down for the Sunday, with someone I've entirely forgotten. But in between these two dates, on the Saturday night, the name of D. D. Sparsholt appeared, coupled, amusingly, with C. Farmonger – Charlie took a very dim view of his friends' obsession with this freshman.

'I wonder what they'll talk about,' I said.

'They won't talk about anything,' said Evert pertly – but he coloured as he went on: 'I've done a swap with Charlie. I'm going to fire-watch with Sparsholt – with David.'

'And how will you explain the change?'

'Oh, I've got to do something else on Sunday,' said Evert.

'I see. Well, you'll have a decent chance to get to know each other.'

'We'll spend the night together,' said Evert, and the prospect of it seemed to haunt his smile. He poured the boiling water into the cups.

'There could be some very colourful activity,' I said. The Blitz was still raging, and we were only fifty miles from London. 'How are your parents?'

They seemed to preoccupy him less now that Sparsholt was the focus of his worries. 'My father's sent my mother off to Wales.'

'You mean, to join your sister?' – I knew that the beautiful Alex had been sent to her aunt in Tenby earlier in the year. At that time I had yet to visit Cranley Gardens, but it seemed from what Evert said that things there were on a generous scale. 'So your father's alone in the house?'

'He has Herta for company.'

'Of course. I hope to meet Herta one day.'

'You might get round her, I suppose,' said Evert, looking at me consideringly, 'though few people do.'

'And aren't you worried about your own things at home?'

'I don't have many things, really. Most of my books are here. My father's put all the valuable pictures in the cellar.'

'I thought you weren't supposed to do that. The firemen's hoses ruin everything at the bottom of a house.'

'Oh, has he got it the wrong way round?' said Evert. 'Still, water does less harm than fire, surely.' He got up to search through the records stacked beside the bookcase. Most of us at that time were in a rut with records, having few of them and playing them over and over. What he picked out was something wantonly emotional by Tchaikovsky; after four and a half minutes his mood had been worked up effectively. He turned the record over, stood with the small fire smouldering in the grate behind him. 'God, I wonder what Sparsholt's doing now,' he said, throwing out his arms as the brass came in with some fateful motif.

'Yes, I wonder.'

'Do you honestly think Coyle's interested in him at all?'

My silence now seemed more culpable than it had before. 'Oh, Coyle's interested in a hundred people,' I said. 'Even if he is, it won't last long.' I felt Evert saw my real meaning – he stared at me and then looked away, so that something seemed to have come between us. The orchestra surged and ebbed.

'I think I'd like to be an artist,' he said, after a bit.

'I've a suspicion,' I said, 'that artists don't have nearly as much fun as they like us to imagine.' But I could see that in Evert's mind they had an infinite freedom.

As it happened, I ran into Peter in Blackwell's the next morning. He was with a dark young man he seemed reluctant to introduce – I wondered if he even knew his name. 'I'm Freddie Green,' I said. 'Oh, George Chalmers,' said the stranger, and we shook hands. Peter looked vaguely irritated. 'How did it go with Sparsholt?' I said.

'What, last night, you mean?' – he peered dimly, as if at a much more distant memory. 'I wasn't there very long.'

'But you did a drawing?'

'Just a quick sketch or two, you know.'

'And how did you get on with him?'

'I wasn't really in the mood, Freddie,' said Peter. 'Sometimes it just doesn't happen.' He smiled at George Chalmers, who was perhaps his next sitter.

I went on, 'What on earth did you find to talk about?'

Peter looked at me rather oddly. 'If you must know, we talked about you. He doesn't know what to make of you.'

'Oh,' I said, both amused and very slightly wounded, 'I thought I was nice to him.'

'No, no, he said you were. He's probably just not used to your style. He's from Nuneaton.'

'Oh . . . yes.' There was something null about it, as a fact, though the only fact I knew about Nuneaton was that George Eliot also came from there.

'Well, we must press on,' said Peter, and led his silent model, if that's what he was, out of the shop. In fact George Chalmers must have spoken, because I heard Peter saying quite sharply, 'No, he's not,' as they stepped into the street.

5

There were now enough of us going out from Oxford to Woodstock for a special bus to be laid on – it picked us up in St Giles': filers and typists, who'd been billeted in Keble College, a small body of students which expanded in intriguing ways, and half a dozen dons, linguists mainly, who had not already joined up. We trundled out the five or six miles through the autumn countryside, as if on an excursion away from the War; though once we turned in through the gates of the Palace we found a scene disfigured with the guard huts, Nissen huts and paraphernalia of a wartime base. I was there for two or three days a week, and was often back in College quite late. As a result I saw Evert less, and was so busy with other and, on the whole, graver secrets that I rather forgot about the Sparsholt thing.

I came up the stairs one evening about nine o'clock, and bumped into Evert coming down. 'Oh, thank God,' he said.

'Come and have a drink.' He followed me back into the room. 'How are you?'

He stood and gazed at me with a remote smile, as if it should have been obvious. He was wearing a finely cut suit, as usual, with a soft blue cravat at the throat; he seemed to have put on quite a lot of some rather florid scent. He also looked as if he hadn't slept for days. 'Oh, Fred,' he said, 'you're the only person I can really talk to. Most people would be horrified, or disgusted, but you understand.'

'Well,' I said, cautiously, 'I don't know.' I made him sit down, and poured him a glass of port. 'So much of that sort of thing went on at school it would seem very odd to me if it suddenly stopped at Oxford – especially now, you know, with things in such a muddle and no one knowing what's round the corner.'

'I couldn't bear it any longer,' he said, 'I can't think, I can't do any work. Garvey gave me hell over my Dryden essay.'

'All because of Sparsholt,' I said.

'I even wrote him a poem, and left it in his pigeonhole.'

'Garvey's . . . ?'

'David's, of course.'

'And what did he say about that?'

'I went back a few minutes later and took it out again.'

'Not good enough,' I said sternly.

'It was a beautiful poem.'

'I mean, you've got to do something, Evert – at least get to know him a bit.' And when you do, I thought, you'll see he's not worth all this trouble.

Evert sipped his port and stared at the carpet. 'I just have done something – I've just been to his rooms.'

I sat down too, and Evert stretched out on my little sofa, looking away from me, like an analyst's patient. The narration that followed was pained and hesitant, and he seemed to run away several times from his own decision to tell the story. But I give it here as I summarized it later that night in my diary, which even now makes me hear particular phrases in his soft deep voice. With the blackout he had been unable to tell from the quad if Sparsholt was in. He had gone upstairs very quietly, two at a time, and found that his oak was open, and stood there for some minutes listening and hardly daring to breathe. He believed he could hear an occasional sound. I said had it been rhythmical creaking? Evert said no, and I couldn't tell if he smiled. It was perhaps 'like someone turning the pages of a book'. He remained there in the dark for five minutes or more, but simply couldn't bring himself to knock. There was only a little light leaking out under the door. 'It was quite an eerie feeling to be so close to him, without him knowing.'

I couldn't help feeling it would have been more eerie for Sparsholt, had he found out. I said, 'You didn't stoop to peering through the keyhole.'

'Of course I stooped, but the thing was down on the other side.'

'Do tell me you knocked in the end.'

'I did,' said Evert, pausing to drink and nod ruefully at the recollection. But there had been no reply. He waited for a while, then knocked again. Whatever the noise was that he thought he could hear had stopped, but he didn't know if he had been imagining it, or if Sparsholt was sitting just feet away pretending not to be there. So with sudden decisiveness Evert turned the handle and went in. There he was at last in the room of the loved one in all its unguarded ordinariness. No one was there but he had the strange sensation that the room itself was staring at him, as at a man who was taking advantage of another's innocence. At the same time he was giving the disappointing contents of the room – the few books, the Ladbroke's calendar, the commoner's gown that hung beneath a Boat Club cap on a hook – the most tender and generous appraisal they can ever have received. Next to the desk some barbells and Swedish clubs were placed against the wall. There was a fire in, and

Sparsholt had got in some logs, which Evert saw must have been the noise he'd heard. They were crackling behind the old wire fireguard. It was warm in there, and of course with the shutters closed and the curtains pulled across it was quite snug; it had the emptiness of a room which seems to expect any moment the footsteps of its owner on the stairs below. The door was open into the unlit bedroom, and Evert drifted towards it and looked in, and had hardly taken a step inside when there was a sudden rustling noise in the shadows and a voice said, 'Oh, hello!'

The feeling of being caught was disastrous, it meant the scandalous exposure of his desires. He hardly knew what he said, as he backed away into the sitting room, apologizing for waking him, and watching fearfully as Sparsholt got off the bed and came towards him into the light – and it wasn't him. Evert stared and laughed. He thought for a second he must have gone into the wrong room, that all the drama of waiting had been an absurd waste of time and anxious emotion, and that the bar-bells and the cap and the books on dynamics were mere effects in some bewildering coincidence. But no, he was sure, it was Sparsholt's room, his bedroom, but with another man in it.

'So what did you say?' I asked.

'I said I was looking for David, which was perfectly true, of course. And he said, so was he, but he'd just had a little lie down while he was waiting.' Evert sat forward slightly to take another sip of port – I saw the moment's calculation as he left a quarter-inch in the glass.

A strange conversation had ensued between the two intrud-ers, though Evert was so thrown that it didn't strike him at first that the other man's story was a very odd one. Both of them were confused, which saved the situation up to a point. They introduced themselves; the stranger was called Gordon Pin-nock, he was at St Peter's College, and he came from Nuneaton

– he had been at school with Sparsholt, and claimed outright to be his best friend.

Over the next few minutes Evert seems to have found out a good deal about him, though whether he revealed as much of himself I doubt. They had quite a chat; and Evert found him attractive, in a peculiar way, with a smile he couldn't help thinking somehow suspicious. If Pinnock and Sparsholt were such close friends it seemed horribly likely to Evert that Sparsholt must have mentioned him, the strange second-year man who was always staring and hanging about in odd places. And it was certain that after this present encounter Pinnock would tell Sparsholt just what had happened – Evert himself was now listening for footsteps outside, while conscious of the need to use the small time available to make his case. I didn't like to say I thought it quite likely that Sparsholt had hardly taken Evert in at all.

Pinnock looked at him a bit comically and said, what was it about? Evert said he just wanted to leave him a message. And of course Pinnock said, 'Oh, I'll tell him, what was it?' – which made Evert feel there was definitely a game of some kind going on. 'I wonder where he's got to,' said Pinnock. Evert said it was all right, he'd leave his message in the lodge, and he mumbled something about the fire-watching roster. He was turning to go when Pinnock surprised him. They were standing beside Sparsholt's desk, with the heavy discs of the weights on the floor beside them. And Pinnock said, with a strange little smile, 'Are you an admirer of the male form?' 'Well . . .' said Evert. 'I know, funny isn't it,' Pinnock said; and then he told him something very revealing, which was that up until two years before Sparsholt had been 'a total weed', he was 'weak and skinny'. As a schoolboy he was always being pushed around, and the only sport he was good at was running – running away, in effect. So at some point, he decided to make a man of himself. 'Get him to show you a picture,' said Pinnock, 'the next time you see him: you won't believe the change.' 'Right, yes, I will,' said Evert. And with that he made his excuses and left.

He emptied his glass and turned to face me. 'Well,' I said, 'that doesn't sound too bad.' But I could see that his mind was lurching round new loops, and had seized on Pinnock, who sounded to me like a hundred other affable and lonely freshmen, as a new hazard and a further rival.

When Evert had left I went over to the lodge to see if some papers I was expecting had arrived, and found a brown cardboard tube in my pigeonhole. I recognized the Art Nouveau writing on the label, and felt I had better not open it till I was back in my room. Once there I coaxed out, tightly rolled so that it seemed to spring free (or half-free, since it kept the disposition to curl), a sheet of pale grey cartridge paper. In fact it curled up coyly in the second I reached away for a book to weight it on the desk. On the back were the pencilled initials, 'D. S.' and 'P. C.', and the date, 30. X. 40. Was I supposed to imagine a heart and an arrow between them? I held it down flat with Myles on the Papacy and *The Code of the Woosters*, and had a look at Peter's effort.

What did I think of it, really? I was torn between wanting to see genius in a friend's work and a very much drier view. I had a sense of being provoked. Why, after all, had he sent it, or possibly given it, to me? I suppose it was to prove his point, his seducer's speed; but I felt he was mocking too at my interest in the matter, which he seemed to feel was excessive: I think he thought he could excite me as he himself had been excited.

In fact my position gave me a larger scope for criticism, since I'd seen very nearly as much of this model as Peter had: in the strokings, or fingerings, of red chalk, there was a rush to enhance and ennoble Sparsholt's body beyond the already enhanced reality. Those two years of incessant press-ups and

34

weights had been outdone in ten minutes. It was the portraitist's usual flattery, no doubt, but fed by Peter's own desire to worship: a somehow unwholesome collusion of two men with quite different tastes over a question of male beauty. I have always thought the male nude drawing a sadly comical genre. At one time my half-brother Gerald collected those woeful 'académies' produced by the thousands in the art schools of Europe – the moustache, the ropy muscles, the merciful cache-sexe, or if not that the intractable silliness of the genitals themselves, were obstacles only the finest artists could surmount. Well, David Sparsholt had as yet no moustache, and no silk pouch was seen in Peter's drawing of him. Had it not been for the pencilled note, the heroic torso might just as well have been his gardener from Corpus, or any other of his subjects. In an art so prone to exaggeration it was hard to tell. What Peter had created was a portrait of a demigod from neck to knee, the sex suggested by a little slur, conventional as a fig leaf, while the neck opened up into nothing, like the calyx of a flower.

6

It was meatless dinner in Hall on Friday – perhaps a bad night to have signed in Jill as my guest. She fell on the charred pilaff with greed and dismay, forking through it in search of bits of carrot and cauliflower; she might almost have been on one of her digs. Her decisive gestures, her bunchy brown hair pushed back behind her ears, those large grey eyes and that jutting jaw, all stirred me more now than they had before – I watched her fondly, and I seemed to watch myself, intrigued by my own deepening feelings. Our talk was academic, in fact archaeological, for the most

part. She spoke with earnest excitement about some small Etrus-
can cups or jars she had been allowed to handle when the
contents of the Ashmolean were being packed up and sent away
in case of bombing. I'd never been interested in such things
myself, but I smiled at her enjoyment and after five minutes I
started to wonder if I didn't share her enthusiasm. We sat facing
each other between the yellow lamps, the sleeves of our scholar's
gowns sweeping the table. With those small artefacts, I felt, she
must have shown a delicacy of touch she had not yet shown to
me; or perhaps to any other person.

After dinner I sensed she would have liked to come to my
room for coffee, but I was due to start my fire-watching almost
at once. I lit her through to the Canterbury Gate, and this time
as she shook my hand I leant over it and placed a light kiss on
her cheek: I still remember its surprisingly available softness
and warmth, just threatened by the cold November evening.
Her own reaction was hard to make out exactly in the dark, but
horrified alarm seemed the main part of it; she muttered something as she quickly went off. I popped up to my room, rather
pleased none the less with what I had done. It paved the way
for doing it again. Three minutes later I was crossing Tom Quad
for my vigil with Barrett. I brought with me, as well as a Thermos flask and a coat and scarf, *The Wicket Gate*, volume one of
A. V. Dax's *Dance of Shadows* trilogy. As I was to introduce
Evert's father at the Club, I wanted to be sure of my footing in
the crowded twilight of those earlier novels.

Barrett was another Brasenose refugee, a small northern
scientist of some sort, but it struck me he might know Sparsholt
and might throw out inadvertent titbits that I could pass on to
Evert, before his encounter with him tomorrow night. I was
uneasy about this deviously engineered plan, and afraid that
Sparsholt himself might think it so odd as to turn against him.
As Evert's confidant I wished the painful story a happy con-
clusion, and as his friend I saw my duty to prepare him for the

worst. When two friends are pursuing the same hopeless object, one with more apparent success than the other, all advice is subtly compromised. I went carefully up the steep dark stair of the tower, and into the square ringing-chamber that was our base for the night, with the sallies of the bell ropes, striped red, white and blue, looped up like bunting just above our heads. It was now four months since they'd been used, and I imagined the bells overhead in their downcast vacancy, and seemed almost to hear the strange creaks of ropes and wheels on the day, perhaps not too far off, when they would be raised again and rung. A few church chairs, with slots for hymn books, had been brought up, and a folding table. The small window was blacked out and the room was starkly lit. Barrett and I would each spend half the night here, and the rest of it up on the leads above, looking out for any kind of trouble from the sky. It was the duty of the one who was resting to run with any message called down by the watcher. So far it had always been wearily eventless work, enemy aircraft sometimes at the limit of hearing: in the black early hours after midnight, while nightly raids were burning London, Oxford, in its bowl of hills, was fixed in a new and generalized silence.

I made a little study in the corner of the room, and found myself growing critical as Barrett was five and then ten minutes late. At last I heard the door bang dully down below, and rapid footsteps on the stairs. I turned away to conceal my impatience, 'Oh, hello . . .' he said from the doorway behind me, and I looked round to see a greatcoated figure pluck off his cap – it was David Sparsholt. 'Oh, hello!' he said again.

'Oh, David, hello' – I had spoken without thinking, from a feeling of closeness he could have had no sense of. In his quick blink and shake of the head, his pleasure that I remembered his first name outweighed a trace of awkwardness. It was clear from his little grin, as he took off his coat and looked for somewhere to hang it, that he didn't know what to call me. I was conscious of what Peter had said – that Sparsholt mistrusted my friendliness. He said, 'We've met before, haven't we.'

'We met shaving,' I said. 'I'm Freddie – Freddie Green.'

'Oh, yes, that's right,' he said, and we shook hands again. He wore a heavy brown Army jersey, tight on his powerful frame, and his grasp was strong and his gaze direct. I wondered if Peter had made up his story, to tease me; he had a merciless eye for others' insecurities.

'But we've seen each other a few times since.' Did he really not remember these? If the first time, waiting under Tom Gate for the rain to slacken, he had been a little unsure how to meet my eye, the second time, when we passed each other in our quad, he returned my nod gratefully enough. 'I wasn't expecting to see you tonight.'

'No. I'm sorry to be late,' he said, 'I swopped with Tom Barrett.'

'I don't mind at all,' I said. I was immediately relieved that Evert would be spared his misconceived night alone with him. 'When were you supposed to be on?'

'I was down for tomorrow.' He looked at me straight, though he coloured as he spoke – a little sequence I remembered from before. 'I'll have my fiancée here this weekend, you see.'

'Your fiancée – aha!' I said, perhaps overdoing my surprise. I entered into it clumsily, 'Yes, you don't want to be stuck on the roof all night when she's here!'

'Well, no,' said Sparsholt, so that I saw I had been abruptly intimate. 'Now how are we going to do this?'

I started to describe the way I had done it before, but he spoke over me and said he would take the first stint on the roof. He put his coat back on, and his cap: he had found the small military element in the night. I went up the stairs behind him just to show him the way, and he pushed open the low door on to the leads. In a minute we adjusted to the quality of the night. It would grow darker yet, and when the moon, in its last quarter, had slipped down behind Merton tower, the whole city would sink into mere muddled shadow, as if a vast grey net had been thrown over a table heaped with once familiar objects, now enigmatically confused and obscured. I said I would come back in an hour and went cautiously to the door and then down again; decanted some coffee in the lid of my flask, and sat down at the table with my book, but all the time something else was sinking in, the degree to which his presence had intensified. In straightforward terms he held no interest for me, except as a figure from a world so unlike my own that it might be instructive to observe it; but by proxy he had assumed an aura. I was abashed to think that in my room, hidden among jerseys and vests, there was a drawing of him in the nude. It would be difficult now to deal with him as if unaware of how other people desired him, or of how they would envy our spending the night together. What I thought I might find out, in the course of the night, was how much he sensed all this himself.

In my first hours below decks I ran quite far through *The Wicket Gate*, ignoring for as long as I could the failure of the magic and the grey dawn of disillusion. It is hard to do justice to old pleasures that cannot be revived – we seem half to disown our youthful selves, who loved and treasured them. There was the scene where Enid returns to Mark Gay at Garstang Hall: 'Great was his joy to find that she was come' – in my school dorm the words had brought a new constriction to my throat and given me a glimpse through tears of the wild landscape of adult passion; the archaic solemnity of the prose had clutched at my heart. Now they struck me as an awful simulacrum of literature, though written, I none the less felt, with perfect sincerity. It was a sham that had convinced the author himself. I went up at ten to start my shift with a feeling of relief.

At first I couldn't see Sparsholt. By now the moon had set, and I sent my weak torchlight flitting over the sloping leads and the step-shaped battlements. In the centre of the roof, but hidden from the ground, rose the simple wooden housing of the bells, as functional as a shed, and high enough to conceal anyone standing behind it. I made my way round, with an oddly racing heart. There was no one here either. I wondered if he had climbed on up into one of the small corner turrets, which were something like watchtowers, bristling with gargoyles instead of guns. 'Who goes there?' – in a sudden angry shout. I gasped and jumped and looked upwards. Hollow footsteps sounded above my head. He had clambered up somehow on to the pitched roof of the shed, and a few seconds later my narrow beam caught him there, massive against the sky, then twisting away from the light. I saw his big white smile, or snarl, before he crouched and slid to the edge and dropped down, almost taking me with him as his feet hit the angled surface and he fell forward and stopped himself on the high parapet. For a second he had clutched at me, saving himself or protecting me, I wasn't sure. I think he hoped to frighten me. *Who goes there?* – it was a challenge from a film, from a children's game, but when Sparsholt said it I caught the thrill, for him, of the game becoming real.

I found my first watch the strangest. It was still early, though the indiscriminate darkness disturbed the sense of time. Seeing little but outlines of steeples and pinnacles under a thinly clouded night sky, I observed in another way, with the ears. Standing quite still I was at the centre of a townscape drawn not only in charcoal but in sound. At its outer rim there was the mild intermittent noise of cars on the Abingdon Road, which seemed to merge and lose themselves in the episodic sighing of the breeze in the tall elms of the Meadow. A keener ear still might have heard leaves falling and milling on the paths beneath. Now and then there was the muffled rumble of a late bus or car in St Aldate's, unavoidably drawing attention to itself. For ten minutes there was something close to silence, broken by a moment's music from an opened door somewhere, and then the quick footsteps and unconcerned conversation of three men crossing the flagged terrace of the quad below. I peered out through the battlements and saw their torch switched on and off, its beam mere momentary scratches on the dark. None of them of course looked round or looked up – I was a secret observer of these trivial happenings, my head unsuspected in the night among a hundred unseen Gothic details. Then a silence that was that of 4 a.m., so that it was a shock, and a bore, to turn the light on my watch and find it was barely eleven.

When a further hour and five minutes had passed I went downstairs, thinking Sparsholt might have fallen asleep. In fact he was sitting at my little table with his back to me, his head propped on his left hand as he read a book. 'Anything doing?' he said, as he looked round, and stood up, and stretched, and seemed to expand by some further factor of rediscovered muscular power, his fingertips swinging a looped bell rope overhead.

'Not a thing,' I said, unwinding my long scarf, and glancing down at the open page – a spread of scientific diagrams, with graphs crossing and diverging. 'Oh, I thought you might be reading my novel.' I'd been slow to see that I had a subject.

'Mm, I had a look at it,' he said, with a smile and a lift of the eyebrows, as if to say it confirmed his impression not only of novels, but of people who read them. The wary humour was new, and appealing.

'You might not like it,' I said. 'I don't myself, really – but its author is coming to talk to our Club next week, and I have to introduce him.'

'Oh, I see . . . who is it?' – turning over the book. 'A. V. Dax . . .' He shook his head.

'I used to love his books, but now I've seen through them – if you know what I mean.' I took off my overcoat and dropped it over the back of the chair.

'Well, we all go off things,' he said.

I winced. 'It's a bit delicate because his son's a good friend of mine.'

'Oh, is he?'

'In this College,' I said; 'you may have met him?' Again a little moue of unconcern. 'Evert Dax, he's reading English, in the second year.'

Now he nodded hesitantly. 'Evert . . .' he said, as though something improbable were being confirmed. 'Yes, I think I've met him. I thought it was Evan.'

'It's a Dutch name – his father's partly Dutch.'

'And he's a friend of yours' – reassessing me in the light of this. I had a confused sense that I might have to defend Evert – that Sparsholt had already marked him down as a pest. Should I concede that he had strange habits – was, as we said then, 'over-emotional'? Loyalty seemed pliable, for a moment. 'Well, if he's the person I'm thinking of,' Sparsholt said, 'he seems very decent.' He pulled his cap down low on his forehead and shrugged on his greatcoat.

'Why don't you come along?' I said, ' – to the Club.'

But he shook his head again. 'I've got no time for reading,' he said, and with that he clambered off up the narrow stair into the dark. I savoured the dry comedy of his remark, as I sat down and poured another inch of coffee into the Thermos lid; and then there was the knowledge that Evert, in so far as he figured at all in his mind, was 'decent': he'd been friendly, surely, was what he meant, unlike others in this cold college. Evert, besotted by this great hunk of a boy, his thoughts about him no doubt indecent in the extreme. I picked up Enid and Mark's romance again but distracted and even guilty at the thought of the longings that had so far escaped young Sparsholt's detection. My eyes passed across the scant features of the room, barely seeing the gilt-lettered boards that gave the age and weight of the bells, and the framed testimonials to feats of change-ringing.

I can't now recall the exact order of our passing encounters, on the difficult ribbed leads or on the steep companionway. But as the slow night turned and intermittent winds piled up and then dispersed high continents of cloud, we fell into conversation of a kind that I've known only in the War, brief dislocated intimacies, a blurring of boundaries between person and person in the surrounding dark. One time he came up quickly, and stood next to me, saying nothing – I knew from the way his breathing stilled and he shifted almost noiselessly in his greatcoat that he was glad of the company, the mere proximity of another person watching. I pictured a dog, brought back on the invisible leash that links it to a man, standing panting at first, then merely waiting and breathing. Soon a plane was heard, the first of the night, silent after the first doubtful rumble, then more sustained, though distancing already: still we said nothing as we recognized a Wellington – the rumble of reassurance rather than fear. We were standing on the north side of the tower, the squat spire of the Cathedral close by, and beyond that mere conjecture. It was the moment when I sensed the real tenor of Sparsholt's concern – I saw I had been slow, although something in him repudiated sympathy, or the weakness of requiring it. In that vast northward view (or lack of view) was the world he came from. I said, 'By the way, I hope your people are all right?'

He said they were, so far, though they'd had a dozen or more air raids already. I asked what they did. His father was a manager at a steel-plant, and his mother worked on the drapery counter at Freeman's, the local department store. He was an only child – 'though we also have a cat,' he said.

'I suppose your father's in a reserved occupation?' I said.

'That's right,' said Sparsholt. 'To be honest, though, I'm more concerned about him getting killed up there.'

'Yes, of course.'

'It's been bad already but we're still expecting, you know, the big one.'

We stared blindly into the darkness, and I felt for him. To me home was a place tucked away, unsignalled, with the great stone bulwarks of the Moor between it and Plymouth, to the south, which had already been the target of the bombers. But to Sparsholt, gazing north, the world of home lay open as if on a tray, the factories, foundries, munition works offered up to the beak and claws of the enemy. They would have AA guns, he said, but we both knew these were badges of hope and faith more than practical defences.

'Let's hope they come through,' I said. His silence might have covered any number of things, and I wasn't sure in the dark if we had both settled down on the idea of his home, or if we had drifted apart into separate reflections. He didn't ask about me; I felt my exemption from service made him uneasy, as if there might be something shameful and embarrassing about the whole Green family. I could have told him that my half-brother Gerald was in Crete right now, a captain in the special forces; and there were things I was prevented from telling him about what I was up to myself. 'Right, I'll go down,' I said, and for a second I was startled to see, in the quick play of my flashlight, the face of a determined young stranger – in the darkness he'd softened into quite another figure, with subtle elements of several other people I knew, and who was I suppose a mere fantasy fathered by his presence.

At another change of the watch he must have found me asleep – and sleeping heavily too, with the weight of sleep postponed. A noise in a dream brought with it a complete rationale of history and consequence, which fled away as I opened my eyes to find Sparsholt staring into my face with mingled apology and impatience and saying again, 'It's five o'clock,' or whatever lonely time of the night we had reached. I apologized myself, with a fuddled sense of foolishness and a trace of something else, a kind of mutinous pleasure in having succumbed. 'It's no good falling asleep,' he said, as if about to list the reasons; but making do with a stare and a quick nod. I saw that something almost hidden was playing out through the night, a little game of seniority. As I pulled on my coat and reached in the pockets for my gloves I felt that my greater age and experience, the people I knew and the thousands of books I'd read, counted for nothing in his eyes. The War had levelled us, and on this platform he was already standing taller and stronger. I might have won the Chancellor's Essay Prize in my first year, and the Gifford Medal in my second; but to him I was just an eccentric weakling, close friend of other eccentrics, with whom he was thrust into a fleeting alliance.

And yet there was something unguardedly boyish about him too. There was even a strange moment towards dawn, when it felt colder than ever, when he asked me what some vaguely emerging landmark was, and leaning by me in the stepped opening of the battlements he put his arm around my shoulders, while with the other hand he pointed and I squinted down his finger as through the sight of a gun. I had never been used to physical contact, and his loose hug flustered me before it warmed me and even cheered me. He gave off, at this late end of a long day, the faint mildewed smell of someone thirsty, unwashed and unshaven. 'Thanks for being so decent, Green,' he said. He half-turned in the grey early light, and I thought, as I peered up at him, that he was smiling. He gave me a squeeze, a quick sample of his withheld power, as he let me go, and his train of thought was no doubt subconscious: 'Well, I'll have my Connie here today!'

'She's Connie, is she?' I said, and nodded. I felt I should have asked about her before. He paced off to the far end of the roof, where I saw from his stance he was relieving himself into the corner drain – delayed and just audible came the thin cascade through the gargoyle's mouth on to the flagstones far below. It was his turn to go down but when he strolled back he said, 'I'll stay up a bit and see the day in.' In fact he had his own question, put with that throwaway air which doesn't quite conceal a longer curiosity:

'So do you have a sweetheart?' he said.

Like his 'decent', the word touched me. 'Well . . .' I murmured. Something in me longed to say yes, and dress up a mere hope as a certainty, or a boast. But could Jill, even if things went well, ever turn into a sweetheart? I said, 'As it happens, there is someone, yes.'

'Is she in Oxford?'

'Yes, at St Hilda's.'

'You're lucky,' said David. 'Do you think you'll get married?' This was rather a jump, and I felt my claim had been put to an immediate test.

'Well, it would be nice to think so,' I said. 'What are your plans?'

He seemed conscious of speaking beyond his years. 'We're hoping to do it as soon as I leave. Connie's moving to Oxford at the end of the month.'

'Well, you're the lucky one, in that case. Is she a student too?'

'No, we're friends from home. She's just managed to get a job down here.'

'In the university, you mean?'

I could see him lean forward and peer down, as though even here we might be overheard; but all he said was, 'No, something else.'

'Well, there's a lot of something else going on in Oxford these days,' I said and looked at him slyly to see his reaction.

'She'll be putting up at Keble College,' he said. 'She's a qualified shorthand typist.'

'Ah, yes, I see,' I said, 'I see.'

He seemed warily relieved that I did. 'Can't say much more about it,' he said.

When we left the roof he said, 'I had another look at that book of yours,' and he made one or two remarks about how 'fancy' the writing was, and how far-fetched the narrative. 'I don't know what Enid sees in Mark Gay,' he said; 'I don't think a real woman would have felt like that about such a boring bastard.' He laughed briefly, conscious but not ashamed of his disrespect. I thought it was the kind of criticism that might have ensued if readers with no literary training were to write the newspaper notices instead of professional reviewers; but I was on the back foot as I found myself trying to defend Victor Dax, since what Sparsholt said, though ignorant, was lethally true. 'I think there's rather more to it than that,' I said, regretting my superior tone. 'You know it's all based on Arthurian legends.'

We turned off the light and began our descent from the ringing chamber to the quad and the blessed humdrum of gowns and breakfast. Our conversation had again that air of inadvertent candour: I was coming down rather cautiously with the back of his cap and his close-cropped neck a foot or two below me. 'Do you know a man called Coyle?' he said.

'Well, I know Peter Coyle,' I said, glad he couldn't see me – it was the very first time I'd been caught unawares by the Sparsholt affair, and I blushed hotly. 'Why do you ask?'

'He asked if he could draw me. Now he wants to paint my picture, for some reason.'

'Oh, well, I hope you'll let him,' I said.

There was a pause as he felt for the light switch for the lower stair. 'I suppose he's a bit of a pansy,' he said. I felt the word itself was a bit of an experiment for him.

'Peter? Lord, yes,' I said. 'But I imagine you can look after yourself.'

Now I wanted to see his face. There was a good deal in reserve in his short laugh.

Once on the ground, I pulled the door to and locked it – in that detail, I hoped, regaining my dignity. As I pocketed the key we stood looking at each other, two friends who'd seen something through. Or merely two chance colleagues? There was no knowing what the relations were between us. Was he, were both of us, chafing to be free? Or did we mean gracefully to carry our alliance through to the moment after breakfast when, like husband and wife, we would have to part and get on with our separate days? It struck me that if I saw Evert as I went into Hall I could ask him to join us, and break the news of the double swop that had given me the prize he longed for: I could bring them together then for a few minutes at least. But I doubted at once if Evert would be able to carry this off – I saw myself reassuring each of them, out of my intimacy with the other. It was a kind of reprieve when Sparsholt was hailed by a rowing friend, and taken off without a backward glance to their table nearest the door.

7

I met Connie a few hours later. I had slept all morning, and after lunch went out for a stroll round the Meadow. It was a dazzle of autumn sunshine, eights and fours flashing by on the river, and on the faces of passing couples the wartime pleasure in daylight. As I came back down the avenue I saw the lamp on in Evert's window, and had a troubled image of him shut up in there, in his fury of desire and suspicion. He was furious, at least, about my night with Sparsholt, and had reacted to the facts I passed on over breakfast – the stuff about Nuneaton, and the steel-works and the marriage plans – with envious mistrust.

I was almost at the College gate when I saw a couple approaching down the centre of the Broad Walk, among the spinning and drifting leaves, the man a good head taller and leaning over sideways to keep his left arm round the girl's shoulders. There was something clumsy in their linked progress, and I wouldn't have looked at them again if he hadn't raised his right arm and held it high – a command as much as a greeting. I stopped, nodded, and moved slowly towards them, seeing him tell her in a quick phrase (what was it?) who I was.

'Green!' he said. 'I want you to meet my Connie.'

I came up to them, smiling with a mixture of pleasure, curiosity and faint irritation at Sparsholt's matey tone. Connie was a healthy-looking girl, with thick dark hair under a red beret, rather prominent teeth, and a bosom which was all the more striking in a woman of modest height. Tightly covered in green jersey, and crossed by the broad lapels of a belted mac, it seemed to come between us, to be a kind of brag on Sparsholt's part, unmentionable, but undeniable. I didn't find her otherwise especially pretty, but she had the interest of being what he wanted. 'Hello,' I said, 'Freddie Green.'

We shook hands and Connie said, 'I've just been hearing about last night.'

'Ah, yes!' I said. I saw that Sparsholt was anxious for a moment about what she might repeat. He said cheerfully,

'So did you get some sleep?'

'I did,' I said, 'I missed two lectures,' and smiled complacently rather than utter the question which lurked in the air about us, as to how much sleep they had had. 'I thought you might be on the river,' I said airily.

'Not this weekend,' said Sparsholt, and grinned, as did Connie, colouring but confident. If she hadn't been there I'd have said a quick word to him about keeping his scout sweet, all the more important if he was unpopular on his staircase. A fiver (or so I'd heard) would buy a scout's silence about having a woman in College overnight.

'I hear you're a great reader,' Connie said. She had the West

49

Midlands twang more clearly than he did, and a directness, a curiosity as she looked at you, that I enjoyed. There was a flattering suggestion that they'd talked about me quite a lot. 'What have you got there?' She nodded at my coat pocket, square with the bulk of *Horseman, What Word?*. I tugged the book out, wondering how to describe it, and she craned forward to see it. 'Oh, A. V. Dax,' she said, 'yes – do you like him?'

'I'm not sure any more,' I said. 'Do you?'

'Well, I love the trilogy,' she said. 'I've read it three times.'

'I know what you mean,' I said, anxious again not to sound superior. 'I'm re-reading them all at the moment, as it happens. You know Dax is coming to speak to this club of ours – if you're free next Thursday evening, come along. You'd be very welcome.' This appeared a mere kindness to a new arrival in Oxford, but I felt too I was making a bit of mischief.

'Oh, drum,' she said, and grinned eagerly but narrowly at her fiancé. I took this at first as a genteel curse, like 'oh drat', but she shook her head. 'Drum won't want to come. He never reads a thing.'

'I do!' said Sparsholt happily. I had a salutary sense of their differences exposed and forgiven long before they'd taken their wedding vows. 'Drum' must be his nickname – or of course his second name, short for Drummond. It suited him much better than his first.

'Well, I'll see,' said Connie.

'No, you go with Freddie,' said Sparsholt, 'I've got training on Thursday night.'

It was touching that he trusted me, even if again he took a lot for granted. I saw that in his eyes I presented no threat. I said smoothly: 'I'll drop you a line. I think you'll be at Keble?'

'Yes . . . yes, I shall,' she said, and I saw she was surprised not only that I knew, but by the idea itself – it was still a novelty to her.

'You'd better tell me your surname.'

'It's Forshaw,' she said, 'yes,' and nodded as if hearing all that was satisfactory in the word.

'Are you coming in?' I said.

Sparsholt said, 'We're on our way to see a pal in St Peter's,' and Connie smiled and snuggled under his arm – the pal, I suspected, would be Gordon Pinnock, that true intimate of Sparsholt's, whom I'd never met, but whom Evert envied and almost detested, after their encounter in the loved one's rooms.

We turned and separated (Sparsholt wasn't one for saying goodbyes), they slipped at once into their own murmured talk, and it was ten seconds later that Connie called out – 'Oh . . . *Freddie* . . . Won't you join us for a drink tonight – in the pub?' She spoke as if there were one pub in Oxford, rather than two hundred.

'Well, if I can,' I said, as they came back to me.

'We'll be at the Gardener's Arms,' she said. 'At half-past eight.' I noted the way she threw out the name of this place she could never have seen. I had no real desire to go, and believed it would look odd, a third-year man out drinking with a freshman and his girl; but the strange mood of the Sparsholt affair made me feel I might regret missing it.

'Bring your girl along,' said Sparsholt.

'Oh, well . . . yes. I'll find out if she's free.' I didn't suppose she had a very full diary, but I couldn't see her in a pub – unless she took it, in her resolute way, as a challenge.

'What's her name, by the way?'

'She's called Jill.'

Was there something charitable in his hint of a smile? 'Ah, that's a nice name.'

'Well . . .' I said. It had always made me uneasy, it was too close to *chill*, and to *jilt*, and not at all far from *gill*, a quarter-pint of cold water.

As I left them and turned back to the gateway I glanced up at Evert's window and saw him standing there, staring down.

I nodded and raised a hand, but there was no response, and I went back to my rooms in a muddle of unexpected guilt and excitement.

I hadn't been to the Gardener's Arms since my first year. It was one of those dim little locals in St Ebbe's, with a front of glazed ox-blood brick, and a Public and a snug. I could picture the mild glow of its windows, the cheap Windsor chairs, the shove-ha'penny board by the door at the back. In the blackout it wasn't so easy to find. I made my way cautiously through the narrow streets, self-conscious in spite of the darkness. It was a pub where you might run into your scout, or people from the market. In fact I made a wrong turning, and took two or three minutes to find the way back. There were others about, of course, indecipherable signallers with their taped-over flash-lights; but the dark doorways and alleys re-awoke my sense of being watched or even followed by noiseless figures. I knew the pub, when I came to it, by the noise it made. In its entrance-way two curtains were fixed, with a narrow lung of changeable darkness between them, from which I groped half-panicking into the commonplace light of the saloon. I saw Sparsholt and Connie in the far corner and decided I would leave as soon as I'd done my good deed.

I nodded, left my hat on their table and fetched a glass of Ind Coope. I've never been a beer-drinker, and the wartime beer was especially foul, but I felt it was the thing to order. We sat for a minute admiring the sooty atmosphere of the pub – the soft thwack of the dartboard and murmur of scoring could be heard from the Public just visible beyond the bar. 'Have you been here before?' Connie asked – she was slumming it cheerfully with her Drum, but a certain fastidiousness peeped out. I said how my half-brother Gerald had brought me here when he visited in my first term; and how he himself had been brought here as a freshman by Wystan Auden. 'Auden liked St Ebbe's,' I said. 'He liked to show people the gasworks.' 'Oh, yes . . .' said Connie, and laughed unsurely; if her taste was for Dax's romances, she was probably less attuned to the angular new poetry of railways and revolt. I quite wanted to add that Gerald had gone to bed with Auden later that day, but I felt that just now it was a subject to steer clear of. I said merely that I remembered the cat, which seemed not to have moved in the past two years. There it lay, fat, hot and possessive in front of the coke fire, deaf to endearments and hostile to all strokes and tickles. The old man who was the only other occupant of the snug shook his head and said, 'Ah, Tiger . . .' in the tone one might use of a long-lasting problem, like arthritis, or the War itself. Connie smiled sternly at it. 'And what about Jill?' she said. She seemed to picture a feminine ally in this dingy place.

I sensed Sparsholt paying careful attention to my answer. 'She's awfully sorry but she can't come. She has an essay to write.' I felt sad that this respectable excuse would not last any of us much longer. And before she could put more questions, 'In fact I've asked my poet-friend Evert Dax to join us – I hope he can make it. He's A. V. Dax's son, and I thought since you like his books so much you might care to meet one of his other productions.'

'Gosh,' said Connie, pleased but a little flustered; and Sparsholt, who never admitted to surprise, said,

'Yes, he's a good man,' and nodded as he lifted his pint.

'You never said you knew him,' said Connie.

'I know all kinds,' said Sparsholt, and winked at her over the top of the glass.

'Oh, Drum,' she said; but she was preoccupied for a minute by the prospect of the encounter.

There was no sign of him after a quarter of an hour, though, when a new round had to be bought. I went to the bar and Sparsholt joined me, leaving Connie to her attempted seduction of Tiger. 'Won't you call me David?' he said, and I said of course I would. The barmaid, not specially friendly to students, took her time to turn round from the counter of the Public, framed through an archway like a picture of a brighter and more natural life. She carried on talking over her shoulder as she drew our drinks (stout for Connie, another bitter for David, and a gingerly half for me). David said he was paying (he had a sort of hard purse, the coins shaken out on to its leather tongue), and as he waited for the change his eyes studied the barmaid's round backside until he said, 'Isn't that your friend?' I was puzzled for a second, then looked through into the further space. It was clever of him to have known that the figure in a cap on the far side of the room, turned away from us as he bent over a newspaper, was Evert. 'It's Evert, isn't it?' he checked; then said 'Evert!' in such a sudden and carrying way that the dart-players turned, and Evert himself twisted round, alarmed as he was by any public attention, and overwhelmed to be called in this way by Sparsholt himself. He stood up, red-faced, grinning, channelling his confusion into the mime of taking his glass and his paper, going out into the street and fighting his way back, through a convulsion of curtains, into the snug.

'I didn't know you were in this bar,' he said – but the muddle had turned into a success, an endearing little incident, and he himself, in his time in the Public, had found the Dutch courage he needed. 'I'm so pleased to meet you,' said Connie, and Evert somehow found it in himself to say, 'And you too!' I seemed to see, in a crowded few seconds, his judgement of her voice, her look, his snobbish reserve at odds with his keen and jealous curiosity. I saw too that he focused his attention on her because he was too shy to look at David himself, who said, in the same hearty way, 'Evert, what are you having?' He'd got the name now, and he was using it as freely as he used mine.

Evert didn't look at me much either, but somehow conveyed a reluctant gratitude. I changed places and put him next to his idol, who sat forward with his splayed legs and their big boots tucked round his chairlegs and his knees in casual contact with Evert's. 'Well, this is nice,' said David, 'cheers, Evert!' and they jogged their drinks together, Evert's hand trembling and the thin spume of his pint slopping down the outside of the glass.

'Yes, cheers!' he said. If I hadn't been his chaperon I'd have laughed at his eagerness and terror. He had the nervous lover's long-held habit of backing away from what he most wanted, and here, although no one but me knew it, he was knee-to-knee with the man he adored. The whisky he'd had in the other bar must have helped; he was staring furtively at David's profile as if to confirm and explore his incredible situation. Connie said,

'I just wanted to say I'm a huge admirer of your father's books.' Evert said nothing. 'A. V. Dax,' she explained. If his flinching 'Oh, thank you' was meant as a snub, she was only a little discouraged. 'I expect people say that to you all the time . . . I just can't imagine growing up in a house where those wonderful books were being written' – and she gave a happy shudder.

'No, well . . .' said Evert. She wasn't to know of the difficult atmosphere at Cranley Gardens.

'It must have been so exciting,' she said.

'It wasn't a bit exciting,' said Evert, and with a brief smile, 'quite the contrary, I'm afraid.'

I thought I'd better step in, though it's hard to know what you can say to a stranger about a friend's private affairs. 'I don't believe Evert saw much of his father when he was growing up, just because he *was* so busy writing.'

'Well, I suppose,' said Connie. 'Yes, I see. They often say having a famous father isn't easy.' I'd never heard anyone say that myself, but I saw what she meant. 'Did he read aloud to you from his books?'

'Good God no . . .' Evert said, as David stared amusedly over his head, raised his chin and said, 'Gordon!'

Connie too looked relieved. 'There you are at last,' she said, as the drama of the curtain subsided, and a neat little fair-haired man in a trench coat stood smiling beside us. I waited to be introduced, while Evert folded himself over his pint and hid his face.

'Freddie, this is my old mate Gordon Pinnock, from back home' – David was already a bit noisy with drink.

'Hello . . . !' – and seeing Evert, 'Ooh, hello! *We*'ve met already. Gordon Pinnock.'

'Oh yes . . . that's right . . .' said Evert, in a negligent drawl at odds with his high colour.

'Oh, aye . . . ?' said David.

I said quickly, 'So were you two at school together?'

'That's right,' said Gordon.

'But not you?' I said to Connie; and by the time a small discussion of the matter had been got through, the question of Evert and Pinnock's earlier meeting was, perhaps shallowly, submerged. Gordon bought himself a gin-and-tonic, which I wished I'd had the sense to do too.

David was amused by the speed with which Evert downed his first pint – we all felt he had set a new pace, and knocked ours back too. Now the evening would be got through in a cheerful and approximate way, David would grow louder and more physical, Evert would be even more intoxicated, and the friendly closeness would grow all the more painful, with Connie holding David's hand on the tabletop, the pale blue stone of her engagement ring sparkling in the light. I felt I'd done my bit and I reached for my hat, but Connie looked truly upset. 'Please don't go, Freddie,' she said. I smiled regretfully. 'I want to talk to you about . . . Woodstock, and everything.'

Evert said boldly, 'Fred's got an ancient aunt who lives in Woodstock, but no one's ever met her.' I thought it was probably time to explode my aunt, but I couldn't do so here, in this company. I said,

'Ah, yes . . . well, excuse me a moment,' and went out to the foul-smelling gutter at the back, with its one light bulb and conspectus of venerable graffiti. Ten seconds later I heard footsteps and glancing sideways found David had come straight in after me – making loud grunts and sighs of urgency and enthusiasm. I valued a certain discretion at the urinal, the mild embarrassment covered by genial remarks unlikely to lead to conversation, a certain huddled concentration. But to David it was a chance for a confidential chat. He stood well back on the wet raised step, hands on his hips as a lively tide swept down the gutter towards me; he seemed almost to invite me to admire his performance. 'What do you think of my pet, then?' he said, and for a moment as I glanced at him I thought pet was his word for his organ. I studied the undead jokes in front of my nose, the intercalations by two or three hands in particular. 'Oh, I like her very much,' I said, and when I glanced again I found him looking shrewdly at me. 'Yes . . . yes, she's a great girl, isn't she,' he said, nodding steadily and relieved that I'd given my approval.

It wasn't a long evening, and we left before time was called, hurried through by the beer which they all had more stomach for than me. I was dismayed by how plastered I felt; and next day, when I wrote it all up in my diary, I was dim about the end of our session. I remembered my growing interest in Connie, and her extraordinary figure, which walked the giddy edge between comedy and dream. Much of the time Evert talked with David, exchanges hard to analyse, and which I was keen not to monitor too closely. At times it was as if the crisis was over, as Evert, after the shock of contact, was confronted by the cultureless blank of David's personality; certainly he had no other friends like him. But I noticed two other things. David himself seemed excited by contact with Evert: there was a subtle mixture of teasing and respect in the way he looked up at him through his eyebrows as he listened to the stories that Evert, in a tipsy and hit-and-miss attempt at impressing him, was excitably reeling out. And then there was that gleam of Evert's, controlled but breaking through the fug of the room, the grubby gloom of the pub, in passionate flashes, when he in turn listened to whatever David was saying.

Sometimes David asked Connie something, or put his hand on hers or on her knee, but he was happy to let her gossip with Gordon, the old friends reunited. They had the whole world of home to talk about. In Gordon's earnest attention to her, and his occasional shrieks of laughter, I quickly saw something else – that he was no threat to David, who looked on them both, almost smugly, as people devoted to himself. In fact Gordon, in his way, was more feminine than she was. Connie, with her coat thrown back on the chair, her hair down and feet sturdily apart, was reaching forward for her pint of stout, while Gordon centred his gin and tonic on the damp cardboard mat and made a private gesture with his tongue to tell her she had foam on her upper lip.

David had been eyeing the shove-ha'penny board and towards the end we all had to have a game. We huddled round the small bar-room table, I with the bland resignation of the born loser, but encouraged by the occasional astonishing pressure of Connie's bust against my arm. We smiled as the slipping and lazily revolving coins coasted over the board, smooth-worn old halfpennies with the profiles of Edward and George in helpless indignity as they swivelled and smacked off the frame at the top of the run. The right side of the board was faster than the left, and the middle was almost sticky. It was a question which was the cleverest way through, to bring the old coin up short in the topmost band, or to sail on past and deflect back into a good position. I was happy, briefly, to make an ass of myself, while Gordon made wild comic shots right off the table, followed by a grope between our legs on the grimy floor, David already lining up his next shot. It was a study in competition, and its avoidance. Evert played with the uncanny precision of the first-timer: the coin hovered and then halted between the lines as if drawn to a magnet. David gave us a valuable talk on the physics of inertia, but he wasn't nearly so good. He muffled his shame in quick heavy embraces, so that Evert had to shake him off to play, and at the end his wounded pride was almost concealed by a staring grin of congratulation. Gordon had kept score and announced the final order: '5th Green, 4th Pinnock, 3rd Forshaw, runner-up Sparsholt, winner Dax!' He squeezed Evert's arm, and it struck me he'd taken a shine to him on this second meeting: some hinted feelings had passed between these two men, and I wondered if they might not bury their shared passion for Sparsholt in a much more suitable tendresse for each other.

8

'What nice cups you have,' said Jill.

'Oh, yes, they're Meissen.' She had seen them several times, and had never appeared to notice them. 'Of course I'm flattered – I know you like your tea-things a millennium or two older.' Jokes were always a risk with Jill, but she made a comic moue I hadn't seen before, a little snubbing of the nose which struck me as a momentary foretaste of intimacy, in its unguarded gestures and feelings. She was in a new mood, more trusting and intriguingly less sure of herself. I set the low table in front of the fire. Behind me on the hearthstone the electric kettle had shifted from its first sharp sighs and creakings into a more enthusiastic rumble. 'I brought them from home,' I said.

'You have nice things then,' she said – and in her smile at the cup, with its tiny picture of pink hills, I saw a further prospect opening, in which I took her down to Devonshire with me to see other things we had, and to meet my mother.

'A few passable pictures, I suppose,' I said, 'but nothing exceptional. Don't forget my grandfather started as a humble grocer's boy.'

She surveyed this fact with a touch of complacency. When I'd made the tea she said, 'You've never asked me about my family,' so that her own reticence appeared almost to be my fault.

'Well, I'd love to hear about them, Jill dear.' I was charmed to watch her enter such personal territory for the first time – more than I was by the story itself.

'I had a difficult upbringing,' she said, tucking her chin in to suggest the unforgotten stress as well as her firmness in facing it.

'I'm very sorry,' I said, as I took the place beside her on the little sofa. She budged up slightly but kept on talking.

'By difficult I mean harsh and loveless and . . . confusing.' I thought she might have been describing a historical era, not the girlhood whose closing years she still inhabited.

'From the start?' I said.

'It was reasonably happy at first – I think you know my father was a solicitor, and my sister . . . well, I had a little sister.'

'You had?' – I turned sideways as I listened to her, and laid my left arm along the back of the sofa.

'She was knocked down by a van and killed, when she was six.'

'Ah, I'm sorry . . .'

'My father blamed my mother, and my mother frankly rather hit the bottle.'

'She felt she was to blame.'

'Well, she was to blame, she was with her at the time. This was in Fordingbridge,' she explained.

'You must have been a great consolation to them.'

Jill sighed emphatically but said nothing for a moment. 'I was away at school, and when I came home for the holidays I found my father had left.'

'Oh, I see . . . so just you and your mother . . .'

'Indeed. And before long my mother was quite unable to look after me. She sent me away to an aunt in Lancashire.' I don't know why I was smiling at this terrible precis of her family history. I laid my right hand consolingly on her wrist; she looked blankly at it for a second and then swiftly sat forward to reach her cup. 'I never had anything of my own,' she said, in a petulant tone, and took several quick, dissatisfied sips of tea.

'And what of your parents now?' I said. 'Your mother must—'

There was a rap on the door and Peter Coyle came straight in. 'Aha!' he said. 'My dears . . . well, well.' His smile was awful but flattering too. For some reason I justified myself:

'You know Jill's taking tutorials from Marley at Corpus, so I asked her to look in afterwards.'

'Very naturally,' said Peter.

Jill herself seemed conscious of the imputation in the air. 'I haven't seen you for ages,' she said. They'd never much cared for each other, but I could tell Jill was pleased he'd come in. Whether because she liked to be seen with me, or because it put an end to our tête-à-tête, it was hard to say.

'I've been so hideously busy,' Peter said, walking round the tea table with continuing mild amusement at what he'd found, 'painting the sets for this bloody *Triumph of Time*. And any number of other things,' he added slyly as he turned away and took off his hat and coat. 'Is there more in the pot?'

'There are more cups over there,' I said, rather sullenly, and my tone itself made him chuckle. He served himself, topped us up too, and looked sharply at Jill.

'Well, since you're here, Jill darling, perhaps I'll draw you.' It was quite as if she had barged in and not him.

I watched uneasily as he took his pad from his satchel, and a little tin of chalks. Jill seemed flustered but not displeased. Her attention was now divided between Peter and me, with Peter in charge and my own remarks a stilted sideshow to the portrait sitting. I started to feel I was the one who had barged in. He pulled round my desk-chair and sat with one leg cocked across the other to support his work. From time to time he slurped in his uncouth way from the teacup beside him on the desk.

'I was fire-watching at the Ashmolean last night,' he said, looking briskly up and down at Jill, who was in profile and pretending to read the book he had given her at random – pretending but soon almost furtively turning the pages while trying not to move her head. 'You don't have to sit still,' he said. 'The sort of thing I'm doing won't require it.'

'Oh . . . all right . . .' she said, adjusting cautiously to the idea of something freer, and perhaps not wanting to move much anyway; she waggled her head once or twice obligingly. Peter was sketching in great sensuous arcs which it was hard to associate with his sitter.

'It's marvellous up there – you should come, I mean you both should, of course.'

'Jolly cold, I should think,' said Jill.

'We could try it,' I said.

'While we were downstairs Gardner got the magic lantern going – we ran through thousands of slides, one after the other. The whole history of art in about two hours. Well, I suppose not the whole history of art. Giotto to Munnings. Plus all those naughty Attic vases, which sadly aren't there at the moment themselves.'

'Just as well,' said Jill, with a chuckle, but she coloured, perhaps the more so under Peter's scrutiny. She had a way of facing down her embarrassments – it was less embarrassing than letting them creep in and confuse her further. 'The Greeks were sex-mad,' she said firmly.

'Weren't they just!' said Peter.

'I don't suppose the Greeks carried on like that all the time,' I said, rather rattled myself to be talking about sex in Jill's presence. It was just the sort of awkwardness Peter liked to bring about. I recalled that even the Burgon Collection, mere water-colours of ancient objects, with descriptive captions, had caused Jill discomfort: '*Three nude men dancing*,' she said to me once – 'oh dear!'

Peter didn't explain why he'd come, and I guessed it was something even he was too delicate to mention in Jill's company. I was anxious Jill's portrait might be more like a caricature; but felt shy about going round and checking his progress. I made some nervously genial remark about the problems of drawing from life and when there was another firm knock at the door I jumped up quickly to see who it was. To my surprise David Sparsholt was standing there, in cap and greatcoat, and with a formal but distracted look. 'Oh . . . hello,' I said, with a small bored feeling that he'd got the wrong idea, and that I, the mere duenna in Evert's courtship, had become the object of his devotion instead. 'Who is it?' called Peter over his shoulder. I saw Sparsholt glance past me into the room. 'It's David Sparsholt,' I said. 'Come in, Sparsholt, old man!' said Peter, his surprise absorbed at once in the prospect of mischief; at which point I ushered him into the room.

Peter seemed quite tickled to see him, but kept steadily at work; Jill, still wary of moving, turned her head a little when he was introduced. Each knew something about the other, since Jill had been there on that evening in first week when we'd watched him half-naked across the quad; and David of course had coaxed certain romantic claims about her from me. So they each had the gleam of being in on a secret, or a joke – which was possibly disconcerting to the other. It was clear from David's bland politeness, as if to some old lady don, that he could never have fancied her himself. He pulled off his cap and gripped it in his hands throughout his brief visit.

'And what can I do for you?' I said. There was an idea (though we all showed how ready we were to overlook it) that it was odd of him to have dropped in like this on his elders.

'Am I interrupting you?' he said.

'Well, hardly' – I gestured at the sitting in progress, both artist and subject curious about the interrupter. It was clear that he wanted something, and had come to get it, but like Peter before him was inhibited by Jill. But then Peter too made him uncomfortable; he surely remembered their own sessions together, which I pictured like some regretted seduction never to be repeated. I also thought of the red chalk nude rolled up in the drawer in my bedroom. He looked over our heads, as if to far more important matters.

'I was wondering if you'd seen Mr Dax,' he said, the 'Mr' jocular but chilly too.

'How is Evert?' said Peter, mockery compressed in his frown at Jill.

'I haven't seen him for a day or two,' I said, 'but I've been in the country, you know.'

'Oh, yes,' said David, with a momentary smile. This was what we had now been told to call our activities at Blenheim Palace.

'Shall I pass on a message,' said Peter, 'if I see him?'

David paced to the window, where he stood and seemed to take in for the first time its relation to his own window, up under the pediment on the far side of the quad. Was a tremor of suspicion a part of his quick bracing movement, the shoulders thrown back, furled cap smacked softly in his palm as a colonel might have done with his gloves? 'No, it's not that important,' he said.

Peter's concentration darkened on the pad and the chalk and

his sharp glances at his subject seemed slightly overdone. 'And how is your fiancée?' he said.

'She's all right,' said David. 'She's had to go back home for a few days. Her uncle was killed in the air raid last week.'

'Oh dear,' said Peter, 'so you're all alone for a bit' – calculating as much as condoling, it seemed to me. I said,

'I'm sorry to hear that. And she'll miss Evert's father's talk tomorrow.'

'Yes, that's right,' David said, with reasonable curtness.

Jill was plainly surprised by how well we all seemed to know each other, and turned a page of her book with the stiff look of someone left out of a game.

'I'm not happy with it,' Peter said. 'Jill darling, I'm going to try again, next week.' He put his things away without letting us see what he'd done, and left abruptly, like someone who has been offended, though no doubt he merely had an assignation elsewhere. Something told me that David no longer mattered to him, and David as ever barely said goodbye to him.

Jill peered round and then stood up, as if slowly coming back to normality from a spiritual experience of some kind – an unusual look for her. She bent her attention graciously on David. 'It's strangely tiring, posing,' she said.

'You were only posing for ten minutes, dear,' I said.

'But I imagine you've had your portrait done' – her remarks were all for him.

He turned and smiled: 'Yes, I have,' though his pride in the fact was somehow compromised. I sensed he didn't want Jill to know that Peter had done him too.

'I hope you were painted in uniform?' she said, jutting her chin and as it were inspecting him, from bright boots to curly crown.

'No – no, I'm not in uniform yet, in fact,' said David, and glanced at me with a breath of a laugh. 'And anyway it was just a drawing.'

Jill kept smiling, in a rather fixated way. 'I'd very much like to see it,' she said. I think I coloured now myself – it was almost as though she knew I had it.

'I'm not sure – oh . . .' – this third knock at the door had the signature of farce, but it was only Phil, come to fix the blackout. As always at dusk he edged in to the room half-concealed by the oblong screen for my bedroom window, steered it through the further door and installed it first of all. The dusk itself had crept forward two hours since the start of the term, and made me wonder, in a bleak sideways thought, what progress I had made in my own affairs in that time. It was only when Phil came back that he noticed who was in the room; he busied himself with the fire with the look of someone with-holding criticism. 'Oh, excuse me,' he said, almost brusquely, as he went to the window and David, absorbed again in the view of the quad outside, seemed to wake up, and got out of the way. It was Phil of course who'd first told us about Sparsholt, that there had been some trouble, the rhythmical creaking a problem in itself but also perhaps a signal of further problems he had no wish to mention. Who knew what the scouts talked of, in their stark little pantries under the stairs, where they visited each other and drank tea? Phil would never have been openly rude, but there were times when a frustrated wish to sort us all out would darken his features. He heaped all the tea-things on the tray and left the room.

It felt to me high time that Sparsholt went too, but Jill was holding him there with a seductive intent she had never shown to me. It seemed the little hints of closeness she'd shown me when she arrived had been merely provisional, and had now fastened on to a worthier subject. I suppose the truth was I'd never till then thought she had desires. I said something to remind her the future Mrs Sparsholt had only gone out of town for a day or two; but it had no effect. She even said she'd love to meet her.

'You should have come to the pub with us the other night,' said David.

'Well,' said Jill, 'I would have done if I could' – a mercifully ambiguous answer. 'Where do you like to take her?'

David went quite pink at this. 'She only got here last week,' he said. 'We went to the dance at the Town Hall on Sunday afternoon.'

'Oh, goodness!' said Jill, in the tone one might have used before the War of a trip to Paris. 'I bet that was fun.'

'They had a pretty good band,' said David, as if he'd heard a fair few bands in his time. He was warming to her warily. 'You should get Freddie to take you.'

This seemed to remind her that I was in the room. 'Oh,' she said, 'Freddie doesn't care for dancing' – as if the question had ever once come up between us. I didn't know whether to grin, in the role of comical curmudgeon, or earnestly protest that she had never mentioned the subject. I said, 'Jill dear, I love dancing, if I've had a few drinks.'

'You can do anything on a few drinks,' said David.

'Well, you can get drunk,' I said, which wasn't quite a joke. He stood and waited a second, and then smacking his cap in his palm again he said goodbye and crossed the room.

'Bye . . .' said Jill, watching the door close.

'Sorry about that,' I said, as his heavy tread diminished down the stairs; then a moment later was heard in the quad. 'He's only seventeen.' Jill didn't quite look at me, she had for the second time the smile of someone under the spell of a recent experience, and reluctant to be brought back to reality. 'You're only twenty yourself,' she said.

This came as a slight surprise even to me. I said, 'What I mean is, I'm afraid he's rather a bore.'

Now she looked at me with droll disparagement. 'He's gloriously handsome,' she said – I could see her own words excited her and deepened the feeling they expressed. It was the exalted tone I knew all too well from Evert. 'Like Clark Gable.'

He really didn't look like Clark Gable, but I answered pleasantly, 'Well, I never know. I suppose he must be, from the effect he has on all my friends.'

'For God's sake,' said Jill, with an odd chuckle.

'In form and moving how express, and admirable . . . maybe,' I said.

'Mm?'

I laughed. 'Jill darling, if you had to talk to him for more than five minutes you'd be yawning your head off.' I'd never called her darling before and I couldn't tell if she took it as a tribute or a liberty. She smiled remotely as she put on her coat.

'Who's talking about talking?' she said.

'Ha-ha!' This was a mad leap from anything I knew of her, and I saw how in twenty minutes the whole occasion, which had started so sweetly, had slewed out of my control. Now it was her turn to tease me, with her admiration for this teenage star, in whose dull square face she claimed to see beauty, where I saw only the vacuum of culture, the cheery indifference to everything Jill and I, surely, most prized. I said with a forced grin, 'Well, we'll go dancing, then. I'm going to take you.'

'I'll hold you to that,' she said, inattentively, as she looked for her hat.

I found it for her and guided her to the door, as if about to start dancing there and then. I slipped a hand round her waist and just before I turned the door handle, as I stooped my head with a questioning smile, she said sharply, 'Freddie, this kissing must stop.'

Even now I feel the reproving force of those words. She blurted them out, but they had a considered ring, a fatal formula she might have rehearsed many times and which, if so, represented in one stiff phrase a very deep disgust. I stood astonished, and making those immediate convulsive allowances with which one tries to save a person who has been startlingly rude, and almost to reassure them that they haven't been. I flinched, I blushed, and I believe I giggled, in spite of myself, just for a moment. 'Freddie,' she said, 'you haven't understood at all.'

9

November 14 had arrived, the day of Victor Dax's talk to the Club. Before lunch I quickly rewrote my two-page introduction, and then stood to rehearse it, looking out at the quad through rain-streaked windows. As secretary I liked to speak without notes (last week I'd surprised myself with a ten-minute eulogy on Cecil Day Lewis, who'd said drolly that it ought to be published); but Victor was making me anxious. It wasn't only my mixed feelings about his work (I thought much of Day Lewis was windy and derivative), or the fact of his being Evert's father. It was to do with the portrait of him Evert had created, inadvertently and piecemeal, in my mind: a man with few friends and little humour, proud of his gift and disdainful of his contemporaries; a man of fanatical habits, who worked each day from eight till four, seen by no one but Herta with her lunch tray; who had, like Brahms or Balzac, a coffee-making device and dosed himself into a mania of production, but then emerged and moved, full of remote benignity, among his family; whose children, even so, lived so much in fear of saying the wrong thing that they barely said anything to him at all. Most worryingly for me, it seemed that praise – a full-page notice in the *New York Times*, the award of a prize or the Légion d'honneur – made him specially touchy, as if it were too late, too small, or itself somehow belittling. Still, praise him I must, and I was changing my little essay once again in my mind when I saw Evert coming across the quad towards my staircase. His umbrella concealed him from the chest up, but there was no mistaking his walk, the quick small steps. 'My dear, what a day!' he said, when he'd come into my room and then gone out again to leave the opened brolly on the landing. ('Bad luck,' I heard him say, 'but still . . .': the War combined with the Sparsholt affair had made him madly superstitious.)

'I think things are more or less in order,' I said.

'Mm . . . ? Oh, good . . .' Evert had the look of hollow sleeplessness I'd grown used to, and today he was smiling too, a tense, persistent smile, as if refuting a series of arguments. I'd known from the start that his father's visit was a challenge for him, which only added to the worry I felt about it myself. A note had come to me from Victor's secretary announcing his arrival on the 4.30 train, which left us with nearly two hours in which to amuse him before dinner.

'This weather's not encouraging, but perhaps your father would like to see the tombs in the Cathedral.'

'Oh, Christ!' said Evert.

'Or I thought some of the Rawlinson manuscripts in Bodley, for instance—'

'My father's coming.'

'Well, yes. You mean you'd forgotten?'

Evert looked at me and shook his head. 'Oh, Fred,' he said. 'That's not why I'm here, you know.'

'Well, it's a good job you are, none the less.'

'No, no . . .' He walked around abstrusely for a minute with a hand raised to forbid questions. Then he took an envelope from his breast pocket. 'I really wanted you to see this,' he said, but held it and pondered it for a while before passing it over; then he sat down and crossed his legs, and stared ahead as if mentally ready – for triumph or despair, or simply perhaps to reply. In the envelope was a standard white postcard with the College's embossed address, and beneath it a mere three characters, in careful blue ink:

$$\alpha \ \& \ \Omega$$

'Little alpha,' I said, 'but upper-case omega.'

'Yes,' said Evert, still gazing ahead, 'he's a scientist, not a classicist.'

I winced, stared again at the card, played the part of the slow-witted friend. 'So you know who sent it,' I said. I had my ideas, but felt there must be an element of doubt.

Evert said nothing, but gazed at the cornice, still with his provoking hint of a smile. He said, 'The question is not who it's from but what the person who sent it means by it.'

'I feel to know that one would have to know who the sender was. It might be, as you say, scientific, it might be religious, it might be, well, some other kind of symbol.'

'It's from him, Freddie – from Drum.'

'Drum is it now?' He stared ahead. 'In that case not religious, I think.'

Evert laughed briefly at my tone but he trembled, or rather a single shiver passed through him, before he said quietly, 'I spent last night with him. This was in my pigeonhole at ten o'clock this morning.'

This was a mad way of speaking, and I treated it lightly. 'You spent the night.'

'I had him,' said Evert.

I was never a bit rattled by the sexual anecdotes of my friends but I may have shown that on this occasion I was shocked. Shock no doubt was part of the effect he was aiming for, the shock of the fact and of the brutal little phrase; I think he was startled by it himself. I felt the burn of something darkly secret, even wicked, and I hid the stiffness of my features by returning to the window and gazing down into the quad, as my tutor did when pursuing a complex argument. I saw that likewise I had to test what Evert had said. It was something Peter Coyle threw out once a week – 'I had him': but quite what this 'having' was one never knew, and hardly liked to ask. Nor could I ask now. I said, 'What about Connie? It simply doesn't make sense.'

'Connie's gone home for a couple of nights for her uncle's funeral. And anyway, there's a side of Drum that doesn't make sense.'

'Well, no doubt—'

'I mean he doesn't make sense in the sense that you mean sense.' There was something tryingly riddling about Evert today, a mixture of defiance and anxiety. But he was probably right. I thought of Sparsholt's unexpected visit to my rooms the day before, and the question he'd asked, almost reluctantly, as to where Evert was. And now I glimpsed, with a wary curiosity close to envy, the two of them together. It wasn't envy for Evert's act, however I pictured it, that troubled me, but for his having acted. His body held a knowledge that could neither be expressed nor forgotten, but which invested it, in my young eyes, with the indefinable aura of experience.

I'm not sure if I provoked him into telling me the story, or if he was set on doing it anyway. He seemed still astounded himself that it had happened, that love had flowered in this unlikeliest of places. He wanted to get it clear, and I felt that what I was hearing was the primary text: it would be no good deciding later on that something different had been said or done. I don't rule out to this day that he may have exaggerated certain points; and I sensed a strange relish that his victory over Sparsholt was a victory over me, of whom he had long been pointlessly jealous. But I saw even so that I was the recipient of the essential truth. Again I give the story as he let me see it.

*

During Hall the previous night they had twice caught each other's eye: the first time, David looked instantly away, but the second time there was the flicker of an eyebrow and suppression of a smile as he turned his head to speak to his neighbour, and Evert believed that over the following minute David was conscious of him, and that something had not only been acknowledged but promised. Something tiny, no doubt – it was the frail first chapter of a friendship, that might still be screwed up and thrown away without much sense of loss on David's part. But that they were friends, since their evening in the pub, was surely beyond question. When they stood for grace there was no more than a glance before the bowing of the head – but it now felt to Evert inevitable that on the stairs outside, as they made their way down in the dark like so many fireflies, a hand should grip his elbow and a light flash upwards on the face beside his own. He looked devilish like that, and still gleamed on the eye in the darkness half a minute later, when he could barely be made out in fact; though it wasn't at all clear what was happening, and neither of them said a word till they were out in the quad, where they would normally have turned in opposite directions. The blackout was no place for polite indecision – in a moment Evert might have lost him. He knew that the grip, and the flash of the torch, might be no more than childish clowning; he foresaw the scene of misunderstanding, the mortified return to his own room, alone; but his pounding heart made him walk on beside David, and then quite accidentally he stumbled against him in the dark – he felt his strong hand grab at him again and steady him. 'All right there, Evert?' he said, with a quick laugh; and then, in a very flat voice, in which all the things he would rather have done seemed to loom and die, 'So what are you doing tonight?'

'Oh . . . nothing,' said Evert, with a half-glimpsed image of Roderick Random and Peregrine Pickle, the subjects of this week's essay, tumbling into a dark chasm, where Dryden's plays and the *Life of Johnson* already lay abandoned.

'You don't fancy a pint, later on?' And now it was all the other men David might have gone drinking with that Evert pictured, in a shadowy crowd.

'Oh, well, yes – if you like,' he said, sounding nearly reluctant with excitement. It was the question he'd failed to ask a dozen times himself, and he thought he detected a slight airy nervousness in David, as if he too had rehearsed it. But he kept his head. 'Will Connie be joining us?'

'No . . . no, she's gone home for a couple of nights. Her uncle's been killed.'

'Oh, I'm so sorry,' said Evert – and in his happiness he almost was sorry for her, in a generous overspill of feelings. Though of course what this meant was that David simply needed someone to fill the time with: no doubt this peculiar second-year man who seemed to quite like him would do as well as any. Evert's job, very likely, would be to condole with him on Connie's absence, and to say repeatedly what a great girl she was. 'What time would suit you?' he said.

'I expect you're too busy,' said David.

'No, no – really,' said Evert.

'Then what about eight?'

'Yes, perfect.' There was something in him that seized on this forty-five minutes' reprieve, and he went to his room and paced back and forth, glancing at his watch and thinking by turns it had stopped or was running fast.

When he went down to the Tom Gate, David was already waiting, and sounded impatient. 'Do you want to go to the Marlborough House?' he said. Evert felt he might be regretting his invitation.

'Wherever you like,' he said amiably, though his heart was racing. A smooth remoteness of manner covered him sometimes, the trance of tension. It was a ten-minute walk to the

Marlborough, over Folly Bridge and away from the centre of town, into a part where fewer students went. He felt David had chosen it because he wanted to be alone with him; and it was only once they'd set off down St Aldate's that he saw it was just as likely he didn't want his rowing friends to see them together. Well, perhaps both things were true. 'Good to get some exercise,' he said.

'If you call this exercise,' said David – in the dark it was hard to tell if he was teasing. Evert felt already his humour was a thing of situations more than tones, and that irony might nettle him if it didn't elude him altogether.

'Not to you, of course,' said Evert firmly, and rubbed shoulders with him for a step or two. He knew that he was older, and much more sophisticated, but he'd surrendered so much in advance to the figure beside him that it was hard to remember they were barely friends. He saw the heavy disproportion in their feelings for each other, but was too light-headed to worry about it. Surely both of them felt the novelty of their first walk alone together. They heard the far-off drone of planes passing high up to the west, and David grunted and looked skyward. The moon, nearly full, was hidden by the high walls of the College as they went downhill, and disappeared behind cloud as they approached the river. He seemed to Evert both uneasy and determined.

There was a square way round to the pub by road, but half-way over the bridge Evert felt David touch his arm and they crossed to the far side – thirty seconds later he was following him down the narrow footbridge that breaks off through a gap in the parapet to the riverbank below. Evert would never have taken the towpath alone at night, it seemed even darker than the street they had left, the river nothing at first but a quick and irregular licking sound, and then, as they walked on, a broad barely visible presence, curving northwards – the sheds and chimneys of the gasworks on the far bank just beginning to show against grey cloud. It was a further little test of nerve, Evert flashed his torch with an anxious laugh, and David said, 'Best not to use that' – as though they might give themselves away.

At the pub they groped their way into the cheering glare of the public bar, where a few heads turned, and Evert himself stared at David with disbelief. He said quietly, 'What will you have?' But David seemed puzzled, not by the momentary attention of the room or by Evert's gleaming look but perhaps by the bar itself not matching the idea he had had of it when they set out.

'There's another bar, isn't there?' he said; and after they'd peered through the door into the empty snug – 'Let's go in here.' To Evert it had the air of taking a room in a hotel – he pushed the door to behind them and found he couldn't quite look at David. They unbuttoned their coats and hung them on the stand, Evert purchased their pints of mild and bitter, and brought them over to where David was sitting, beneath the dim ceiling light, in the odd raw smell of the blackout curtains and the banked coke fire. He saw now that David had changed to come out, into old flannels and a home-knitted jersey surely made for the much smaller boy he had been two years ago. The low table had a beaten copper top, and the glass roared a little as he slid it towards him. He raised his own glass to his chin, met David's eye, and for the first time in his life said, 'Cheerio!'

When they left the pub they had each had three pints, and Evert found himself in the most unexpected, exciting and worrying position – he had made a huge advance, but into territory he had never dreamt of. The rush of drunkenness and the immediate return to the dark outside world made things all the more confusing and inescapable. The three pints themselves were like the acts of a drama – a strange, experimental one, spoken in fragments and murmurs, but to Evert the most intense he had known, dark with surprises and decisions; the decisions seemed almost to make themselves, in the liberty of drink and the irrefusable presence of the man he adored.

To begin with their shyness made them rush at things. The outing was David's idea, but he hadn't suggested it had a purpose, and to Evert simply being with David was purpose enough. Still, he heard something forced and masochistic in his own first question: 'How's Connie getting on in her new job?'

David looked into the barely smouldering fire. 'Oh, all right, thanks, Evert – it's, you know, very long hours.' He spoke consciously as one of a couple. It was a place, a view, that Evert had never inhabited, but he took some small amusement from the frown.

'So you don't see much of her?'

'It's not perfect,' said David, flatly stoical.

Evert left a considerate pause. 'Still, it's better than nothing!' he said. David grunted and looked again at the fire. He perhaps didn't want to talk about his private life, any more than Evert wanted to hear about it; even so, to hear about it was to move in the magic zone of his confidence, to be privy to his secrets. 'I wasn't quite clear the other night what she's actually doing. She's . . . well, she's so bright!'

'Oh, aye,' said David, as if that were both a proud fact and a bit of a problem. Was it possible something was wrong, there was some intimate obstacle with which he needed help? He spoke bluntly, as though impatient with Evert for not knowing: 'Well, you know she's at Blenheim Palace, she's working there.' For a second he had the glare of efficiency, he was the soldier in mufti, the opposite of Evert, the essential civilian; who said,

'Ah, yes, I see,' though in fact it was mere rumour to him what was going on at Blenheim. He sensed he'd missed hints before.

'Along with our friend Mr Green,' said David.

Evert said, 'Quite so . . .' as if discreetly concealing his own knowledge of this confidential matter. He was surprised, and pleased, by that cool 'Mr Green'. Then he found David was giving him a sly but rather beautiful smile, and he held his gaze for as long as he could, and then looked down in confusion. He wasn't sure what had happened, but he hoped to take advantage of it.

Evert of course couldn't judge how David saw their evening going – perhaps just a pint and then a quick walk back to College. He loved sitting close to him, looking at him as much as he liked, laying his hand on his arm now and then to make some amusing point – the smoky drabness of the bar was to him a golden privilege . . . but it was painful too, because it forced a recognition: he was his friend now, but he would never be more. As Evert finished his beer David stood up and said, 'The same again, then?' as if in his view the evening was going well – perhaps only just getting started. There was the same small fraction of play-acting, as there was in his being engaged, or at other times in rowing kit. Evert watched him at the bar, the old flannels tight too around his over-developed backside and thighs, and almost worn through under his seat – he was standing a drink but it was obvious he had very little money.

It was only when David sat down again that Evert saw he had something particular on his mind, and thought for a second it might be some gentle but awful rebuke, and that their first time alone together was designed exactly to be their last. 'Cheers!' said David again. 'So you haven't heard about my bit of trouble?'

'Oh, no!' said Evert. 'Back home, do you mean?'

'Not that, no – though that's pretty bad' – and he seemed ready to talk about the air raids instead, but stopped himself: 'No, I mean this business in College.'

'I haven't heard a thing,' said Evert, sounding slightly indignant. A number of ideas appeared to him like figures glimpsed in a room before the door is shut. 'What is it? – if you want to tell me, that is.' He thought it would be very hard after that for David not to.

David glanced at him with a quick provisional smile and took a swallow of beer before he answered. 'I'm in trouble with the Censor.'

'Oh, yes . . . ?'

'I didn't know the ropes, you see – I see that now.'

'Ah,' said Evert, pretending even to himself he didn't see what was coming. But then, 'You mean to do with Connie?'

David pursed his lips and nodded. Was he going to make Evert come out with it for him? 'I see,' said Evert, feeling there was still some welcome ambiguity.

'Yep,' said David, and drank some more. 'No, what happened, if you want to know, was that my scout came in first thing two days ago and found us together. And he's reported me to the Censor. He's never liked me, since that business with Sangster downstairs – well, you wouldn't know about that.'

'The scout hasn't, you mean . . .'

'Well, or the Censor.' It was that baffling idea, for Evert, of anyone not liking Sparsholt, or giving him the widest licence.

'So what did the Censor say?' Evert found he was picturing the moment of discovery, the threshold of the blacked-out bedroom where he himself had first met Gordon Pinnock. He was appalled to think David might be about to leave in disgrace, never to be seen again. 'He can't send you down for that,' he said, in solid defiance of the truth.

'Oh, he's not sending me down,' said David. 'Don't worry.'

'Ah good,' said Evert.

'No, he says in view of the fact that I'm about to leave anyway, he doesn't want to mess up my service career.'

'Well, that's a relief.'

'And of course the fact that we're engaged, which must make a difference.'

'Yes . . .'

In the pause that followed, while David nodded and then drank and set down his glass, it was as though there were no problem after all. 'No,' said David, 'but he is going to fine me.'

'Oh, well . . .' said Evert, and thought he sounded too careless. 'A lot?'

'Twenty quid,' said David.

Evert winced sympathetically. '*Quite* a lot.' It was exactly what he was going to pay his North Oxford contact for a second little landscape by Stanley Goyle – in another two weeks, when his December allowance from his father came through. 'Can you manage?'

David flung himself back in his chair, in a gesture of defeat that was also a kind of display. He showed his wounded magnificence, his sweater tight across his chest as he spread his arms and shrugged. And he looked directly at Evert, with the perfect blankness of someone calculating a move. 'I can't ask my parents, of course' – he gave a curt laugh, and now his look at Evert seemed faintly accusing.

'I can see that might be difficult.'

'I mean, they're very strict – you know what parents are.'

'Yes,' said Evert kindly. He thought his own father, though he'd complain about it, would be hugely relieved to hear that he'd had a woman in his room. David sighed deeply, and slid further down in his chair, in a strange abandonment of his normal alertness; one leg pressed against Evert's calf. 'Will you be able to manage?'

'I haven't got it,' said David, curtly. 'We've got a bit put away, you know, for the wedding. But that's untouchable.'

'No, quite,' said Evert.

'That has to be untouchable.'

The word seemed to Evert oddly provoking. His eyes

played over his friend in a stunned inventory of his merits. It was a reckless, sickening decision, that must be made briskly and completely. 'Can't I help you out?' he said. David stared back at him, with respect, as well as the proper gloom of someone who must decline the offer they have just solicited.

'I couldn't accept,' he said; but there was something else, as he sat up and leant forward, the dull glint of the tactician, to whom winning is everything.

'I don't have a lot of money,' said Evert, 'but I could probably lend you, you know . . . what you need . . . tomorrow.'

'Really?' said David. Now he seemed all anxious solicitude for him. 'Isn't it too much? It's a hell of a lot. Well, that's grand' – sticking out a hand, to shake on it, in a way both gracious and inescapably businesslike. Before he let the hand go he jerked Evert forward, flung his other arm round him and hugged him; did he even kiss his ear? – clumsily spontaneous, it was too as if he'd found a moment to do something long planned. Or so Evert was to feel the next day. 'You're a real friend.' And he sat back, manly and capable again, staring at the table as at the barely doubted outcome of a daring act: he seemed to see his rightful future given back to him.

With the third pint they moved away from the fine and the loan, though the question still gaped darkly for Evert. The beer carried them along for the moment. 'So tell me more about your family,' said David, a diplomatic new line. And for a minute or two Evert did so, but stumbling and exaggerating out of worry that he wouldn't find them interesting. David nodded and gave occasional small smiles of recognition. His question was (Evert sensed it already) the inattentive politeness of a man who still wanted mainly to talk about himself, or who had not yet quite learned the art of conversation. Evert said how his sister was living in Tenby with their mother.

'Is she pretty?' David wanted to know.

'Yes, she is,' said Evert, 'well, they both are!' – annoyed by his mechanical interest in Alex instead of himself.

'Perhaps she'll come and visit you,' said David.

'You can meet her if she does,' said Evert. 'If you're still here.'

'Ah . . . well!' said David, and nodded over his pint at the justice of the remark. 'Anyhow, you're not bad-looking yourself, you know.'

'Well . . .' said Evert, astonished, and grateful, but caught at once in the maze of impossible replies. David's own beauty was the unspoken context, and of course his incalculable modesty and vanity shaded any such compliment. 'As I say, my mother's very pretty,' he said.

'There,' said David, almost reproachfully, and for the first time, miraculously, he blushed.

It was on their brief walk back to College, in the barely penetrable dark, that the new possibility took shape, unseen, between them. That it couldn't be happening, was only a possibility, gave it a kind of terror to Evert. The walk by the bickering river, that had been stiff and self-conscious on the way out, now was hurried along home on a giddy-making swirl of altered meanings. When David abruptly took his arm Evert stumbled to get into step – 'Shape up!' said David, and the unstated promise of the light grip and then squeeze of his elbow against David's ribs had to struggle with the wild unlikeliness that anything further could happen. The white rings painted round tree trunks marked out their passage to the footbridge. Surely it was a mean and wicked game, to encourage a belief without putting it in words, ready to rebuff it if Evert dared to act on it. But not to dare would leave him with tormenting regret. Their element was the night and the unspoken, in all its queasy ambivalence. When they reached the great gateway and ducked through its small postern Evert's pulse was bouncing in his ear. Then inside, with the vast unseen courtyard a mere intuition beyond them, he said, 'I've got whisky in my room, if you're on for another drink.' There was something in him that hoped David would say no, and restore him to his accustomed state of unbreachable longing; but something else that made him smile in the face of the darkness when he said, 'Yes, all right,' and then, 'Show me the way!'

Evert seemed to retain just a few impressions of what happened in the room. To him it raced with tension, and David himself showed a jocular unease as he hung up his coat and flung himself down in the armchair by the grey fire. Then he sprang forward, poked the embers gently to uncover them before he put on the last two pieces of coal from the box. They both watched the fire as if it were the most important thing in the world. Evert saw that the room, which he disliked, and its precious books and pictures, were not of the slightest interest to David.

He poured out a good inch of whisky, and offered water, which David rejected. There was something quite rough in his reach for reassurance, the stiff fix of alcohol. Evert hovered near the window, smiling like someone alone at a party. After a minute David sat forward to tug off his sweater, and barely looked round as he chucked it on the floor beside his chair. Evert stared at it, talking distractedly as he made his way slowly towards it. He picked it up, while discussing with elaborate pointlessness the essay he was meant to be writing, which itself was as pointless and remote as starlight when he held the warm homemade mass of the sweater, with its smells, soft or sharp, of David's person against himself and then slowly folded it and set it on the table as if quite unaware he had done so. David's look, his near-smile, tongue on lip, was mocking and as it lingered almost tenderly questioning. 'You're as bad as my Connie,' he said – and the mention of her seemed to reassure him, and to clarify perhaps his sense of whatever it was he was doing now. He slid forward in his chair, head thrown back, boots straight out across the hearthrug. Evert knew already how David took drink, and noted the way he mugged being drunker than he was. He saw for three seconds David was showing him a thing beyond speech, and looked away and back again in hot-faced excitement. Then David dropped his hand and covered himself loosely, as if Evert were indeed a pervert to peep at a man's lap. In his other hand, flung out across the arm of the chair, the whisky glass was at an angle, only lightly held. 'Careful . . .' said Evert, and David, lifting his head, saw what he meant, and drank a slug of it as if swallowing a pill. Now his sly little smile had faded, the instinctive command of mere gesture became a scowl, as if something faintly unreasonable had been asked of him. 'Well, we'll have to have the light out,' he said.

It was with an incredulous tension, as if carrying some large delicate object, that Evert, with his eyes fixed on David's, slid back step by step towards the bedroom door. In there too the blackout was up, the dark air, as he pushed the door open, as cold as a pantry. He didn't dare disobey by flicking the light switch, or feeling for the bedside lamp. He felt he had a look of terrified coquetry as he stood there, and watched David get up, with the sigh of a strong man who's been called on to help, the nod of almost concealed satisfaction, and come towards him with the whisky bottle in his hand.

In the calm after David had gone he thought lucidly of the Goyle that he'd seen and would perhaps never now own; the strange economics of the thing appeared to him – the loan had been made for love, it was the unexpected surrender of something lifeless but lasting for something impulsive and unrepeatable. His collector's obsession seemed mere consolation, a sad shadow of his obsession with David, whom he would never own, but had borrowed for an astonishing few hours. For the moment the heat of the memory peopled the chilly room where he lay, with the blankets pulled up, staring into the darkness. He was awake, and alone in a new way, pulsing with hope and triumph and a quite unexpected prospect of despair. The beauty of the thing was that the surrender had been wholly unnecessary for David – he had won the promise of the loan already, on the sheer intuited force of Evert's feelings for him. He showed a leader's strength, a sixth sense of what others would do for him. But then to come to his room, to encourage him and submit to him, was pure will and hunger, and a taste for danger – freed from one kind of sexual trouble he entangled himself at once in another. Evert imagined him a few months ahead, as a fighter pilot of idiotic daring and brilliance. And then, as the first sounds of day began, and he waited for his scout to come into the next-door room, open the black curtains, and take out the ashes and the empty glasses, the thought of David on the far side of the world, in the unknowable future of the War, turned him suddenly cold. He got out of bed, put on his dressing gown and went into the sitting room, where old Joe, who was always so tickled and confused by the Anders Zorn woman, big-hipped, heavy-breasted on a Nordic beach, was plumping the cushions in a genteel mime of curiosity and reproach. 'A bit of a session, sir?' he said.

Evert's yawn and stretch as he crossed the room disguised a sudden horror of discovery; he pretended unconcern at whatever Joe was doing. 'A friend came round for a bit of a . . .' – for a moment he couldn't decide . . . 'I suppose it *was* a bit of a session,' he said. He peered out at the dull dawn – no, there was nothing to worry about here, but in the bedroom? For a wild few seconds he saw himself being called up by the Censor, on grim evidence from Joe, and being made to pay a further £20 to get out of trouble. There was the slight noise of the gate being opened down below to the left, and as he half-knelt on the window seat, and looked out, he heard a quick shout and saw the squad of two dozen men in dark running gear swing out at speed on to the Broad Walk and cross in ten seconds into the avenue beyond. The dark path as much as the gleams of the reflected room had swallowed them up. But he had seen David there, in the thick of the other men, in their fast forward rush. He seemed restored to his rightful element – nothing made the chasm between them clearer than this instant unswerving return to the life of the crew, and their charge to the river at first light.

Evert cut his tutorial that morning, and it wasn't till after ten that he went to the lodge and found the postcard he had shown me, and which he now took back, with a look of slight mistrust. It seemed very likely to me that David would regard the night-time favour as itself the repayment of the promised loan, but I couldn't tell if Evert had yet made the calculation of his own folly – a feverish two or three hours in bed at a cost of £20. He said, 'So we return to the question of the card, Fred, the alpha and omega. Does he mean that I'm the be-all and end-all?'

'Well, indeed,' I said. 'Or does he mean,' and I was as tactfully objective as possible, 'that that was not only the first time, but the last time too?'

Evert and I went down to the station to meet his father, and said nothing more about the matter; our talk was bright but empty for the lack of it. And in that evasion I saw something else – that this Sparsholt affair, which had consumed my friend's life and pressed for a few weeks so oddly on my own, was surely quite unknown to the rest of the world. Evert, I felt certain, had no other confidant, and it was unthinkable that Sparsholt himself would speak of it. It had already assumed its true scale, something fleeting, and entirely personal, too hidden to rate even a footnote in the history of its time. I doubt anyone has spoken a word of it till now. I glanced at Evert as we hurried down past the Castle. 'Did Dad write to you about the train?' he asked.

'Well, I had a note from his secretary.'

'Oh, yes? I didn't know he had a secretary. What's she called?'

'I can't remember.'

'It's probably just the woman who does his typing: Miss Hatchet?'

'Perhaps,' I said, though it didn't sound quite right.

The train was late, of course, and we sat for ten minutes in the blacked-out waiting room, sharing a discarded copy of the *Oxford Times*. Unlike Evert I was hungry, but the once friendly chocolate machine had been empty for months. Still, I tugged at the drawer. Then the train was in the station, and we had to jog along beside it towards the first-class carriage, in which Evert had spotted his father sailing past as the engine slowed. I'd caught a glimpse of a severe pale face and of a figure behind him, hovering or reaching up to the rack above his head, a woman in a wide-brimmed hat and a ginger fur. The grinding scream of the brakes lent an edge to my nerves.

I had no idea how Evert would greet his father – in fact they both avoided a greeting, Victor turning as he stepped down to address the woman behind him, with the wide hat, who I saw was a complete surprise to Evert. 'This is Miss Holt,' Victor said, 'my secretary.' We all shook hands, Miss Holt hanging back and looking after a large briefcase as well as her own handbag and two umbrellas. Victor wore a grey trilby and a red paisley scarf, between which his smooth blue-eyed face looked out blankly. His book jackets bore no photographs, but I had seen his picture in the paper, and imagined a much larger man. Evert stood two inches taller, but no doubt saw him in all the psychological grandeur of a parent; to me the first impression was of a humourless businessman of superior rank, neat, pre-occupied, more likely to be a slave than a master of the word.

'I don't know what you'd like to do,' I said, preparing my small menu of amusements.

'We'll go straight to the Mitre,' he said. 'I need to press on with an article for Sweden.'

Evert looked relieved, and I'm not sure what I felt.

A taxi was an expensive rarity, and I proposed that we go into town by bus. A bus was waiting, nearly full, at the station entrance, and we clambered on, Victor absorbing the indignity by pretending not to be in a bus at all; I paid their fares. Evert sat beside his father, and I squeezed up with Miss Holt and her bags in the seats behind them. Every now and then Victor turned and said loudly, 'That's Worcester College, Miss Holt . . . That's Elliston & Cavell's . . .' At another time Evert might have been embarrassed by his father, but today he was barely with us; his yawns were his helpless tribute to the night before. If Victor was conscious of the minor stir he caused on the bus he perhaps put it down to his being known; and there was something unaccountably distinctive about him, it seemed to me, which made anyone who'd glanced at him once do so again. His voice *carried*, even in Oxford, a city of unstoppably self-confident talkers: it was crisp, autocratic, he had caught to perfection the drawl and snap of the upper classes, but with the charm and oddity of an 'r' rolled lightly in the back of the throat. In his mouth such familiar monuments as the Radcliffe Camera and the Clarendon Building emerged in a subtly glamorized light. 'That's Christ Church down to the right, Miss Holt, where my son is.' Evert turned and smiled in confirmation and apology.

Evert, Charlie Farmonger and I went over at five-thirty to collect our guest for dinner; we planned a drink in the bar first. He came in with a small cigar going, and Miss Holt again just behind.

'There's one thing I'd ask,' he said, as he took his glass of gin. 'Will you be introducing me later on?'

'I will, sir, yes. I thought—'

'Keep it brief, if you don't mind.'

'I won't go on long,' I promised.

'I gave a talk in Paris last year – chap went on for a good twenty minutes, full of praise, of course, finest writer alive and all that, but it eats into one's own time.'

'I'll have to praise you a bit,' I said. But this was close to teasing, and Victor showed by his congested frown over his cigar that I wasn't to try anything in that line. I'd wondered for a second if Victor was teasing himself, but of course he wasn't mocking his French introducer – he was in strict agreement with him. It appeared Miss Holt agreed with him too, though with a hint of anxiety, as if telling herself to concentrate.

When we sat down at a small round table with our drinks I looked more closely at her. She was about thirty-five, slender but not frail, with hesitant brown eyes, and dark hair pulled back from a face more intelligent than beautiful. 'Have you been with Mr Dax long?' I asked. 'Hardly any time,' she said, with an uncertain smile. I said it must be fascinating. She thought for a moment before murmuring, rather sweetly, 'I'm still learning the ropes.' Her accent was refined, she seemed to say 'the reps', and I guessed she was an educated woman making ends meet. I couldn't help seeing her in that moment as Lorna Monamy in *The Heart's Achievement* or Christine Lant in *Horseman, What Word?*, those obscurely troubled helpmeets to the war-blinded artist and the disillusioned sage. Her delicate fingers trembled slightly, and I noticed when she reached for her glass the soft ridge where a long-worn ring had been removed.

Poor Evert wasn't really with us. He'd produced his famous father and now sat beside him with an empty beer glass, as if hardly knowing who he was. We shared a few long glances, which made me feel uncomfortably not merely his friend but his accomplice. Victor carried on as if his son weren't there, and after a while Evert seemed to feel the need to remind him that he was. A silence had fallen over all of us before he said pleasantly, 'How's Herta, Father?'

'Why do you ask?' said Victor, rather crossly; and Miss Holt too looked uncomfortable. 'I don't know if you've heard about the German Blitzkrieg presently being waged over the very roof of your family home' – he looked quickly round at us to enlist us in his sarcasm. Charlie laughed loudly, and Evert said he had heard, that was why he was asking; he was as unsure as the rest of us what he had said wrong. A silence fell, and I changed the subject and nervously asked Victor about the name Dax – was it Dutch? I think I must have known it was his mother's family who were Dutch. 'No, it's an old Shropshire name,' Victor said, 'as a matter of fact.'

'I wonder then if it's a Norman name,' I said, 'that has lost its apostrophe.' I thought myself it was extraordinary how he elicited this kind of flattery and submission merely by sitting there and staring at us over his drink. He seemed to compute the relative problems and advantages of the Norman idea – he blew up a big cloud of smoke in busy, rather wounded-looking thought before he said, 'You may well be right,' superbly making no claim himself to such ancient lineage, and making it sound as if I cared far more about the matter than he did.

Jill came to join us just as we were leaving the hotel. Victor perked up a bit at the sight of another woman, and as our little group trailed back down Alfred Street towards the College, they walked together, in the noncommittal good humour of such brief moments between strangers. Jill held the torch, Miss Holt and I came just behind, with Evert and Charlie in the rear. The night was so clear, after the earlier drizzle, and the moon already so strong that the torch was barely needed. The roofs across the street gleamed steeply, and the reflected moon slid from window to dark window like a searchlight. By now I was measuring the length of dinner, which was all that remained before my speech, but I watched Jill too. Her confidence with Victor had a touching new note of bravery to it – she flattered him, which was what he demanded, and where from a man the flattery, once secured, was treated with disdain, from her he was prepared to take it. 'I hugely enjoyed *The Gift of Hermes*,' I heard her say, and Victor said something about enjoyment being the least he hoped readers would get from it. 'In my *considered* opinion,' she said (and here I regretted that dear bossy tone of hers), 'it's the finest thing you've done.'

'Well, it's a great book,' said Victor briskly, as if there were no point in either of them pretending otherwise. But he smiled as he turned to her. 'Though not as good, I hope you'll think, as the one I'm writing now.' Like others of our writers he took no interest in his hosts, but with her there was a glint of engagement through the cigar-smoke. I suppose I was jealous.

We came in through the back gate of the College, the achievements of the Boat Club chalked up in the quad all glimmering in the moonlight. Though he was the guest of our Club, Victor dined with the Fellows on High Table: there was just a moment, when Evert left him at the SCR door, when I glimpsed the straightforward affection of father and son, a quick nod, a light pat of Evert's upper arm as the great man turned away. In Hall he was seated next to the Dean, and I glimpsed him myself now and then between the backs of the nattering dons with a kind of proprietary affection, and a real anxiety, now the thing was unstoppably in motion, about how he would go down with the undergrads. Evert had stuck by me, counting on my understanding, and we wisely sat where we couldn't see David. Even so, his presence somewhere behind us made the starving Evert turn his meal over incapably and gaze into the dark oak of the table as if it hid untold marvels, or miseries.

It was when we came down from Hall into the moonlit Tom

Quad that we started to hear the noise. We were pulled up short as the crowd of undergraduates pressed behind us and around us. The sound was of a weight and penetration and strange gusted density we hadn't heard before, outside London: the sickening irregular drone of the Heinkel 111. In a quick flick of the flashlight I saw Evert and his father, side by side, stock-still and staring up at the nearly invisible spectacle. Victor's head was back, his mouth open, so that even he, with his famous indifference to the Blitz, appeared for a second like a figure witless with fear. On and on it went – no one could count, but there might have been fifty, a hundred, two hundred enemy aircraft, Heinkels and Dorniers, passing high overhead towards the north. I felt a hand grip my elbow and sensed more than saw that it was David. I did my best to stand steady, a little anchor for him, as he swung round on the flood of the crowd, and with his other hand seized on Evert. I had the impression we both held him up, as he stood gaping at the thing he had dreaded above all.

Sparsholt's home was destroyed that night, though it was two days before he knew for sure what had happened. Hearing the siren, his parents had gone out as always to the air-raid shelter at the bottom of the garden; the noise of explosions was already loud when they found that the cat wasn't with them. Frank Sparsholt ran back to the house for it, and died there together with the cat while his wife sat trembling underground thirty yards away, terrified by the noise and by what she had allowed to happen.

My affairs at Woodstock took more and more of my time in what was left of that Michaelmas term. I saw Connie Forshaw now and then on our special bus, but surrounded by a group of other girls – I raised my hat to her and smiled, and once only she gave me a nod. Had she somehow found out what had happened while she was away? If so, was her coolness towards me a sign that she thought me to blame? At the Palace she worked among the labyrinth of filing cabinets in Vanbrugh's library, while I had my desk in a Nissen hut out on the freezing forecourt; so we were kept apart. But two small incidents connected with her fiancé remain.

I gave Peter's drawing of Sparsholt's torso to Evert. He was the person likely to value it most, and I felt uneasy keeping it in my bedroom closet. It wasn't beyond that old investigator Phil to find it, and fiddle it out of its tube, and leapfrog his way to all kinds of conclusions – I imagined already the strained courtesy of our subsequent dealings. It was a relief to pass it to Evert one evening, and a teasing, curious pleasure to see how he took it. As he unrolled it in my room and turned it to catch the light from the fire, I edged my question into his distracted attention. The red chalks and the fire-glow made the drawn image lively and a little satanic. 'I suppose it *was* omega?' I said. He didn't answer at first. 'Well, I had to see him to give him the cheque.' 'Oh, yes, of course you did.' 'Thanks for the drawing, though.' 'No – I'm glad you've got it' – we both considered it for a minute. 'And have you, you know,' I said, 'seen him since . . . ?' 'Mm, what's that . . . ?' Evert murmured – red-faced himself as he hung over the drawing. I found that I couldn't repeat the question; and saw that he knew I couldn't.

Then in eighth week, with its more than usual flurry of packing and departure, I saw David Sparsholt in person for what proved to be the last time. I had been down to Magdalen to visit a friend who himself was leaving prematurely for the Army, and I went on from there, in a melancholy mood, to the Bodleian Library. I was on the first broad stretch of the High Street, with the glowing windows of Schools across the way looking almost friendly in the bitter December morning. An enormous convoy was approaching from behind, over Magdalen Bridge, and as the first lorry drew level with me I became aware of a figure running in the opposite direction on the far side of the street. He was in white shorts and a singlet, as if about to leap into a boat, and his breath made vanishing white plumes round his head. His powerful thighs were pink from the cold, but he seemed almost madly unaware of the weather, and loped forward with who knew what mixture of pride and indifference. A figure so unstoppable was alarming as well as splendid. I slowed as I walked but didn't wave to him – he was in his own world, and besides it was too late. It was in two successive gaps that I saw him, as the convoy passed, like a man in a Muybridge photo, in exemplary motion: first here, then there, then no longer there, as if swallowed up by his own momentum.

*

This narrative, written for, but never read to, the Cranley Gardens Memoir Club, was found among Freddie Green's papers after his death.

TWO

The Lookout

1

'You like drawing,' said Norma Haxby.

Johnny was sorry to be caught out. 'I like drawing people.'

Norma took her cigarette case from her handbag. 'Aren't people rather hard?' She treated him like a child, but as she flicked the lighter and raised her head she seemed to assume a pose.

'That's why they're interesting,' Johnny said, beginning to shade in the background, then coming back slyly to her nose.

'I could never draw at all,' she said. 'Do you get your artistic side from your mother, I suppose?'

'He doesn't get it from me,' said his father, quite sharply. He was just outside the French windows with the rolled oilcloth of his toolkit spread out; he was fixing the patio light.

'Well, you're more practical, aren't you, David,' said Norma, and Johnny could see from the way she lifted her head and blew smoke towards him how much she preferred this; there was something provocative in her voice.

'Connie's the arty one,' his father said; 'always has been.'

'Well, I know Connie's a great reader, isn't she,' said Norma, stretching her neck with a kind of idle satisfaction. 'I can't think when I last read a book.'

'Oh, well, Jonathan doesn't read,' said his father. 'Never quite got the knack, have you, old lad.'

'Ah . . .' She looked at them both uncertainly.

'Of course he's only fourteen.'

'You don't read much yourself, Dad,' said Johnny, holding out for justice.

'I don't have the time,' said his father, 'do I?' – passing back through the lounge into the kitchen. 'Is your pal about? We leave in ten minutes.'

Norma smiled after him, then, left alone with Johnny, blinked, stubbed and squashed her cigarette, and stood up. 'I hope it'll stay fine for you,' she said. She stared out at the gusted palm tree, the Falmouth ferry coming in, the cloud that dragged and blurred above the headland beyond. 'I don't know what your mother and I will do if it rains.' She perhaps hoped to see his drawing but wasn't going to ask to do so; Johnny closed his sketchbook anyway.

'I'd better find out what Bastien's up to,' he said.

'The Lookout' opened in front on to a patio and steeply dropping lawn, with a broad view of sea above the roofs of the town below; but at the back it was half quarried out of the shaly hillside. The boys' bedroom looked over a narrow gully at the side wall of the garage of the next house up the hill; so far they'd found it best to keep the curtains closed. Their beds were bunk beds, kids' beds which Bastien, a year older than Johnny, was already too big for. The spindly structure shuddered and lurched when he clambered in and out of the top bunk, and when he turned over. Johnny was condemned to lie under the low meshed ceiling, under Bastien's shifting weight, staring upwards for long minutes in the first dawn light at a dangling sheet or sometimes an unconscious left hand, dimly pulsing inches from his face as Bastien slumbered on his front and Johnny listened, hypnotized, to the tone of his breathing. Bastien didn't have pyjamas, he slept in his underpants – Johnny lay beneath him picturing him from above. Whenever he finally got to sleep the light would be on and Bastien would be going to the lavatory. Yesterday his mother had suggested not flushing at night, she'd broken the rule and used French words to explain. 'I don't mean "rougir",' she said, and did so, to Bastien's sly fascination. She was the person he paid most attention to, and he followed her from sunroom to kitchen and almost into the lavatory with fixated courtesy.

Johnny went along the landing with a gloomy feeling, but when he opened the door the room was bright: there were the unmade bunks, Bastien's open suitcase covering half the floor, and Bastien, up, dressed, and lacing up his plimsolls. Johnny checked what he was wearing in one oblique glance: the tight dark-blue jeans with frayed hems, a red polo shirt; now he stood and stroked back his hair and pulled on his 'Coq Sportif' cap, with the peak angled high, and there being no mirror in the room he turned to Johnny for approval.

On the narrow path Johnny fell behind, glad no one would be looking at him for a minute or two. His father was some way in front, moving faster, with a coil of rope round one shoulder, as if about to scale a cliff; Bastien scrambled after him, carrying the two oars; and Johnny came last, clutching the slippery life jackets.

The path was romantic, twisting, up-and-down, thrown sideways by large stones and the roots of the thorns and hazels that closed it in for much of the way, with glimpses here and there of the weed-covered rocks below. It was a sequence Johnny was still learning – the fenced-off stretch where it turned inland round the back of Parry's yard, the dip where a rising tide forced you up into the hedge if you wanted to keep dry, the five or six back gates with the names of houses that were hidden in high trees above the estuary, some broken, blocked and over-grown, some giving glimpses of exotic Cornish gardens climbing the slopes. To him the names blurred, 'Pencawl', 'Pencara', but each gate had its different magic. Now called-out words were heard behind a hedge; here a tumbledown gateway was choked by dank elder, with fox-paths through the nettles. Ahead of him Bastien stopped to look at something Johnny's father had of course ignored, scattered parts, a wing, stray feathers, a knot of grey gristle, of some not quite nameable bird. Johnny peered at him warily before he pushed against him and as they stooped to examine it he found the warmth of him so painful both to feel and to resist that he was glad when Bastien stood straight again with a sickly smile and moved suddenly ahead. The short oars lodged aslant over each shoulder kept Johnny at a distance all the way to the kissing-gate at the end; here last year he had always claimed a forfeit from his mother, until the day when she told him not to be daft. He burned with the memory of it. Now Bastien edged into the narrow pen of the gate, the paddles tilting and banging on the wall as he tried to hold them with one arm and swing the gate back with the other. Johnny hovered behind, his freedom neutered by the armful of life jackets. 'Merde!' said Bastien – Johnny threw down the jackets, leant forward to swing the gate through its tight quadrant, and watched his friend step free. He picked up the jackets again, with a dismal sense of the slavery to tasks that was his father's ideal of a holiday, and said, 'You're meant to kiss me before you let me through.' But Bastien by now was some way ahead, at the top of the Club's concrete slipway, where Clifford Haxby was waiting for them.

2

First they had to put on their life-jackets. 'You can all swim, I hope,' said Clifford as he passed them round.

'You mean you can't, Cliff?' said Johnny's father, with a concerned little smile, at which Clifford tutted scornfully.

'Only in the bloody Navy, wasn't I.'

His father looked puzzled for a second – 'The Navy . . . ? Oh, didn't I hear something about them once, in the War?' and he winked at Bastien, who stared blankly and then, alarmingly, winked back.

Johnny pulled the cord through and tightened it. He retained a subliminal sense of his father's strong hands holding him, above and below, then pushing him away, the fluid sequence of security, cold fear, freedom, but he couldn't remember not being able to swim. And Bastien was all right – Johnny pictured him at the big public baths in Nîmes last summer, smashing around, with no fear and not much skill, then surging up out of the pool so fast that his trunks were half torn off by the water. In fact he'd pictured it quite often. Today Clifford was in dark shorts tight across his backside, revealing lean white hairless legs; he had a blue sailing cap pushed back, his oiled forelock fell over his left eye in a ragged comma. He might have been in the Navy in the War but he seemed to be play-acting more than Johnny's father, in his old khaki running shorts and blue windcheater, taking up the oars Bastien had thrown down and wading into the sea in his deck shoes to get to the little tender. In a minute they were all in, riding low down under their joint weight, and moving off now with the first thrust and quiver of being out of their element. Heavy in the centre, held steady by the boys, lay the motor, sleek white body and two long screws. Clifford watched Johnny's father rowing, seemed to take the measure of his neatness and power. 'It's not the bloody Boat Race, you know, David,' he said.

Johnny's father smiled and raised an eyebrow. 'So which one is she, skipper?' There were fifty boats out there at least, different sizes and ages, sleek floating homes one or two of them, riding high above little brown craft that felt more homely and more loved, *Doris*, *Jeanetta*. Leslie Stevens's boat was moored way out beyond the biggest one of all, *Aegean Queen*, all closed up, curtains drawn, sinisterly private.

'It's just like *Thunderball*, Dad,' said Johnny.

'All right, there she is,' said Clifford, as they came round, clear of her anchor cables, stretched out by the outgoing tide. Johnny construed the strange word *Ganymede* in white on the blue strip above the white hull – the letters strange though he knew the name and hoped Clifford didn't know the story, he was bound to harp on about it if he did.

'Is this what they call a destroyer, Cliff?' said his father – he was terribly humorous today. Clifford found it more captain-like to ignore him.

'She's just a pocket cruiser,' he said, 'twenty-five foot,' and looked approvingly at the little boat, which as they clambered on to it from the tender had a comparative stability and even a slightly worrying size. 'Leslie had her out with his boys at the weekend.' Bastien seemed nervous as he stepped up on to the narrow edge of it and groped forward for a hand-hold as the tender pushed up and bobbed away. 'Has he sailed before?' said Clifford.

Bastien shrugged and said, 'Yes,' and looked away, which Johnny assumed meant 'No'.

'We'll have different words for things,' Clifford said. 'Port and starboard.'

'They'll be the other way round, won't they, in France,' said Johnny's father.

Clifford said, 'Just tell him to do what I say.' He handed up a can of fuel, which Johnny took and stood holding with a looming sense of all the discipline of sailing, the shouting and blaming cutting through the fun.

The boys looked into the small sunken hutch of the cabin, with its two converging seats and Formica-topped table, then scrambled forward to explore, if that was the word – it wasn't much bigger than the dinghy they'd borrowed last year, but it was to be their world, for the next hour or two, and seemed already made of tiny territories, occupiable surfaces. They stood clutching a diagonal cable with neither of them knowing what its name was or what it was for – but they were allies, brothers, it seemed to Johnny, within the narrow bounds of the boat and the trip. 'Who is Leslie? This man's wife?'

'Leslie,' said Johnny, 'no it's a man, it's a man's name too, like ... well, you wouldn't know him, probably, Leslie Crowther, on *Crackerjack* ... no ... Leslie Stevens is an MP.'

'Oh,' said Bastien and wrinkled his nose.

'A Member of Parliament. He's quite important,' said Johnny. 'You know Leslie?'

'Me? No. Not personally,' said Johnny. 'He's not our MP.'

'And this man is a Member?'

'Who? Mr Haxby?' – he glanced round but Clifford and his father were caught up in some quiet-voiced routine of their own, business as well as sailing, business as usual. 'No, he's on the County Council, you know, very important too, Dad says.'

Bastien smiled, and scratched his balls. 'All very important,' he said.

The sun, that had been promising the past ten minutes, came out, a great distance of blue showed high over the cloud. Johnny swung on the cable, half seduced by Bastien's mockery, but not quite ready to forsake so much reflected glory.

They were going to go out on the motor; a powerful one, only roused past the curt roar of the start-cord into continuous untroubled action when Johnny's father nudged Clifford aside, strength hoarded all year for these rare and richly satisfying moments. Clifford pursed his lips in a funny way at this further show of muscle, nudging his way back, and when he'd done so revving up the engine in a quick smoking snarl as they cast off. In the estuary still, million-sided sunlight on water green as the woods above, a dazzle over weeded rocks, sudden dark drops below, they went out unhurriedly, responsibly cutting their wash as they passed children kayaking, a couple rowing a skiff with a terrier in the bows. Still, there was a sense of lurking mischief between the two men that Johnny was unsettled by. Threaded along the shore, barely followable, was the path they had taken, and then round the steep point past Parry's yard the whole painted panorama of the town curled forward into view, Johnny not knowing if the daring and privilege of being out in a boat was worth more to him than the warm solid pleasure of going to the café and the pasty shop and watching the half-naked boys on the harbour wall. 'I say, David,' said Clifford, 'when Archer Square's done you'll be getting something a bit bigger than this.' It was a name out of the air of the recent months, the 'really big job' Johnny's parents stopped talking about if he came into the room, though it wasn't exactly a secret. A photo of the model had appeared in the paper, blank white cuboids surrounding a blank white tower, 'the tallest building in the Midlands', raised roads beside it, dotted with balsa-wood cars.

'Well, we'll see about that, Cliff,' Johnny's father said.

'We'll have a bloody shipshape crew too – not this school-boy shower – eh?' – Clifford beamed alarmingly at Johnny, who said, 'Yes, sir,' and looked down. The Falmouth ferry was coming past, turning in towards the harbour, and Clifford seemed to flirt with it, running in close, holiday-makers on deck looking down at them, and in a moment they were riding and smacking along the larger boat's wake, among seagulls dropping and screaming and lifting off. A child at the back of the ferry waved. Clifford twisted the throttle and their bows rose by a few degrees as they curled out beyond the point towards the open sea. Bastien turned his head aside and stood down with Johnny in the step of the cabin. 'All right, Cliff,' said Johnny's father, unruffled but not, Johnny felt, especially impressed.

The rhythmical jolts across the surface of the sea, the wind making you cry unconsciously and flipping Bastien's cap off his head without warning (Johnny jumped and saved it where it wrapped for a second round a cable) were things he knew he was meant to enjoy, but almost made him long for the dreaded part, when they put up the sails. It wasn't a speedboat, after all; he wondered what Leslie Stevens MP would think if he saw his friends using his *Ganymede* like this, Clifford grinning like a bully to show he at least was having fun. Then he turned the speed quickly to nothing, so they seemed to lurch forward where they stood; they settled down and back. Clifford told the boys to untie the cords that bound the sail to the long horizontal boom, and the other small sail that was in front of the mast. They got on with it, and there was something too interesting to look at closely in Bastien obeying orders, a sort of absent-minded competence worth more to him for an hour or two than his usual effort at showing he didn't care.

When the big sail went up it was suddenly serious, and they were all responsible. The uncomfortable fun of the first bit was over, and now there was going to be tacking and being shouted at, hanging on the side with the sea always dashing to get you as you slid over it and giving you a wet slap now and then. Again Johnny's father seemed more in his element than Clifford, it was a practical lesson in physics, whose laws he had long ago mastered; the two men stared and smiled at each other as the sail ran up in half a dozen hard yanks, hand over hand, and tautened as it had to. And it went as it was meant to, Johnny was proud of his father, watching the sail, which cut off the sun, a new presence among them and above them. Johnny had one of the two ropes to the boom, and after a while his father nodded and passed the other to Bastien. 'Steady, young feller,' he said. For two or three minutes they scooted on, sail curving, in their sound-world made only of the creak of the mast in the rush of air and the splash and concussion of the waves on the little hull, Johnny feeling the delight of it after all, and being able to do it – he grinned at Bastien, and looked back at Clifford, and away across the glittering sea at other boats sailing, crews out and about on courses of their own.

Without warning Clifford shouted, 'Ready about!' in a clipped hard tone that had been waiting for its moment – the boom swung across, the sail indecisive, robbed of all will for a moment and then jerking and filling out with a thump and a snap on the other side, as Johnny snatched at Bastien's shirt-hem and brought him under. Still, they got in the rhythm of it, and again it wasn't something Bastien saw any point in being bad at; though he had, once he'd settled in, a blank look on his face, as if tiring of his own obedience. Sailing required such effort and concentration that time itself speeded up and it was hard to enjoy the real beauty of what you could see as you went skimming along – the dazzle of the broken sea and the coast beyond all the while slowly turning, advancing, and falling away. Johnny thought Bastien himself was beautiful, half-unwillingly woken up and with a strength he perhaps didn't know he had as he gripped his rope and held the boom firm and thrumming against the wind. The wind made the sunlight cold and shaped Bastien's shirt tightly round him; it went for his cap again, and in the second he snatched for it he let the rope go, and in the second after that his plimsolled right foot caught Johnny in the ribs as he dropped, on his back, into the sea.

It was a disaster, a fall from a far greater height, in Johnny's mind, staring back, heart racing, knees locked straight against the new strain on the sail, imagined injury and death all condensed in the few dilated seconds it took to happen – in his life-vest Bastien barely went under, he shouted once, beat the water with his arms as he twisted round, left behind in their long wake, and the cap now twirled and hurried away, far off beyond it. Clifford yelled, Johnny's father leapt up and in just a few seconds tore the main sail down in armfuls, as if tackling and smothering it; and somehow then they brought the boat about. Bastien, in the water, doggy-paddled towards them, waited, sploshing about over the light swell, and with a strange look as if he wasn't in communication with them. Johnny thought he was reconstructing his dignity, the idiot emerging as the hero of the story. Then his father threw out a pink life-saving ring on a rope, it splished into the water close to him, and he bobbed his way in a few strokes towards it and clutched it and was pulled steadily in as the *Ganymede* twisted and threatened to swing round again. Johnny joined his father to tug him up, leaning down and reaching out a hand, which Bastien grasped with the fear he was hiding behind a distant attempt at a smile. Very heavy, a big fifteen-year-old boy was, in saturated clothes – it was as if by a magical expansion of his own strength that he saw Bastien rise almost vertically from the water in his father's two-handed grip on his other arm.

'Well done, laddie,' said Clifford harshly. Johnny stared at Bastien, wanted to hug him and kiss him with relief as he laughed at him, streaming beside him, the cause of concern, and the public menace, the soaking wet person among the still dry. Bastien laughed too, but he was trembling as he undid his life jacket, and took off his shirt. It was a crisis, dealt with by David Sparsholt in swift wordless actions, over almost at once – in a minute the fall was repeating in Johnny's mind as allowable excitement, even comedy, the interest of talking about what had happened flooded in to replace the fright itself. Bastien, dripping, wiping himself with his hands, pushing his hair out of his eyes, seemed to know and not to know. He didn't thank anyone for saving him, and it was Johnny who said, 'Well done, Dad!'

After a while Clifford started up the motor again – it took a couple of goes. 'Tell him to take his fucking trousers off,' he said, 'we're all men here' – with an odd cut-off laugh, Johnny tense at the sound of that word in his father's presence. He looked nervously at him but he seemed, blank-faced, to allow it. Bastien turned away as he unbuckled his belt, and prised the clinging jeans over his buttocks and down his thighs. His wet underpants hinted at transparency, a flesh-tone through white cotton grey with water, but were decent still. To Johnny it had the hot-making magic of those sudden but longed-for moments when sex ran visibly close to the sunlit surface. Bastien snapped down the hem at the back and gave him a quick smirk from the summer before – which seemed now to throw the scene on the boat in a colder light, Johnny no longer his secret friend but one of the three watching Englishmen. 'And don't forget your . . . *bloody* life-vest,' said Clifford under his breath, turning the throttle and taking the *Ganymede* round in a long arc.

It wasn't clear what they were doing now – sailing, at least, seemed safely to be over. They were perched out here in the middle of the sea with a worrying new lack of purpose. 'Dad, shouldn't we go in?' said Johnny.

'We're still OK, aren't we, David?' said Clifford – Johnny looked from one to the other, the uncertainty about who was really in charge more serious now. Johnny's father shook his head and shrugged. 'Then we'll catch something, shall we, something to show the girls when we get back?' He stared briefly at Johnny, 'You like to fish, don't you?' – something about his unease with the boys conveyed in the way he never used their names. 'Well . . .' said Johnny. He knew from last summer there was pride in sitting down to a fish you had caught, and with it something that soured and spoiled the taste, the effort to shut out images in the mind, hooks in the throat and the brain. He sat down now, to excuse himself from helping, as Clifford cut their speed and they puttered on with the engine down low, the screws frothing as they came out of the water on the drop of a swell. It turned out there was a gadget in one of the lockers, which could be taken out and clamped at the back of the boat, and half a dozen lines run out from it with what looked like silver spangles hiding the hooks. Clifford set it all up with oddly intent seriousness and thoroughness. Johnny watched the lines paying out from their spools, hoping he would fail.

When the lines were all set, Clifford said, 'Gentlemen, refreshments.' He stooped down into the cabin and took the lid off a plastic box of sandwiches wrapped in grey greaseproof; there was also a Thermos. 'Your missis prepared this,' he said, 'though you might like a drop of something stronger, David.' He had a flat metal flask, which he unstoppered and took a shot from, and clenched his lips.

'No, not with the boys to look after, Cliff.' The tea, with milk and sugar in already, was passed round in the cap of the Thermos, Johnny avoided the side Clifford had drunk from, refilled it and passed it forward to Bastien, who sipped and screwed up his face – he never drank tea. Then the sandwiches were offered, paste – again disgusting to Bastien, so that Johnny, crouching in front of him, amazed by his near-nakedness, in his underpants and life-vest, ate his share too, making faces at him as if they were delicious. Bastien grunted and looked away.

It was hot after all in the relative calm, and once the sandwiches were finished Johnny's father, steadying himself against the small pitch and slide of the boat as they chugged on, unfastened his own life-vest and pulled his top over his head.

'Going to soak up a few rays, David?' said Clifford. 'Good idea.' He looked up at him with confident blankness – as he said, they were all men here; though Clifford himself, it seemed, was keeping his shirt on.

Johnny was used to the sight of his father's heavy upper arms, the rounded-out chest just shadowed with dark hair – he watched him fold up the windcheater, proud of him, and minutely embarrassed too by the display, or by his father's own pride in making it. 'Don't get sunburn, Dad,' he said.

His father tutted, turned their attention away from himself to a luxurious white cruiser that was coming in ahead of them towards Falmouth, two uniformed crewmen active on deck.

'I'd say you keep pretty fit, then, David?' Clifford said.

His father swung round, as if not expecting the compliment. 'Oh, I like to keep in shape, Cliff,' with a modest but competent laugh.

Clifford made an odd gesture, squaring of the shoulders in forlorn competition. 'Mind you, we were all pretty fit, weren't we, in the War.'

'Yes, well . . . I've always kept fit,' Johnny's father said, raising his arms casually, halfway, and letting them drop, his fingers clenching and flicking. 'Twenty minutes every day before breakfast. You're ready for anything then.'

Clifford smiled, nodded slowly, seemed to take this in, as a possible new regime, sizing the other man up as an example of what could be done. Johnny's father smiled back, raised his chin: 'I think you've had some joy there,' he said. It took Clifford a moment to see what he meant, but Johnny hadn't forgotten about it, the activity on the lines. Clifford got up and leant out and started reeling them in – ambiguous at first among racing ripples and refractions on four of the hooks, but then clearer and grimmer, the sleek fighting black-arrowed shapes of mackerel, and on the end hook something else that Johnny'd never seen, a paler more golden fish with dark fins, curving and jerking frighteningly in the air as it was pulled from the sea, though it was the frightened one, of course. 'Well, don't just stand there gaping,' Clifford said, as he brought them in over the edge of the boat, and it was safe (though not safe for them) to grip them as they fought, and then prise them off the hooks. The first mackerel landed on the boards at Johnny's feet, and he jumped back, as the fish jumped, bucked and slithered, head and tail beating the floor in mortal desperation. His father, just beside him, with a hand on his shoulder, smiled strangely, at the flailing death, and also, Johnny felt, at Clifford's furious excitement.

The boys sat up at the front at an angle, legs hanging down and feet drenched in the irregular buffeting of the waves as they picked up speed; Johnny's father standing behind them with his hand on the mast, and a feeling too subtle to be explained that he was pleased with him, and forgiving of Bastien, and somehow protecting them both, while Clifford drove the boat. Bastien's shirt and jeans blew like some makeshift signal from above their heads. Johnny looked round and up at his father, watched him as he turned and went aft balancing himself at each sure stride, and dropped down on to the square of the deck. Pendennis Castle was riding in then out of view as they came in close to the headland, the castle set back, not big, but with the magic of any keep or tower to Johnny, who made Bastien crane round to look at it just as it disappeared. Clifford seemed concerned about a chart, said something inaudible in the bluster to Johnny's father, who perhaps was looking for it. Now the top of Pendennis appeared again, round and squat, above its low circular wall, no flag on the flagpole, no cannon between the battlements, but Johnny was fixed on it – far more rode on it than he could express or the others would understand. And it would be so easy to go there – he almost wondered if they could land now and clamber up over the rocks and climb through the woods. He got up carefully and saw the engine had been left on a set course while Clifford spoke with his father in the cabin. He scooted aft, glancing up at the castle, and down into the little sunken deck. At some point the two men had dealt with the fish, which lay, dead, gleaming, striped like moving water itself, and seeming, with the thrum of the engine, still to shudder with unrelinquished life on the wet boards below. Perched on the edge of the boat Johnny peered down into the cabin. Clifford and his father were looking closely at something on the table: Johnny couldn't see their faces, but in their hunched figures there was a sense of something nice being planned after all, a surprise it might be a shame to spoil. His father's right arm lay loosely across Clifford's shoulders as they bent forward. 'Where are the lads?' said Clifford.

'Both up front, I think,' said his father.

'That French kid's a piece of work,' said Clifford.

Was it 'Difficult age . . .' his father murmured, as he leant over, some private joke, odd bit of grown-up clowning, which made Clifford suddenly grip him round the waist, white hand on brown flesh, in a little rocking tussle, his father distantly amused and turning his face close to Clifford's as if thinking of something, as Clifford said, 'Now, now,' and tapped him lightly on the bum.

'Dad!' said Johnny.

His father tensed, annoyed as always by a childish interruption. 'Yes, what is it, old lad?'

'I just thought, can we go to Pendennis Castle?'

'Oh . . .' He stood back, stood up straight. 'Well, we'll see. You'd better ask your mother.'

It was nearly good enough. 'Oh . . . OK,' Johnny said.

His father was suddenly restless. 'We'd better get them back home now, hadn't we, Cliff?'

Clifford turned, with a tart little smile that bunched up his moustache. 'Yes, no castles for you today, I'm afraid, young man,' he said. He leapt up and took his place by the tiller, flash of tightly clad backside and bare thighs, little ouch, adjusting himself, as he sat down. In five minutes they were cutting their wash as they came in past the town again.

*

'Ah, look who's there,' said Clifford drily.

But Johnny had made them out already, his mother and Norma, among the stretched weedy cables at the top of the slipway. He waved confidently, and had to do it again before he got a response, Norma a moment later, as if reluctant. There was a sense, as they stood talking, his mother with her arms crossed, Norma lighting a cigarette, that they'd come down to tell them something was wrong. The muffled greeting was a preparation for it. Then they were hidden from view by the silent and secretive blue-and-white bulk of *Aegean Queen*. It took a while to get *Ganymede* moored, the sails fully furled and bound, the decks sluiced clean of blood and guts – 'The scene of the crime,' his father said, naturally orderly, Clifford worrying about Leslie Stevens, double-checking everything. Bastien hunched in the cabin to pull on his jeans, and button up his damp shirt, watched obliquely by Johnny. Then the boys climbed into the tender, the food box and then the engine and then the two threaded clusters of mackerel were passed down, with the other fish, which Clifford said he thought was a pouting. 'A what, Cliff?' Johnny's father said.

'I will . . . how is it? . . . *ramer*?' Bastien said. He didn't get through at first, seemed to be fighting for some unknown reason with Johnny's father who was holding the little oars. 'I,' he said.

'You're going to rammy, are you, laddie?' said Clifford. 'Well, well.'

Bastien took a few strokes to get used to it, skimming, unbalanced, under the sceptical scrutiny of the rest of them; they were a heavier lot than he'd expected, but he got the hang of it, the kind of pull it needed. Johnny watched and called out to steer him through the other craft in the way. He came in fast for the last bit till Clifford shouted, 'Christ! Look out . . .' and they were nearly aground, he stopped abruptly, let both oars go with a splash and looked round with a grin at Johnny's mother.

'How did it go?' she said, as Johnny ran up to her and un-expectedly flung his arms round her. He wanted to say Bastien fell in the water. 'How far did you go?'

'Right out past . . . there' – Johnny gestured, but from here, in the shelter of the estuary, the vast windy curve of the globe they'd been bouncing across was completely hidden. 'Bastien fell in the water.'

His mother looked at him narrowly. 'He had his life jacket on?'

'Yeah, yeah,' said Johnny. 'He was fine'; and it was another lesson of the day, the dark underlying fact that his mother and father were wholly responsible for Bastien, however much they thought him a pain in the neck.

'What did Dad say?'

'Dad and I pulled him in, it was fine.'

She smiled narrowly, 'You make him sound like a fish.' A few moments later Bastien himself came up, with a serious, almost shy look, and presented her with the mackerel. 'For you, Madame.'

'Good God . . .' – she laughed, put her hand to her throat.

'I catch them all for you.' He looked at her earnestly. 'We eat for dinner.'

'We'll be eating these all week. Look at them, Norma.'

'I know,' said Norma, standing back.

'And what about your clothes?' – she patted his shoulders, and he held his arms out with a smirk, still holding the dead fish.

3

'Is he getting up?'

Johnny sprinkled sugar on his cornflakes. 'I shouldn't think so.'

His mother moved round the kitchen, tied the apron over her pink cotton frock as the tap filled the washing-up bowl. 'We'll just let him stew, then, shall we? It is meant to be a holiday.'

She was sunny, but after a moment Johnny said, 'Sorry, Mum.'

'Well . . .' – she looked down at him frankly for a second: 'I don't think you're having much fun, are you.'

'It's OK.'

'Was he talking in his sleep again?'

'Oh . . . yeah . . . a bit.'

'You know, I can go back in with Dad, if you want to use the other room.'

'Dad's snoring's much worse!' said Johnny. 'No, I'll be OK.' There was something he didn't want to lose in the broken nights . . . Bastien clambering in and out, the brief functional rocking of the bunk beds as he had his wank, and then when he slept the loud fragments of speech which suggested an inner life far more dramatic than he gave any hint of when awake.

'Well, you will say,' said his mother, 'won't you?'

'Yes, Mum.' The house, downstairs, with just the two of them, was so peaceful. 'Where's Dad?'

'Clifford came up just now in the car – they've gone off somewhere . . . just for an hour.'

'Oh . . .'

She tucked her chin in, smiled at him firmly as she turned

back to the sink. 'We'll all do something nice together this after-noon.' There was a thump overhead, creaks, the slam of the bathroom door. 'Ah, here we go . . .'

Johnny scrunched on his cereal, in the now familiar tension of longing to see him and dreading his coming through the door.

Bastien had arrived in England a week ago, but the awful dis-appointment of his visit had begun (Johnny saw it now) many months before. In Nîmes, last year, he'd been Bastien's gullible pupil, and almost at times his slave. He had gone there to work on his French, his stumbling innocence shown up the more by the barely grasped murmurs and exclamations with which Bastien bossed him around. It went on all the time, Johnny blushingly at war with his own modesty, at the Pont du Gard, on the beach near Aigues-Mortes, in the bedroom the Marcs had thought it would be nice for the boys to share. Nothing like this had happened at school, no one would survive such a scan-dal, he had had to go to France for it. When they were alone together their roles were easily maintained; when the family were present Bastien, with all the distractable energy of a four-teen-year-old boy, forgot the strict terms of the drama – he was lazy, rowdy, unobservant. Johnny sensed the mysterious force of the parts they played, a structure in the dealings between two friends that kept them going and could never be escaped. Bastien was disdainful, and mocked him each morning and night for wanting the very things he had taught him to ask for. His genius, even then, was his perfect selfishness, a beautiful smile that he must have learned early in life brought him any-thing he wanted. Mme Marc herself seemed obedient to it.

Johnny remembered his own laboured efforts at politeness, when the family had taken him to see the sights. None of them had much English and they pretended, to be on the safe side, that they had none at all. Johnny had too little French to say that he thought one particular church they'd seen was very ugly: when he mentioned it they all assumed that he wanted to praise it. 'Ah, oui!' they said, 'la basilique . . .' Johnny didn't know the word for *ugly*; he temporized: 'Elle n'est pas belle' – with an instant sense of the difference. Mme Marc, seeing a worthwhile subtlety, said, 'Pas belle, tout à fait, non, mais assurément magnifique à sa façon.' Johnny caught his breath and had another go, but felt constrained already by this first demurral. After a minute, the potential offence of what he wanted to say had grown in his mind as these far milder objections were imagined and cautiously allowed (it was very large . . . it was a bit on the dark side . . . it was nineteenth-century), and to insist on its ugliness now would have been positively hostile. When Mme Marc suggested they should all go to Mass there on Sunday, since he was so interested in the building, he gave up, watched mockingly by Bastien who was leaning in the doorway behind his parents with a blatant erection in his little black shorts. Ah, that was what had made all the difference; that was what had been truly *beau*.

Nîmes had been different in every way from what he'd been used to – the meals, which either failed his needs and habits (a breakfast of milk coffee and hard-crusted French stick) or heavily exceeded them (rich meats, crêpes for pudding, a small disorienting tumbler of red wine); the movable duvet, the two-pin plugs, the button light-switches, the taps that switched themselves off to save water – all the things with which they, and Bastien above all, were unthinkingly intimate. He was humble, hesitant, in the presence of these fixtures, which had, like the French words for them, an educational quality; and aware of his own good manners in using such starved, stiff and miserably designed things without criticism, even at times with hinted admiration.

The Marcs' house, modern, medium-sized, was very close

to a busy road out of town, and with its electrically operated shutters and narrow strip of garden behind a green mesh fence hardly looked like a house at all – a closed office, maybe. On the side away from the road it had red and white awnings over the windows as well as steel shutters, a patio crazy-paved in dirty white marble, a dry lawn stretching down to some shrubs and another chain-link fence. The house was completely without character, and the first afternoon, as he unpacked his case dumbly homesick in the twin-bedded room, he saw nothing to console him; it was only after supper, both the boys stoned with the wine, Johnny headachy, dry-mouthed, that Bastien started wrestling with him. By the end of the long three weeks the featureless house, yellow-white pebbledash, the telephone wires coming in at an angle above the lawn to a bracket between the bedroom windows, had something ideal about it. Johnny felt more clearly than before the imperative to draw – he sat at the end of the garden with pencil and paper, aghast at the thought of going home. The Marcs themselves were welcoming, somehow both earnest and relaxed. Mme Marc, source of Bastien's large lips and dark eyes, looked steadily at Johnny when they had their exchanges in French: she wanted them to understand each other. And maybe she understood too, from stray glimpses, stifled phrases, the stink of semen in the boys' room, that something was going on. But he didn't think so; and if she did, her looking him so firmly in the eye was a sign of her French intelligence on all things to do with sex. The blank-looking house, with its cactuses and spider-plants, and the traffic at the back all day and much of the night, was infused with the mood of permission, experiment, things not to be spoken of yet, in English or French.

In the long months since then, Johnny's troubles with reading, his parents' squabbles, the worry of resitting the Common Entrance, his father's embarrassment on the subject, and his none the less repeatedly telling people about it, had all been offset by a sequence of memories, melting and reforming, a secret theatre on the edge of sleep where at last, a year on, Bastien himself would be welcomed on stage when he came to Nuneaton for more. Best of all, he would join the Sparsholts for their week in Cornwall, allowed by Johnny's father as a special privilege.

Johnny had gone to Birmingham airport with his father to meet him, with a breathless sensation, in the slow, congested traffic on the A45, of running much faster towards something dense and inescapable. They were late, and found Bastien in the arrivals hall chatting with a tall blonde girl in a miniskirt and black halter top. Johnny saw him, went towards him, slowed now by his own wordless calculation, and after ten seconds said to his father, 'There he is!' Bastien seemed not to have seen him, or even, when he stood beside him and said 'Hello!', to be expecting him. He said something with a smirk to the girl before he turned and came over with a little upward nod to meet Johnny's father. Of course memory was out of date: he was three inches taller than last year, his lips, nose, chin, fringe still beautiful but all larger and coarser and in a somehow different relation with each other. He wore tight blue jeans of a kind Johnny wasn't allowed, a black-striped rugby shirt and a blue baseball cap which he didn't take off when introduced to Johnny's father. They all shook hands, the long-imagined hug and lustful murmur in the ear obstructed by his huge black suitcase, bound round with red elastic straps. Johnny grappled the case towards the exit, panting and grinning and with a sense of foreboding at its unexplained weight.

Bastien got into the Jensen as if it was any old car. Johnny climbed in behind, and sat looking fearfully at the lost profile of his friend – there must be an element of nerves in his indifference, his refusal to be at the disadvantage of admiring anything. Johnny's father was friendly and straightforward with him, but wasn't a great talker himself. They couldn't tell yet how good

Bastien's English was, and he gave them little chance to find out. They came into Nuneaton the long way, perhaps to avoid traffic, but almost the first thing they saw was the works, the high brick end-wall of the building with its large white-painted lettering, D. D. SPARSHOLT ENGINEERING, which seemed to Johnny to dominate this side of the town and compel the attention of anyone coming in. His father said nothing, and Johnny, afraid Bastien was missing it, leant forward and touched his shoulder: 'That's us.' He thought it registered, that little upward nod again of guarded, almost sceptical interest, a glance through the gate into the yard as they passed. When they turned off Merivale Road it was still only half an hour since they'd met, and once they were alone without Johnny's father, things would surely change, Bastien's heart-turning smile would break out of hiding and the wrestling would begin. They swung into the drive of 'Hornbeams' and Bastien took in the red brick, the creeper-covered porch, the half-timbered gable, with a strange throat-clearing, as if about to say something difficult, though it seemed from his distantly matey tone when he came into the hall that he didn't really consider himself to be there. Johnny's father said, 'Welcome,' and smiled rather oddly: 'I'll let Jonathan show you round.' But the expected tour, run over a hundred times in his head as if 'Hornbeams' were Haddon Hall, now felt threatened, a contest of his desire and the visitor's coolness. They went upstairs. 'So this is *your* room!' he said, and sat dumbly on the bed, while Bastien glanced out of the window and then opened the wardrobe. 'And I'm just next door!' They went into Johnny's room, and he put his arm round Bastien's shoulders and showed him his Danish biro, with the bronzed young man on the side whose swimming-trunks vanished when you turned it upside down. Bastien turned it over himself, lower lip sticking out, and said, 'You like that,' as he gave it back. Then Johnny explained some of his drawings, taped up above the bed; he saw these also needed to be taken in the right spirit. It was starkly unlike how he'd imagined it would be, having Bastien at last in his own room.

Johnny's mother was staying with her sister, who'd had an operation, so the set-up for these first three days was odd, his father out early to work, and Mrs Doyle coming in to clean and make lunch. In the evenings June Palmer, his father's secretary, came back to have dinner with them. There was a feeling of substitute mothers, as there might have been if his real one had died rather than gone to London for five nights. She seemed to be the one thing Bastien was curious about. On the first tour of the house, when they came back downstairs, he picked up the honeymoon photo in the sitting room, taken at Swanage, with the weird grey shapes on the beach behind them. 'That was in the War,' Johnny said, leaning forward into Bastien's breath, then a hand round his shoulder, warm through the rugby shirt. 'Those were the concrete things they put up in case the Germans invaded. You see Dad's in his RAF uniform – he was a fighter pilot; in fact he won the DFC.' Bastien was smiling. 'That stands for the Distinguished Flying Cross.'

'Elle est bandante, ta mère,' said Bastien in a murmur, and when Johnny, uncertain, hungry for approval, looked up at him, he made a gesture with his free hand of outlining and then grasping a woman's breasts. Then he nudged Johnny, pushed against him as he put the photo down, in a momentary overflow of physical feeling that was also a clear signal of where his interests now lay.

4

There was nowhere to hide at 'The Lookout'. Bastien had made the boys' bedroom his own, and for long half-hours the bathroom too. Johnny found himself corners to draw in, there was a semi-private place between the carport and the dustbins where he could sit and puzzle out the effects of sunlight and clouds on the sea. Norma Haxby spotted him there when she came in next day; 'Still at it, then?' she said, and tried to make him show her what he was doing. He showed her the palm tree. 'You've got the shape of that all wrong,' she said.

In the house itself there was nothing much to look at. It was the holiday home of some people from Devizes, who came here several times a year themselves; above the phone in the hall a framed colour photo of the family in sailing gear showed them having more fun than their present guests seemed able to manage, the big teenage son beaming and holding an oar. The house was just five years old, and everything in it sturdy and primary-coloured. There were three flashy blue-and-white paintings by the same person, of sailing boats at sea, whose garish deficiencies were shown up each time you lifted your gaze to the real thing. The chairs and tables were modern and plain. There were rag rugs that slid and rode up, and lamps made from bottles, with lampshades of newspapers, overlaid, and repeating, like a wallpaper pattern, with half-hidden head-lines and corners of pictures. You made up the stories yourself. Norma tilted her head, semi-sozzled one evening, to look at them. 'Nothing about you, Cliff!' she said.

The Haxbys were round a lot, Johnny's father taking all this in his stride, as the expected working out of a plan Johnny's mother seemed not yet to know the extent of. The Sparsholts were never invited to 'Greylags', the bungalow just down the hill that the Haxbys had taken, though his mother asked Norma airy questions about its kitchen and provision of crockery. When Johnny's father needed a discussion with Clifford about the Archer Square plans or some such subject they walked off together to one of the hotel bars – Johnny had seen them once through the window of the King Mark, sitting over pint glasses, smiling about something. Clifford and Norma were town people, away, but not really on holiday. Where the Sparsholts wore old shorts and moccasins and pulled on unfashionable waterproofs if it looked like rain, Clifford was generally turned out in sharp grey flannels and looked ready to chair a meeting of the planning committee at any moment; a bit of blue piping on a jacket or a bell-bottomed trouser-suit were Norma's main concessions to the seaside. She was good-looking, in her hard, immaculate way; and Clifford, too, with his black moustache, low broad brow and oiled-down hair, clearly thought himself very dashing. There was something instructive to Johnny in seeing him side with a man as famously handsome as his father. After supper, when they were watching *The Saint* on the portable TV, Johnny sitting at the table could capture them, under cover of general doodling, without making them self-conscious. He drew his father almost shyly, knowing he needed to do justice not only to the strong clean features in profile across the room but to who he was, something larger and harder to get. Mainly of course he drew Bastien, who wanted the TV on because he was bored but was bored by the programmes themselves which he could hardly understand.

Johnny found a book at the house called *Cornish Landscape and Legend*. 'Bloody fairies!' Clifford said, hanging over his shoulder and breathing on his neck. 'Ooh, not in Cornwall, Cliff!' Norma said – not a joke at all, but they laughed and Johnny darkened with sullen embarrassment, for himself but really for them. Then they left him alone with it, and that small devaluing of pleasure that you had to fight against for a minute or two. It had lovely photographs, in a process called Dufay-colour, sand and cliffs gold and bronze, the sea in the coves the extravagant blue of (he searched for the likeness) the toilet-flush in this house. He was charmed by the chemical magic of the colours, even as he worked out what was wrong with them – well, not wrong, but inaccurate. In a broad stretch of heather on Bodmin Moor the purple and brown were nearly fused, the distant tor either grey or green. He went back over them. The book had been published before the War . . . MCMXXXVII . . . not thirty years old, but a peculiar gel of romance seemed to fix the scenes further back, caught at times of day, early morning, early closing, when no one was about, small boats bobbed at their moorings and no car or coach was seen on the pink and fawn ribbons of the roads.

Always facing was the text, which he sometimes looked at with his abstract, edge-of-the-eye apprehension of a page – the occasional chimneys that ran straight down between words, line after line, or climbed like diagonal flues across a long para-graph, the odd accidental poolings of ascenders, descenders and inverted commas into small abstract images, knots, mouths, sea anemones, and the teasing habit of glimpsed capitals to suggest and then withhold his own name – it happened all the time in the paper, July Sales, Junior Sports, he was abruptly famous, then not, and it seemed to lurk here, in the fabric of Cornwall, with its string of particular saints, St Just, St Piran, St Pinnock.

On the Thursday the Sparsholts escaped by themselves to see Pendennis Castle, just as Johnny wanted, and had lunch in Falmouth, Bastien begging a sip, and then another one, of his mother's lager and lime, until his father bought him half a pint to shut him up. In the back of the Jensen afterwards Bastien fell asleep, Johnny looking out through his small side window as his parents' talk moved cagily round a subject Johnny hadn't detected starting. 'Well, I don't think he's very nice to Norma', 'She has nice things, doesn't she?', 'Things aren't everything', putting her hand as if absent-mindedly on her husband's knee; he glanced in the mirror. 'He's certainly not a ladies' man,' his mother said. 'No, he's all right, though. There's a good brain there.' She said, 'Well, he's got the good sense to think well of my husband, anyway,' rubbing his knee awkwardly before she took her hand away. And there was the sign, 'Treterrian. 14th Century Church' – it was pictured in brown and gold in Johnny's book.

'Oh, Dad!' he said, and his father was oddly amenable – they were having fun by themselves after all; he braked hard, and took the turning. It was up and then down a long sequence of lanes and though marked three miles from the main road was what his mother called 'psychologically much further'. 'I'll get out my psychological map in a minute,' said his father, braking again and reversing very fast into a passing place for a van to go by. Johnny was excited but tense – his wish had been granted and now he was responsible for it being worthwhile. 'There it is!' he said. In a moment they had passed the church gate, and there was nowhere to park. 'I'll go in this field,' said his father, which added another kind of worry as he swung in through an open gate on to rough grass. 'We'll only be a minute.' When the boys were let out from the back, Johnny went ahead across the road, strangely aware he was acting out what he really felt, the pull – the fascination mixed up with fear – of an old building. He was obliged to like it, and if the others didn't, he would have to like it even more.

In the churchyard there were lines of slate headstones, sliced an inch or two thin and with rich orange lichens spreading over the inscriptions. His mother always enjoyed reading gravestones, and they made out the lettering together, sharing the

problem for once. He was a terrible reader but he loved lettering – at school last term they'd done tracings of epitaphs in
the abbey churchyard, and followed the change of styles over
time. Here each line was in a different font, cut into the hard
grey surface, and drawn out in curlicues to fill the surrounding
space. The later tombs were heavier and as his mother said
'more preachy'. His father came and stood behind them:
'"Most sincerely regretted by his family" – an unfortunate way
of putting it!' and chuckled, and Johnny laughed too, uneasy
that he meant something more by it.

He raised the latch and held it for a second as he held his
breath at the imminence of unknown space beyond. The church
they stepped down into was primitive but well kept – in fact a
lot of holiday-makers, scratching round for some point of
interest inland from the beach, made their way here. There were
welcome signs, enough flowers for a wedding, and a massive
collection box made from an iron-bound chest. Even so, it was
chilly on bare arms and legs, the old walls were thick and the
nave windows small and dark with Victorian glass. Johnny saw
in a minute it was the transepts that made the church, with their
tall clear windows, and several old marble tablets on the walls,
each with its own little commonplace quirk of design. Light
from the south transept lay tall across the darker nave: the high
pulpit with its rough oak panelling and brass candlesticks
glowed, and the hymn-numbers stood out vividly above. His
father studied them for a second, looked down at the floor, and
told them the Highest Common Factor. Johnny wanted to sit
and draw, but knew he would be trying his patience – it was out
of the question. His mother went round with a distant smile, of
having signed away an interest in these odd old things. His
father wasn't at all at home in a church, he took the building,
like the hymn numbers, as a problem. 'The obvious thing to
do,' he said, 'would be to close off those two side bits.'

'The transepts, Dad.'

'They're probably never used anyway, and you'd save a bomb on the heating.'

Johnny called them back to sign their names in the visitors' book. His father always put 'D. D. Sparsholt' and underlined it, his mother wrote 'Constance Sparsholt' though the surname sort of gave out, and Johnny added the signature he had practised at school all last term, with the crossbar of the final *t* running on and swept downwards and back to cradle the two words in a stylish curve. He could draw curves and near-perfect circles freehand, but the biro gave out on the final upswing and he had to go over it again in small strokes which spoiled the line. Perhaps for different reasons none of the Sparsholt family wrote a comment in the column provided. They went out into the sunshine again, Johnny darting back to add 'DFC' after his father's name, and then staring one last time at the great slant bar of light across the nave to fix it in his mind for ever before he closed the door. 'Now, where's Bastion?' said his father, un-French as ever. They had left him to sit in the sun, but he was nowhere to be seen in the sunny south churchyard sloping down to the road.

'Perhaps he's round the back,' said Johnny.

'Run and find him, old lad?' said his father.

'We may just have to leave him,' said his mother.

'Well, we can't hang around here all day.'

Johnny marched back up the path and cut off across the grass between the tall slate tombstones. With a phrase like that his father cut at the root of the pleasure he had just so unexpectedly allowed. Johnny glanced at the fanciful inscriptions, their circus-like mixture of lettering – he was never, ever given enough time to look at the things he liked. He came round the west end of the church into the shadowed and neglected far side of the graveyard, with the heaped grass cuttings and the ugly jutting vestry and a water butt. He needed a slash, and looking all round went into the corner where a downpipe from the roof ran into a drain. Before he'd finished he heard voices and hurried to be done. They were coming from round the east end of the church – Bastien, certainly, and some English people. Johnny found them, a middle-aged couple with a teenage daughter in a skirt pulled over a bathing suit. Her blonde hair down over her shoulders had darker matted streaks where it hadn't quite dried from the beach. She had the look, which Johnny understood in a flash, of being fascinated by Bastien and unable to respond under the moronic supervision of her parents, though perhaps she wasn't entirely sorry they were there.

'Do you like it here?' said the father.

'It is so beautiful.'

The mother said, 'Rather like Normandy, I expect you find.'

'Oh, it is nicer here,' said Bastien, and smiled outrageously at the girl, the seducer's smile of self-love, filling Johnny with contempt and envy. Bastien stood with his hands clasped in front of him, like a child wanting to pee, though that wasn't of course the reason now.

'Well, we mustn't keep you from your friends!' the mother said. Bastien came back, undecided if he was sulking or quietly triumphant, to the car.

'Here he is!' said Johnny. As he slid past him into the back seat Bastien thrust against him. Johnny's father started the car, and Bastien said quietly to Johnny, without looking at him, 'My friend, now you see why God created woman.'

'Church seems to have gone to his head,' said his father, turning, tongue on lip, to reverse out through the gate. And his own mood had changed – the unplanned ten minutes at Treterrian had filled him with a weird but familiar urgency, as if to make up for the time lost. 'We can get back this way,' he said, taking the road that ran on, past the church, and appeared to rise, three-quarters of a mile away, a grey line on the high moorland slope beyond. They went down very steeply, to a farm at a crossroads, a fast narrow stream under a bridge. Johnny's instinct was to turn right, and work back eastwards towards the main road they had left. His father, after a second's hesitation, went straight on. But the road ahead had its own long-established ideas, slowed them down with a sequence of right-angled bends, which resolved, after four or five minutes, in a clear steady climb to the west. 'Well, this'll join the Truro road,' his father said.

'Your father's never lost,' said his mother, more boldly than he would have dared to.

When they reached the main road ten minutes later, the Jensen asserted itself, down the open expanse, in a punching ascent through the gears ('Here we go,' said Johnny's mother), up the first long hill, overtaking a lorry, two cars, cutting in, a second lorry, until, just over the crest, they dropped fast in three roaring descents to take their regretted and ignoble place as the last and then not the last vehicle in a queue that stretched round the bend and out of sight: in half a minute the second of the lorries drew up with a great sneeze of its brakes two feet behind them.

Well, they were familiar with holiday queues – they'd been held up for an hour on the drive down from Nuneaton, Johnny's father humorous but far from patient. Some of these old crates didn't even have synchromesh: you saw the panicky back-sliding gear-change on a 1-in-4 hill and from time to time, down one hill and up the next, the immense glinting line of cars behind a stalled and steam-wreathed Morris Minor which should, as his father observed, have been sent to the crusher ten years ago. The crusher was the ultimate weapon in his peace-time arsenal. They sat looking out at cows behind a hedge, breathed the local warmth of the place through the open window; then ran forward a bit, even moved into second gear, before slowing again to a halt. It appeared there was a narrow lane to the right up ahead. Johnny's father looked in brief concentration at the road map, closed the book, and driving in a sudden stately spurt up the empty other side of the road, swung off at the turning – a wild road to a small high village, with the plunge beyond to the next oddly named place. What happened wasn't nearly an accident, thanks to his fighter-pilot reactions, but in the high-hedged lane, with its breathtaking drops and sharp bends and only occasional passing places, you needed to be quick and agile as he was to avoid the odd slow-witted trippers in their ancient jalopies. And now there was a nick, just a brush, but they felt it, with a toiling Austin Cambridge, driven by a little old man who lacked David Sparsholt's instinct for timing and space – he just kept coming. The two wives stayed in the cars, while the men all gathered by the blue off-side fin, Johnny's father drily practical, Johnny joking but lightly frightened saying there was no scratch at all, while Bastien dropped his head from side to side as if to say he thought the old man had a reasonable case. The old man of course was the frightened one, and not quite in control of his temper. 'Ruddy playboy,' he said. 'And your children with you too.' This was something they laughed about more than seemed quite explicable once they'd got back in the car.

5

The next day the Haxbys, who'd come up the hill for tea, stayed on for a drink and kept starting up the talk with jocular remarks when the Sparsholts had let it run down. 'Have I got to make them dinner?' said his mother, when Johnny joined her in the kitchen. She ran her hand through his hair and pulled him to her abstractedly as she made up her mind. 'You don't have to,

Mum,' Johnny said. At 7.30 it was *Take It or Leave It*, which she always reckoned to see. She went back into the living room, went round topping up with the gin in one hand and the tonic in the other, and then switched on the set. Clifford took his drink into the hall and shut the door; in a minute he was heard using their phone. The TV at 'The Lookout' was a portable, brand new, but the reception, through a long red-tipped antenna, was unsatisfactory. The problems with the picture and the sound compounded the trickiness of getting anyone to watch a programme they didn't know; but his mother made no apology and said nothing about Robert Robinson and the rest. Johnny helped her – the thing was that touching the aerial or even standing near the set affected the picture, which tore people's faces sideways in zigzags the moment you sat down again; or it milled mechanically downwards at two-second intervals. 'You'll just have to stand there,' said Norma, lighting a cigarette.

Johnny sat on the floor against his mother's knee; he always watched the programme with her, his father not interested or not home yet, and her love of books shown off in his absence to her son, who loved the ritual of the questions, read out by an actor from a wing-backed chair, and of his mother's groans, hand raised as if to stop him from saying the answers himself, while she stared at the screen. Often she got them right, or it turned out she'd dismissed the right answer on her way to the wrong one. Just as the theme music started, Johnny's father got up to pull the curtains across, since the evening sun made it harder to see; and as he did so slipped behind them through the French windows into the garden. 'God, I never look at this,' said Norma, as the music ended and the four contestants were revealed as if in the depths of a smoke-filled bar. Each of them was introduced in turn, stared at the camera and after a strange pause said graciously, 'Good evening.' 'Oh, jolly good evening to you too!' said Norma, and waggled her head. This week there was John Betjeman, Johnny's favourite, who always knew a lot, and the man called John Gross from Cambridge, who made even the rare times he didn't know the answer into darting displays of what he did know. On the other team were a man and a woman he hadn't seen before. Bastien said, 'Excuse me, Madame, erm . . . I am hungry,' clutching his tummy and rocking his head, but he'd picked the wrong moment, and had to sit down. 'Have a Twiglet,' said Norma, pointing sternly at the bowl.

The first extract was read out by the actor. 'Oh,' said Johnny's mother, 'oh . . .'

'What is it, Connie?' said Norma, as if she might be ill.

'Oh!' she said.

The man called Freddie something in a spotted bow tie said, 'Carlyle?'

'No . . .' said Robert Robinson, 'not Carlyle; Elizabeth Jane Howard?'

'Is it George Eliot, I almost wondered?' she said.

'George Eliot, Mum,' said Johnny.

'Not George Eliot either, I'm afraid.'

'No . . .' his mother said.

It was obvious as they switched to the other team that John Gross knew it, but he let old Betjeman have a go first. 'To me it very much has the ring of Ruskin,' he said.

'Yes, yes, *Præterita*,' said John Gross, as if applauding him.

When the next gobbet was being read out there was the jangle of phone-call ending and Clifford came back in. 'Don't worry, there's nothing on,' said Norma.

'It's Freddie Green,' said Johnny's mother. 'David knew him at Oxford.'

Norma seemed to be watching but she said in a minute, 'He was never at Oxford.'

'Oh, yes,' said his mother, putting on a silly voice, 'he was up at the House, you know.'

'Oh, I see,' said Norma, 'I thought you meant Oxford University.'

'I'm being silly,' his mother said. 'He did one term before he joined up.'

'Hah . . .' said Clifford, and looked rather put out by this fact.

'Very good, Freddie,' said Robert Robinson.

'I knew it too!' said Johnny's mother.

'Well, I knew Victor Dax a little,' said Freddie Green, through the sideways drift of Elizabeth Jane Howard's cigarette smoke. 'I think you did too, John?'

'A curious figure, and a fascinating writer,' said Betjeman. 'People were very keen on him in the twenties, when I was at Oxford.'

'A highbrow taste, would you say, John Betjeman?' said Robert Robinson.

'He seemed highbrow, but I'm not sure he was really.'

'John Gross?'

'I'd be surprised if he was read again; but yes' – he smiled regretfully – 'I read them all when I was younger.'

'There was a rather good play, at least it seemed good at the time, based on one of them,' said Betjeman. '*The Heart's Achievement*. With Celia Johnson.'

'Yes,' said John Gross, 'of course it changed the ending.'

'Well, there we must leave it. Our next extract . . .'

'Silly old fool,' said Clifford.

'Who's that, Cliff?' said Norma, ready to agree.

'Bloody Betjeman . . . .'

'I like him,' said Johnny.

'I used to love A. V. Dax's books,' his mother said, to no one in particular. The actor was reading out the next gobbet when Johnny's father came back in from the hall.

'So you knew that man, David?' Norma said, Johnny wishing she'd shut up.

'Who's that?' He peered at the little screen as if thinking it unlikely, and it took a few seconds for him to work it out. 'Oh, God, old Freddie Green, is it?' He got closer and the picture lurched sideways like stretched knitting until he stood back. 'We were in the same college. He was a fair bit older than me.'

'He looks about twenty years older!' said Norma, glancing round for agreement.

'I say, David,' said Clifford, 'was your friend Freddie a bit of a fruit?'

His father laughed quickly but there was some lingering annoyance in him as he went for a moment into the kitchen. 'He had a bloody great girlfriend, Cliff,' he said, 'I can tell you that.'

'He looks like a fruit,' said Clifford.

'Con met him as well, you know.'

'Did you, Mum?' said Johnny.

'Don't tell me you were up at Oxford too,' said Norma, as if it was getting beyond a joke.

'Not really – not at the university'

'You know my wife was a spy, of course,' said his father.

'You weren't, Con . . . ?' said Norma.

'Well, hardly,' said his mother, though she seemed not to mind the suggestion. 'We did the spies' typing.'

'I see . . .'

'Typing and filing.'

'You must have seen quite a lot then.'

'Well, we signed the Official Secrets Act,' said his mother, her eyes to the screen.

'You'll not get a thing out of her,' said his father. 'I never have.'

'I can keep a secret if I have to,' said his mother.

'Oh, so can I,' said Norma, and looked round rather fretfully for her cardigan.

*

By the time they finished dinner, everyone but Johnny was drunk. His mother had drunk enough, it seemed, to forget her annoyance at having to make them all dinner in the first place. Bastien had wangled a glass of red wine, and topped it up when he refilled Norma's glass. Then Johnny's father had got out a bottle of brandy. Johnny helped clear the pudding plates and took them to the kitchen. In the other room the TV had been switched on again. 'Turn it up a bit,' said Norma, 'I like this.' Johnny heard and saw, as he went back through with a quick rush of the pulse, that it was Tom Jones, smiling and nodding, hips, knees and shoulders starting up like sliding pistons as the music started, tight black trousers with a huge-buckled belt like a cowboy's crowning the famous unmentionable bulge, which the set made it hard to see in enough detail. The top three buttons of his shirt were open, a cross glinted in black chest hair as he danced. He was singing 'It's Not Unusual' as he swayed and swung about, girls in the audience screaming and staring, Johnny knowing all the words and feeling them slide like hands around Bastien, and also a little bit around Tom Jones himself. He blushed at his thrusts, and looked away blankly. Clifford was sitting forward, peering mockingly at the little screen. 'Ah, that's what the ladies like . . . !' he said, and knocked back the rest of his brandy.

Johnny took the wine glasses and the crumby cheese plate into the kitchen, regretting every missed second of the song. When he came back he saw his father, with a little mock-serious bow, trying to dance with Norma. 'Ooh, David,' she said, 'you'll have my husband after you.' But Clifford only tutted, as if he had better things to worry about. She looked down to make sure of her footing. 'Cliff never takes me dancing.' She laid her hand, as she must have been taught, along his upper arm, and her right was swallowed up almost in his left. They moved off quite fast round the end of the dining table and out on to the lit square of the patio, where he steered her with a pilot's skill between the white chairs.

'Oh, David's a good dancer,' said Connie, rather irritably, and looking let down. There was a sort of implication that Clifford should ask her to dance, though a quick cold smile passed between them as they agreed to avoid it. The song ended, to studio applause, and Tom Jones started on 'What's New, Pussycat?', the girls screaming dementedly as they heard the first phrase. It was then that Bastien came forward, swaying from the hips and with his arms raised in front of him, clowning, but not entirely. He stopped by Connie's chair.

'You like to dance?' he said, with a welcome glimpse of nerves in his big grin.

'No, you cheeky monkey,' said Connie. Bastien, still grinning, not wanting to show he minded, kept up his jiggling movements round her chair, his thighs in trousers almost as tight as Tom Jones's. 'Oh, come on, then,' she said, and got up and fitted herself to him – 'And not too close!' as his hand went round her waist and Johnny sat down at the far end of the sofa from Clifford, and they watched, each with his own thin smile.

6

The Jensen crept forward with a crackling sound over the small rough stones of the drive: the beauty of its slowness was its mighty potential for speed. At the gateway the tail-lights flashed red for two seconds, and then, with a turn so fast that a short spray of stones leapt out across the road, it powered out of sight up the hill to the left. Three whooping growls were heard as it climbed through the gears, but at the fourth the sound was lost in the deep lane. They had gone. The mid-morning sun beat down on the lawn; it was wholly still, until, for a moment, a breeze off the sea shook the pampas grass and opened the *Daily Mail* on the patio table.

'So it's just us!' said Connie. In the general relief there was a small unplaceable cause for worry – perhaps about what they would tell the two men they had done when they got back.

Norma sat down again at the table and lit a cigarette. 'What are we going to do?'

'Let's go to the beach, Mum,' Johnny said.

Norma blew out a slow stream of smoke. 'Oh, I don't know about the beach,' she said; though she liked to be coaxed into agreement with any plan. Small reminders of her goodness in yielding spiced up the day. She was wearing her white bell-bottoms and the floppy straw hat with a blue ribbon. 'Look at me!' she said.

'Mum, we've been here four days and we haven't even been to the beach yet' – to Johnny it was a long-imagined scene. 'In fact Bastien was complaining about it.'

'Well, if Bastien wants to' – with a weary laugh at what things had come to. 'You'd better get the Zulus.'

Norma stared at her, ignorant of Zulus, and Johnny said, 'I'll get them!'

'You don't mind, Norma? And see if Bastien's up, while you're about it . . .' But here he was, scuff and flap of his flip-flops, blinking as he stepped out through the French windows, voice still throaty from sleep, and it seemed with a small worry of his own.

'Your husbands have both gone?' He smiled and spread his hands with bleary chivalry towards the women, as if faced with a double duty in the men's absence.

'Yes, it's just us,' said Johnny.

'But where are they?' said Bastien.

The women ignored this question, but Johnny said, 'They've

gone to Truro in the Jensen. Truro' – and he thought perhaps he shouldn't say this again – 'is the county town of Cornwall, I told you . . . with the cathedral.'

'I think Cliff just wanted a go in David's car,' Norma said.

Connie gave a dry laugh at this childishness, said, 'Your car's just as good, Norma,' but added an adult note, 'They're going to have lunch with Leslie Stevens.'

'Oh, Leslie Stevens, well . . .' said Norma.

'Well, they're cooking something up.'

'We're going to the beach,' said Johnny, laying his hand on Bastien's strong shoulder.

'Is there some coffee?' said Bastien, looking seductively past him at his mother.

'I'll make you some,' she said. 'We'll leave in ten minutes.' From her mouth such orders were wonderfully lacking in authority. Norma had to totter down to 'Greylags' to change and fetch her bathing suit; Bastien cajoled his way into bacon and eggs, then went to the lavatory for fifteen minutes; and it was nearly lunchtime when they set off down the hill, crossed the big road and picked their way down through the ginnels and steep stairways between cottages to the high sea front, and its dizzy gap from which a further steep stair, mere stone blocks jutting from the harbour wall, with a frayed rope passing between rings as a rail, descended to the bright underworld of the beach.

The choice of a spot to lay out their towels was a tug of small calculations – there were strips of fine sand between diagonal ridges of rock, exposed now by the outgoing tide, some further away from the big outlet pipe and slimy cascade across the beach below it, but too close for Johnny's mother's liking to a noisy family with transistor and dog driving people away, and a sun-browned blond son or son-in-law in green trunks drawing

Johnny in furtive abstraction towards them. Further along, but right up at the rocks at the top of the beach, was a woman with two daughters, and Bastien, still partly in role as the senior male, made a firm move towards them. Norma stood in ladylike patience until the decision had been made. Johnny watched the blond man amble down into the water and with a quick unflustered gesture fall forward into a lazy crawl. Connie, free of the men, seemed more open than usual to the charm of having no plan, and almost no will. They settled in a minute at a place a few yards above the tideline, the sand smooth and warm in front of them but still damp to the digging toes.

Now the two baskets, carried by Johnny and his mother, were set down and emptied – towels and sun cream, a book, lemon squash, and the swimming things, glimpses of furled linings and straps. 'Do you want a Zulu, Mrs Hardy?' said Johnny.

'I'll just sit here for a bit, thank you,' said Norma.

'Bas?'

Bastien smiled at him narrowly as he took it in both hands. No one knew why they were called this, it was some very obscure connexion with the film, which Johnny had seen three times at the Ritz. Mrs Sparsholt's Zulus were made for modesty, old bath towels sewn together and worn like a poncho with a hole for the head. Inside them you could change in and out of your swimsuit on the beach; and after a swim dry and warm yourself. Bastien unrolled it and stretched it out under his chin like a shapeless frock. 'What is this bloody thing?'

'Oh dear,' said Norma.

'It's to change your clothes in,' said Connie firmly, 'or under.'

Bastien shook his head – 'I don't need,' and rolled it up again loosely.

'He can just use a towel,' said Johnny, in a reasonable tone; but in a moment Bastien had tugged off his shirt and was unbuttoning his jeans. They all looked or didn't look. He had his trunks on already, thin blue and white stripes, he stepped out of the jeans and folded them and put them safe in the basket.

'Voilà, Madame!' he said, and looked down at himself, pleased as he had been last year, on the burning French beach, by his own sleek elegance and indecency. Johnny had a breathless intimation of the warmth and tightness of the swimming trunks worn under clothes, the lucky loop of the drawstring now tucked inside. Getting changed himself, he found his pleasure in the Zulus drain away, he felt prudishly British beside the French boy's simplicity.

Next it was his mother's turn to cover herself in the long towelling smock. Johnny noted, while not quite looking at her, the little active bulges, the intuited moments of release from bra and so forth as she got undressed. The never-seen nakedness of his parents was never more present to him than when they were hopping and wriggling in their Zulus. When she emerged, in her black one-piece, she seemed confident but self-conscious – or maybe Johnny's self-consciousness leaked into her: she looked oddly at him for a second, stooped for her red bathing cap, put her hair up in a few quick tucks under its snappy rim, and walked down, lively, heavy-footed, to the lifting and tumbling water's edge. Bastien watched her going in, something awestruck for a second in his impudence. Then Johnny ran down and joined her, the cold grip of the water shocked him in a way she hadn't hinted at, in her quick duck and rise, the steady breaststroke that took her out, red head bobbing. He wanted to swim with Bastien, tangle with him in the waves, in the element where he was superior; but he knew, he'd known from the moment they left the house, that Bastien was not going to put himself at that disadvantage. He pushed out fast, then lay back in the water, the shore as if seen by periscope, with the background restored, white-painted houses lined above the sea wall. He waved, as though Bastien might have missed him: 'Come in!' Bastien was being talked to by Norma, who had laid down her hat – she must have asked him something, he stared at her, then came over, reluctant, with no escape, to help her with her Zulu: he dropped it over her head like a cloth on a parrot's cage. She struggled out, fussing about her hair. Bastien turned away from her, with his fastidious smirk, and it struck Johnny, as he swivelled and swam on again, that probably no one much cared about Norma undressing, however she did it.

It was fun swimming with his mother, little bits of talk if they were close, 'Hello!' like delighted friends, then unannounced races to and fro, and companionable circlings, in breast-stroke, round a moored dinghy, *My Boy Lollipop*, or the two red marker buoys. He was a stronger swimmer now than last year, and his mother acknowledged this, with a hint of distance in her laugh. They were different in the water, daily habits dissolved, his mother all features with her thick hair sleeked away, and the chill of the sea not to be ignored. He felt it once or twice, with the pitch of a small unexpected wave in his face, her look, entirely used to him but not quite sure what she was seeing. He loved his father not being here, but he wished his father could see him, hanging for a moment on an upstretched arm from the gunwale of the dinghy, with an easy new sense of his own strength. 'Oh, he's off,' said his mother, and Johnny swung about almost reluctantly to see the shore, further off now, church and trees in the picture above the town roofs, and Bastien a hundred yards away from Norma, walking calmly towards the far rocky corner that led round, at low tide, to Crab Beach.

When they came out, and ran up the sand, and stood dripping and drying themselves in front of Norma, the indescribable alertness to change, to his own unmannerly growth, seemed to glow off them both, as the breeze ran across them and the force of the sun took over from the cold of the sea. He was nearly as tall as his mother now, in a year she would look up to him, as she did to her husband. She had sturdy legs, scratched around the ankles from walking in sandals, her large breasts were squashed together by the black bathing suit, her high cleavage goosefleshed under droplets of water. He knew she was forty-four, an age not mentioned, far ahead in the dense tangled stasis of adult life, whose language he still hardly understood, though he was learning to hear new tones in it, hardness and significant silence.

No point in following Bastien to Crab Beach, the rumour of topless women . . . he hoped it wasn't true . . . but ached at the thought of him there with them, while he was left behind here, with his mother and her friend. He squatted down by her while she rubbed sun cream on his back, feeling her take stock again, unseen, of the new size of him. He thought about how Bastien had changed in a year, the hair on his legs, the shadowed upper lip and chin, and how when he himself went off next month to boarding school he would surprise his mother each time he came home. 'Don't go too far,' she said, as he walked off, not knowing really where to go. His mother and Norma settled down, saying nothing; he went where they couldn't see him, past the family with the dog and the striped canvas windbreak, the young man was changing, Johnny a second too late as he pulled up his pants with a snap and stood wringing the wet from the tiny green trunks. Johnny could be so absorbed in looking he forgot he was visible, and being looked at. 'All right?' said the man – a clench of shame for Johnny, but it was just pleasantness, unsuspecting. The dog ran over, and Johnny scratched its head with sudden rough energy and relief.

Talk had started up when he drifted back behind his mother and Norma – he went perching and shifting over the ridge of rocks, little creatures in the trapped weedy pools hiding from his shadow. His mother had her book from the library, *The*

Red and the Green, and Norma, excluded, made conversation in idle, vaguely nettled resistance to it. The niceness of his mother glowed through, her book turned face down, answering, hitching one thing of no great interest to another, and keeping it going. He knew very well she didn't care much for Norma Haxby, and not at all for Clifford – it was a keen little glimpse into the marital machinery to overhear her talking for her husband. 'I've brought the *Mail*,' she said, 'if you want it,' and reached over to the basket; Norma took it, but perhaps couldn't read it in her sunglasses. He was aware of her turning her head and watching him, and wondering perhaps where the other boy was. He hopped down to a place where he could make drawings in the firm wet sand. He could only just hear them through the general noise of the beach and the gulls, and they spoke now with confidential flatness. His mother looked up over her book, 'I hope they're getting on all right. I think Bastien's rather bored.'

'It's that age, I expect, isn't it,' said Norma vaguely.

'He only seems interested in girls.'

'How old is he?'

'He's fifteen.'

Norma peered out to sea. 'He could pass for older, couldn't he.'

'Mm, I know what you mean.'

'Good-looking . . .' said Norma.

His mother peered humorously down the beach. 'Lazy puppy. I wish he had some other things to wear.'

'Well,' said Norma, 'I suppose they grow out of things, at that age.'

'Actually, I don't care, but he'll need something smarter for dinner at the Boat Club.'

'They're quite relaxed, aren't they?'

'They may be, but Drum isn't. He won't take him there in those trousers.'

'Ah, I see . . .'

'He's very proper, is Drum!'

'Oh, well so's Cliff,' said Norma.

Johnny had made a face, like a great luscious boy doll, huge eyes and lips: sand was a tricky medium. He erased the whole thing in a stamping dance, smoothed it again with a stick of driftwood. Then he lay down on his front and closed his eyes. The talk ambled on, his mother's reasonable tone each time Norma brought her out of her book.

'I say, Cliff was quite surprised about David being at Oxford University.'

'Well, it was only for one term, you know.'

'He didn't want to go back, then?'

'He could have gone back, of course, after the War. But, you know, Norma, he was twenty-three or something, youngest ever squadron leader, DFC – he just couldn't see himself getting back into student life.'

'I should think you were jolly glad, too.' The repeated click of a lighter, and in a few seconds cigarette smoke in the ozone. 'No, Cliff was saying he'd had a very good war.'

'Yes, he did. He loved it all really, that was the thing.'

Norma said nothing about Clifford's war. 'You took a while to get round to starting a family, though, Connie.'

'I suppose we did, we both had so much energy – you know what it's like—'

'Well . . .'

'And there was the business to set up – that was all-consuming for five years. And anyway we wanted our fun.' He felt the pause here, she must have looked round. 'Not that it wasn't fun having Jonathan . . . David always wanted a boy.'

'Oh, did he? You never wanted another?'

'I wouldn't have minded, but he wasn't keen – strictly between you and me.'

'Of course . . .' Two busy puffs and a sigh as she screwed

the barely smoked cigarette into the sand beside the others. 'I expect David's very busy with work all the time, anyway, Cliff is. It's nine o'clock sometimes before he gets in.'

His mother said quite humorously, 'Yes, I don't always feel I have his undivided attention.'

'Well, this is it,' said Norma, perhaps not sure how vexed she was.

'He's on the Council now, too, of course. And he's taken on the RAF benevolent thing, which he feels very strongly about.'

'Oh, well . . .'

'But Cliff must have a lot of dinners and so on.'

'Oh, dinners, meetings . . . Dinners he can take me to, not always of course, and there's the Masonic. But I go with him if I can – well, it saves me having to cook!'

It was hard to picture Norma cooking – sausages on sticks seemed about it. Connie said, 'And Drum has his sports things too, some evenings, and most weekends.'

'Ah . . . yes,' said Norma. Here she was unable to compete.

Johnny ran off down the beach, the tide some way out now, and their little encampment stuck where no one would choose to be. He looked about as he jogged and slowed, made detours round rocks where there was a possible boy to see, a taut contour, a heart-racing moment of nakedness, went within a foot of near-naked couples, in the borderless democracy of the shore. What he hoped to see was Bastien coming back over the rocks from Crab Beach, and telling him nothing had happened. He hopped up on to a long concrete casing like a walkway exposed by the tide – there was a boy about his own age playing by himself just below on the other side. He looked out and there Bastien was – Johnny waved and shouted, and thought he saw the upward nod, his sign of greeting and dismissal. The boy, in red swimming trunks and with a child's spade, digging for something in the saturated sand, looked up too, turned and peered at Johnny.

'Is that your friend, then?'

Johnny still saw the merit in saying yes.

'What's his name?'

'Bastien – he's French.'

'Oh, yes? . . . I've got a French friend,' said the boy, as if he knew both the pleasures and the problems of having one. He stared at Bastien approaching, small against sea, sand and rocks but unique and magnetic. 'They're very smooth, aren't they.'

'Yeah, I suppose so,' said Johnny, and blushed annoyingly.

The boy clambered up on two rocks and stood beside him, looked at him cautiously. He said, 'Is it your dad's got the Jensen C-V8?'

'What, the Mark III, you mean?' said Johnny.

'Is it? I didn't know it was the Mark III.'

'Yeah,' said Johnny. 'We had the Mark II before.'

The boy looked at him, hesitated. 'Is it made of fibreglass?'

'Yeah, yeah,' said Johnny, frowning out his own faint unease at the fact. 'The doors have aluminium skins, of course.'

'Oh, right . . .' He stared down the beach at the collapsing waves, in the strange gravity of these facts. 'I should think it could take off,' he said.

Johnny tutted. 'Not with that engine – it weighs a ton.' He heard his father, in his brusque defence of the car against any sidling suggestion it was lightweight, and not what it seemed.

'I suppose so,' said his friend. 'How fast does it go, then?'

'Hundred and thirty-six?'

The boy seemed to make some calculation of his own. 'You've never had it that fast,' he said, as Bastien came up, and rather than joining them looped further up the beach, past where the mother and two girls were still sprawled, all three it seemed sound asleep. Johnny's new friend stood assessing him as he passed, then ran off without a word the other way.

Johnny homed in on his mother and Norma just as Bastien strolled up, gave them all a more friendly nod, kicked off his flip-flops and flung himself down on the towel he had left an hour before, the corners now curled up by the wind and the edges strewn with sand. Norma looked at him, from under the wide brim of her hat. 'So where have you been, young man?'

He rolled over, glanced up at her, sand on his bottom, hair stiff and quilled from the sea and the breeze, something sly in response to her boring adult tone. 'I've been walking, on the coast.'

'How far did you go?' said Johnny pleasantly, siding with him but dreading his idea of what he had got up to even more, now he was back and lying there in all his glorious capacity.

'Not so far,' said Bastien. 'No, it was nice,' and when Norma turned to find her bag he winked at him – Johnny gasped, and looked away, pierced by the thought, the muddled impossible image, of Bastien seducing the topless women on Crab Beach.

'You need some protection from the sun, Monsieur,' said Connie.

He smiled and cringed – 'I don't have . . . Madame.'

Norma, in her strictness, with its shy shade of experiment, childless woman among teenage boys, said, 'What do you need?'

'I think you have . . .' he said, and watched as Connie dug in the baby-basket, and held out the plastic bottle with a palm tree on it.

'I have some,' said Norma, peering down through her sun-glasses into the bag where her own more expensive creams were carried.

Now Bastien was helpless, grinning at Connie – 'Madame, can you put it on to me? I can't reach . . .' and he flopped back, face down, lifting his buttocks just once, to make himself com-fortable.

'Well, I can . . .' said Johnny, sitting forward, heart in mouth. 'Oh, I'll do it,' said Norma, 'for heaven's sake.'

And now Bastien lay on his back and slept, or seemed to, in a sated surrender to the heat. It was as though he had given himself to Johnny to look at, there was trust of a kind in the complete indifference of sleep; and also a kind of contempt, since looking, it seemed, was all Johnny was left with. Of course they slept together each night, one above the other, in their squeaking bunks, 'more fun for you both' as his mother had said . . . Norma wandered down to the sea, stopping here and there and staring blankly at the family with the dog; she didn't really go in, just stood, smart and solitary, where the waves could swill over her feet, and back again, sucking the sand out from under them. It seemed his mother too was asleep now, under her floppy hat, *The Red and the Green* sloped side-ways, her hand over the page. Johnny looked at Bastien for spells of five seconds, then ten seconds, together. The dip of his smooth stomach, the hidden navel like an orifice, not a button, the thin gap under his taut waistband narrowed with each slow breath . . . Because of the sea and the sand Johnny hadn't brought his sketchbook, but what he saw was indelibly drawn on his mind.

'What about lunch?' said Norma. It was another experiment of their husbandless day that mealtimes were so neglected. Now it was after two. Johnny's mother must have seen there was no point in resistance.

'I'll make us all something when we go up.'

And a few minutes later the women were tented and chang-ing. Bastien showed no sign of moving, and the possibility of a short sunny nearly naked time alone with him took possession of Johnny. 'We'll come up in a bit, then,' he said.

'It'll just be salad,' said his mother. 'Take your time.' She stepped free of the Zulu, the damp heap of her things. Norma too emerged, in her white shorts, and started to pull up and shake the towels, Bastien wincing and shrinking from the blown sand.

'Please,' he said, 'we will bring everything back for you.'

Norma smiled narrowly at this unforeseen offer. 'Oh . . . well, if you like, Bastien.'

'Yes, yes, we'll bring them, Mum,' said Johnny, the tone of cheerful drudgery.

'Yes, Jonathan will carry them,' said Bastien, and smiled at him as he got to his feet. He was already a few yards down the beach when he said, 'I race with you,' and jogged down towards the water, turning to a sprint when Johnny came up fast beside him, shouldering him, all the force of longed-for contact in the riding of arm against arm. They went into the sea together, went under – it was as if all Bastien's meanness, the awful act he had put on for the past week, was banished in a glittering splash.

Larking in the water, dragging each other down, just the edge of panic once from Bastien, he disguised it in two seconds, jeered at Johnny as he pulled himself to him, an arm round his neck, and Johnny, in a dream, without thinking or asking raised his legs and circled Bastien's waist with them. They laughed, steadied, gasped in each other's faces, Bastien stared at him as if thinking how to phrase something or more probably planning his next attack, jutted his lips forward, and kissed Johnny on the mouth. It was very quick, and then he'd fallen back, catching Johnny out in the instant of surrender. 'Salope!' he said, and laying the flat of his hand on top of his head, pushed him under.

It took them a minute to feel the heat, when they came out and ran up the beach with the water all over them still. With a touch of clowning Bastien picked up a Zulu, and slipped it over his head; Johnny did the same, and they stood pulling the towelling round them from inside, to get roughly dry. Then Johnny realized Bastien was untying his trunks and with two stooping twists pushing them down: they appeared round his ankles, and he stepped out of them. Johnny did the same as calmly as he could, picked them up, and wrung them out, and took them up to the baskets, thrilled by his own hidden nakedness. When he turned back, he found Bastien had sat down on a towel, was huddled up but with his knees apart under the Zulu.

It was something Johnny had done, last year, with the secret daring that seemed nothing when the impulse was so strong. He thought at first Bastien was pretending, as he sat down facing him, and then he knew, with a piercing sense of a last and only chance and at the same time of cruel exclusion, that it was for real. 'I race with you!' he said. It was a jolt, a sudden opening, and Johnny was doing it too, with quite new feelings of not wanting to race, of wanting it to go on for a long time, to be saved and postponed into something different and better. If it was a race it would soon be over, Bastien could come unbelievably fast, forty seconds from starting last year, when they'd tried it, but in bed then, together. He stared at him avidly, saying nothing. He was part of the game but the game kept them apart, each of them focused on his own desires, though Johnny's, he knew, burned in his face: he doubted how long he could look at Bastien and think of him in that way. Bastien smiled at him, was he mocking him or saying that of course he loved him? He had the intense private look of the approaching climax, it seemed terribly obvious, but no one was watching, and his eyes twitched away beyond Johnny's shoulder in a last hungry stare at the two girls up by the wall.

The boys gathered up the things and started back to the house, the mood cool, quiet, souring in the sun on the steep path, the clamber up steps encumbered with the baskets, but with something strange still binding them, the one shared act that neither of them mentioned. The relief of being part of Bastien's mutiny rather than its target carried him through, and gave a new twist of hope, and anxiety, to the remaining three days. On the final lane climbing out of town – the sunroom windows of 'The Lookout' glimpsed above and to the left, over the pampas grass – Bastien seemed uncertain. Was it better to drag behind, with sullen thwacks of his flip-flops, or to stride ahead, competent and careless? The driveway to 'Greylags', cut from the shaly bank, climbed sharply on the right to its covered carport, and it must have been because Clifford Haxby's Daimler was already parked in it that the maroon back end of the Jensen, pulled in behind it, jutted out. Johnny stopped for a second, in surprise and disappointment that they were back, and the unusual freedom of the hours with the women at an end already. It seemed too soon – how far was it to Truro? About fifteen miles, but on twisty roads. He looked at his watch and it was ten past three, on the beach they had forgotten time and now it had caught them out. Bastien came up behind. 'This is their house?' he said and of course there was no one else he could be referring to.

'It's Dad's car,' said Johnny, 'the Jensen.'

'Ah,' said Bastien, and nodded.

'They're back already.'

'Perhaps it was not far?' said Bastien, going a few steps up the drive as if to check Johnny was right, seeing some interest in the situation when he might have been counted on to shrug and pass by. He stood peering, with his basket, as if delivering something.

'Come on,' said Johnny, 'I'm hungry, let's have lunch,' and when Bastien went a bit further, 'They're probably still talking business.'

Bastien said, too loud, 'Have you seen the house?' He was at the top of the drive. 'It's nice.'

'No,' said Johnny – he'd wanted to see it, but the Haxbys had put a bad spell on it for him. 'Come on.'

'In a minute . . .' with a flap of his free hand. He put down the basket and went on out of view.

So Bastien was being difficult, again, after all, and he was left at the gateway, scuffing the stones in his plimsolls. 'I'm going home.'

He went a few steps up the road, hoping Bastien would follow, but when he didn't he stopped again. Clifford Haxby hated Bastien, and his father would be furious if he caught him creeping about while they were having a meeting. They were friends but it would seem like trespassing.

When he reached the top of the drive, Johnny couldn't see him. 'Greylags' was a bungalow, expensive-looking, clad in reddish wood, and with French windows on to a front lawn. All the windows were closed: they could only just have got back, and there was a feeling almost that no one was in, they had parked the car there and gone away – gone over, it struck him in all its simplicity, to 'The Lookout' itself. There was no one here, and he studied the house across its smooth lawn with a gripping impatience, even so, for Bastien to reappear. A car came down the steep lane behind, slowed, but went on, to the left, into the town. A great screaming jabber of seagulls broke out, echoed round from the harbour below, the horn of the ferry sounded distinctly, a man close by behind the fence of the next house spoke, and a woman answered; and still the Haxbys' house, or the house they were renting, sat closed and unresponsive, while Johnny made up excuses, breezy and hopeless, for standing and staring at it. Here Bastien was now, coming out from round the side of the house, moving quickly but with feet clenched to silence his flip-flops. Had he been seen? He gave Johnny the quick grin of someone who has kept a friend waiting. 'No one here,' said Johnny.

Bastien shrugged, and looked vaguely disgusted at the pointlessness of the thing. Then, stumbling, scratching back at one point with his foot to capture his shoe, he started to run down the drive. 'Come on!' he said. 'Lunch time, I'm hungry.'

'What, did they see you?' Johnny said.

'Nothing to see, my friend,' said Bastien, 'nothing to see,' and reached out to bring him with him, sudden brotherly warmth of his body against him, marching him out under the strength of his arm, Johnny's hand in a moment round him, the beltless waist of his jeans, nothing on, of course, underneath.

'Oh, your basket . . .'

He had to break out of Bastien's embrace to go back for it. He reached the edge of the lawn, snatched up the basket, and in the moment that he turned he saw, or thought he saw (the reflections of sky, cloud and blue in the wide windows), the unfolding ripple, the slow wink of light and shade, of the fine slats of a Venetian blind swivelled upwards and then downwards on their cord and closed.

THREE

Small Oils

1

'Hello. You're new!'

Johnny gave a cautious smile. 'Am I?'

'And what have you got for us there?'

'Well, it's for Mr Dax, in fact.' He showed the flat brown-paper parcel, with its pasted label, *Evert Dax Esq., Cranley Gardens*. 'It's a picture.'

'Of course I thought it must be.' The man peered at it teasingly, his lean, humorous head on one side. He wore a bow tie, a brown velvet jacket and flared tweed trousers surprising on a man of sixty. The woman with him, who was younger, red ruffles at her bosom under a red coat, said defiantly,

'Well, we're going to take the lift.' They crossed the hall to where the cage of a lift ran up in the narrow embrace of the stairs. 'I'm Clover, by the way.'

'Oh, Johnny,' said Johnny, 'Johnny Sparsholt.'

She half-turned and looked at him for a moment more closely. 'Oh, yes. And do you know my husband.'

'Freddie Green, hello,' said the man, 'hello.' He smiled again, and Johnny wondered if he did in some sense know him – he seemed to expect him to. 'It may not be working, love.'

Clover pressed a worn brass button; there was a sequence of pneumatic clacks, and after a longish pause, in which they all peered upwards, the hanging loop of cable dropped slowly into view, and then the tiny cabin itself, a cage within a cage. 'I'm not going to ask you what the picture is,' said Freddie, as the lift came to rest. He pulled back the folding grille, and let Clover, who was rather larger than him, go in first.

'I'll tell you if you want,' said Johnny, wondering if Freddie would have heard of the artist. There was really only room for two in the lift, and if the power went off, as it did almost daily, they might be trapped there, testing the warmth of their new-found friendship for an hour or more. Freddie gestured gallantly, Johnny stepped forward—

'Oh, don't worry, I'll take the stairs.' He held up the wrapped painting.

'I'm sure we can all squash up,' said Clover.

'You know it's the second floor,' said Freddie, stepping in with a humorous stoop of submission.

As Johnny climbed the stairs the lift creaked steadily upwards beside him, and at each turn he saw Freddie and Clover from another angle, pressed together and speaking quietly, in a register between public and private. Freddie glanced out, at some remark she made, met his eye and gave him a friendly nod. Johnny smiled and looked down, at the shabby stair carpet, and up, at the gilt-framed paintings climbing in the gloom beside him. It wasn't a race, but he was there already on the second floor to hold back the grille for them. He could hear the muted noise of voices from nearby.

'Evert's father had the lift put in,' said Freddie as he emerged – 'you know, having only one leg.'

'I haven't actually met Mr Dax,' said Johnny, not sure if this father was still alive – much less still living here. He imagined Evert Dax to be getting on a bit himself.

'Oh, you haven't . . . ?'

'I only know his secretary.'

'Ah, I'm not sure . . .' – Freddie jiggled the door closed and made sure the latch had engaged.

'Denis Drury?'

Clover laughed. 'Oh, you know *Denis*,' she said, and as she went along the hallway, she turned and looked at Johnny again. 'I suppose you'd call Denis his secretary'; her smile seemed both to put him in the wrong and to give him a mischievous hint. They threw down their coats in a small bedroom. Johnny said, unexpectedly caught up, 'I'm only staying a minute . . .' and then, 'Well, when I say I know Mr Drury . . . It was him who brought the picture in to be cleaned, you see . . .' He remembered his unnerving stillness, in the shop, and his dark unblinking eyes.

Mr Drury himself wasn't to be seen in the room they then went into, where a small crowd of people were talking quietly, as if at a funeral, a group of women on a sofa below a tall mirror, and a darker huddle standing by the fireplace. The dusk seemed to have taken them unawares. From the big west-facing window there was a view of chimney stacks and a church spire against the last faint pink of the sky. 'It's the deterioration of money in general,' a grand but piping voice was saying, as Freddie and Clover were greeted and absorbed into the standing group, while Johnny hung back, looking shyly at the nearest pictures, which he'd been told were worth seeing. There was a small off-white relief by Ben Nicholson, behind glass, and another large abstract painting in a stark black frame, whole areas of the grubby white paint, when you looked closely, cracked and pooled like a skin on boiled milk. Next to it was a print of an airborne blue cow, with a pencilled inscription, 'À mon ami Dax – Chagall'. The pictures seemed to confer a quality on the people in the room, too familiar with them perhaps to bother looking at them. On the table behind the sofa stood what must have been a Barbara Hepworth sculpture, a hollow globe of auburn wood, its white-painted aperture strung with white wires. Johnny saw the curved back of it in the mirror, and himself slipping past, meeting his own eye for reassurance.

'Are you going to join us?' said one of the seated women.

Johnny looked down at her and grinned – again he thought it would be rather a squash. 'Is it a party?' he said.

'I wouldn't say a party' – she shook her square grey head. And it was true no one had a drink – it was a meeting of some kind, just about to get going, and best avoided before it did so. He looked at the window again and from here the reflected room half-concealed the dark mass of the house-backs beyond, the lamp beside him equal for a minute to the light that had come on in a bedroom there.

'You must be a friend of Denis's,' said the second woman.

'Yes, of course,' said the third.

'Well, not really,' Johnny said and gripped his parcel, and peered round. In a room of middle-aged and elderly people he was much the youngest, and he felt now like a child under the lightly teasing scrutiny of a trio of aunts. 'I'm working for Cyril Hendy, you know, the art dealer.' There was still a novelty to saying this, though he knew he could hardly speak for the great Cyril, who himself hardly spoke at all.

'Ah,' said the first woman, 'you're a picture person. We thought you might be going to read to us.'

'Read to you?' said Johnny, with a giggle.

'Well, Evert will be reading tonight himself,' said the second woman, looking round. 'You know he's writing this book about his father.'

'Oh I didn't know,' said Johnny, 'no.'

'You know about Evert's father, at least,' the grey-haired woman said, with her slightly arch severity, as if to suggest he would feel foolish when he realized who she was.

'He only had one leg, didn't he,' said Johnny.

'Well, there was rather more to him than that,' said the second woman.

'Oh God yes,' said the third woman, who'd been gazing up at him in a preoccupied way. A smile spread slowly across her face. 'You must forgive me if I say I'm madly envious of your hair.'

'Oh, er, thank you . . .' said Johnny, feeling he mustn't look too closely at hers, which was fluffy and dyed a strange rust-red; he glanced up into the mirror again.

'But isn't it an awful nuisance to you?' asked the second woman, with artless curiosity, and a sense she was glad the subject had been broached.

'We haven't been told your name,' said the first woman.

Johnny told them now, and on one face at least he saw the familiar momentary suspicion, and its tactful suppression, and the lingering curiosity, half cunning, half sympathetic, that ensued. As if to discountenance all this, the third woman said, 'I'm iffy, by the way.'

'Oh . . . um . . .'

'Iphigenia,' the second explained.

'Old, old friend of Evert's.'

'Mm, you go back a long way, don't you,' said the second woman.

'But look, do you know Freddie Green?' – Iffy sat forward as if to make an introduction.

'He doesn't know anyone,' said a man's voice at his shoulder; and as he turned Johnny saw Denis Drury's face in the mirror and felt a hand placed lightly in the small of his back. 'He's completely new.'

'Hello!' said Johnny, and put out his free hand, which Denis took without looking but kept hold of and squeezed as he went on,

'I hope you've all been nice to him.'

'Oh, we have,' they more or less agreed. Evert Dax's secretary looked just as he had when he came into the shop, formal and old-fashioned, in a dark suit with waistcoat and striped tie, speaking without moving his head and with the tiny suggestive concession of a smile on his small, plump mouth. His hair, cut short above the ears, was sleek and black, his dark eyes large and challenging. His age though had grown mysterious – in the shop he was like a snooty school prefect, but close to, in the softly raking lamplight, Johnny saw that he might be forty. Denis let his hand go, in a conditional sort of way, but the pressure in the small of his back seemed to count on some further understanding between them. Johnny was worried what the women might think; he said firmly,

'Well, I've brought your painting back.'

'So I see,' said Denis, surveying in a long second the parcel and Johnny's corduroys and of course his hair. 'We'll all have a look at it afterwards. I know Evert will want to meet you.'

'Oh, you see—' said Johnny, and all the lights went out. There was a staggered sigh of annoyance and weary amusement, while Denis, raising his voice to say 'It's all right, it's all right,' let his hand drop as if inadvertently across Johnny's backside as he moved away. Someone flicked on a lighter and held it up, above the subtly altered group. 'My dear, it's like the War,' a woman said. 'But not half so much fun,' said someone else. 'Well, we're all a good deal older,' said the grey lady, in a very steady tone, and got a laugh. After a moment Iffy said, '*Was* the War so much fun? I must have missed it . . .' and a high-pitched man said, 'Gordon, can you just get on to the Prime Minister and tell him to sort this nonsense out,' at which everyone laughed and a deeper voice from the hall said, 'Too late for that, I'm afraid,' and then, 'Now don't panic!' as the beam of a torch swung in through the door: 'We've got this down to a very fine art.' The torch flashed upwards for a second to show the speaker's face – a ghoulish impression of a grey-haired man in glasses, with a preoccupied smile as he turned to light the way for the person behind him: 'Herta is here . . .' – and a small white-haired woman with a tray followed him into the room. On the tray was a collection of old candlesticks.

'Ah, Herta . . . !' said two or three of the guests, rather warily.

'We have the candles,' said Herta, absorbed in her task to the exclusion of social niceties. 'Please take off the books.' She came forward, in the beam of the torch, like a figure in a primitive ritual, people clearing the way in front of her. Johnny wondered why the man didn't carry the heavy tray, and Herta the torch; but something told him their roles had been unchangeably fixed a long time ago. She bumped the tray down on a table, and the man, who must surely be Evert Dax himself, watched her with a certain impatience while she struck a match and then another match and got all the candles lit. By their light Dax himself lit the two candelabra on the mantelpiece, with their twisted silver arms and driblets of red wax. Soon the room was glowing, with an effect that Johnny found beautiful. It was a little experiment in history, like the oil lamp in Cyril's workshop, and the half-lit streets, and the other lamented but enjoyable effects of the present crisis, which had lasted the whole six weeks of his London life so far. He put down his package, and helping to pass the candles round he found a role, so that one or two others made spaces for him and introduced themselves. There was a friendly superfluity in these proffered names of people he would never see again. The last thing on the tray was an old brass candle-holder like one his father had, with a snuffer and a square slot to hold a box of matches, and he set it down beside Freddie Green with a fairly certain feeling of some ongoing joke.

'And there was light,' said Freddie.

'Mm, but was there drink?' said Iffy.

2

When Evert Dax started reading, Johnny took his small sketch-book from his pocket and held it closed on his knee. It gave him a sense of purpose, and security, while he sipped from his glass of punch, smiled with the general laughter at something Dax had said, and looked around in a curious prickle of feelings. There had been a strange moment, as people were finding their seats, when Denis mentioned he'd asked 'the boy from Hendy's' to stay on. Dax had peered at him pleasantly over his glasses, Johnny came forward to shake hands, raising the candle in his other hand as if to see his way, and said his name – and then, instead of the usual quick blink or two of absorption and adjustment, Dax blushed, laughed rather oddly, a queer five seconds while his blue eyes ran quickly over Johnny's face and then away, as if too shy to look at him again: '*Johnny*, you say? . . . yes, indeed . . . well, of course – please!' before he turned his back, 'Right! Right!', raising his voice and calling them all to order. These days the fairly rapid deduction that Johnny was David Sparsholt's son rarely led to such obvious confusion.

He was glad he was at the back. He opened the sketchbook and tilted it discreetly towards the candle beside him. It was really a subject that needed colour, the room reimagined in soft-edged zones of crimson and grey, with a dozen little flames picked up in the mirror and in the broad still depth of the window. The elderly faces were hollowed and highlit by the candle glow, caressed and gently caricatured. Dax's boyish head, with its wavy grey hair and blurred glasses, was a subject Johnny could stare at without being rude – and Dax himself still seemed shy of looking at him: he sat forward, the bright edge of the typewritten sheaf trembling slightly. On the wall beyond him were six or seven pictures, hints of colour and dim reflections lost in shadow. The event he was describing took place in Oxford during the War – it seemed his famous father was a writer, who had come to speak to a club that Dax was a member of, an occasion when various things had gone wrong. There was no mention of his only having one leg, and Johnny wondered if this was another thing this group of old friends took for granted. The tone was ironic and old-fashioned, and Freddie

Green himself appeared in the story, which added a kind of nervous humour to the reading: people glanced at him all the time. Beyond that, the article was bobbing with names that meant nothing to Johnny, and he knew from the start, with the buzz of the drink and the distraction of drawing, that he wasn't going to take much of it in. The present gathering of unknown faces had opened at once into another, a crowd without faces and even more ungraspable.

He peered across the rough half-circle of guests, who were drinking and smoking and paying attention in their own ways, one woman with her eyes closed but moving her hands on the arm of her chair to show she wasn't asleep. Furthest away, by the window, and almost hidden behind Dax, a middle-aged man with a grey goatee was leaning into the light to take notes. Johnny quickly captured the tilt of his head, and the way he kept glancing at Clover, who was on the floor, curled like an enormous cat at Freddie's feet. They made a base for the drawing, with the bearded man at the apex, a triangle of unguessed relationships, with all the teasing oddity and secret connectedness of London life.

He tried to get Freddie's long comical face, fixed in a self-deprecating smirk, which slid, before Johnny could get it right, into a listener's unwitting look of regret and boredom. Iffy, leaning on the arm of the sofa, was smoking, her head lowered and eyes raised towards Dax, nodding now and then as if taking instruction from him. When the others laughed she carried on staring and nodding, then gave a rueful grunt and stubbed out her cigarette. Next to her the grey lady sat with her empty glass in her lap and her left eyebrow raised a sceptical quarter-inch, as if she'd already thought of several things to say.

Behind them both and leaning on the console table Denis Drury stood watching. Had he given up the last chair for Johnny? Or did he, as Dax's secretary, prefer to stand, like a servant, while the guests were seated? He didn't laugh with the others, he had the functionary's blankness of respect or indifference, his thoughts possibly focused on what was to follow the reading. The candlelight suited his pale clear skin, arched eyebrows and large brown eyes; Johnny outlined the fine nose, small full-lipped mouth, the glossy black lick of hair, shaded it tight over the ears. Maybe his mother was Italian, or Spanish? He was like the Carreras twins at Johnny's school who came from Tenerife. Denis Drury was hardly an exotic name – unlike Evert Dax, though Dax himself, in a well-cut tweed suit, looked wholly English, and spoke in a pleasant deep voice like an ideal family doctor, or solicitor. 'Such,' he said, 'were my father's troubles, equipped with a wife and two mistresses who lived, unknowingly he supposed, within half a mile of each other. Faced with such troubles, his reaction was naturally to make them worse.' Now Freddie was grinning again, and Dax himself, with a sudden smile, paused and looked at Johnny before going on. One or two of the others turned, and then looked away with the tact that betrays itself. Denis himself slowly turned his head, stared at him for four or five seconds, then closed his eyes with an almost invisible smile. Johnny blushed and reached down for his drink; a minute later he turned back the page and went again over the lines around Dax's mouth and neck, knowing he was spoiling it.

Over by the window, the grey-bearded man caught his eye, shot him a narrow smile, looked down, stared up at him through his eyebrows, then looked down again: Johnny looked down quickly too, at the simple but confusing recognition that he wasn't taking notes, and that all the while he'd been drawing he was being drawn himself. He closed his little notebook, sheathed the pencil in its spine, and tilted the last oily drop out of his glass. The man frowned and rubbed and peered again, as if the relation had acceptably cleared between them, and put in what Johnny knew were the long swoops of his hair. He couldn't help a quick shiver under the inspection, as he turned his head.

The reading seemed to end sooner than anyone expected, after a moment there was a scatter of thoughtful applause and a few nods and murmurs of praise, as people reached for their glasses and several stood up. It wasn't clear if Dax also expected more – as he tidied his papers he had the haunted look of someone who must adjust in ten seconds to a smaller success than he'd hoped for. Johnny picked up his parcel and came forward quickly. 'Yes, very good, Evert,' Freddie Green was saying, and Dax said, 'Was it all right?' as though he'd already forgotten it.

'Someone should write a history of the old Club.'

'I think Evert sort of has,' put in Iffy, who standing up was taller than both of them, and a striking figure with her red hair and long red skirt above brown suede boots.

'That year I was in charge, it was really rather marvellous,' said Freddie. 'I got Orwell later on, of course.'

'Well, indeed,' said Dax, 'I was in the Army by then,' smiling anxiously at Johnny as though his opinion was what he most wanted: 'I hope that wasn't too dreary for you.'

'Oh! . . . not at all,' said Johnny, and feeling as he said it that he might sound rude, 'I'm afraid I didn't know who most of the people were.'

'Ah, no, I suppose not . . .' said Dax.

'Sic transit,' said Iffy.

Johnny felt he must be clear. 'The reason I came was to bring you this, from Mr Hendy' – handing over his parcel crumpled at the edge now from carrying.

'Ah, yes!' said Freddie, as if the evening had suddenly become interesting.

Johnny bit his lip gently while Dax tore the wrapping and let it drop away when he took hold of the inner cocoon of tissue paper. 'Mr Hendy says he's done the best he can, but some of the damage was quite severe.'

'Right, let's see,' said Dax, with a little throat-clearing at the mention of damage.

'Oh, that's come up nicely,' said Freddie, as Dax discarded the tissue and held the picture under the light from the candelabra. 'I'd quite forgotten it was that colour.'

'What's this?' said the grey lady, coming up.

'It's the little Goyle, Jill, you may not remember, it used to hang in my study. One of the first pictures I ever bought.' Dax turned it over – it was signed on the back 'Goyle 36'. 'I don't know what Stanley did to his blacks, but they always crack up. And no doubt thirty years of coal fires and cigarette smoke had rather dulled its impact.' To Johnny, in the shop, the wonder had been that something so modern could look already so injured and antique; though out of its frame, the original colours, covered and squashed by the off-white slip, had showed brightly round the edges, as if still wet. Now, restored, the small abstract landscape, thick blocks of black and green beneath a stripe of white, gave no hint of these indignities. 'Well, there you are.'

Jill seemed cautiously satisfied. 'I'm sure Ivan will be pleased,' she said.

'Oh . . .' said Iffy. 'Ivan's not here tonight.'

'I've just seen him,' said Jill.

'Do you know Ivan?' said Freddie, with raised eyebrows and a wondering shake of the head, his amusing readiness to picture Johnny's confusion.

'Um, I shouldn't think so,' said Johnny. 'Who is he . . . ?'

'Ah, there he is!' said Dax, warmly focusing attention away from himself. Just inside the door now was a smiling young man also in a tweed suit, talking to Herta as if she were the Queen and not just the grumpy old woman handing him a drink. He gave a hoot of laughter, then charmingly pursued an anecdote of some kind, while Herta, head on one side, looked

up at him with coy signs of the approval she had firmly withheld from Johnny.

'You *don't* know him?' Jill made sure.

'I don't know anyone!' Johnny said.

'Oh, you'll like him,' said Iffy, with her heavy nod.

'We've all grown awfully fond of him,' said Jill. 'He's Stanley Goyle's nephew.' Johnny wasn't sure if this was offered as
the reason for their fondness.

'Oh, I see . . . really . . .'

'Oh, yes,' said Freddie, with another humorous shake of the
head, 'you won't easily dislodge Ivan from our affections.'

Now Ivan slipped across the room towards them, neat,
self-possessed, with the hunch of playful apology, dark eyes
glittering in the candlelight. Johnny felt curious, relieved, and
under some kind of social expectation, as in childhood, when
there was someone else his own age he would have to play with.
He tried not to take Ivan's suit, not new, but smart, and worn
with a waistcoat and wide red tie, as a comment on his own
tight cords, bush jacket and open-neck shirt. Ivan greeted his
elders with rapid nods, 'Hello, hello . . .' and grinned at Johnny,
and shook his hand. 'You must be Jonathan,' he said, with a
Welsh lilt and sense of meaning something more: 'I'm Ivan.'

'You missed a marvellous talk,' said Freddie.

'Oh, I know, I know, I'm sorry . . .' said Ivan, kissing Iffy,
nodding to Jill, and then kissing Dax himself on both cheeks,
which caused a fleeting self-consciousness in them both.

'Ivan's been helping me with it,' said Dax. 'He knows all
about it' – looking at him, Ivan's suit somehow mimicking the
older man's style. 'He's been a terrific help.'

'Isn't that Denis's job?' said Jill.

'Oh, Denis has got his own work to see to,' said Dax.

Jill looked round for Denis. 'I thought *you* were his work,'
she said.

*

Johnny went to the lavatory, and waited politely some way from the door but not too far off to claim he was next. He was happy to escape from Ivan and then as soon as he'd left the room he was anxious to get back. Along the carpeted passage-way many pictures hung, and he picked up the candlestick from the table to see them better. There was a large brown portrait photograph of a man with a bald head and a white moustache who Johnny thought might be Evert's father; two framed cartoons of impenetrable pre-war humour; and nearest the bedroom at the end (beyond whose open door his candlelight bobbed back at him from a mirror) a red chalk drawing of a naked man, with a body-builder's chest and ridged stomach, artily cut off at the knee and the neck, and with a high-minded blur where the cock and balls should be. He heard the loo flush just as Denis came towards him along the hallway. 'Aha . . !' Denis said, and stopped to peer briefly at the drawing too. 'Ancient pornography – is there anything more sad.'

'Oh . . .' said Johnny, as if nervously agreeing.

'Or perhaps you like it,' said Denis.

'Well,' said Johnny, 'no, not really my sort of thing,' but seeing it almost as a symbol of the London life – it could certainly never have hung in his father's house, or even his mother's.

'No, I'm sure.' Denis pondered for a moment. 'Come and look at this,' he said, going past him into the bedroom.

'Is it urgent?' said Johnny, and laughed apologetically – the lady who'd been interested in his hair was emerging at that moment from the lavatory.

'It won't take long,' said Denis sharply, but then stopping and giving him an abruptly courteous, almost grateful smile. Johnny had to leave the candle where it was for the lady and followed Denis stiffly into the bedroom. It was more than a mere reflex that made him flick the dead light switch on and off. The glimmer from the passageway showed red curtains hitched back, the side of a wardrobe, and the shadowy edge of a bed. He saw himself stoop forward, in the mirror, in cautious silhouette.

'There's a flashlight here somewhere,' said Denis, feeling on a bedside table behind the door – there was a clatter of small things knocked over. Then a beam of light, stifled at first in the shrouded hump of the pillows, then swinging round, blindingly reflected for a moment in the uncurtained window. 'Ah, there you are.' Denis played the torch up and down, with the murmur of uncertain judgement, over Johnny wincing and turning his head. It was a game whose rules had yet to be explained. 'I thought, since you like art' – he let him go, sent the beam across to where a dark-framed picture hung above the fireplace. 'Yes, that's right, you're the art-Johnny.' He reached out to steer him across. 'Come over here,' taking Johnny's wrist.

'Oh yes . . .' – dazzled and cringing he saw Denis was mocking him for suspicions they both knew he was right to feel. The white glare of the torch floated on his retina, jumped and floated across what seemed to be a large Graham Sutherland, its hooded picture-light now casting shadow, the red skeletal plant or tree dramatic in the gloom. 'Mm . . . great,' said Johnny, who'd been taught to respect Sutherland but had never really liked him.

'I knew you'd like it,' said Denis, relaxing his grip – at which Johnny took his hand back. 'I've never cared for it myself, though I'm told it's worth a packet' – and he laughed, as he had stared earlier, with an odd mixture of respect and disdain.

'Yes, I suppose so . . .' said Johnny. The unworldly ethos at Hoole, when he was a student, discouraged all talk about the price of a picture, and he still felt unhappy with the subject now he found himself working for a dealer. Denis toured the torch's beam across the painting, which showed it as eerily material, a surface blankly unconcerned with what it depicted; the rough sweeps of white and grey flared back.

'So are you often to be found in the Notting Hill station Gents?'

'What . . . ?' Johnny said, blinking as the light swept into his face again, and feeling for a moment as if the sudden arrest he'd felt almost certain of there had come for him now. The idea only lasted for a dreamlike two seconds, but the blood rose to his face. All he managed to say was, 'I don't know what you mean.'

'You probably couldn't see much through all that hair' – Denis seemed to dare him to move as he reached out and lifted Johnny's hair and pushed it back past his right ear and held his scared but indignant gaze with his large dark eyes. 'But I saw you,' he said, 'very clearly,' just as he turned off the torch and tossed it on to the bed. He laughed distantly, pulled Johnny hard against him, made him gasp and in that same moment stuck his tongue into his open mouth. For a breathless five seconds of surprise and curiosity, Johnny let it happen, not quite responding as Denis's tongue, neither warm nor cool, and abnormally long, seemed to worm its way into him – until he twisted his head away. Denis had him caught against the side of the bed. 'What?' he said.

'Sorry . . .' said Johnny, 'please . . .' pushing at him, but with an anxious sense that perhaps this was what people did, he was rejecting a compliment, even a privilege – Denis, under that waistcoat and silk tie, was hard and sinewy, his breath in his face as he pressed against him, but visible only as a dark obstruction against the faint candlelight from outside. It was confusing, the moment Johnny gave in, Denis lost interest, and had let him go.

'I see you're not your father's son,' he said.

'Oh, for fuck's sake,' said Johnny, and Denis gave a surprising laugh, as if pleased at a show of spirit after all. Johnny slid round him and out of the room, and locked the lavatory door behind him with a gasp of relief, though his face in the mirror revealed something further, the little flinch of guilt, whatever happened.

Ten minutes later he was sitting on the window seat with Ivan, their plates on their laps. He smiled at him and said, 'So you were expecting me.'

'Mm?' said Ivan, shaking the tip of his fringe from his eyes.

'You knew my name.'

Ivan smiled back. 'Oh, well, Denis said you might be coming.'

'Oh did he?'

'A little surprise for Evert, I think.'

Johnny wanted to say he'd had a bit of a surprise himself, but he didn't like to sound stupid. He had the soft burn in his mouth still, and kept it to himself, but imagined just mentioning it, not sure if Ivan would think he was complaining or boasting. Denis was going round with two wine bottles, and when he got to them he refilled their glasses with a bored look as if he barely knew who they were.

'Why would it be a surprise?' Johnny said.

Ivan looked at him and after three seconds gazed out and nodded at the rest of the room. 'Well . . . fresh blood,' he said.

'Oh . . .'

He lowered his voice. 'The thing is, Denny's still quite young, and as you can see most of the rest of the gang are getting on a bit. You know Freddie and Evert were at Oxford together – well, you've just heard. So was Jill. Freddie's going to be fifty-five on the fourth of June.'

'Is that all?' said Johnny.

Ivan shot him a glance. 'The old lady talking to Evert was one of his father's girlfriends, Glynis Holt. She's the one Evert mentioned in his reading. I thought she looked a bit shocked; but you know that's the point with the Memo Club – they have to tell the truth.'

'Oh, do they.'

'Not all the time, obviously! – just on the third Tuesday of the month . . .'

'Right . . .'

'You know, that's when someone reads a memoir.'

'And how do you fit in, then?'

'I sort of come and go,' said Ivan. He peered at them all fondly.

'I'd have thought you were a bit young to write a memoir,' said Johnny.

'Yes, but I'm saving things up,' Ivan said.

'I wouldn't know where to start.'

'Ooh, I don't know about that.' Ivan looked at him oddly, Johnny felt the attraction of his soft pale face and brilliant dark eyes that he watched the tips of his fringe slide into and be blinked away. His small white teeth leant inwards in a moistly carnivorous way. 'So how *is* your father?' he said.

'My father . . .' Johnny blinked too. 'He's fine.'

'Because he remarried, didn't he, after . . . all that?' said Ivan quickly, and as if David Sparsholt's personal happiness were his main worry. He went red but he went on, 'His secretary – if I've got that right.'

'Well, yes, he did – it was a while ago now. Six years.'

'Ah . . . good, good' – and perhaps sensing he was going too fast on the question, 'And what have you been getting up to in London?'

Johnny told him, flatly, taking a moment still to get over the previous question: working all day on pictures and picture frames, with the bus down to Chelsea each morning from Shepherd's Bush. 'I'm living with my aunt,' he said.

'And is that OK for you? Your father's sister?'

'No, my mother's. It's all right,' said Johnny, though Kitty's determined attempts to look after him only made him miss his mother more. 'I don't want to be there for ever.'

'We'll have to see what we can do about it,' said Ivan, whose confident grasp seemed to reach into the future as well as the past.

'And the three-day week, as well, it's all been a bit strange.'

Ivan tilted his head towards the group sitting nearest them, where the situation was being talked about. The man who'd been speaking when Johnny first arrived, a tall, red-faced man with a bow-tie, said, 'The City's virtually ground to a standstill. I wouldn't be a bit surprised to see total collapse within a month.' One of the people with him looked crushed by this, the other slyly sceptical. 'You know what Gerry's saying – sell up while you can, the Communists will be in charge by the end of February.'

'What am I supposed to sell?' said the worried man. 'You mean the house?'

'And I've been going to some concerts,' Johnny said. Ivan smiled sympathetically. 'I went to hear Haitink conduct Mahler 6 last week.'

'How was it?' said Ivan.

'It was amazing,' said Johnny, 'as you can imagine.'

But it wasn't clear Ivan could. 'You'll have to talk to Evert about that – he's mad about Mahler. I think he may even have been there. Is it the very loud, very long one?'

'Well, yes . . .' Johnny said, not feeling that this told the whole story, or indeed distinguished it from half a dozen other Mahler symphonies. 'It was the first time I've heard it live.'

'*Brian*, of course,' said Ivan, his smile redirected at two older people who'd been going round with their plates and not finding anywhere exactly right to sit down. One of them was the pointed little man with a grey beard and half-moon glasses who'd been drawing Johnny earlier, now with the small pretty woman who'd been worried about his hair; the subject seemed still to be between them, a possible link or embarrassment. The boys shoved up together, thigh to thigh, and when Ivan reached round Johnny's shoulder to put his glass on the windowsill behind them Johnny felt the first glow and lift of nearly certain consent and concealed his excitement with his napkin.

'I'm Brian Savory,' the man said, as they settled.

'Oh, Brian and Sally,' said Ivan: 'Jonathan Sparsholt.'

'Johnny,' said Johnny.

'That's a good name,' said Brian, with a quick smile, spreading his napkin. 'Yes, we had a Sparsholt generator at our last place – started up like a dream, never gave us a moment's trouble.' This was a kind of blundering tactfulness Johnny was used to, and didn't mind. 'You must be connected? . . . It's an unusual name.'

'Yes, that's right,' Johnny said.

Sally seemed more conventionally sensitive to the matter. She gave her hesitant smile: 'Did you say you work with Cyril Hendy?'

'That's right,' said Johnny again.

'Wily old Cyril,' said Brian.

'You know he knew Sickert?' said Sally.

'Yes, I did, actually,' said Johnny.

'I expect he talks very fascinatingly about it. He worked for Sickert when he was a boy.'

In fact Cyril was reserved, nearly silent, on all subjects of such obvious interest. 'He doesn't talk much,' said Johnny.

Sally narrowed her eyes for a moment. 'I think he even knew Whistler.'

'He can't have known Whistler, love,' said Brian. 'Whistler died seventy years ago.'

'Well, how old's old Cyril . . . ? No, I suppose you're right. But Sickert he certainly knew – knew him very well. And a lot of the painters, I think.'

Brian sawed off a square of cold beef and balanced some coleslaw on top of it. 'Evert's memoir was rather good, I thought.'

'Mm,' said Johnny, with a mouthful himself, a valuable delay.

'Do the young still read the great A. V., I wonder?'

'Oh,' said Johnny, swallowing, 'well, I haven't . . .' He looked to Ivan, who said,

'Did you know him, Brian?'

'I met him once, very briefly. I'm not sure I could read him now.'

'He's not my author,' said Sally.

'Not much fun, is he, love,' said Brian. He smiled at Johnny. 'You're a friend of Denis's.'

'Well . . .' said Johnny. 'Does Denis have a lot of friends?'

'Oh, you know, a certain amount,' said Brian. He glanced across the room. 'I keep meaning to say, I like your trousers.'

'Oh, thank you . . .' said Johnny, confused, though he loved them himself.

'Elephant cord, aren't they?'

'Are they, yes, I think . . .' – feeling now that Brian was trying to put him at his ease about being so casually dressed.

'Jolly snug, I bet.'

Sally peered at Johnny's knees with a smile of timorous interest. 'They're certainly a lovely colour.'

'*Honey*,' said Brian; then flinched and looked away again. Johnny ran his hands down his thighs and leaning forward flapped a crumb off the wide triangle of the flare. He felt hurried into boldness,

'I want to see your sketches.'

'Ah!' said Brian. 'So you shall. But only if I can see yours.'

When he spotted the first people coming in with trifle, Johnny took all their plates for them and went into the kitchen, where Herta told him curtly to leave them on the table; she seemed annoyed at being helped, or at least at being helped by him. On the landing as he came back Freddie and Clover were doing up their coats. 'Oh, are you off?' said Johnny, amused by his own tone.

Freddie nodded, and looked round with a quick wince; Clover, throwing her hair back over her coat collar, gave him an expectant look. 'Yes, we'll slip away,' said Freddie. There was something confidential in his smile. 'We like to be home in time for *Kojak*.'

'Oh, well . . . !' said Johnny, as Freddie, picking up the candlestick he'd given him earlier, moved to the top of the stairs. Above them, a further flight rose into immediate darkness. 'But the telly won't be working, will it.'

'Of course I take your point,' said Freddie. 'But it would be awful to miss it if the power comes on. You know the plots can be quite hard to follow, and we've found if you miss the start . . .'

'Right,' said Johnny. He was puzzled to be still here when they were going, but he had already a preoccupied sense that he had to get back to Ivan.

'We'll see you again, I'm sure,' said Freddie, while Clover nodded in her oddly teasing solidarity with him, and they set off carefully downstairs, with one or two sharp admonitions to each other. Johnny watched the candlelight inattentively pass a dark portrait below, and then fan and fade when they'd turned the corner and were hidden by the cage of the lift.

'Oh, are they going.' It was Ivan, beside him, amused but unsurprised.

'Oh hello!' – with the soft jolt of happiness he touched his arm. Then, 'You're not going too?'

'I'm not going anywhere.'

'Oh, good,' said Johnny boldly.

Now Ivan leant to his ear: 'My dear, I live here.'

'Oh, do you? What, in this house . . . ?'

Ivan stood close, looking over his shoulder as if quickly assessing the situation. 'Come and see my room if you like.'

Johnny's heart skittered with worry, and pleasure too, and he said, 'So how many people live here?'

'Oh, more than you'd think,' said Ivan, turning but with his left hand resting still in the curve of Johnny's back, where Denis's hand had laid claim to him before. He led him upstairs, and in the stumbling shadow of the next landing took a pen from his pocket and turned a narrow line of white light on the doorways to left and right.

'So what does Mr Dax do?' said Johnny, just behind him.

Ivan looked round, seemed surprised. 'Well, he's a writer, and an art historian, obviously.'

'He seems very nice,' said Johnny, not sure if he meant it.

'Evert? Yes, isn't he heaven – now careful here . . .' – at the far end of the landing a door like a large black cupboard opened on a narrower, steeper stair. The short ascent was a muddle of shadows and lost bearings.

'My God . . .' said Johnny, chuckling, careful but not wanting to be left behind. Now in the space under the roof the spindly beam jumped across bookshelves, heaps of books, a desk with a typewriter, a small bed that had been made and then lain on, the cover screwed up. It was extremely cold, and Johnny hugged himself before he hugged Ivan, hands slipped round him inside his jacket, and then he found he had kissed him.

'So this is my room,' Ivan said, holding him back with his free hand, as if overlooking what had just happened, and delaying whatever might happen next. Johnny laughed in the dark just at the moment the overhead light came on: 'Oh shit!' From far downstairs the noise of jeering relief just tinged with regret made a weird acoustic comment on their situation, squinting under the bright bulb of the attic room.

3

Evert started to undress, observing himself in the mirror with an anxious new interest: how had he seemed to David Sparsholt's son? Alarming and absurd that someone half his age should wake in him the need to be admired. 'I knew your father,' Evert had said – awful phrase that a number of loyal old men and cagey old ladies had said to him over the years, but which he himself had never uttered till now: the motto of obsolescence. He rolled up his tie as he thought of the boy's answer, which was a kind of reproach: 'You should get in touch with him.' And Evert had said humbly, 'I really must.' He had no idea what was allowed, in talk about David – about Drum, if he was still called that. He took off his shirt and looked at himself in his vest with the same sense of newly awoken confusion: a man whose unnoticeable small changes were revealed after thirty years in one cumulative picture of shrinkage and slippage, skinny, paunchy and puckered around the armpits and waist.

And the fact was that he had been in touch, as lately as seven or eight years ago. At the time of the crisis, the 'Sparsholt Affair', he had written Drum a letter, of wary and perhaps rather futile support. And a few days later a policeman had come round, to have a word with him about it. What had he known about David Sparsholt's private life? How well did he know him himself? Had there ever been any suggestion of impropriety on Mr Sparsholt's part towards him? 'Absolutely not,' said Evert, frightened by the question but amused by the private perspective in which he saw the answer, as if naked figures were holding their breath behind the curtains or crouched under the desk. 'We knew each other slightly at Oxford' – not sure these days if this mere fact would deflect suspicion. 'But of course we were both called up almost at once' – which he thought had a better chance. 'One knew about his marvellous war, squadron leader at twenty-two, wasn't it? The DFC . . .' Perhaps this was overdoing it, but the policeman paused respectfully. 'I simply felt sorry for him – I imagine anyone would.' When the door opened and Denis came in, behind the inspector's back, Evert said, 'I'll give you those letters in a minute,' in a very sharp tone which made Denis jump and then with a quick calculating look from one to the other of them go out and pull the door to with almost farcical discretion till it made its sharp click. As he saw it now Denis was wearing yellow shorts and sandals, and looking about as queer as you could get. Evert had always more or less done what he liked, but it was risky still, in 1966, as the Sparsholt business showed. He remembered the inspector's wintry hesitation, in the hall as he was leaving, as if to say he knew exactly not only what had happened then but what was happening now.

There was too much of David in Jonathan – was it partly to dodge this biblical ghost of a joke that he offered himself as Johnny: with immediate modesty and hesitant intimacy and as with all Johnnies a half-hidden plea to be indulged, and forgiven? To introduce yourself as 'Johnny' was to say 'You won't have heard of me, but I think you'll like me' – and as 'Sparsholt' to say 'You know me all too well.' And of course Evert did know him: the squarish face and large mouth and something guarded about the eyes, for all the ingenuous smiles. His hair was like a girl's, coarser probably; one day he would cut it all off and see the relief in his friends' faces. Evert pictured Drum, as he'd appeared in the papers, the 'flawed hero' with his airman's crop and small thick moustache: what did he make of his son's disguise? He saw it perhaps as just that – saw the need for concealment in the forward-sloping curtain of hair (though of course the boy stood out on account of it). Perhaps it was a way of embarrassing his father, in return for the years of embarrassment he must have inflicted on him. Evert went to wash his face and clean his teeth, and without his glasses on, a further faint estrangement, he saw something blurred but still seductive in the smile that the mirror returned. Since his twenties he had rarely been seen bare-faced by anyone but lovers and barbers. Now going to bed was a surrender to suggestion, glasses laid on the table. He'd been able to see all right in the War, but Drum had preferred being fucked in the dark. Memories of that were the ineffable hauntings of touch, fingers on smooth skin . . . and kisses, reluctant, then intense, then regretted, and repeated.

Evert climbed into bed, and sat up with his hands on the covers, like a patient. On the bedside table a carafe of water, beaded with standing, waited on a crocheted doily, one of the hideous artefacts Herta made for him that had to be found room for somewhere in the house. How had it all blown up, so suddenly, seven years ago, a dim nexus of provincial misconduct that for a month or more was news? A foolish Tory MP was involved, which made it a national scandal, but it was Drum in his beauty and wartime glory who emerged as the hero – if that was the word. Evert found even now he didn't want to think about it – a horrible mess in the life of a man he'd once adored.

He reached out for the book he was reading each night, in small well-intentioned instalments – his father's third novel, *The Heart's Achievement*, which he had never got so far through before. It had come out in 1933, and was dedicated to Evert's mother, at a moment his recent researches had shown to be one of hair-raising infidelities. It ran to 634 pages, a monstrous length, and had been a comparably huge success, especially in France, where it seemed it was still spoken of as a key work of modern English fiction. In England it had been turned into a play, with Celia Johnson, which Evert had been thought too young at the time to see. Now he put on his glasses again and found his place; he was on page 107, the beginning of the second of five 'Books' it was divided into. He found it as hard as ever to imagine his father writing it, though it must have been going on, day after day, in the study downstairs, opening on to the garden, where he and Alex were never permitted to play before lunch. It took a kind of mania to write like this, in vast unparagraphed sweeps, with sentences sometimes two pages long. The challenge now was to look both kindly and objectively at A. V. Dax's peculiar style, and technique.

There was the sound of Denis cleaning his teeth, and then he came in, barefoot, in his dark red pyjamas with black piping. 'What page?' he said, slipping into bed, so that Evert closed the book and moved over. 'I thought they would never go.'

'You know Iffy,' said Evert, with a smile that indulged her and Denis too.

'Yes, I do,' said Denis. The sleepy provocation of his pyjamas, the dim peppermint of his breath, his hard knees as he pushed for more space, were as natural as yesterday. He let Evert kiss him between the eyes. 'Mm,' he said, yawning. 'I thought Freddie was a bit funny about your reading.'

'Did you?' said Evert – it was just what he didn't want to think.

'You can tell he wants to write about the famous Club himself.'

Evert grunted. 'Well, no one's stopping him.' He saw that Freddie's approval was what he most needed; and hadn't he been very nice about it afterwards? But Denis was a great diviner of motives. His excitement showed through his odd flat tone as he went on,

'You haven't said what you thought about young Sparsholt.'

'Oh – well, he was certainly a surprise,' said Evert.

'I'm afraid he got awfully drunk,' said Denis.

'Did he? Yes. He seemed very quiet to me – I didn't get much out of him, I'm afraid.'

'He's just a bit shy, Evert. You can all be quite intimidating.' Denis seemed not to include himself in this image of the gang; and shifted himself away as if to get comfortable. 'Anyway he knows about art – he's a picture person.'

'No, you're right – he said he wants to be a painter,' said Evert, who in the past had loved their treacherous bedtime breakdowns of their friends' behaviour, but now longed to change the subject.

'Very nice bum though,' Denis said.

'I really didn't notice.'

'You lying old queen,' said Denis.

'I am not!' – Evert grinning and running his hand almost nervously over Denis's chest. Denis had acutely sensitive nipples – he scowled but there was a gasp of a smile as he said,

'Ivan was wildly excited to meet the son of a famous criminal.'

'I'd hardly call him a criminal – what he did would be quite legal now.'

'You're forgetting the detail.'

'Am I?' Evert didn't want to lose the nearness of body heat, and the prospect, surely still not impossible or unworthy, of their getting inside one another's pyjamas. He took off his glasses, reached round Denis and put them on the table. 'You're probably right.' But there was a sense, all too familiar in recent months, that Denis hadn't yet made his point.

'I thought it would be nice for you to have someone new, Evert, someone a bit younger.'

Evert said, with anxious brightness, 'You're quite young enough for me.'

'I'm not nearly as young as Ivan, of course.'

'No, Ivan's a mere baby.'

'He hates me.'

'I don't know why you say that. I can't see Ivan hating any-body.'

'Isn't it obvious? He's completely besotted with you.'

Evert tutted mildly at this idea, which didn't interest him or displease him. The truth was that he was in bed with the person he wanted most. 'He seemed to get on well with Johnny.'

'Ivan only likes old men.'

'Well, I may be too young for him,' Evert said gamely, and encouraged by the thought he slid his foot between Denis's calves. It was absurd to be driven, after fourteen years, to these tense gambits of a first seduction.

Denis resumed, 'Anyway, I'm glad you liked Jonathan.'

'Hm, well I hardly know if I do like him yet.'

'Well, it feels as if you like him' – Denis slipping his hand into the fly of his pyjamas.

After a tense few moments Evert said, 'For god's sake, I like you' – and had already pushed himself up half on top of him—

'Ow, careful.'

'Oh?'

Denis made a quick cold sigh and turned his head sharply aside from Evert's lips. 'Not now, Evert, please,' he said, in that tone of renewed disappointment that Evert had come to dread and detest. He disengaged himself, slipped aside and sitting up slid out from under the covers. 'Well, I'll see you at breakfast, if you're up.'

Evert lay there, saying nothing, knowing that a scene, an outburst of rage, would only be met with puzzlement and faint disgust. He was doubtless meant to see, against the light from the landing, the triangular silhouette of Denis's pyjamas, like a drawn bow being slowly lowered . . . Then he snatched up *The Heart's Achievement* and hurled it against the wall. He flinched as it struck – he had the impression the thick slab of pages was ripped from the binding. Once he had heard the inevitable click of Denis's door, he got out of bed, and picked the wounded volume up.

After breakfast, Denis went to the room he had claimed as his study, up on the third floor. The 'work' he was engaged in lay on the table . . . Beyond the table was a window, and it was this rather than the notebooks and typewriter that absorbed his attention this morning. Up here the views were both wider and deeper – a sweep westwards, over the tops of the next street, two Victorian churches, great bare plane trees between houses, three or four chimney pots with glinting cowls, which revolved and beckoned to each other no matter how still the day; but also a steep view down, over low roofs into the mews. He stood there now and stretched, with the unconcerned look of someone who thought he might be being watched, and then leaning against the left side of the window, with the pushed-back curtain bunched behind him, he peered down at an angle. But the black doors of the repair shop were closed, and not a soul about.

Denis was as touchy as Evert himself when asked how his work was going. His manner as they parted after breakfast each day was one of apparent impatience for study, though in fact most mornings went by in a distracted daze of doodling and wanking, from which he broke off now and then to make trips of indefinite length to the bank or the shops. Sometimes an errand for Evert kept him out all day, on a crazily sparking circuit of excitements, his late return unexplained and the evening enacted, as they moved round each other, poured drinks and shook out the newspaper, to a faint, strange sound, the hum of unvoiced thoughts.

He wondered if he had an inordinate sex drive, and how many other men of thirty-three gave so much of their lives, when not actually doing it, to the rapt distraction of imagining it. Of course he knew them when he met them, nameless but identified by need, in a dozen locations, and a lot of them a good deal older than he was. It didn't matter. It was a lesson itself in the power of lust, and in their eyes as they stared and gasped he read his own beautiful fate: for him too it was going to go on and on. The problem really was old Evert. When they'd met all those years ago he was a still virile forty, and a great educator in life and sex to a ravenous new arrival from Jersey, a mere nineteen years old. Now Evert was a lot older, 'knocking sixty' as Denis said, and matters were much less satisfactory. To see the silly old thing with nothing on and his bottom in the air was as laughable as it was depressing. The cheeky taunt, 'Come on, old man!' that had once thrilled them both as Evert 'tupped' Denis twice a day, was now barely usable for its note of pathos and criticism.

Denis got up again and peered down into the mews, where the doors of the garage at last stood open on an empty strip of cobbles. He didn't want to go out and enquire about the car unless Roy was there, and there was no sign of him yet. A keen restlessness and jealousy of Roy overtook him – the very thing he liked about him now seemed a great disadvantage. Roy was his ideal kind of cockney (extending the term louchely to any working-class Londoner): he was twenty-five, a bit shorter than Denis, 'coarse-featured', it had to be said, but, as Roy himself said, 'the living end' when doubled over to examine the entrails of an engine. He had a girlfriend he bragged and complained about, and like Denis he had a surplus of energy that spilled out readily and (it had to be faced) indiscriminately. There was a kind of adulterers' honour between them, but not the least question of fidelity. In fact even the honour was mixed up with mockery of Denis for being posh, and complaints about his meanness. It was very hard to make Roy believe that he had no money at all of his own.

At last there was some action. Old Harris, who ran the

repair business, was out in his overalls, and giving Roy a hard time about being late, no doubt. He too knew not to believe a word Roy said. On the landing below, Denis put on his overcoat and was checking his silk scarf in the mirror when Evert emerged from his study. 'I'm just going down to see if that imbecile's got the magneto fixed yet,' Denis said.

'Ah, yes,' said Evert. He frowned at the break in his chain of thought – it was that maddening look of having to get on with things without the expected help, a little squinting challenge quite wasted on Denis. Then he smiled rather nastily. 'I've always envied your grasp of mechanics.'

Evert had been asked to write 500 words about his work in progress for a column in *The Author*, a task he found almost as hard as writing the memoir itself. There was so much to explain, and his father's position was a tricky one. In his life Victor Dax had been a vaunted novelist, as well as a traveller, collector, philanderer, all interesting roles; but now, some twenty years after his death, he was best known in England as an unread writer – he was almost famously neglected. When anyone asked, or a survey was done, 'Who are the great forgotten novelists?', A. V. Dax was likely to be cited. Sometimes such polls could lead to a revival in an author's value, reprints, even a film; but Dax's name was always mentioned with a strange collective suspension of will, an abstracted pause after which people moved on to talk about other writers they really did mean to read one day. Evert hoped that a memoir of his father's rackety life might form a sounder basis for new interest in his work; but he found it the stiffest thing he'd ever had a go at. Though never a demonic writer like Victor, he had always produced with reasonable ease: *Modern British Painting*, the monographs on Pasmore and Goyle, countless reviews for *The Burlington* and the *TLS*; now he was very nearly stuck, unmanned by his own father. He was glad at least to have read that short extract to the gang, though this morning at breakfast Denis had suggested that Jill hadn't liked it either. Well, Jill had never been easy to please, but hadn't several of the others (not members of the long-ago Oxford Club) said how much they'd enjoyed it? Having shared it he believed a little more in its existence.

In truth the memoir was a game of postponement – a trick he played on himself almost daily, and fell for every time. There would be a poor and evasive morning, with letters to write as well, and a number of phone calls that had to be made; then lunch, at a place not necessarily close, and several things to do after lunch, with mounting anxiety in the two hours before six o'clock: and then a drink, a glow of resolve and sensible post-ponement till the following morning, when, too hung-over to do much work before ten, he would seek infuriated refuge, about eleven forty-five, in the trying necessity of going out once more to lunch. Over lunch, at Caspar's or at the Garrick, he would be asked how work was going, when it could be expected, and the confidence of the questioner severely in-hibited his answers – they had a bottle of wine, no more, but still the atmosphere was appreciably softened, his little hints at difficulties were taken as mere modesty – 'I'm sure it will be marvellous' – 'It will take as long as it takes' – and he left fractionally consoled himself, as if some great humane reprieve were somehow possible, and time (as deadline after deadline loomed and fell away behind) were not an overriding question. In the evenings especially, and towards bedtime, half-drunk, he started seeing connexions, approaches, lovely ideas for the work, and sat suffused with a sense of the masterly thing it was in his power to do the next morning.

Herta was hoovering expressively upstairs, so the pert triple tap at the door could only be Ivan. Evert tugged up his zip and pulled down his jersey and sat forward. There were further little knocks, timidity conquered in a comical crescendo. Evert called, 'Come in!' He hadn't been thinking about Ivan at all, but he coloured at Ivan's intrusion on his brutal little reverie. This was another thing that slowed up work on the memoir, though he wasn't going to tell the readers of *The Author* about it; his hung-over mornings often started with these easy and absorbing diversions from impracticable work. 'Hullo, poppet.'

Ivan closed the door and came towards him; kissed him on the cheek as Evert turned in his chair, but stayed seated.

'Did you want to start with the photos?' Ivan said. Did he scent sex in the air, however swiftly muffled?

'Oh, goodness . . . well! . . . how's your head?'

'Oh, not too bad at all – I was drinking Pepsi later.'

'My god . . .'

Ivan looked at him from under his fringe, and Evert smiled back with a hint of caution. Ivan was dressed this morning in large corduroys cinched at the waist, brown brogues, a collarless white shirt, black waistcoat, and a red paisley neckerchief – most of it from Oxfam ('My tailor,' Ivan said when they walked past the King's Road shop); he was like an extra in an opera, *Peter Grimes* perhaps. The second-hand look seemed to fit with the boy's strange attraction to the world of thirty or forty years ago, when Evert and his friends had been young themselves. He claimed not to feel the cold, which was a blessing for a lodger in Evert's attic in a national fuel shortage. Today, though, was a day, downstairs at least, of glowing lamps and a smell of burnt dust from the two-bar fire.

The photographs were heaped in a cardboard box with the appealing legend 'Château Granjac / Pauillac / Douze Bouteilles' on the side: old bursting brown envelopes, little Kodak wallets with the negatives in milky paper strips, a slew of loose pictures where nameless Edwardian ladies were mixed with Evert's childhood holidays and small colour snaps of the early 1950s. On top like a lid was a heavily bound album kept by his mother, in which over time the concealed paper mounts had one by one perished – now when you opened it the last photos slithered together in the gutter of the binding or tumbled out on to the floor, leaving only her inscriptions in white ink – 'Edwina', 'Cousin Patrick' – under the empty spaces. Ivan's brainwave was to get a new album, and mount all the photos of Victor's life together and in sequence, with new captions of his own. First they needed to be sorted and dated, and the people in them as far as possible identified. It was the kind of thing Denis might have helped him with, ten years ago; though Denis had surely never been so keen.

Now Ivan cleared the books from the table under the window, and tipped all the loose photos out on to it. They did a first glancing shuffle through, like looking for sea or sky in a jigsaw, grouping pictures loosely by period or type; sometimes there were several of one event. Ivan, when Evert glanced at him, had a look of gleaming good luck at the treasure swimming under his fingers, curbed by a responsible frown and simple sense of strategy. 'Is this Victor?' he said, holding out a creased snapshot of a young man in a white suit and straw hat. 'Um . . . yes, it must be,' said Evert, piqued for a moment by the first-name terms, and a moment later puzzled at himself for minding. He saw it touched on a larger worry. What was he going to call him himself? 'Victor' might look like cheek in a son, a patronizing closeness. But to write starchily of 'Dax' would be a weird discipline, silly and spooky by turns, for the biographer who shared his name.

Here was a photograph of his father as a boy, at the seaside, this one with a pencilled date on the back, the now well-known scrawl of his grandmother, whom he'd never known in person: 'Scheveningen, August 1888' – Victor eight years old. Already he knew how to wear his hat; he stood with his beach spade at an angle like a dandy's cane. He'd been a very nice-looking boy, whose face had slowly lost distinction as its owner had gained it. Here he was aged thirty-two, in front of the large theatrical portrait of him by George Lambert, barely completed. This was the time, just before the Great War, when he wore a beard, the twisted ends of the moustache pointing upwards, and a broad-brimmed black hat that added swagger and already concealed baldness. In the photo, with the painting unframed, still on the easel, he seemed pleased by it, amazed, happily outdone by the panache of the painter, while giving just a hint of the sitter's inadmissible sense of disappointment.

'What became of that portrait?' said Ivan.

'The Lambert? I let my old college have it.'

'Oh, I see, right – because the papers are at the University of Lichfield.'

'Yes, indeed.' Evert didn't need reminding of that; he felt some small and unreasonable guilt at the arrangement. It had been an undeserved relief to find so eager a home for something he'd so wanted to get rid of. The papers had been welcomed and catalogued, and the gift had led to the naming of the A. V. Dax Theatre – Evert thought at first a stage and stalls, a little Duke of York's, but of course it was a lecture theatre. He had been there only once, for the opening, when he sat under humming strip lights and heard Professor Jack Bishop talk in confident and surprising detail about the man they were honouring. Now Evert was going to need a good two weeks in Lichfield checking up on details he should have made sure of before the papers went, the whole thing typical of his indecisiveness and delay.

At eleven Herta came in and asked if they wanted coffee. Ivan was on all fours squirrelling for dropped items under the table, his round rump sticking out. Her gaze settled on it for a moment. 'And for Denis?' she said.

'No, Denis has gone out to see about the Triumph,' said Evert, with her German way of saying the name, and glanced at his watch to see how long it had been. 'The fuel injection . . .' He gave a bland smile.

'Still the injection,' said Herta heavily, and went off to the kitchen.

'That Treeooomph,' said Ivan from under the table.

'Now, now . . .' said Evert, looking as if thinking about something else at the taut brown corduroy, the appealing dip of his lower back. 'How are you getting on down there?' Ivan wriggled out backwards till it was safe to raise his head.

'I don't want you to miss anything,' he said. He passed three little snapshots back over his shoulder to Evert in his chair; then he sat back on his heels, ran his hand through his hair and smiled, as if at something else they both might have in mind.

When the coffee came in Ivan stood by the window holding his cup and saucer daintily and peering into the street. There were various telling and touching little ways he made himself at home here, which today Evert wondered about more than before. His eyes seemed to follow someone on the pavement below as he said, 'Oh, I was wondering, what you made of Jonathan, by the way?'

'Sparsholt, you mean?'

'I do.'

'Oh, he seems nice enough.'

Ivan looked at him, as he turned from the window, in a humorously suspicious way – or so Evert suspected. 'I didn't know you knew David Sparsholt.'

'Yes, our paths crossed early in the War.'

'Well, lucky you,' said Ivan.

'And why do you say that?'

Ivan hesitated nostalgically. 'Oh, I had quite a crush on him.'

'That seems unlikely.'

'You know, when I was at school. I used to cut the pictures of him out of the paper.'

'Extraordinary child you were.'

'I've still got them somewhere. You remember the famous photo taken through a window, with Clifford Haxby and another man.'

'Oh God, Clifford Haxby . . .' said Evert.

'Do you remember?'

'Hardly' – the name now a tawdry token of its moment.

'They never found out who the third man was.'

'Oh, who cares?' – at which Ivan looked crestfallen. 'To be honest I've forgotten most of it – certainly all the business side of it.'

'Well, it was rather complicated,' Ivan allowed.

'And the MP, I couldn't even remember his name.'

'Leslie Stevens. He was the one with the house parties in Cornwall,' said Ivan. 'That was when I first learned that there was such a thing as male prostitutes.'

'Oh, really . . . ? Oh, dear . . . !' Evert felt the stale squalor of the thing seep over him again, the prurient press, of course, but also the imagined and salaciously reconstructed events themselves. That was all people kept, of a scandal, as time passed and the circumstances were lost – a blurred image or two, the facts partial or distorted, the names eluding memory. Still, he said, 'Why shouldn't people have a bit of fun if they want to?'

'No, I quite agree,' said Ivan warmly, and looked away before he looked back at him.

'Awful for the boy, of course,' Evert said.

'If they'd been called Brown, it wouldn't be half so bad.'

'Or indeed Green,' said Evert.

Ivan laughed. 'And being, you know, queer too.'

'Ah . . . yes,' Evert said. 'I see.'

Ivan put down his cup and saucer on the desk. 'Did you fancy his dad, in the War?'

Evert peered, as if trying to remember – his sudden decision, like a kick under the table, that he wouldn't tell Ivan broke out in a blush which Ivan noticed and no doubt made his own sense of.

*

Today Evert wasn't going out to lunch, but a new anxiety made him feel he would rather not share his cottage pie with Ivan. He looked at his watch. 'Will you come back after lunch?' he said.

'Oh . . . Yes, well, I need to go to the London Library anyway.'

'Ah, good,' said Evert. 'And you might pick up a copy of Freddie's new book at Hatchard's – put it on my account.' He hoped the little task would muffle the little snub.

The afternoon post brought a letter addressed in watery blue ink, the writing itself the trace of a memory. Surely an old lady's hand, formed long ago, eccentric, the tremor and charm of a voice obliquely conveyed in its broad-nibbed strokes, now made with more effort. It was from Doris Abney, a two-month-delayed reply to his letter to her, asking, in vague terms, about something specific, the affair he was almost certain she'd had with his father. He hoped he'd judged the tone correctly. People of her generation did just the same destructive lustful things in 1925 as they did now, but they talked about them differently, if they talked of them at all. 'My dear Evert', she wrote, as she had done when he was at school, and with a touching trust, surely, in resuming correspondence after thirty-five years; but she signed off 'Affly, Doris Abney', as if she'd found a certain inescapable formality settle on her in the course of writing and saying, in essence, no. Not the unequivocal no of refusal, or of saying she had not been seduced by Victor. 'I'm rather blind now,' she said, 'and getting ga-ga, though Gilbert and Jasmine have been marvellous. I don't know if you'd heard . . .' – and then a string of gossip about people whose names meant nothing to him. Gilbert was her son, a surgeon, and that was the family in which her history had been furthered, and sheltered. A month or two's indiscretion fifty years ago with a man himself now dead for twenty was something she hardly cared to remember. Did she want her friends, her grandchildren reading about it? If secrecy had been of the essence at the time, why boast about it now? Boast, or confess – these were the two ways of speaking up, sometimes artfully muddled. Doris did neither. It was in a PS that she said, 'I hope you will be able to convey your father's charm as well as his more forceful aspects!' There it was again, several of them had mentioned it: 'charm' – a transient magic hard to convey in a person's absence, and against the grain of other, more lasting, evidence. Evert lifted the spring and added the letter to the rest in the black box-folder, replies from his father's friends, some of them now dead too and their words stale in his mind with lying there, pressed together.

To be friends, to be among the little group of regulars at Cranley Gardens in the old days, was to be a devotee of Victor's work, though it was rarely talked about in the house itself, since he was so absurdly touchy about it. Evert could see them still, from the fifteen-year-old's vantage, arriving for a dinner party, their look of walking simultaneously on air and on eggshells. They gleamed with the privilege of proximity, and the terror of saying the wrong thing. Sometimes a naively direct question from a woman who was very attractive, or possibly titled, could produce a simple and illuminating answer – Evert noted how the others listened, with concealed attentiveness, while smiling in friendly pity at the questioner. But in general Victor's books were taken as read. Was it, oddly, as if to mention them by name might expose them to ungovernable breezes of humour and doubt? Only his mother ever got away with it, in the years before the War, at her end of the candle-lit table, when she struck a glass and proposed a toast and won from her husband a brief flushed smile of consent, or defeat. After the War the arrangements were so original, with the upstairs and downstairs flats, that his parents' social scene disbanded – and Victor, with his new prosthesis, stumped around up above unobserved, if not unheard. Evert, working at the Tate, had his own little flat in Chiswick, and when he came to visit his mother he did occasionally see (what she must have seen very often) an unknown woman creaking downwards in the lift, and then hurrying to the front door.

Evert feared he was painting the portrait of a monster, when what Victor Dax should be remembered for was his dense, unfashionable but not insignificant writings. A harrowing exposé was all very well if the subject was famous and pretended to be virtuous; but Victor, disagreeable in life, was now almost unknown to the reading public. Evert imagined a cocktail conversation: 'Have you heard of someone called A. V. Dax?' 'Haven't, I'm afraid.' 'Well, nor had I, till I read this book, and it turns out he was a swine.'

He thought about the days after his father died. The undertaker was a genial little man, who referred to the dead person as 'the party'; it was just the wrong word for Victor, and helped Evert get through the day, the arrival of the hearse at the house, going down rigid-faced with Alex on his arm to the big black limousine that followed it, the long half-defiant, half-apologetic crawl through the London streets to Kensal Green, and the unstoppable burial, which wrenched up emotions in him that seemed quite apart from his wary feelings about his father in life. After that there was the 'party' itself, the oddest gathering there had ever been at Cranley Gardens, a black matinee at which Herta, as mourner and ministrant, was in commanding form. It was the moment she had switched her loyalties, completely, emphatically, to Evert, whom up to that point she had generally obstructed. She seemed to manage and embody, quite cannily, the inevitable process of change, and descent. The survivors from the little group of admiring friends had come together to mark the passing, there was the unavoidable heaviness of occasion, and just audible beneath it a letting-out of breath.

4

All these weeks, the old stove in the workshop was kept drowsily going, with its small scratchy whispers, now and then, of combustion and collapse, and when the power went off it was Johnny's job to open the air vent, rattle out the cinders, hook up the cast-iron disc of the lid and slide in another helping of coke from the hod. Cyril lit the kerosene lamp, replaced its glass chimney and turned the little wheel to bring up the flame. Once his eyes had adjusted Johnny liked the lamp's heavy brilliance, renewed, at an angle, in the sloping glass roof above, where he looked up from time to time and watched their upside-down movements. They seemed to twitch and sidle, like creatures in an experiment, according to their own laws and needs, which careful study might explain. The whole crisis was a nuisance and potentially a disaster, but it had these accidental beauties, winter evenings out of the past. There was something banal in the first startled seconds when the radio spoke and the strip light blinked back into life.

What Cyril's views were on Edward Heath and the miners Johnny never learned. The radio did most of the talking, when the power was on, the news edging forward with small adaptations through the course of the day. Sometimes Johnny looked up, at a joke or some provocative remark by Arthur Scargill, but Cyril seemed never to have heard it. Johnny sensed that the old man's fondness for the radio had little to do with what was said on it. It was a kind of clock, often speaking the time, but more palpably parcelling out the day into news and weather, *Farming Today*, *The Archers*, even *Woman's Hour*. It made other talk unnecessary, and more difficult. It was a form of starvation to a child of Radio 3, which Johnny imagined going on like a better life in a nearby room, but didn't dare ask for, all the time he was rubbing down frames, making moulds of broken details, or learning from Cyril the invisible art of touching up a painting. It was one of Cyril's lessons that most oil paintings more than a hundred years old had been restored, and even much younger ones needed a bit of work. What was more vulnerable than a painted surface, screened only by varnish which itself darkened and distorted and sometimes even damaged what it was meant to protect? Cyril shared his knowledge with a certain reluctance, and expressed approval in a tone of disappointment. 'Yes, well you've got the hang of that,' he would say, and turn away with a pinched look. When the wireless was silent in the power cuts so too, for the most part, was Cyril. Johnny said helpfully they could get a transistor, but Cyril seemed to see this as meddling. It was the ignorant good sense of someone fresh to the job, and no doubt to act on the suggestion would have put him, slightly but unacceptably, in Johnny's debt.

Now the day had come for Johnny's first date with Ivan: he was going round to Cranley Gardens after work, and all afternoon, as he cut down one frame with the mitre saw and curled the wet tip of his brush into the old carved flowers of another, he was picturing repetitively how it might be. In the few days since he'd seen him he had lost the look of him, and wished he'd had a chance to draw him. If he took himself unawares he could catch the brown fringe and the sexy slant of his teeth, and hear the chime of his speech in little phrases which seemed to flirt with him and hold him off at once. They'd kissed, but the kiss had been nearly nothing, and not yet repeated, though Johnny still held a mysterious trace of the feel of him in his hands, the rough warm front and the cool silk back of his waistcoat. He sensed it was best not to hope for too much from Ivan; but his thoughts ran back to him again and around him, and the last two days as soon as he'd woken he'd made love to him triumphantly before getting up.

Sometimes a picture drew him in – it exacted a surrender with no show of force, it seduced by something precisely unsaid. Last Saturday, out of the cold London morning, he'd gone into the National Portrait Gallery, and seen they had a show called 'Londoners at Home'. He hadn't heard of the photographer but was drawn at once by a newcomer's feel for the subject, the curiosity and the dream of assimilation: he imagined resilient cockneys, eccentrics posed with their lapdogs and Afghan hounds, aristos in evening dress – that air of nostalgia for itself that pervades the life of a great city, ubiquitous as fog and soot. It wasn't like that at all. The photographer, an American woman not much older than Johnny, had her own curiosity, and had found a different London, so real that it was hard to recognize. The reality was that of anxiety, confinement, a slowly forming despair. Almost all the subjects were alone, in their rooms, with a TV, an unmade bed, some worthless but probably treasured object. They stared, rarely smiled, but seemed madder when they did. Occasionally there were a couple of figures, two men, friends or brothers, father and son. Johnny's instinct was for the lurking hint of sex in a photo, the shock of what a photo could catch. As someone who wanted to paint people he envied it.

A picture, unlike the dim labyrinth of a book, could be seen at once, but to bring it all to the front of the mind's eye and hold it there was impossible. Some quite simple image might house an irreducible mystery: this he seemed always to have known. There was a photograph here with an atmosphere that excited and eluded him. In a room lit from the right, two lean young men sat on the end of a large double bed with a dark candlewick covering. There were psychedelic posters behind them and a blown-up photo of Mick Jagger dancing and pointing on the nearer side wall. Close up in the foreground, items on a tabletop loomed large, two glass ashtrays, a gleaming packet of Benson & Hedges, a painted bowl in which objects had been heaped, surmounted by a square white adaptor plug, strangely prominent. They didn't have much, these two men, but they were tidy, and the adaptor was nothing to be ashamed of. Was it also the photographer's way of saying something the men themselves couldn't make so explicit? He got closer and closer to the glazed threshold of the photo, the world behind him receding. He seemed to stare into the room through a two-way mirror – from which, at that moment, both men looked away, as though on the brink of some hesitant exposure. Both sat forward, elbows on thighs, smoking. Both were sexy in the wild new way, the one on the left in a tight patterned sweatshirt, dark hair swept back to the collar, long sideburns, rings on two fingers; the other man, head sideways as if cradling a phone in his shoulder-length hair, was shirtless, with tattooed arms, brushing the tip of his roll-up against the rim of the fluted glass ashtray.

Johnny stood there as if lost, but conscious now of another man, a live one, reflected in the glass as he strolled and scuffed and stopped along the far side of the room, a bit older than himself, with short dark hair and an amusing face, black flared jeans and a duffel coat; the waiting and pacing deepened his appeal, as did the risk of him passing on, a missed chance. In a minute he came alongside, craned forward to search for what Johnny saw in the photo, while Johnny shifted from one foot to the other as if magnetized and touched shoulder to shoulder with him. The man stepped back a fraction and peered quizzically at Johnny, then back to the photo, as if finding a likeness and then accepting how absurd, and hilarious, it would have been if one of the long-haired men in the bedroom had been Johnny himself. Johnny was slow to see this, and when the stranger said, 'Not you, then?' he was able to laugh, 'Oh . . . no!' with sufficient surprise and briefly touched the man's arm.

Their conversation went by loops and catches then, while

they drifted from picture to picture in an English uncertainty about how seriously to take them. They touched shoulder to shoulder again as they tested each other's tone, and knowledge. It was beautiful the instinct of it, quite new and alarming too to Johnny, though the idea that he fancied the man grew as it was encouraged and returned, and was smoothly akin to their joint enjoyment of the art, which now mattered rather less. He found he was called Colin, not a name he liked, but he adjusted to it – it made him fancy him more. Still the polite uncertainty sur-vived, after the last picture, and they drifted back through the two rooms, nodding and saying yes to the ones they'd agreed on before. Then they were out in St Martin's Place together, a cold wind blowing and a quick decision made.

It was cold in Colin's flat, too, above a busy main road just south of the river, but they jumped into bed in their underwear and got hot kissing and tugging it up or down. Johnny hadn't been with someone so hard and rough as Colin before, and he watched him for signals as to how he should behave – he was eager but there was a fractional delay, which oddly made the game more intense. Colin showed how much he liked him as he held him down and pushed him around – 'Your hair!' he said, grinning and tutting. He did just what he liked, so that Johnny's shyness smiled helplessly through in the moment of throwing it off. But it all worked out, and seemed inevitable, the pain as well as the brutal excitement.

They lay around, Colin hopped out and lit a cigarette, which he shared with Johnny, specks of ash on their chests, as they lay side by side, Johnny's foot trapped between Colin's feet. It wasn't only the area, with the motorbikes and lorries revving at the lights below, but the room itself, clean, carpetless, with a sheet for a curtain, that was so alien and convincing. Of course he thought of the room in the photograph: Londoners at Home. Colin asked him what his name was, and when he told him he said, 'Oh, yes? Any relation?' 'Yeah – well, he's my dad,' said Johnny, 'if that's what you mean.' He didn't want the whole thing of blame and pity; and being in bed with another man, of course, made it awkward. Colin smiled and nodded slowly as he blew out smoke, 'Would you believe it,' he said, then dropped the cigarette in a cup by the bed and in a minute they were having another go, a humorous start that led to a quick, almost savage finish. It was amazing, and it was enough. After this they smiled and kissed as they stood close together in the curtained-off end of the bath which was also a shower. Johnny's hair grew heavy and dark under the falling water, and unwaved itself into a shiny point between his shoulder blades. Colin's hair was short and neat – he perhaps didn't know yet that it was thinning on the crown. They towelled each other, which wasn't easy to do well, and in the way Colin let Johnny dry him between the legs and half-excite him as he did so there was a vision of what day-to-day life with another man might be, everything he wanted of love and coupledom constantly granted. But Colin, with what seemed to Johnny his lavish gift of intimacy, was not one to repeat himself, and so far they had not met again. After two unanswered phone calls, a reawoken bashfulness kept Johnny from making a third.

Johnny didn't tell Cyril he was going back to Cranley Gardens – any more than he'd told his father, on the phone, that he'd been there in the first place, and met a man who'd known him at Oxford. He was back in the house, on and off, all week, in his mind, among the pictures and the people, who seemed obscurely the key to a new life which would be damaged by contact with the old. It wasn't just because of Ivan, he felt somehow home-sick for it, after one visit, in a way that he didn't for either of his parents' houses. As he put on his coat and scarf he popped into the little cold lavatory at the back of the premises. At work he kept his hair held back in a rubber band; now he looked in the mirror as he folded the thick ponytail upwards and quickly pulled his corduroy cap over it, the peak high at the front, the elasticated hem at the back tight across his nape. As always he saw what he hoped someone else would see in his eyes and lips and broad cheekbones, and then with a turn of the head, as if in a hologram, another lurking image, mouth too big, nose not straight, skin touched up into spots by the oily tips of his hair. He called goodbye to Cyril, and went out into the February night with a chill round his ears.

Outside, the street lights were glowing at half-power, arrested in the dim early mauve of their sequence. People peered quickly at each other as they passed from shadow to shadow, in doubt, and then brief solidarity. A breath of mist had seeped up the street from the river, and the pavements were slippery in the wan gleam of the lamps. Johnny crossed the Fulham Road, where the car-lights and lit buses were the brightest things; after that the houses grew taller and darker and more densely packed with that quality that was still raw and new to him, in every street name and sitting room glimpsed through unclosed curtains, the self-confidence and difference of London life.

When he got to Evert Dax's house he stopped on the far side of the street and looked up. The faint light of the street lamp was lost among the curved wrought iron and dead winter shrubbery of the first-floor balcony, and he could barely make out the balustrade at the top in front of Ivan's attic window. There was a trace of music, and between the curtains of the bay window on the ground floor, five steps above street level, he saw a boldly dressed woman with white hair and a gaunt man in a dark suit and tie waltz mechanically past the spider plants and standard lamps: the Polish couple – Ivan had mentioned them. The windows on the first floor, behind the balcony railings, were all dark. The two floors above that, with their smaller windows, were where Evert Dax lived and worked, curtains closed but a hint of welcome in the pink gap between them; and above that again, the shadowy balustrade, the dormers of Ivan's room, the tall party-wall of chimney stacks and aerials spectral against the sky. Was he going to spend the night up there? It was all too vague, silly drunk talk of drinks, and even dancing. Johnny said should they go to a nightclub, a gay disco, something he hadn't had the nerve to do by himself? Ivan beamed, 'Yes, of course!', a silver promise that tarnished in seconds in the air. And if so, would they come back here at one or two, when everyone else was asleep? And what then? What about the morning? The Poles downstairs, the unseen banker on the first floor, could come and go as they pleased, but Ivan's daily life must be tangled with Evert's, their comings and goings known to each other.

When he climbed the steps it was hard to see the bells . . . he pressed the top one and stood looking down into the basement area, a huddled below-decks sheeted in shadow. A voice crackled 'Hello?' – 'It's Johnny . . . . Johnny Sparsholt' – the only response a dull buzz and he was in. The entryphone was the glamour of London itself, magic as routine. He felt for another button by the door and lights came on in the hall. Then he closed the street door and stood for a second, alone this time in the limbo of admittance, known to be there but not yet seen. Through the further closed door on the right the waltz music could be heard going on. The lift was down and waiting, but he took the stairs as before, wanting to look at the pictures on the way but then fearing the impatience of whoever had answered the bell.

He stopped on the second-floor landing and peered upwards into the shadows; where was the next light switch? Talk came from the half-open door of the sitting room – Evert Dax himself, sounding fretful, and Iffy's gruff voice, and a lighter, very posh woman. 'I can't sell,' Evert said, 'with sitting tenants, and anyway what about all the stuff.'

'I certainly wouldn't *want* to move,' said Iffy.

'Anyway it's my home, whoever's running the bloody country.'

'Mm . . . well, I suppose nothing's for ever, is it, love.'

'I think you should all stop listening to Gordon,' said the other woman. 'He's just upsetting you for his own amusement.'

'I only hope you're right,' Iffy said, rather grimly. 'I don't fancy living in a Communist country. It's a subject I do know something about.'

Johnny found the switch and plunged the whole staircase into darkness. Evert called out, 'Oh! Is that Johnny?'

'Sorry!' said Johnny, and went cautiously across the landing. When he looked round the door he saw Evert and Iffy sitting by the fire with a tea tray on the low stool in front of them while, standing at the window with her back turned, a slim blonde girl in a Davy Crockett jacket and tight black jeans gazed out through her own reflection at the night. Iffy looked up at him briefly, and said, 'Hullo,' as if still thinking about something else.

'You'll want to see Ivan,' said Evert, 'but say hello to us first.'

The young woman stayed watching the scene in the window, and it was only when Johnny, unsure if he was being favoured or gently ticked off, said, 'If that's all right . . .' that she turned round and looked at him directly:

'Of course it's all right,' she said.

'Jonathan,' said Iffy, 'you haven't met my daughter Francesca.'

He said hello over the intervening space, the backs of chairs. Francesca nodded at him, smiled a fraction and raised an eyebrow – like Ivan before her, she had the look of knowing something about him already. She had a severe pale beauty and the poise of a woman of her mother's age – indeed more poise than Iffy, who today in a yellow Indian skirt with tiny mirrors sewn in rows and a large woolly top had a ramshackle air, and had surely never been so nice to look at. There was a faint pale swooping line round Francesca's throat, where in a man the Adam's apple would be, and in an older woman a first fine crease of age. Johnny saw it was where some tight ribbon or necklace had been removed perhaps minutes before. She said, 'Freddie's been talking about you.'

'Oh, has he . . .' said Johnny, while Evert smiled and cleared his throat.

'Have you read his new book?' Francesca said.

'I haven't actually,' said Johnny.

'I wonder if you'll like it,' said Francesca.

'I'm not a big reader,' said Johnny.

'Francesca hasn't read it either,' said Iffy. 'Pay no attention.'

'Oh,' said Johnny, and started to blush. 'Who *is* Freddie, exactly?'

'Ah . . .' said Evert, with a gasp and a smile, 'who is Freddie?' – appealing to himself as well as the others.

'Oh, well . . .' said Francesca, drawing her head back.

'Where to start,' said Iffy and shook her head.

'No reason you should know,' said Evert, so courteously as to suggest the opposite. There was a pause as they considered how best to educate him in this large subject.

'I know his name,' said Johnny.

'So you haven't read *The Lion Griefs*?' Francesca said, biting her lip.

'I'd be amazed if he'd read *The Lion Griefs*,' said Iffy.

'What is it?' Johnny said, not even understanding the title.

'It's a memoir,' said Iffy, 'but of course he also writes fiction.'

'Mm, and not always easy to tell which is which,' said Evert.

'He keeps a famous diary,' said Iffy, 'which we all live in terror of.' She sat forward over the tray, the ruined cake on its doily. 'Are you sure you don't want a cup of tea?'

'Oh – no thanks.' He was dying for a beer, or a glass of wine.

'Well, sit down anyway,' said Evert. 'Take your coat off.'

Johnny did so, laid his coat over a chair, sat down and looked around, explored the view of the sitting room in its normal and private arrangement, books on the floor, the small red light of the stereo, the Nicholsons and what he now knew were the Goyles in their everyday habit of being seen and ignored.

'I want to have a look at your work, by the way,' said Francesca.

'I'm not doing much at the moment,' said Johnny.

'Oh, Brian Savory said you were sketching the old gang the other night.'

'Oh, did he?' said Johnny, and laughed.

'Were you drawing us?' said Iffy. 'You must let us see.'

'Well it wasn't anything – it's just a habit of mine.'

Francesca came towards him, coolly inescapable. 'Do you have them on you?'

'Well,' said Johnny, feeling it was dangerous territory – not only his skill would be assessed but his view of the people who'd welcomed him in. He unbuttoned his jacket pocket and pulled out the little sketchbook. It might be one of those occasions when you had to explain the pictures as you showed them. It went to Iffy first.

'Oh, yes . . .' she said, nodding slowly as she turned the pages. There were really only four quick drawings, and she flicked back through them pretending not to have seen the sketches of something quite different that followed. She passed it to Evert.

'I messed up the one of you,' Johnny said, wishing he hadn't shown them. But Evert looked at it as if he could take anything. Francesca leant over him to see, and though she didn't say a word she looked across at Johnny in a way he found both friendly and unnerving. He was putting the book away as Denis strode in, striped shirt and tie under a dark blazer.

'Ah! How nice: Jonathan.'

'He's come to see Ivan,' said Francesca.

'Are you all ready for a drink?' said Denis, crossing to the table by the window where a dozen bottles and the soda siphon were. 'Iphigenia?'

'What? . . . For once I won't, love, thanks.'

'Jonathan, how about you?' Denis smiled at him, as if any answer he gave would be wrong.

'A gin and tonic, please,' said Johnny.

'A gin and tonic.' Denis snapped the cap on a new bottle of gin.

'Though I should probably tell Ivan I'm here . . .' He found he had seized on the unexpected diversion from being alone with him.

'And what are you young people doing this evening?' said Denis.

'They're going to the Sol y Sombra,' said Francesca.

'What fun,' said Denis, holding up the tumbler like a chemist as he poured in the tonic.

'I hope so . . . !' said Johnny, amazed to hear a gay club mentioned so matter-of-factly among adults of his parents' age, who seemed less bothered about it than he was himself.

'No, I must say I give full marks to Ivan,' Denis said. 'I'd always had him down as a gerontophile.'

Johnny smiled and looked from side to side; through some association with the name Geraint he guessed this was a word for a Welshman. He said, 'I don't really know him yet.' He remembered how in thirty minutes he'd been violently kissed by Denis and had then more affectionately kissed Ivan, and how the memory of the first had interfered like a lingering but more exotic taste with the milder but nicer second. Then Ivan came in, so suddenly they all wondered if he'd heard them, Johnny smiled, his heart raced, feeling his desires were somehow on view to the whole room, but no one seemed to mind or to notice, and it was as if Ivan himself hadn't seen him, he nodded to Evert, and to Denis, who offered him his 'usual' as he crossed to the drinks tray.

'We've had another loss,' said Iffy.

'What's that?' said Ivan, and now he smiled and raised his eyebrows at Johnny as he came round and sat on the sofa beyond her.

'Poor Evert has.'

Evert hesitated. 'Oh, just that little Chelsea figure that was on the mantelpiece.'

'The dear little Falstaff,' said Iffy.

'When did you last see it?' said Ivan competently.

'You know I'm not sure – a week ago?'

'Herta must have broken it,' said Denis. 'She's getting awfully clumsy, poor old thing.'

'It was my mother's,' said Evert, 'but . . . well, it doesn't really matter.'

'So you haven't seen it, Denny?' said Iffy, in a flat tone, as if voicing a general suspicion.

But Denis merely snuffled as he sat down and crossed his legs, and said, 'Cheerio.'

'I can't abide losing things,' said Iffy. 'A lot of Daddy's stuff has gone – or I can't find it. Quite valuable things, probably.'

Evert said semi-obliquely, 'Iffy's father was a rather important architect.'

'Oh, yes?' said Johnny.

After another pause in which the others nursed their shared knowledge, Francesca said, 'Yah, do you know, Peter Orban.'

It was a further room suddenly opened beyond the remarkable one they were already in. 'Oh wow,' Johnny said.

'It sounds as if you've heard of him, then, that's good!' said Iffy.

'Well . . . *yes*,' said Johnny, sitting forward with a small shake of the head and a cautious feeling he might have something to say. 'You see, I did my fine art diploma at Hoole College. So I lived in a Peter Orban building for two years.'

Francesca looked at him narrowly, as if to signal that a lot hung on his answer. 'And how was it for you?'

'Oh, it was marvellous, it was beautiful.' He grinned at Iffy with a new fascination, as if to compare this other product of the great Hungarian Modernist. All his artist's instincts, and loyalties, acclaimed the Hoole campus, though it was a divisive matter, and many people hated it. There were certain impracticalities – the studio windows leaked, the classrooms in summer were stiflingly hot, in the halls where they lived you could hear your neighbour turn over in bed, and you had to get out of bed yourself to turn off the light. Horrible smells came up through the shower outlets. 'I loved it, anyway.'

'I didn't know you were at Hoole,' said Ivan, an airy admission followed smoothly by a claim: 'I expect you know Peter designed a house for my uncle?'

'Oh, no, I didn't.'

'It was the first thing he did in England, almost. Well it's not in England, of course, it's in Wales – you'll have to see it!' – his dark eyes glittering over his raised glass, his mouth hidden.

'I'd love to,' said Johnny, not sure how this would be arranged. 'You mean Stanley Goyle?'

'Uncle Stanley, yes.'

'What part of Wales is it exactly? We used to go to Criccieth each year.'

'As a matter of fact it's in Pembrokeshire,' said Ivan.

'It's become a bit of a worry,' said Iffy, 'I'm afraid. Your grandfather's buildings tend to need a great deal of care.'

'Indeed they do,' said Francesca piously.

'As, I may say, did your grandfather . . .'

They laughed mildly at this, Johnny naturally curious.

'Peter wasn't an easy man, was he,' said Evert.

'He could be bloody difficult,' said Iffy. She looked at Denis. 'Perhaps I will have a drink.'

'So, we've all had difficult fathers,' said Evert, looking

kindly at Johnny, who coloured again and saw Ivan watching him.

'Well, can I just say: I didn't,' Ivan said.

'No, but yours died, didn't he, love, when you were still awfully young,' said Iffy.

'You mean he might have got difficult later on?' said Ivan. Everyone laughed, though Johnny sensed from the way she did so that Francesca thought Ivan an interloper in her mother's world – perhaps she'd been the favourite here before. She glanced aside as she laughed as if to find something more worthwhile to do.

In the pause that followed, Johnny peeped at Evert, half-wanting to ask about his father at Oxford, that brief period of which no word or image seemed to survive. *I knew your father*, he had said, and something merely myth, or hearsay, took on colour, and might darken with a dozen details if he asked him more; but Johnny was so deeply in the habit of avoiding and deflecting talk about him that he said nothing.

5

Johnny closed the shop door, went quickly down the street, and as soon as he turned the corner into the King's Road reached up and with two deft twists freed his hair and shook it out – a man in a passing van whistled, and a middle-aged woman getting into her car said sportingly, 'I wish I could do that.' He saw himself in a couple of shop windows, and in the angled doorway of the Bazaar there was a full-length mirror, where he peered as he parted the jackets on the rail outside. It was after eleven, but the boutiques woke up late, and at some the doors were just being unlocked. He could have taken the bus the whole length of the street, but looked forward each time to the life of the pavement, where even on a dull Tuesday morning odd fashionable figures were about, the first drifters and shoppers alongside the regulars waiting by the pubs. Joss sticks burned somewhere as he passed and from a cave of knotted scarves and batik hangings came the worrying smell of sesame. He was glad Cyril trusted him with these little jobs that got him out of the shop in the daylight hours; though making his way past all this colour and temptation, the Man Boutique, the weird owl windows of the Chelsea Drug Store, the shop he had not yet been into called SEX, he started to resent being made to do anything at all.

At Sloane Square he jogged down to the station platform with a sense almost of truancy, and had to go in a smoking carriage to follow an Italian couple, the man in white jeans so astonishingly tight that he travelled on two stops beyond Victoria just to look at him. Then he quickly changed platforms and came back, he ran up the escalator and the stairs, but the queue was slow at the booking office and when he reached the platform the blank back end of the train he was meant to be on was jolting over the points and out of view.

There was another train in half an hour, and he could still be in Gipsy Hill with a clear thirty minutes before the auction started. He tucked his ticket in his wallet and wandered looking up at the departures boards, and at the men looking up at them; then stood shifting in the onward rush of arrivals from two trains – fantasies of greetings in faces that held his own for a second as they swept past. It was arrival in London, and Johnny felt its excitement as well as the subtler pleasure of noting, as a Londoner himself, the blind air of routine in most of the travellers' faces. Some slowed and waited, roaming, half-preoccupied. A space opened up and he saw the movement round the entrance marked Gentlemen, men going in hurriedly and down the stairs, past others coming out with a businesslike look. He thought he might just go himself – in and down. The copper coin in the turnstile was the price of admission, the admission in his case of a guilty thought – overseen by a man in a glass box for whom any interest in the endless traffic in and out had long been exhausted.

Johnny passed a row of blue doors, all engaged, towards the step and the white wall where the pitted copper pipe started hissing and rasping over the tiles. He saw himself in the mirror above the basins, but in his mind he was hardly visible, the mere magnetized observer of the man who dried his hands for ever on the roller towel, the three men spaced along the gutter, workman, businessman, old gent. He leaned forward and peeped past the curtain of his hair as he tried to piss, stopped up by the presence of the others and the gripping sensation of standing on the brink. The businessman was shockingly hard, the workman, thirtyish, with a roll-up kept dry behind his ear, floppy but bigger. Johnny blushed, looked down with a racing heart, the quick ratchet and thud all the time of the turnstile behind them and a man setting down a big suitcase and pushing in between himself and the workman, heavy-built, coat and hat, off the boat train perhaps, and perhaps unaware of the tense patience of the others who waited him out, frowning as if at their own stubborn failure to make even a dribble. And as he waited with them Johnny saw himself drawn into the criminal collusion of the other men, and under cover of the visitor's last sullen shakes and wheezy buttoning up he stepped down too, as he zipped, and was away through the turnstile and up the stairs with the still-panicked heartbeat of a narrow escape; and a feeling growing, after four or five eventless minutes, while the businessman emerged without seeing him and strode off to the taxi rank, that if he didn't catch a train he would have to go back in again; and that the going in again, past the attendant who seemed neither to condone nor prevent what was going on, would set a visible seal on his guilt.

But the thought of the workman being down there still, down there all morning perhaps, in thick jeans and boots and a donkey jacket moodily used to reveal and close off what he had on offer, was so thrilling that the air in the great noisy concourse above seemed to pulse with a barely concealed new purpose. A cloud shifted and the sun angled down through the high glass roof. He looked boldly at one or two men who were waiting like him for their trains to be announced; but the boldness was met with irritated puzzlement and Johnny drifted away and looked blankly at the cafe and shops. Just inside the open door of John Menzies Ivan was standing. He was at the counter, in a duffel coat and a knitted green scarf which for a long ten seconds seemed to isolate his sleek pale face against the muddled background in a woolly nimbus. Johnny turned away to absorb the shock, the abrupt opportunity, on top of the others, missed and ebbing. He hardly knew if he wanted to see him. Then he turned round just as Ivan came out of the shop with a magazine, and walked towards him with the unseeing look of someone looking for someone else. Ivan seemed aware of a person smiling before he had his own little shock – 'Oh, hello!' and stuck out his hand, which Johnny, disconcerted, took a moment to accept, and shake. It was a fleeting fragment of time, ten seconds again, in which something was irrevocably exposed – though Ivan scooted round to cover it up. 'Oh, gosh – I'm . . .' – he grinned at him. 'I didn't expect to see you out and about in the middle of the day.'

'I didn't, either,' said Johnny: 'expect to see you.'

'What are you doing?' – and now Ivan tapped him on the arm, almost reproachfully.

'I'm going to an auction,' said Johnny, as if it was his own idea.

'In Brighton?' said Ivan vaguely.

'Brighton? – no, Gipsy Hill.'

'My dear . . .' said Ivan.

Johnny wasn't sure of the implication – he looked down at Ivan's magazine: *The Yachtsman*. 'Oh, I didn't know you were . . .'

'Oh . . . !' He looked at it too, and laughed distantly. It was odd, but Ivan's discomfort seemed unrelated to the soreness in Johnny's own mind about their supposed night out, though it wasn't Ivan's fault it had all gone wrong. Ivan rather stalled, he said, 'Well, fancy meeting you at Victoria.'

'I'm glad,' said Johnny, moved again by his presence, his glow in the cold air heightened by the morning's mood of chance and temptation – his fringe had grown longer and caught in the long lashes of his right eye as he blinked and then shook his head.

'Freddie says everyone has their terminal. His is Paddington, you know, coming from Devon, and then going to Oxford all the time, of course.'

'Oh, yes.' It was the sort of London game he could see Freddie playing.

'I'm Paddington too, of course, what are you – King's Cross, I suppose?'

'I'm Euston.'

'Oh, Euston – shame,' said Ivan.

Johnny tutted humorously at this, though he knew what he meant, about the new station. His first London memory, at seven or eight, was of the Euston Arch – just before it was demolished: the six huge gilded letters EUSTON, cut deep in the blackened stone, seemed to dance, more a spell than a name, not like any other word, beneath a deep blue sky. 'Well, you don't spend much time in the station, do you.'

'That depends . . .' said Ivan, and looked away as if he'd said something else.

'Anyway, where are *you* going?'

Ivan stared at him, baffled: 'Oh, I'm not going anywhere,' and then laughed, 'No, I'm waiting to meet my uncle, and he seems' – he craned round again – 'to have missed his train.'

'Oh, I see!' said Johnny, saddened and obscurely relieved. 'I thought your uncle was dead.'

'What? Oh, not Uncle Stanley!' said Ivan. 'No, no, he died years ago, two years, anyway. No, this is another uncle, I haven't seen him for absolutely ages.'

'Right. Where's he coming from?'

'Mm?' said Ivan – his gaze ran with momentary adhesion over the cascading departure boards, in which the trains jumped with a fluttering rattle from column to column as their time grew nearer. Johnny saw his own train had gone and panicked till he saw it drop with its long list of stops like a Venetian blind two places to the left: nine minutes to departure and the plat-form now announced, platform 8, through the gates just ahead. 'He's coming from Horsham,' said Ivan.

'I don't mind waiting with you,' Johnny said. 'I've got a few minutes.'

Ivan smiled again, and pulled back his inner sleeve to look at his watch. 'No, you mustn't,' he said. 'But look, I'll see you soon – come over to the house.'

'Oh . . . yes,' said Johnny.

'I know Evert would love to see you.'

Johnny, stung, had to touch him – it was a pat on the shoul-der, as he turned and went towards the barrier with the idea of a kiss that was lost for ever stiffening his face. Ivan too had turned and moved away, and once he'd shown his ticket Johnny was gripped for the second time by the pain of not having acted, and under it, a little salve, the sense of having escaped. The midday trains leaving London were largely deserted, and he got into the first carriage, still dotted with commuters' litter from hours before. He sat staring across the platform, but then since he had five minutes more he got out again, stood and glanced

casually back into the concourse of the station. He couldn't see
Ivan now, and it struck him with a quick burn of jealousy that
he might have gone into the Gents himself. Or had he been
a fool – Ivan wasn't here to meet his uncle at all, he was after
the unmentionable, the workman in the donkey jacket, with
Johnny for a minute a blundering obstacle. But no – there he
was, talking to a man by the coffee shop and then moving
away: he stood, checking the board, not of course the departure
board but the arrivals one. Now a long train was pulling in two
platforms across from where Johnny stood, and Ivan came
hesitantly forward as the doors all along clattered open in the
faces of those stepping down, who doubled and redoubled on
their way to the exit. Ivan was staring at them as they came past
him, but hanging back, as if wanting to be discovered by his
uncle. He held his magazine, with its bright blue masthead,
across his chest.

Then he put his head on one side, with a questioning smile,
as a man of about sixty stopped in front of him – Johnny
couldn't see, through the stream of other passengers, quite what
happened. There was a quick greeting, and a sort of discussion,
about what they were going to do, perhaps. He had a clearer
feeling now that Ivan hadn't wanted him to meet the uncle, who
looked very smart, with combed grey hair and a darker moustache, and also, in the way he held himself, in his short dark mac
and pink paisley scarf, a bit camp. The whistle blew twice and
Johnny got back into the train.

Rustin's Auction Rooms were in a former Sunbeam garage, a
few hundred yards from the station. The first time he'd come
was with Cyril himself, to look at a landscape catalogued as a
Bargery – 'after Bargery' had been Cyril's dry judgement, and
he'd watched with a cunning hint of self-denial as the auctioneer, raising his eyebrows towards him as the price jumped up

and up, sold it for three times its estimate to a well-known collector from Hove. Standing there beside Cyril at the back of the room, Johnny saw them both at an angle in a tall cheval mirror, a surprising pair, the stout old man in his brown mac, Johnny in his father's RAF greatcoat, loose on him, large-lapelled, double-breasted, his hair pulled up in his corduroy cap. He'd never been to an auction before – he was bored and excited almost at the same time, as the short tight dramas of the bidding ran on one after the other, lulls now and then of dead lots that no one raised a hand for, buyers coming in from the tea room next door as particular items drew near. Then Cyril nodded resignedly at a batch of drawings no one had noticed, but of course they noticed him, there was a flurry of interest which he weathered with small impassive flickers of the eyebrows – Johnny glanced at him nervously, in the mirror his movements were so slight as to be invisible, but the auctioneer, leaning forward, grinning with surmise about this overlooked lot, seemed to dance on the spot for him and bring down the hammer with a smack as if to say this was what made his life worth living.

If it was a Sickert, tucked in amongst them, as Cyril explained on the train going back, it was much the best thing in the sale – if not . . . well, the whole racket of money and dealing and grubbing around was as mad and as seepingly depressing as Johnny felt it was now, walking into the sale room alone and taking his first breaths of its musty ambiguous air. Today it was merely some frames he had to look at, and then bid for them himself. He found them, several lots, stacked against the wall at the back; a red-haired man in an anorak was looking at them, picking them up and turning them over and clattering them back. Johnny waited for him to move away, feeling he hadn't got the knack of indifference yet, the dealer's surly way of handling the goods. He came forward, squatted down, peered at the frames and handled them too, checking for damage, and wondering how much more damage would be done to them before they were sold. It was a small ebonized ripple-moulded frame Cyril was after, but it came in a lot with three others. There was a Watts frame in another lot, in need of repair, but which Johnny was told to buy if he thought it worthwhile. He held it at arm's length, which seemed to draw others to look at it, so that he was displaying it to them, his potential rivals. He made a disillusioned snuffle and shake of the head and put it back with as much roughness as he dared. Cyril had taught him what to look for, and he felt pretty certain the black Dutch frame was seventeenth century, but the decision was his, and the whole business of the auction weighed on him in a new way.

He dawdled off, to fill the time, between the long tables crowded with clocks, vases, canteens of cutlery, stacked dinner services with unequal numbers of plates and bowls. There were things here he recognized from last month's sale, one lot-number sticker on top of another, estimates on the roneoed sheet perhaps a bit lower: the bronze Mercury tiptoe on a globe with his raised right hand missing, the Viennese wall clock that lacked all but one of its bulbous brass finials. 'Losses' was the word for damage to any kind of artefact. There were two portrait heads, called 'manner of Epstein', life-size in painted plaster: a lank-haired, long-nosed young woman, and a man like Thomas Beecham whose thickly moulded goatee had suffered some losses since Johnny had last seen him. He thought they must have come from local houses, local figures in effigy that no one after twenty or thirty years had wanted to hang on to. Perhaps some of the older bidders in these sales had known the sitters; and if you hadn't known them it was very hard indeed to imagine wanting to possess these forlorn lumps of matter. Johnny thought of his father's friends: would you really want a head of Ken Cudlip leering at you every time you went into the sitting room? Even put in the loo as a joke it would soon grow oppressive, and perhaps with time unnerving.

He went through a box of photographs, but thinking about Ivan – was the meeting at Victoria in any way a positive one? It was another event in their story, it gave more substance to their friendship, though it hadn't exactly been friendly in itself. In his fantasies Johnny had run way ahead of where, in the sudden chance of this morning, he confusedly found himself. He thought of his meeting with Colin at the Portrait Gallery, and Colin's flat, which seemed from here, over the ramparts of commodes and chests of drawers with chipped veneers, like the inaccessible room where real life went on, tormentingly separate from his dusty day-to-day dealings.

The sale opened with a section of jewellery: old pins, brooches, necklaces, the bidding sometimes dragging on unconscionably for items of no interest. Or so it seemed to Johnny, taking in the auctioneer, the same bow-tied whimsical gent as before, the small solid gavel in his left hand, the right used to brace himself on the desk or to summon rival bids from the corners of the room and sometimes, it seemed, to pluck them from the air. He was smilingly both enemy and friend. Johnny watched for a bit, and his anxiety had a saving touch of smugness to it, that he wasn't remotely covetous of these trinkets, triple strands of pearls shown on velvet charm pads, pre-war ruby rings with damaged but mendable settings. The weathered old dealers, barely raising their chins or lifting their biros from the catalogue to indicate a bid, and showing no joy in success or gloom at defeat, were welcome to them. Already his heart was beating noticeably as the picture section of the sale approached; his impatience for that was mixed with a nervous longing for delay. Now there was a silver and diamond brooch in the shape of a pug, very nearly like the one his father gave June for their fifth anniversary, and Johnny watched the bidding rise till it topped a good eight times its estimate, £420, and didn't know if he was more impressed or indignant.

He strolled off for a minute or two through the crammed

alley of pictures, hung three deep on the whitewashed brick wall of the old garage – a dark unframed canvas with a tear in it, several naked men dancing, warily titled *Mythological scene*, other po-faced descriptions, 'Interior with the artist's wife and a chest of drawers (£5–8)', 'Portrait of a middle-aged man (no reserve)'. He was oddly involved as he stared at the bottom left-hand corner of the portrait by the thought that the unknown painter had worked for several hours on it, at an unspecified date in an untraceable place with a sitter perhaps now dead – it wasn't very good but it recorded a serious effort to be so; and it was somehow sad, like the whole place. In the background, with ponderous flourishes and remorseless speed, the lot numbers were called out, climbing up, and the moment of drama in which he was destined to act moved stiflingly closer. He came back past the frames, which had a look now of having been ravished and jumbled, the batches muddled and the Dutch frame propped up on top, for everyone to see. He crossed and stood, which felt more careless and confident, at the back of the room, by the poised foot of the one-handed Mercury.

'And now,' said the auctioneer, 'the first of our lots of frames, lot 93,' looking vaguely but fondly towards them. A perfect indifference, as if he had said nothing at all, hung over the room; then a couple of the men who'd been bidding for jewellery got up and walked across in front of the rostrum on their way to the exit. Johnny's pulse was thumping, and a giddy sense that he alone had heard what the auctioneer said made him focus on his face in urgent embarrassment. 'Who'll start me at eighty pounds?'

There was something brutal in that amiable first naming of a figure. Johnny looked confusedly from side to side, his hand fixed halfway up, open-palmed, as if calming someone, and saw the man in the red anorak go out of the room, pulling a cap from his pocket.

'Seventy, then? A good Watts frame in this lot, a nice lot, four frames in total . . .'

Was no one going to bid? Would he get it, if he bid now? Or would he wait, paralysed, till the lot was passed? He saw a quite unsuspected person, a mere bald patch in the second row, lift an unconcerned forefinger.

'Thank you, sir. Seventy I have; seventy-five?'

Johnny's undecided hand seemed to catch the auctioneer's eye, and amuse him. Found out, he raised it further, and no sooner was his gesture accepted, 'Seventy-five, thank you very much, sir,' than he heard 'Eighty . . . eighty-five . . . ninety, thank you, sir . . . ninety-five,' in quick appalling sequence, his own attempted intervention swept over in the rapid chase of nods and barely lifted hands around the room, men all of them, sitting or standing, now revealed as the dealers. He felt they knew each other, they were against each other, but more than that, without thought or effort, they were against him, absurd pink-faced boy with shoulder-length hair and trembling hand. His secret strength was being Cyril's agent; but Cyril's limit for the lot was £90. Johnny glanced for a moment at the burly old man beside him, the man in the lead, with his thuggish illusionless head and look as if he'd rather be anywhere else. 'I'm selling . . .' said the auctioneer, 'for ninety-five pounds,' and it was obvious this man knew what he was doing, it was worth it, and Johnny raised his hand at the last moment, couldn't look at the man but from the corner of his eye saw him shake his head, and found he had won. One hundred pounds. There was a noise like the noise between songs at a concert, of the audience turning the page, as he called out his number, they didn't hear him and he called it again, and it was written down, his surge of success undermined in an instant by the knowledge he had transgressed.

'Lot 94,' no let-up – but Johnny wasn't bidding for this one. He studied the catalogue and bit his lip, and sensed without looking the sneering curiosity of the crowd about this new buyer. Then the bidding got going and he glanced up and no one was paying him the slightest attention. At once it was lot 95, Johnny double-checked, words and figures in momentary mutiny on the page, but he'd marked it, and it was right. Estimate £70–80, but he could go to a giddy one hundred and twenty, if he was sure of the Dutch frame. It had begun already, a man who had bid before made a shrugging first offer of sixty pounds, Johnny sensing the value of coming in late stood by, there was a bid of sixty-five, as if on the off-chance, and the first man dropped out; and no one else moved a finger, so that almost laughing Johnny lifted his hand, the auctioneer smiled back at him, courteously and to show he'd got him, glanced at the previous bidder, who dropped out too, and repeated 'Seventy pounds . . .' into the unexpectant silence. 'Any advance on seventy pounds? I'm selling . . .' the gavel lifted as he peered, with a knitted brow of humorous disappointment, from row to row, Johnny willing them to keep silent while an awful void, as unexpected as the crush of interest in the earlier lot, seemed to open around him and under him, in cold doubt of the clearly wrong decision he was making. These sour-faced men had been coming to sales like this all their lives, they knew a pukka Dutch ebonized frame from a fake when they saw one. 'Sold! for seventy pounds – thank you, sir,' and they made him call out his number again.

He waited, growing slowly less conspicuous, through a few further lots, and it was half an hour later he came out into the car park, clutching the heavy spoils of less than two minutes' unrememberable bidding: with a Watts frame he'd disobeyed Cyril to capture, and whose losses, out on the street now, seemed starker than indoors, and a Dutch frame that was a weirdly good bargain, but which might, to Cyril's eye, be an obvious fake. And how absurd it was, he had to get all the way back to Chelsea with the bloody things, paraphernalia he would never, on his own account, have had anything to do with. Somehow he managed it, on the train, the small frames tied together on the rack, the bigger ones between his knees as he sat and hoped at the half-dozen stops that no one else got in before Victoria. He angled them out, when they got there, very carefully. People looked at him and some of them smiled. He set the frames down, in the rush of the concourse, to sort himself out, and get them in the easiest order for carrying; it would have to be a taxi, and Cyril would pay. He put back his shoulders, lifted the frames up. He hadn't thought of it, which made it the more uncanny when he saw him, the man in the donkey jacket, head turning as if in its own light against the vast iron pillar, looking with a lazy intent past Johnny and then straight at him for a second through the fast-moving crowd, before walking off, with a work-weary tread, towards the entrance of the Gents. Johnny followed with his eyes, then a short way, hopelessly, on foot, and stood, breathless, unable to adjust or conceal his excitement, the seven frames slung like a punishment round his arms and his neck.

6

It was dark under the trees on the far side of the meadow, though spots of distant light showed through between them, and a late glow coloured the dull green wall of leaves above. In the foreground three pale saplings made a line. The early evening flared before it darkened into deeper mystery. Behind the right-hand sapling, covered by its grey trunk, ran a knotty thread. It was a rough canvas 'laid down' on a piece of hardboard, and damaged later by water down the left-hand edge.

The delicate detachment and re-sticking of the damaged portion had been done by Cyril, but the cleaning and retouching, with a fine brush whose every sleek and graded hair showed distinctly through the magnifying visor, was Johnny's own work.

Never before had he paid such minute attention to a painting, certainly not to one of his own – he saw it decompose itself under the lens, he had a view of it not even the artist had had, although elements in the design, which the artist must have understood, refused to give up their secrets. Evening in Kensington Gardens had been nearly night when the picture came in and was taken from its wrapping, the brittle layers of a twelve-year-old *Daily Mail*. The lifting of old brown varnish had brought out a low fence, a row of mere transparent dashes, across the foreground, and an unsuspected hurrying figure half-seen at the right-hand edge. And in the mid-distance, almost under the trees, was another small vertical presence, that might have been a person, a man in a jacket and hat or a woman in a short cape, but was so slender it could have been a statue, a bust on a plinth. Were there statues like that in Kensington Gardens? The vertical mark, a few quick brushstrokes, was a riddle. Over the week that he worked on the picture (itself painted surely in an hour or two), the image, the finite information of the brushstrokes and the indefinitely large suggestion they made, became somehow secret knowledge, and the presence beneath the trees took on an occult significance, like a figure of London life he was yet to meet. When he raised the goggles there was a second of giddy confusion that the picture he'd come from was only eight inches by five. Johnny had never heard of the artist, Paul Maitland, before last week, but now he felt an eerie involvement in his work. The buyer would see the scratched 'PM' in the dark impasto of the foreground, and never know that a half-inch of grey-gold grass, cut hay perhaps, in the middle distance, and other minute touchings-in among the dim green foliage, were the work of the invisible JS, some eighty years on.

'I'm going out,' said Cyril, 'which means you'll be in charge,' pursing his lips as he looked (which he rarely did) directly at Johnny.

'Oh, all right' – Johnny wiped his hands on his apron. 'Where will you be?'

'I'm going to have a look at something,' said Cyril. He sounded both stern and slightly shifty. 'Try not to sell anything, and for God's sake don't buy anything.'

'I'll just take it in, shall I.'

'Just take it in and give them a ticket,' said Cyril. 'They can reserve things, if they look serious. And of course don't let them in here. Never let anyone in here.' But just as he was putting his coat on the bell jingled and he looked through the door into the shop to see who it was. 'Ah . . . good morning!'

'You're going out,' said a man's voice from the shop.

'It's not at all urgent,' said Cyril.

'I've not been in for a while.'

'No, I'm pleased to see you,' said Cyril, with a drop to another register, guardedly flattering. He slipped off his coat and hung it on the back of the door, which he pulled half-to as he went to talk to the customer. It was a thin-voiced man, with the uncommon vowels, some plumped, some pinched, and the scurrying, dawdling manner that still flourished in the London art world. The tone of the conversation was almost abrupt, and neither he nor Cyril addressed each other by name. In the workshop the radio, on at medium volume, engrossed by the events that had followed the election, muddied the conversation. Johnny went to the bench where the cut-down frame for the Maitland was waiting.

Late Summer, Dusk was very much a Cyril picture. Cyril liked paintings small, and it was one of his hang-ups that subjects were spoiled by being treated on too large a scale – his ideal was the 'big small picture', in which a lot of life was conveyed in a tiny space. To Johnny, who at college had been encouraged to splosh paint over areas of canvas as tall as himself, this took a bit of getting used to. He felt its charm and its constraints. The Maitland also owed a great deal to Whistler, who was Cyril's god: it had the quality of a sketch, the rapid lifelike movement he lacked so completely in himself, but had an eye for in a picture. Cyril didn't deal in prints, and Johnny was told no painting by Whistler had passed through the shop in ten years; so the 'school' of Whistler was the thing to focus on. Once you'd gone for the school, obscurity became a lure, almost a virtue. It seemed Maitland himself was an artist only experts knew of, no one had written about, and no member of the public was likely to find in a museum.

Johnny freed the frame from its clamps and laid it over the painting lying on the workbench. Frame-making, at Hoole, was neglected – they showed their freaky portraits and gigantic abstracts unadorned on their stretchers and boards, or at best with a thin rim of untreated plywood tacked round, no gallery pretensions. Cyril was teaching him the further art of the wooden oblong – this little green and brown canvas now, on its first loose try in its 'Whistler' frame (really one gilt frame inside another), became suddenly focused and desirable, more present and also more covetably remote. It still looked too small – a further narrow slip would have to be cut and gilded in just the right shade to enclose it and hold it exactly in its shrine.

'Perhaps he'd care to bring it through,' said the voice from the shop, with its note of scant patience under perfect politeness.

Cyril looked round the door. 'I've got Sir George Skipton here,' he said, 'he wants to see the Maitland.'

'Oh . . . shall I bring it just as it is?'

Cyril stared and nodded confidentially. For a moment there was a clear understanding between them.

The customer wasn't how Johnny had pictured him. He had a lean hawkish face, his long sideburns a gesture at fashion resisted entirely by his camel overcoat, red scarf and trilby hat, which he'd kept on. He seemed carefully wrapped up against any of Cyril's inveiglements about a rare new picture; his thin smile made it clear that his listening to you did not in any way imply that he agreed with you. It was the smile of someone proud of his own judgement – hence surely the cleverly deferential tone that Cyril adopted with him.

Johnny laid the picture on the table, and said, 'The frame's not quite finished . . .' Sir George moved his head up and down as if surveying a far larger canvas, and made two barely audible noises, the first, with head raised, a momentary high-pitched whine, in which surprise and reserve were both implied, the other, with head lowered, a warm but regretful grunt. Johnny looked from one face to the other, unsure if he was being praised or condemned. Then Skipton's smile slid upwards from the painting to him.

'How do you find it here?' he said.

'How do I find it . . .' – Johnny gasped and glanced at Cyril. 'Working here, you mean. Oh, it's very interesting, sir.'

'You'll learn a lot from Mr Hendy' – at which Cyril looked aside and down in a strange way. 'He knew Sickert, you know.'

'Yes, I know,' said Johnny.

Sir George chuckled. 'Small oils,' he said, 'that's the thing.' His look played round Johnny's head, with a kind of critical amusement about his hair in its ponytail, folded up twice. 'Have you been working here long?'

'Oh . . . two months now, sir,' said Johnny.

'Two months' – again, praise and ridicule in his tone. 'And what do you think? Should I buy this picture?'

This time Johnny didn't look at Cyril, though he used his words: 'It's an extremely nice little painting.'

'Yes, quite. I expect you've done a certain amount to it?'

'We've just cleaned it up a bit,' said Cyril.

'Indeed,' said Sir George with a sigh, but still looking at

Johnny. Cyril seemed unhappy at this turn of events and Johnny himself felt uncomfortable till Cyril said rather brusquely,

'I'm asking ninety guineas for it.'

Johnny couldn't tell if this seemed steep to Skipton – whose face was impregnable to any vulgar shock of cost. 'Look, would you hold it for me, Hendy, and I'll come by next week and look at it again.' Was 'Hendy' how you spoke to a servant, or a colleague? – Johnny wasn't sure.

Cyril said he would, and looked displeased but unsurprised. There was a tempo to the art world – delays were written in to it, as well as frighteningly swift decisions. 'Thanks so much,' said Skipton, and as he went, as if unwilling to waste more time, towards the door he turned back and said, 'No, my daughter told me you were working here.'

'Oh . . . really?' said Johnny.

'The exquisite Francesca,' said Sir George.

'Oh! I see . . .' said Johnny, beaming suddenly and feeling himself in some sort of trap. 'I don't really know her.'

'Oh? Well, she's taken quite a shine to you,' said Sir George, which sounded the kind of parental certainty often far from the truth, and in this case embarrassing in other ways. Johnny felt he could tell one truth at least, but it came out oddly,

'I think I'm a bit scared of her.'

Her father seemed puzzled for a second by his tone, but added very drily, as he opened the door and tightened his scarf round his neck, 'I think I know what you mean.'

When Skipton had left, Cyril put on his coat with resumed impatience, and dashed off. The door banged, the bell protested losingly, and a little Chelsea view hung seductively near the entrance rocked from side to side on its hook. Johnny stood in the eddy, oddly aware of how Cyril, prey to the rival tugs of selling and buying, owned everything here, it was the world he had made and would live and die in; while he himself was merely, barely responsibly visiting on his way to a very different life, where of course he would be painting pictures of his own.

Today was Thursday, early closing, so it was only till one. He stood looking out past the wares in the window at the parked cars by the kerb and the occasional pedestrians, any one of whom might decide to turn in to the shop and set the still air, with its smell of wax and linseed, jangling again. He felt relieved, light-hearted and exposed, and went through to the back of the shop frowning at his own desire to mess around. His rebellion took the form of turning the milled dial of the old wireless ten degrees, to Radio 3. Beethoven, at once, but which symphony? He ruled out Three, and Five to Nine inclusive – he wasn't so sure about the earlier ones. As often in the past at home, or in his shared study at school, where he had to claim odd half-hours between his friends' Doors and Stones for intoxicating shots of Mahler and Strauss, he felt the presence of an orchestra as a private overwhelming luxury; and then, being alone, he turned it up and made noises, not singing along, little hisses and yelps of emphasis and agreement.

He got back to work, painting the fine angled slip with a gold paint that sank into the untreated wood. It gleamed and then dulled in the violent dazzle of the scherzo – number Four, surely? He set it on a sheet of paper to dry, and there was the racket of the bell again, and the repeated jangle that half-covered the closing of the door. He looked apprehensively through the blue and then through the clearer red glass in the door of the back-shop, a woman by herself; then he went in – it took him a moment to recognize her from behind, in a long black coat and red boots, peering closely at a landscape then standing off with a shake of the head. 'Oh, hello!' he said. 'That's funny.'

She looked at him over her shoulder. 'Why is it?' she said.

'Oh, it's just that your father was in here half an hour ago.' He came forward.

'That is funny,' said Francesca, 'very funny.' She looked at parts of him other than his face when she spoke, she examined his paint-smeared old Sotheby's apron. 'So you've met Daddy' – she smiled narrowly at him then, so that he saw her daddy in her, at the moment she distanced herself from him: 'Was he being difficult?'

Johnny sniffed. 'I think he rattled Cyril a bit.'

'That's what he does,' said Francesca, sounding pleased at least by her father's consistency. 'He's a great rattler. I don't suppose he bought anything?'

'He's thinking about it.'

She savoured this. 'Well, he's a great thinker too.'

'He seemed to know what's he's talking about.'

Francesca perhaps found this remark misplaced. 'You'll have to come and see his collection,' she said, in a tone which didn't promise an immediate invitation.

'I'd love to, thank you,' said Johnny, feeling this must be a privilege. 'What does he collect, mainly?'

'Well, he's got three Whistlers, for instance,' she said. And as if that was enough about that, 'So this is where you beaver away.' She looked round again, as if more intrigued by the existence of the shop than by anything specific in it. 'A lot of pictures' – advancing and looking very quickly at two or three in a way that might equally have conveyed ignorance or unhesitating connoisseurship. Then she stared at the half-open door behind Johnny, with its coloured glass window let in and the uninterrupted noise of the radio beyond. 'I suppose all the fun takes place at the back.'

'I don't know about fun,' said Johnny, and felt slightly ashamed. 'No, it can be fun.' He was pleased she wasn't going to see round the back. 'That's where I am mainly, I don't come out here much.'

And in a moment of course she was going towards the door, and Johnny with a pained smile following her. She peered in broad-mindedly, a hand on the doorknob, like an adult shown the children's playroom. 'Gosh, all those frames.'

'I know,' said Johnny, keeping close by her as she crossed the threshold. 'You're not really —': he felt he couldn't say it to her; and she ignored the bad form of what he'd started to say. Anyway, why shouldn't she go into the room? He found he wanted her to see it, it confirmed what was otherwise a mere rumour about what he did all day. He made something chivalrous of it, looking round with fresh eyes at the stove, the tables, the two hundred frames hanging inside each other on the wall: 'Cyril doesn't like people coming in here, I don't know why.'

'Well, Cyril's not going to know, is he,' said Francesca.

The Maitland which her father was or was not about to buy was on the table. She picked up the magnifying visor and fitted it over her blonde curls and was suddenly inside what Johnny had been doing. He thought even so she wouldn't be able to tell. Standing back she was clumsy for a second before she took the visor off. Neither of them said anything about the picture.

'So do you get time off for lunch?' she said, direct but tactful. Who knew what picture-dealers' apprentices got?

'Well, today it's early closing. I'll be shutting the shop in ten minutes.'

'Oh, good. So we can have lunch together.'

'Oh! . . . yes . . . all right' – he had no other plans, but this one was a bit of a jump. 'If you don't mind waiting.'

'Not a bit,' she said, and sat down unnervingly in Cyril's chair.

'I suppose, um . . .' – but anyway he got on with fixing the gilt slip, with the feeling, as she watched him, that he was acting out his own job. He didn't want to refuse her, that was the thing.

She got up after a minute, and looked into the small glass-windowed cubicle, like the office in a garage, which was where Cyril did the books and where there was a square safe under the desk. Johnny had never had more than a glimpse into the safe, last thing on Fridays, which was when the week's takings were carried in Cyril's briefcase to the safe deposit chute at the bank, and when Johnny himself was paid, with an odd little cough on Cyril's part, as if to counter any hint of warmth or congratulation. He had seen that the safe had things in it other than money. 'Is this him?' she said.

'What's that?' He was worried about her making trouble for which she, at least, would not be punished. He put down his brush and went over. She was looking at the framed photo on the wall above the filing cabinet, Cyril thirty years ago, with another man, looking at a picture, which Cyril was holding in his hands. 'Yes, I don't know who the other man is.'

'Oh, well, it's John,' said Francesca, 'John Rothenstein. Daddy knows him – and Evert, all that lot. Evert used to work with him at the Tate.'

This should really have been Johnny's territory. 'Oh, did he?'

'John used to *run* the Tate,' said Francesca, masking her impatience with a sentimental smile at his pug-like Mandarin face and circular horn-rimmed glasses. Beside him Cyril, looking not a day younger, was wearing a remarkable canvas garment with buttons up to the chin and no collar. Its cuffs too were buttoned back, perhaps to save them trailing in paint and glue. It gave him a specialized, ecclesiastical air.

'Cyril hasn't changed,' said Johnny.

'He's still got that silly coat on,' said Francesca, and the joke was funnier than it should have been – a first break in the high-pitched tone.

The bell jangled again and Johnny went through to see who it was. To his horror it was Cyril, closing the door and turning towards him with a picture in a carrier bag under his arm. 'Success?' said Johnny eagerly, stepping forward as if expecting him to unwrap it and share the joy at once. There was no way

Francesca could be smuggled out of the back room, but his instinct, even so, was for delay.

Cyril's response was a clearing of the throat suggesting it was none of Johnny's business. 'Anyone been in?' he said.

Well, it was a chance. 'Actually, Sir George Skipton's daughter came in. Francesca, you know?'

'The one you're scared of,' said Cyril.

'Well, not really,' said Johnny, 'no, no. In fact she's here now.'

Cyril stared. 'Where is she then?'

'Well, she wanted to see the Maitland that her father's interested in, so I said—'

'I'm here,' said Francesca, looking round the door, and coming towards Cyril with her head on one side as if at the great pleasure of meeting him at last. 'Francesca Skipton.'

'How do you do,' said Cyril.

'My father's always talking about you,' she said.

'Well . . .' said Cyril, and with a little nod at them both he went past her and into the workshop. Johnny followed a few seconds later. A dread of almost parental disapproval was mixed with a feeling of defiance that was just as childish. The music carried on, a harp concerto now, and he hovered by the radio, unsure whether to turn it off. Cyril went through to the office, where Johnny saw him stoop to unlock the safe and slide the white carrier bag and its contents into it, and lock it up again.

'Have I dragged you into the mire?' said Francesca when they were out on the pavement – 'I wasn't quite sure.'

'I'll let you know tomorrow,' said Johnny. And now there was the more pressing thing of lunch to cope with. They went up Old Church Street, both slightly self-conscious.

'Ivan's going to join us later,' said Francesca.

'Oh . . . OK,' said Johnny, and his relief that he wouldn't be alone with Francesca was mixed with relief that he wouldn't be alone with Ivan. Again he had a certain flustered feeling of being talked about: Francesca seemed to have a plan. 'I don't know about Ivan,' he said.

'Oh, Ivan . . .' – she chuckled in an odd way that suggested no friend of hers could be safe from ridicule. She glanced at him narrowly. 'No one's quite sure what's going on between you two.'

'Well, nor am I!' said Johnny.

Francesca had a judicious look. 'You don't fancy him.'

'No, he's extremely attractive . . .'

'Just not your type, then.' It was as if Johnny was spoiling things.

He blushed. 'I'm just not his type, I think.'

But it seemed she was on his side. 'Well, you're far more attractive than he is,' she said.

'I think he likes me,' said Johnny, laughing in his surprise at her remark.

'Hmm,' said Francesca. 'So you mean you've never done it with him?'

Johnny had done it with few enough people to feel reluctant as he said, 'We kissed, you know, but that's about it.'

'Well, he's sillier than I thought,' she said, and as they turned the corner on to the busy street she took his arm, as though to reassure him. They were astonishing questions from someone he hardly knew, but they showed she had got his number: she wasn't taking him out with any designs of that kind herself – and at this he felt suddenly light-headed. 'We're going to Bond Street,' she said, looking over her shoulder. 'Blast, that cab's gone.' She left him and went back past the turning to get ahead of the shoppers spaced along the kerb but the only cabs that came in the next few minutes were already taken too.

'If we're going to Bond Street,' Johnny said, 'we can get the 14 bus.'

Francesca blinked distractedly at this. She even ran thirty yards, to catch the eye of a cabbie emerging from the mews opposite, but he turned right, very slowly, ignoring her in his turn. 'Wanker,' she said.

'There's a 14 coming,' shouted Johnny, running the other way, towards the stop, and raising his hand.

They sat at the front of the upper deck, the one place of notional privilege on a democratic bus, amid the sour fug of smokers past and present. Francesca had nothing smaller than a five-pound note, but she paid for them both, when the conductor at last came upstairs. 'This is on me,' she said. 'Well, this is fun.' Of course Johnny felt responsible for the bus, and for the heavy delays it fell into by some clumsy instinct. Francesca watched its progress, and watched the black cabs slipping past it and darting ahead and out of sight. Now the bus lumbered to a bus stop where a large group of tourists in bright rainwear almost blocked the pavement as they massed and funnelled in at the rear. At last the conductor pinged the cord, and they edged out five yards into the traffic backed up at the lights; which, on account of a blockage beyond the junction, changed twice before they passed them, the brief roar of progress braked immediately as they homed in on the person with arm raised at the next stop along.

'I mean, it's hopeless if they're going to keep stopping,' said Francesca.

'Well, it's sort of how it works, I suppose,' said Johnny, with a little shrug at its undeniable drawbacks.

'Do you do this a lot?'

Johnny knew the rhythms and speeds of London transport, knew his Tube lines and four or five bus routes, and in the routines of waiting, letting one bus dismissively go and nodding satirically at the long-delayed sight of another, he still sensed the original beauty of living here. 'Every day,' he said. 'To get to work, you know.' He was pretty sure Francesca didn't go to work herself. 'Do you have a job?'

'Not yet . . .' she said. She might have meant things were not that desperate, but just possibly that she did have something in view. 'No, I'm making plans, about various things – you'll see.'

'Oh, OK,' said Johnny. 'About work, you mean.'

She smiled but didn't quite look at him. 'You'll see.'

It was late for lunch when they got off the bus outside Burlington House, but clearly Francesca had no hidebound ideas about mealtimes. 'So where do you want to eat?' Johnny said. He was ravenous.

'We're going up here,' said Francesca. And as he followed her up Bond Street, past Asprey's and other old jewellers whose names he didn't recognize, past clothes shops English and Italian, the Fine Art Society soon on one side, Sotheby's on the other, with not a glimpse of anywhere to have lunch, he began to feel not only hungry but resentful. Francesca, striding onward in her scarlet boots and black coat, was the match for any of the mannequins in the windows; men and women coming towards them dwelt on her with just a hint of amusement at her style, and looked at him too to see how he was related. He felt he had to absorb, or share, or repel their varying reactions to her, the penalty of the shy with the un-shy. 'Here we are,' she said, leaning suddenly on the tall glass door of Fenwick's and with a second's show of weakness as Johnny reached above her to push and hold it open.

'I've not been in here before,' he said, 'have they got a cafe?' All he could see was the complicated gleam, mirrors among panels of white and gold, the round and square stations of the cosmetics sellers with their glass display counters and further small angled mirrors, among which you had to thread your way to reach hats, scarves and lingerie. A strolling woman in a wide-shouldered suit offered Francesca a squirt from a tester and as she ignored her Johnny bared his wrist instead. In the fifteen seconds before it dried, flapping his hand obligingly, Johnny caught a sweet stab of freesia – it was a game the assistant didn't much like playing, with a woman's perfume. To him it was a memory of a game, with his mother, in Freeman's at home, or for a big day's shopping in Coventry, she quite firm, when they went in, about what she wanted, but testing anything on offer. 'I've no space left,' she would say, 'try it on him!' In the car going home he offered her his wrists in turn, she took her hands in turn off the wheel, and they shared a world of sensation and suggestion, not always agreeing. He saw Francesca on the far side of the shop, and went after her.

She was standing with her hand on one of the tall stools where customers perched for consultations, and gazing at a woman on a similar stool two counters across. The intervening displays half-concealed her, though the young woman in a black frock who was applying the make-up was perhaps aware they were being looked at. The customer was a woman of about fifty, in a green floral dress – she had taken off her coat, which lay on the counter beside her handbag. She had something awkward but committed about her, greying hair fiercely permed, the fading discomfort of someone still hot from the dryer. Francesca said nothing, but her raised hand brought Johnny under the puzzling spell of the moment – were they avoiding an encounter, or springing a surprise, or simply spying? He wondered for a minute if the woman might be a member of the Memo Club (but he didn't think so); a friend of Iffy's, perhaps . . . ? The girl moved round to fill in the merely sketched make-up of the left eye and eyebrow and Johnny saw her now full on. Framed by the upright of a cabinet on one side and by a pillar on the other the cosmetic artist was a work of art in herself, her large oval face burnished with graded layers of pink and something close to gold. Her eyes glittered between long black lashes, her mouth was a glossy purple red. It was flawless, a make-up for the camera, a diva on a box set, and with something underneath it pressing through none the less, a certain heaviness of resistance. She glanced across at them now – with a twitch of the mouth which might have been amusement or irritation at being watched.

Perhaps the customers were stirred by the glamour of the staff, who were advertisements as well as artists. Johnny felt unhappy watching, with other shoppers passing by, but Francesca's outstretched hand made him play the strange game. The woman raised her chin and turned her head patiently, as prompted by the large girl in black; when she could, she glanced in the mirror on the counter. She was unaware of the spectators, but determined to present a new face to the world, to the street, when the session was done. She looked somewhat anxious, but the session itself was a treat, and not to be rushed. There was a sense besides that the girl had nothing else to do, and was lazily stretching the job out, anchoring her customer's attention with a raised knuckle under her chin, two fingers at the temple to steady her as she darkened the doubting lashes into beating signals of attention. She said things to her, barely audible, now and then, calming and convincing her. When the woman looked down, the girl turned to Francesca and Johnny, stared for a second, and stuck out her tongue.

At last it was done, the customer stood, looked quickly in the mirror over the counter, put on her coat. She didn't want to stare at herself, transformed now like the assistant, a Turandot among the Thursday afternoon shoppers. She bought a little box, like Johnny's watercolour tin, coloured squares, and took her purse from her handbag. Francesca came forward, smiling like a waiting customer, her impatience concealed in a cool concern for the customer before her. 'You do look nice,' she said.

'Oh . . . !' – the woman looked at her uncertainly, almost touchily, but a compliment had to be taken for what it was. 'Thank you.' The girl gave her her change, which she put into her purse, and then, very quickly, as if forced to perform some intimate act in public, she took out a pound note, folded it, and slipped it into the girl's relaxed but retentive hand. 'Till next time,' she said.

They watched her go, her tight-curled head passing out into the street.

'Lovely,' said the girl.

'Wasn't she a darling,' said Francesca.

'Mrs Tucker,' said the girl, 'from Guildford.'

'Mm, and where is she going now?'

'She sees her friend Sylvia in Clapham once a month. She always comes to me first.'

'Wise woman,' said Francesca, with a funny chuckle.

Johnny was aware the girl was looking at him, as she tidied the counter. 'Hello,' she said.

'Johnny, this is Una.' Una put her hand out coyly, but when he shook it her grip was firm. He stood there in the well-meaning uncertainty of introduction to the friend of a friend.

'Johnny Sparsholt,' he said. She studied him, as she must have studied strangers twenty times a day, with the still competence of the professional. She saw problems and possibilities.

'We're going upstairs, dear,' said Francesca.

'OK,' said Una, turning to replace her pencils and brushes beneath the counter.

'Who's on this afternoon?'

'Not sure – Greta?'

'Oh, I love her.' Francesca drew him on, with a hand for a moment under his upper arm. 'See you in a bit.'

They went through to where the steep-stepped escalator trundled untiringly upwards.

'Is Una coming up here?'

'She'll come up when she finishes. She's meant to have forty minutes, but if they're busy . . .' – she looked at him, on the step below but level with her: 'Poor thing, she works so hard.'

In the cafe everything was small and expensive, a menu of items you didn't precisely want; he ordered fish pie. As the waitress turned away Francesca excused herself and went off to the Ladies, and Johnny sat back and slipping the coloured band off his wrist pulled his hair into a bunch and snapped the band around it. He looked blankly at the menu in its stand, and was sunk for a minute in the department-store mood, the dim murmur of voices beyond rhythmical escalators, the air of refuge from the street, the interest and tedium of shopping for clothes, toiletries, soft furnishings. It was his own school holidays again, only child of a mother who didn't work, but kept busy, who took him in with her through glass doors, over flashy marble downstairs, along carpeted perspectives above, where men in late middle age fussed for you over measurements and checked on the phone about discontinued lines. All the shop's promise of abundance was pinched and sorted into lines, things in stock, or on order, or no longer available. The most imperious shopper must adjust herself to the available, fall in with the range, the season's styles, become in a way the servant of the shop – or of course take her custom elsewhere.

'Ah,' said Francesca, settling as the waitress brought their drinks. 'No, it's not Greta . . .'

Johnny turned in his seat. 'What is it . . . ?'

'I admire her, though, don't you?'

At this late hour for lunch only half the tables were taken, shopping bags tilted against chairs, and between them, moving patiently and courteously, strolled a tall young woman in a beige tartan suit with a short matching cape and a pillbox hat. With raised hands turning and pointing as if discreetly undecided about which way to go, she gave the sense, none the less, of having a clear purpose. She smiled at the lunchers, her gaze dropping across the tables, as though to note what they were having, but not meeting their eye. She engaged them and released them in a passing moment of goodwill and just perceptible embarrassment: it was odd to be invited to stare – though she was too polite, in her serene revolutions, to stare at them.

'They don't still do that . . .'

'Don't you love it?' Francesca did stare, a calculating look, with a sly lift of an eyebrow when the woman came alongside. 'Is it available in other colours?' she said.

The young woman stopped, though a tendency to revolve still showed itself above the waist. There was a consciousness of drama in asking her to speak. 'Yes, love – I think there's sort of a reddish one? Maybe a blue, but I'm not sure we've got it.' She snubbed her nose. 'Do you like it then?'

'Oh, it's not for me,' said Francesca. 'Do a turn for me?'

And with a subtle feeling, not unwelcome to either, that the rules had been broken, the girl turned her back on them, lifted the cape and angled her bottom first one way then the other.

7

He met up with Francesca and Una again at six thirty, outside Liberty's, and they took him to a small bar in a side street off Regent Street, where you wouldn't have expected a bar to be – was it a new arrival or a survivor? Beyond the pub door with its small opaque window was a heavy curtain that kept the draught from the drinkers and his main effort once they'd skirmished past it was to seem unfazed, even happy, at being the only man there. Una pushed her way through to the bar, though it wasn't a struggle, she was greeted and patted by two friends as she pressed past, and she leant across the counter, unsmiling, for a kiss from the barmaid – if that was the right word. Johnny did spot a grumpy-looking man with short grey hair in the corner, who suddenly got up and came to the bar with the unmistakable arse of a woman. His main worry was that they would object to him, and he nodded his hair forward to conceal himself, without supposing it would fool them.

In fact when they'd been there ten minutes, and Una had introduced him to one or two of them, he had a feeling he'd been briefly admitted to a more civilized place than usual – a kind of high-minded solidarity, untouched by any sexual interest, seemed to support him, without going quite so far as to welcome him. He felt it would be bad manners to stay too long. He saw too that Una, who said almost nothing, was a figure in the bar – not far from where she worked, on the hinge between Mayfair and Soho. Francesca this evening was decidedly Mayfair, played up to her poshness and temperament, and drank beer from the bottle with just a bit too much carelessness. Una and Johnny had gin and tonics. A friend of theirs called Mary, small, dark, beautiful, in tweed jacket and brown jodhpurs, asked him what he did.

'I'm an artist,' he said, 'yes, I'm a painter,' in the palpable spirit of the bar of being what you wanted to be.

'What sort of thing?'

He sensed the question was clever, not philistine. 'At college I was an abstract expressionist,' he said, 'well, lots of us were, not just me! Now I'm hoping to focus on portraits.'

'*Not* abstract . . . ?'

'That's right.' A quick flirty calculation was allowed in his study of her head, and her clothes. She seemed wittily to be a lesbian now and also forty years ago, but he wasn't sure. 'Have you been painted?'

'Oh, not yet,' she said, as though she had a proper sense of when such a thing should happen. But also as if some proposal had casually formed. In the first small lift of the gin, a pub measure, not much, but nicely unfixing, he felt (what he wasn't of course) in love with her, and watching her then, as she drew out a soft leather pouch and constructed a roll-up, was abashed by her quiet authority. 'You wouldn't have so much freedom, of course,' she said, 'being a portrait painter. You have to please people who often have no idea about painting.'

'I hope once I've got started they'll know what sort of thing they're in for.'

'That's true. And it's certainly a more dependable source of income,' Mary said. 'I only say all this because my grandfather's a painter. You may not have heard of him.'

'What's his name?' He sat forward on the low stool and twiddled the ends of his hair.

'You don't have to pretend you're a woman,' said Una.

He blushed and laughed, on his mettle not to take offence. He never thought of himself as feminine, though women looked at him and spoke to him, in rivalry and understanding, on the street, or in the disordering gale of the Underground. And at that moment someone touched him on the shoulder, he turned apologetically, and she said, 'I like your hair!'

'Oh, thank you . . . very much,' said Johnny, and kept on blushing, the centre of all this chaste female attention.

'I'll do it for you, if you want,' said Una.

'Oh . . .' said Johnny, flattered, and unnerved a little, as he hadn't thought it needed doing. Then he played up, shook it back. 'That would be great' – he tried to hold Una's eye as she studied him, speculatively, biting her lip at the scale of the task.

In the restaurant Fran and Una spoke about the Sol y Sombra with a mixture of excitement and scepticism Johnny found hard to follow. 'You've been to the Solly, haven't you?' said Francesca.

'No, I haven't,' Johnny said. 'That's the thing.' It had been dangled in front of him for the past two months; he'd stood outside its door.

'I thought you were going with Ivan?'

Johnny shook his head. 'Well, we went. But the power went

off that night. We got there and they'd put a sign up – they'd had to close.'

'Oh, you'll love it,' said Francesca.

Una didn't seem so sure. 'It's somewhere to go,' she said. 'Anyway, we'll be all right now.'

'You mean, now the power's back on?'

'Oh god, do you think Audrey will be there?' Una said.

'God,' said Francesca. 'I don't believe she'd dare.'

'I think she will,' said Una. And they talked to each other about Audrey for a bit, while Johnny's smile faded. The girls were taking him out and showing him life, and he felt a small shameful reluctance that he didn't have a man to explore with. Well, Ivan was supposed to be turning up later, but he was a worry as much as a help. 'So shall we get the bill?' he said.

Francesca looked at her watch. 'You are keen,' she said.

'So how are we getting there?' he said, when they were outside. He wasn't going to risk the bus again.

'Taxi,' said Una.

'Or we could take the Underground.' He saw his funds for the evening running awkwardly thin. 'It's probably quicker . . .'

'Oh, the *Underground* . . . !' – Francesca stood, in apparent indecision, gazing at a spot a few yards away on the pavement, beneath which she seemed to picture it running. 'Is it still open?'

Johnny looked at his watch. It was ten past ten. 'Well, yes,' he said. And he saw in a moment the Tube as perhaps she imagined it, rather than as he knew it from frequent use – a deep proletarian labyrinth, a sort of human sewer, rumoured to underlie the whole city.

'Oh, but look—' and she ran a few steps into the road and somehow caught the eye of a taxi driver passing the end of the street, who backed up and turned and in twenty seconds was taking her instructions through the open window.

In the cab, as it swept round Trafalgar Square and out into Pall Mall, Johnny had the uncomfortable but elated feeling that his London life had taken off, not how he'd imagined it, but the unimagined, when it happened, had the bite of authenticity. The women travelled side by side, and Johnny sat on the folding seat, looking at them and past them, at the vanishing road and the lights of other vehicles surging up or dropping behind. He still felt hungry, he had only had one thing at the little Chinese, and then the bill was split three ways and he couldn't protest. You ate almost in the kitchen there, with the poor splayed roasted ducks hanging just above your head like lanterns. He pushed down the window an inch but the throb of the engine shivered it shut in two or three seconds. Racing backwards to his first gay club, he felt a little queasy.

'This is it,' Francesca shouted to the driver, and they stopped at a narrow white building on the Earl's Court Road. A small queue had formed outside, and there was a certain defiance in showing so plainly where they were going. The cabbie looked out warily.

'You don't want to go in there, love,' he said to Una, 'it's a poofs' place.'

'Yes, we do,' said Una.

Francesca paid him, and took the change in full, and flapped her hand in front of her face when he drove off in a loud fart of diesel fumes.

Ivan was coming down the other way, from the Tube station, his duffel coat unbuttoned, and the long fringe of his woollen scarf bobbing like a sporran between his thighs. 'Darling!' said Francesca, so that Johnny didn't know where he was, after all she'd said about him earlier. Ivan kissed the two girls, dodged a kiss with Johnny by butting his head against the lapel of his coat. Johnny felt the quick squeeze of tension, was anxious and lustful, watching Ivan unwind his scarf, and was drunk enough to put his arm round his shoulders and leave it there. He seemed as drunk as they were, and engaged with the girls more than with the friend who was loosely holding him.

'Here we all are then,' said Francesca, as they edged a yard closer to the door. She winced at Johnny – 'Sorry about this hideous wait.' It was the disconcerting thing, where a brilliant person is drunk. She turned to Ivan, narrowed her gaze again. 'There's something funny about you. Where have you been?'

'Me?' said Ivan, cautious but pleased.

'You've been up to something.'

'I had to go and see that old friend of mine in Hampstead Garden Suburb . . . you know.'

'I do think it's good of you to go all the way out there.'

'What's this?' said Johnny.

Ivan craned round to see who had lined up behind them, and when Johnny squeezed him he shrugged free and murmured, 'I'll tell you later,' which seemed a promise with a hint of a threat in it.

They went into a narrow space inside the door, music audible now, swing doors beyond like a cinema and a glimpse when they opened of the bare room at the start of a party; the large man in a bomber jacket glanced sceptically at the girls. 'You know this is a gay club,' he said.

'We've been here thousands of times,' said Francesca, looking wanly past him.

'So you're lesbians, are you?' he said.

'Don't be vulgar,' said Francesca.

'How you going to prove it?' said the man.

Francesca sighed and looked away, as if dealing with this kind of person were a quite new indignity; then Una, with a hint of a smile on her large flawless face, pulled her towards her and with a tilt of the head started kissing her with a steady pushing and chewing motion which Francesca, while taking no active part, made no effort to prevent. Johnny giggled in amazement, and felt a sudden knot of excitement that he and Ivan might be made to do the same thing. 'Whoa, whoa, whoa,' said the bouncer, but it took him another ten seconds to separate them. He looked Johnny and Ivan up and down. 'Right you are, gentlemen,' he said, and unhitched the rope for them all.

It turned out you had to be a member – Francesca claimed she was, but this time couldn't prove it, so they all had to sign a list and give their address, which made Johnny uneasy; he imagined them getting in touch with his aunt, and he put a different number in the street. It cost 50p each – 'And of course you get your meal,' said the little Irish boy in the lit cubbyhole. Then it was 10p to leave your coat. 'Shall we put ours together?' said Johnny, 'save money,' but Ivan said, 'No, it's OK.'

From his duffel coat Ivan emerged in a green silk shirt, rather creased, and very tight black flared jeans. It was a startling change from the Oxfam flannels and braces, and Johnny had a shivery feeling of him revealed in layers. He followed him through into the club, looking secretly at his hard round bum and the sliver of neck where his shirt collar was tucked in. They all stopped at the bar, Ivan turning and showing in his strangely amused stare round the room that standing them a drink was the last thing on his mind. 'What will you have?' said Francesca – and while she ordered, Johnny strolled off casually, as if returning to an old haunt, to get the lie of the club, excitement and fear mixed up in his half-drunk sweep through the space. There was the bar, and then round the corner a square room with a diminutive dance floor, a chequerboard five squares by five, the squares pulsing underneath in sequences of red, white, orange, blue, and just two men on it, staring and frowning at each other as they stalked and touched and parted and touched again. They had a long silk scarf that they trailed and drew

across each other's eyes. They were silly, but they were men, a
bit older than Johnny, and they touched again and kissed so that
Johnny looked away and looked back smiling in confirmation
and shock. He went through further swing doors into the
black-painted toilets, which like the rest of the club had an odd
vacant readiness, Price's candles on the ledge above the basins,
cheap smell of disinfectant. He pissed, washed and dried his
hands and looked at himself in the mirror, let his hair down, and
put it up again, judging the effect as if he'd never done it before.
Was he more in hiding one way or the other? No one knew
who he was anyway. He left it up, and went back, past the
dance floor, empty now, swinging his hips as he walked, looking forward to dancing, and into the bar, which was filling and
getting noisy. He came up behind Ivan, gently straightened his
shirt collar, and laid his hands on his shoulders – Ivan looked
quickly back, said, 'Ah, Jonathan,' and passed him his beer
bottle from the bar. 'Cheers!' said Johnny, and clinked bottles.
Ivan touched him lightly just above the waist. 'So here we are
at last,' he said.

Una bagged a table, and they sat leaning forward to hear each
other over the music. 'Did you have any luck at that sale last
week?' said Ivan genially.

It wasn't what Johnny wanted to talk about. 'Oh, yes, well,
I got what I wanted.' He looked narrowly at him for a second.
'It was so funny,' he said to the girls, 'I ran into Ivan at Victoria
last week.'

The girls didn't seem to think it was that funny. 'Mm . . .'
said Francesca, and looked away.

'How was your uncle?' said Johnny.

'Oh, very well – we had a great time.'

'Where did you go with him?'

Ivan seemed distracted by talk behind them. Francesca said,

'Oh, my god, she is here. Don't look now.' Una and Ivan turned their heads, and stared at someone who'd just arrived at the bar.

'She looks awful.'

'*Frightful*,' said Francesca.

In a few minutes Johnny offered to get them more drinks, and they all said yes, Ivan drinking up quickly. In the crowd at the bar he wasn't sure which of the two women the frightful woman was; he had the sense of pressing his way into the gay world, alone among dozens of people all knowing from previous experience what was going to happen. He didn't know what to expect, in his limbo with Ivan, but people smiled at him, a man turning from the bar with drinks lifted high raised an eyebrow and grinned at him. In the mirror behind the barman he could barely see himself between the optics and ranged bottles. He ordered and waited, holding his wallet, and saw enough to know the man leaning beside him was looking at him, then felt his hand on his upper arm. A handsome man in his thirties, with swept-back blond hair and good teeth. 'Are you with Franny?' he said. 'Yeah, I thought I saw you, I'm an old friend of hers – Tony' – and they shook hands. 'What's your name?'

'Oh, Johnny,' said Johnny, pleased to be talking to someone among these strangers, and abashed by Tony's physical presence, the tight blue T-shirt and, glimpsed when he looked down to pocket his change, the big jutting packet, oddly round, as if he wore a cricket box.

'I'll come and join you,' Tony said. 'Really great to meet you.'

When Johnny got back to the table a fat middle-aged man with a tray was hovering there. 'It's your salads,' he said, and started to unload little bowls among the bottles and glasses.

'Oh, god,' said Francesca.

'I'm not hungry,' said Ivan.

'It's all free, it comes with your membership,' said the man, smiling firmly.

'We've already eaten,' said Francesca.

'It's just your salads,' he said, as if a salad were a medicine, and with the air of someone used to resistance, for all his pleasantness. 'You've got to have them.' He put down four forks wrapped in paper napkins.

Johnny peered into the bowls, which each contained a bit of iceberg lettuce, a ring of tomato and (almost hidden, unnameable) a glistening square of meat. He sat down when the man moved on to the next table, and unwrapped a fork. 'I didn't know we got this,' he said.

'Don't eat it,' said Una.

'No?' said Johnny.

'It's the licensing law,' said Ivan, 'they have to serve a meal.' This seemed to Johnny both absurd and quite fortunate, he was more hungry now than he'd been before dinner, and food was here, the shameful stopgap of the boozing student.

'Well, doesn't look too bad.' And with the others gazing at him, and then thinking it better to resume their conversation, he ate his lettuce and tomato, there was no dressing on it, and popped in the pink-grey tongue-sized piece of meat, which he chewed uncertainly, thinking it was probably ham, pre-packed, sweaty, and with a knot of gristle in it that he had to bring out behind his hand and hide in the bowl under his screwed-up napkin. It was dismaying, and connected in a momentary violence of image with the glazed squashed ducks earlier. Sometimes meat disgusted him. He took a swig from his cold beer bottle.

Ivan raised an eyebrow into his fringe and gestured to his own bowl. 'Have mine . . .' he said.

'No, thanks,' said Johnny. 'Or, well, actually . . . ,' and switching the two bowls, he ate Ivan's salad too, it only took a minute, smiling defiantly as he chewed and thought of other things of Ivan's he'd like.

And when that was done, the thing with the force now of some future anecdote, he pulled Una's salad towards him, and polished it off. He rested, he felt some natural deference as he looked at Francesca, then he smirked, and she said, 'What? Oh, go on,' waving her hand over the bowl as she turned her head in mingled amusement and disgust.

Ivan put up a struggle, only partly humorous, when Johnny tried to pull him to his feet. 'Maybe later,' he said, and squeezed Johnny's hand as he pushed him off. So it was Johnny and Una who edged on to the bright pulsing square of the dance floor. Una hardly danced herself; she angled her shoulders moodily and moved her weight from one foot to the other; now and then a powerful quiver passed upwards through her large body, her head nodded and then settled again as the wave passed downwards. She gazed at a spot beyond Johnny, or else at the floor just in front of her toes. Johnny smiled and touched her loyally on the elbow, feeling men rub against him, bump into him, wanting a man to dance with, feeling the tense start of a new freedom, then starting to strut to and fro between the other dancers, and loving dancing, surprised by a desire to be looked at, smiled at, not laughed at – he felt himself balance and sway, cheerful but lonely. Then he turned back to Una, and found she'd given up dancing and gone to the bar. At the edge of the floor there was the risk of being shoved off it altogether by raised elbows and shrugging shoulders. He stood for a bit jiggling, watching, on the margin, in the hollow tension of not knowing where Ivan was: his eyes searched for him among the cute couples and grinning groups of friends, faces hollowed and shadowed as they danced on the upcast light of the floor. Just behind him when he swivelled Francesca was with the

man Tony, looking over the floor like grown-ups at a children's
party.

He could just hear her saying, 'Yah, his father's David
Sparsholt, of course.'

'Oh, really . . .' said Tony. 'Yeah, he looks a bit like him.
Does he talk about it?'

'Oh, god, he wants to get away from all that. He's . . . he's
an artist,' Francesca said, 'a painter.'

'I think I'd like to see his work,' said Tony.

'I knew you'd fancy him.'

'He's got a great arse,' said Tony. And Johnny, thrown by
the compliment as much as the bleak inescapable phrases before
it, pushed his way into the crowd that was swinging and pointing to 'You're So Vain', and swung his arse about just a bit too,
in half-proud, half-indignant reaction. He thought he saw
Colin and his heart sped up – it was someone who looked like
him, his smile barely returned, the wave slid back down the
beach . . . but in his reawakened absence he was gripped by a
longing for particular men he'd fixed on in streets and shops,
the black businessman reading *Le Monde* on the morning bus,
the young barman at the Chairman's Arms: why shouldn't the
world of fantasy step on to the dance floor and show itself as
real, touchable, kissable? Two men dancing with a girl pulled
him in, and he joined the game, pointing and mugging, 'You're
so vain! You prob'ly think this song is about you . . .' – it was
last summer at college, a song he knew all the words to. 'What's
your name?' said one of the boys, hand on Johnny's shoulder
as they bopped. He told him, grinned back at him, unsure if the
question was social or something more, but thinking already,
did he fancy him, if it came to that? But it seemed he was the
boyfriend of the other man, the more handsome one, and they
both danced with the girl, pretty, Indian perhaps, as if the point
was just to have fun. He saw Ivan, standing beyond the dance
floor, looking on, with a faint smile and the hunch, which

Johnny understood, of someone unable to let himself go. He took his new friend's hand, then put his hands on his shoulders and danced with him for a minute, throwing his head back and laughing, and when he looked round again Ivan had disappeared.

At the bar later on there was a huge fat man who could well have been in his fifties, in a blue shirt hanging out all round like a sheet; he was joking to the barman over the heads of the people in front. Johnny and Ivan had to squeeze round him. 'Ooh, hello, mischief!' the man said.

'Hello, Bradley,' said Ivan, and leant in and up over the broad frontage to kiss him on the cheek. 'This is my friend Johnny Sparsholt.'

Happily Bradley didn't hear. 'Are we all going to dance?' he said. It turned out a skinny boy, under-age almost, with dyed blond hair, was with him, and had got them drinks.

'Hello, I'm Jeff,' he said, rather tartly. They all seemed to consider the prospect of Bradley on the dance floor, and the exodus of other dancers it would require.

'I love dancing,' said Bradley, and raising his glass he moved his hips in circles, nodded and bit his lip. He leant forward and said to Johnny, 'They all know me here, darling. I've been coming for years.'

'Oh, right, I see,' said Johnny.

'I don't think I've come across you before, though!'

'Oh . . . no' – Johnny feeling that Bradley was an act and he would have to play along, while the others watched, amused or pitying, he wasn't sure. 'I've not been here before.'

'Oh, I've been coming here for years. They all know me.'

'How do you know Ivan?'

Bradley hesitated, put his arm through Johnny's and pulled him slightly aside. 'I've got a cock, darling.'

'Oh . . . yes.'

'I haven't seen it for years and years, but I know it's down there. And do you know how I know?' Johnny simply shook his head. 'Because I could feel it being teased, darling – teased and teased beyond endurance by Miss Ivy Goyle. Terrible name, isn't it, *Goyle*, sort of goitres and piles, which I don't have by the way, and never have had.' He looked sharply at Johnny, who shook his head again—

'No, nor have—'

'She's the queen of the cock-teasers, is all I'm saying.' Johnny understood at once, and felt he should defend his friend, even so, and at the same time conceal the humiliating fact that he hadn't known this all along.

'Come on, Bradley, behave yourself,' said Jeff, and led him off towards the further room.

Half an hour later Tony was bumping his bum against Johnny's as he danced with Francesca, and then when Johnny got out of the way turning round and pulling him in with a long muscular arm. Tony grinned all the time, it made you look a prude or a bore if you took exception to him. Also he was a friend, of some sort, of Franny's, Francesca's. The three of them danced together, while beyond them, with all the energy and determination of a normal-sized person, Bradley was bopping and thrusting his arms in the air. It seemed in fact everyone did know him, he was a star as well as a fool, and little Jeff pranced round him in delighted orbits. Johnny smiled at the spectacle, fell in with the mood of the club. Now Tony was getting behind him again, he felt him tugging his hair, and Franny too, very drunk as she helped him – it didn't matter to him, he let them pull off the band and shook his hair out, shook it in Tony's face. 'Wow!' said Tony. 'You look amazing.' With a strange wise pissed look Franny moved away.

He didn't like being pestered, but then wondered why not, the feel of Tony's body, as they danced with their arms round each other's waists, was beautiful, warm hard muscle under the thin T-shirt, Johnny mostly avoiding his gaze, and when Tony pulled him in tighter and his hand slid down over his arse he found he was hard in spite of himself. 'There you are . . .' said Tony, but didn't press his advantage. 'You're a great dancer!'

'Oh, thank you,' said Johnny, very gratified but wary of Tony getting round him.

'I can't believe I'm dancing with you.'

'Oh . . .' said Johnny.

'It's so cool.'

Johnny shrugged, he saw what was happening.

Tony smiled at him more narrowly, pushed his right hand through Johnny's hair and said in his ear, as if it wouldn't have struck him before, 'David Sparsholt's son's gay!'

'Well, there you are . . .' said Johnny, pushing back.

'I mean, what does he say about *that*? Could be interesting!'

'I'm sure it could,' said Johnny. He looked away, at the floor between the dancers' feet, the lights changing in their not quite followable sequence. 'I've got to go to the gents,' he said, Tony holding his forearms now, just above the wrist, keeping him captive and certain of success. He held on longer, quelling resistance, and grinned still as Johnny jerked his hands away—

'Hurry back . . . !'

Johnny took his time, roamed back afterwards to the bar, in a growing childish feeling that he wasn't enjoying himself. When he'd bought a beer he had £1.05 left. He went and danced by himself, on the edge of the dance floor, looking round for Ivan. Tony was dancing with another man, dark-skinned, curly-headed, older and more attuned to his game. He looked over and touched Johnny on the shoulder. 'No problem, by the way.'

'That's what you think,' said Johnny, not loud enough to be heard over the music, and taken by Tony perhaps as some kind of gratitude. It was 'Living for the City', it brought everyone out, playing up, friends shouting along with the words, which

Johnny construed in his own way. Una and Fran were locked together, Johnny didn't like to look at them, in their closeness, though they were sealed up too in the obliviousness of drink. He danced beside them, Fran reached out to him, and staggered as she did. 'Have you seen Ivan?' he said. She looked down solemnly as if weighing some much larger question; it was Una who said, 'He's gone.' 'Gone where?' Una looked round rather vaguely, as if she might still find him. Fran leant on him, said in his ear, 'He said to say goodbye, you were tied up with Tony at the time, darling, he said he didn't want to barge in.' It was hard to judge her own feelings about this news, though she seemed, quite promptly, to understand his. She brought him close to her, they danced willy-nilly, bumping each other, and in a minute he felt the almost impersonal weight of Una's arm on his shoulder, and the scented warmth of her as the girls, saying nothing more, pulled him in.

8

'You're not a bad driver,' said Ivan.

'Oh, thanks very much!' said Johnny, and wondered mildly why it had taken him two hours to say so.

'I should really learn to drive.'

'I'll teach you if you like . . .' – Johnny put his foot down as he shifted into the outside lane, and was aware of Ivan glancing at the speedometer.

'It can't be all that difficult,' he said.

'You mean, if I can do it?'

'No, silly' – Ivan tutted and twitched back his fringe as he looked away.

'It's best to start when you're young, obviously.'

'No time to lose, then.'

'Ha, ha. I mean, I was driving when I was about fourteen.'

Ivan thought and said, 'Did your father teach you, I suppose?'

'He certainly did.'

'But how could you drive when you were fourteen?'

'Dad had permission to go on this old aerodrome near us, you could do what you liked.'

'You were lucky, then,' said Ivan, in a tone Johnny'd noted before – of pathos about his own father mixed with hidden curiosity about Johnny's. 'I expect your dad's a fantastic driver.'

'For god's sake. He was a fighter pilot, wasn't he,' said Johnny and not wanting the questions about him to start up again he pressed the black knob of the radio, turned it up. It was something he felt at once that he knew, massive, thickly scored, aerated by the wireless's warbles of distance and dense crunches of distortion. He edged the tuning dial very slightly into someone talking, and back more slightly still, and it focused and held for ten seconds, a quiet passage, hard to hear through the racket of the engine, Johnny pushing his head forward, staring down the fast lane as if at the not quite catchable name of the piece. Prokofiev . . . but he wanted to get it right, in front of Ivan. Now the heavy brass came tramping back, with battering timps and a bass drum too that jammed into a rattling fuzz of sound. He turned it down. And again it cleared, as they cleared the brow of a hill, the march stamped gleefully through to its slamming end, and applause burst out, fuzzy washes of sound, the ineffably judged pause before the announcer said, 'The Sixth Symphony by Sergei—'

'Prokofiev,' said Johnny, a fraction of a second before she did, '*yes*.'

Ivan looked up from the map and said, 'Now, when we've

crossed the Severn Bridge, we keep straight on till the motorway turns into the A48.'

'Just tell me when to go right or left,' said Johnny, and twiddled the volume right down so that the talk and then the music that followed could be barely made out amid the roar of the road and the thunder and whine of the overtaking traffic.

'Ah, there it is . . .' – over a crest in the road, the two towers, the low arc of the roadway, at an angle and foreshortened, the two white arcs descending to kiss it, a haze of rain on the river and the Welsh shore. 'Isn't it beautiful.' He felt Ivan took some pride in it: he looked up from the map, but said nothing. As they approached, it was as if a sketch resolved into a monument, sublime in its abstract absence of scale; then they came closer still and it rose and settled into place and detail. A minute later there was the swerve of freedom, half a dozen lanes, before the dark traps of the tollbooths. 'Have you got 30p?'

Ivan groped in a pocket. 'I'm not sure I have.'

'Look in the glovebox, Auntie Kitty usually has some change in there.' He slowed, joined a queue, wound his window right down. There was something to Johnny's eye quite new as they came in under the canopy, a flash of light against shadow as if a photo had been taken, when the woman in her cabin looked down into the car and saw them together, Ivan beyond him, peering across as he offered the coins with an up-stretched arm. They were a couple, travelling. And then, doubted still for the second or two before it happened, the barrier flicked upwards and rocked where it stopped in the air, in a passing salute.

When they were on the bridge there was no stopping, and the two rows of fences screened off the view of the river, the high-loaded ship that was sliding beneath. The rhythmical pulse of the air through the open window smelt of the sea. After the great bridge was the smaller unheralded bridge, over the Wye – and ten seconds later they were back on land. 'Welcome to Wales,' said Ivan.

'Thank you,' said Johnny, and laid his left hand on Ivan's knee.

Ivan shifted. 'Do you want one of your auntie's sweets?'

'Yes, please.' Ivan eased off the lid of the tin, in which chipped and sugared tablets, orange, yellow and lime-green, had fused long ago in a crystallized lump. 'Can I have orange?'

'You'll have what you're given,' said Ivan, prising off a fragment, and when Johnny kept his hands on the wheel, pushing the sharp sticky lump into his mouth, which Johnny pretended to resist, and licked Ivan's finger as well as the sweet. 'You've got sugar on your chin,' said Ivan; but this Johnny had to wipe off himself.

Twenty miles later the motorway ended, and they were on their own, and within half an hour on hilly roads almost deserted. Now the bluster of the wind in the car had a local softness and smell, freshened to a nice chill when they went fast, then slowing into warmth at a crossroads or a steep bend. They passed through villages and small towns with their chapels and shut houses and not much to look at. Sometimes a farm in the middle distance, in its shelter of old oaks, caught Johnny's eye. 'I can't wait to see West Tarr,' he said.

'Yes,' said Ivan, 'I hope you like it.'

Johnny said, 'As a Peter Orban fan . . .' and smiled at him, picturing the house from a small grey photograph, a thin glass-fronted box on a bushy slope; if nothing happened between them he would have to make the most of the building. He was nervously optimistic – the weekend was Ivan's idea, he was purposeful but mysterious. And at least in a Welsh valley, miles from anywhere, he probably wasn't going to slip off with someone else, as it now seemed clear he had done from the Solly.

Ivan was the host, with a necessary belief in the treat he was offering, and with something new in his tone, once the name of the nearest town appeared on the signposts: a furtive evasion of responsibility. 'Of course I don't know what it's like now, Jonathan. As I told you, no one's been there for two years, at least.'

'But someone keeps an eye on it.'

'Sort of. It's very hidden away.'

'Mm, I like the sound of that,' Johnny warming the talk when he could.

Ivan said, 'Of course you like modern things.'

'Don't you?' said Johnny.

They couldn't see the sea but there was a sense of it in the sky above the long bare hill, a freshness, a deflected lustre. The lane turned back from it, dropped slowly then steeply into the sheltered valley, there were a dozen grey cottages, a chapel, tiny, tin-roofed, and then the messy gateway to a farm, ruts strewn with hay. The broad fields above had just been mown. 'It's after the farm,' said Ivan, 'if I remember correctly.' They passed an overgrown gate. 'I think that's it.'

Johnny backed up, pulled in and let him get out – watched him walk down the short incline in front of the car, small, neat, urban against the unpeopled landscape. It was a light five-barred field gate, aluminium, tall nettles round the posts. Along the verge, and on the far side of the low broken wall, cow parsley held up its tilting crowns. Ivan was fiddling with the padlock. He was a puzzle, a stranger, grey flannels, Viyella shirt, no tie at least today, but a jacket on the back seat with everything checked in the pockets before they left: wallet, address book, fountain pen. At the petrol station near Chippenham, the pub where they'd had lunch, he had seemed embarrassed by Johnny's threadbare jeans, and the way people looked at his hair. Now he turned, and beamed, lifted and thrust the gate wide, and Johnny smiled back and let his foot off the brake.

The way down to the house had a high bank on the left, and a view through a hedge across the valley on the right. Clearly it was used, once in a while, by farm machinery, a tractor and trailer – the tyre-gouged ruts held long shallow puddles. Johnny was anxious about his aunt's Renault; anxious too that it should do the job. He smirked guiltily as they dropped and jolted, brambles tearing vainly at the doors, wild flowers thrusting their heads through the open window and then rearing back. The Calor gas canister thumped in the boot. Round a bend the track swung to the right into a field, ignoring the second gate, straight in front of them; beyond which Johnny saw no more than a pale horizontal, a gleam of glass among leaves, and felt, as he had all his life, the pull of any unknown building, and the odd but essential twist of fear in his need to look at it.

The door was at the side, the narrow end of the box. Johnny stood with the bags, shifting between concern about the blocked gutter and strip of white trim hanging off and a guest's pretence of being happy with everything. Ivan had a further key, a tatty label attached to the key ring, 'West Tarr', in rusted ink, a glimpse, as he pushed it into the lock, of the habits of the Goyles, who had come here thirty-five years ago. 'Are there any paintings by Stanley here?' said Johnny.

'Not paintings, I don't think. There are some of his things – you'll see.' Ivan struggled with the key, there was a moment's smiled-through doubt about it, and then they were in.

In the dark lobby Johnny felt at home, for all the mystery of that first minute, of closed curtains, half-seen objects, the stored and pickled smell of winter damp and baking sun. Hard to know now, in the small kitchen, with bathroom beyond, if it was warm or chilly. Ivan went ahead into a larger room, pulled back one floor-length curtain, then another, the sunshine fell instantly at an angle on low tables and a sofa which kept for a few seconds a look of intimate surprise. It was the living room, and behind a folding wall the studio, two easels, a high window looking the other way. Ivan turned a key, reached for a sliding bolt, pushed open a tall glass door and stepped out, as if his first impulse on being here again was to leave. Johnny followed him, more slowly, smiling, fingers on the metal frame, the tapered wing of the steel handle. He turned, stood, put his arm through Ivan's in thanks and encouragement, but said nothing as he took it in. It was a small house, and the whole point was its simplicity, as he'd known it would be, the very act of construction tempered by a longing to have next to nothing. Not much money, according to Iffy, a house for one artist built by another, both fired up with ideas about space, form, economy, something mystical as well as technical in Orban's soul. For Johnny the sense of being home was partly a feeling of being back at Hoole, where all these precepts still filled the air. Here a platform had been built, bedded into the hillside at the back and projecting in a broad deck at the front. The whole front of the house was glass, gazing out across the valley to the last ridge of hills that hid the sea. He craned over his shoulder at the edge of the deck, a drop of six feet into nettles and grass; then looked back at the house, the trees pushing round, grass and a small bush in the choked guttering, the sun-bleached and damp-stained linings of the curtains against the glass. He said, 'I love it!' and squeezed Ivan's arm.

'Was your college like this?' said Ivan, as they went back in.

'We had the same sort of windows,' said Johnny, making do with a detail, and caught in an unshareable memory—

'Leaky ones, you mean . . . ?'— Ivan scuffed his shoe-tip over the swollen and blistered sill.

'Well, they could be.'

'I just can't imagine living here, can you?'

It was something Johnny was imagining so vividly that he laughed. 'I think it's got everything I need,' he said, thinking really it would need Ivan too. He knew the hard square armchairs were an Orban design, and in the sagging bookshelves on the far side of the room he recognized three or four of the spines, bold lettering on torn jackets, Henry Moore, Mondrian, Kandinsky, old books on modern art. Ivan searched for a moment and pulled out a smaller book, wide-format, and passed it to him: 'Did you read this, I expect?'

'What is it?'

'Evert's little monograph on Stanley.'

'Oh . . . yes . . . interesting,' turning a few pages, 'I mean no, not yet.'

'Ah, I see,' said Ivan, crossing towards a further door. 'Well, have a look at it.'

'I will . . .'

'It's very good indeed.'

'I'm sure it is,' said Johnny, sensing there was a line about Stanley and that he must be careful. He stood looking at the small sameish colour plates for a minute, then put the book down and went after Ivan, who was pulling back the curtains in the room beyond.

There was the main bedroom, which had a low double bed covered by a yellow counterpane but with no sheets underneath – long unused but still with the indefinable presence of a bed a particular couple had occupied for years, its confidence and privacy. And in a windowless room behind there was a narrow single bed, with boxes stacked on it, cardboard soft and bulging, books dropping from the bottom of one as Ivan lifted it and quickly put it down, brown bowls and plates and pitted chrome candlesticks in the other, which Johnny looked at distractedly as the unnamed but undenied likelihood came clear: they would be sleeping together. Ivan went out to turn on the water and electricity, while Johnny picked up the bags and came back alone into the main bedroom. Vacant, cross-lit by the three o'clock sun, the bed was a stage, floating in shadow. The truth was he had never spent the night in a double bed. They had come with four single sheets and Kitty's electric blanket, and he spread them out under the cover, and plugged the blanket in; nothing, then the little red light came on. On the wall above the near bedside table hung a small woodcut: a naked man and woman, Adam and Eve, rough and darkly inked, the man heavy-hung, the woman heavy-breasted. Johnny sat down on the hard edge of the mattress, the Goyles just out of view but present, as a challenge and perhaps a reproach.

To make tea they had to link up the Calor-gas cylinder to the stove, and give the lime-scaled kettle a good clean-out. Johnny liked these tasks, playing house with Ivan, a hand on his back as they passed in the narrow space between sink and table. 'I'll make a fire later if you like, dry the place out a bit.' He felt one eagerness merge and take cover in another.

'Oh, if you like,' said Ivan. 'Or I can do it.'

'I'm just going to look in the studio.'

He found there were paintings, six or seven oil sketches stacked in the corner, unframed and possibly unfinished, in Goyle's later minimal style; they looked feeble to Johnny, routine startings going nowhere. He felt but of course didn't say that there was something depressing in general about the way Goyle repeated himself, to the point of monotony; perhaps to him each new work had been an adventure, but to the casual eye he appeared to be stuck in a rut. In a cupboard in the lobby, smelling of old macs and boots, there was a folder of drawings on an upper shelf. 'I found these,' he said, taking them into the kitchen, where Ivan was pouring boiling water into a brown-glazed teapot.

'It was always said,' said Ivan, as if from a vantage point much later in life than twenty-three, 'that Stanley couldn't draw at all. He said himself that when he got into the Slade he couldn't draw for toffee, but the professor there was very sympathetic and said, "Don't worry about it, young man – just get on with painting" – he saw he had a gift.'

'Yes,' said Johnny, who could see that Stanley had thought

in paint, not in line, there was nothing graphic at all to his slabs of slate colour and dull green and his grey-black sea. He remembered the small landscape, almost an abstract, that Cyril had cleaned and which had introduced him to Evert and to Ivan himself. Without that little painting he wouldn't be here now.

They sat down side by side with their tea to go through the folder of drawings. 'I don't know, they look all right to me. What do you think of them?' said Ivan. Johnny turned over the dog-eared sheets of cartridge paper, faintly damp and spotted here and there with mildew; the sketches seemed to him per-fectly competent, and more varied than the paintings: details of walls, fallen trees, the tin-roofed chapel they'd passed in the village. Tucked in underneath them were three studies of a mid-dle-aged woman in the nude. 'Oh, my god, it's Auntie Jen,' said Ivan, ' – sorry, I wasn't expecting to see that.' He giggled and covered his mouth. And there was something funny in the contrast of Auntie Jen's large-breasted figure and her tightly permed sharp-featured head. She wasn't a nude model, such as Johnny had got used to studying at Hoole; she was a housewife who'd taken her clothes off in the middle of the day. She sat with thighs stoutly apart, and a worried look, as if she'd just remembered something in the oven.

'He was a randy old goat,' said Ivan. 'You know he wrote these poems about her that caused a bit of a stir locally. There was a famous one that began, *I come to you, loins bared.*' They both laughed, Johnny gazed at him and thought, wouldn't it be best to kiss him now, put an arm round him, get the whole thing going?

But there were jobs to do, a start on jobs that could have gone on all weekend. They swept up, hundreds of dead flies, two dead mice, had a go at dusting, the dusters themselves worn through. There was a Ewbank which Ivan pushed squeaking over the three faded Indian rugs. Johnny did the bathroom (narrow, toplit, ingenious), the first water hoarse and rusty from the taps. He went out and picked heads of cow parsley from the bank beyond the house and set them in two earthenware pots on the dining table. It was a pleasure in itself, with a feel of preliminary ritual. 'They're not really indoor flowers, are they,' said Ivan.

'I like them, I'm going to draw them,' said Johnny. At which Ivan raised his eyebrows and said he would make supper tonight. Johnny politely held back, opened the bottle of Noilly Prat that Kitty had given him, and wandered off with the thick green tumbler in his hand, to look at things – the magic of the house and the lift of the drink offset the tension of the long summer evening.

Johnny held his nerve when they went into the bedroom. Ivan saw him take his shirt off, a moment's appraisal as if thinking of something else, then he went out again to clean his teeth. Johnny rolled the band from his wrist and tied his hair back, pulled off his jeans and socks, and slipped in under the sheet and the yellow bedcover, an old waxy smell re-awoken by the blanket beneath. He found the hot oblong in the centre of the bed, his feet in the cold damp margin. Then he got out quickly to turn off the overhead light – just the lamp on the bed-side table: he didn't mind which side he slept, he knew couples had their habits, one side with a small accepted deference to the other, his father, getting up early, nearer the door. Here the person with control of the lamp would perhaps be in charge. In his bag he had some KY jelly, used till now only to practise, breathless tension and yielding to his own fingers, which went only so far: he hid the tube just in reach under the edge of the bed. Ivan came back with a glass of water and a book. Johnny didn't watch him getting undressed, but saw him lift the cover and slide in beside him, in his vest and his string pants. 'Ooh . . .' said Ivan, nudging into the warm centre, where Johnny lay facing him. He sat up with the sheet pulled over his chest, opened the book and uncapped his pen; he wrote something, underlined it, and sat biting his cheek. 'I hope you're not a light sleeper,' he said.

'I can sleep when I have to,' said Johnny, edging over and with a small yawn raising his knee over Ivan's left leg and sliding a hand round his stomach.

Ivan shook his fringe out of his eyes as he wrote. 'You must be tired after all that driving, aren't you?'

'Mm? Not really,' said Johnny. 'I'm quite drunk, though . . .'

'You drink too much,' said Ivan, and turned the page with a nod. He wrote fast and vigorously, little rocking and circling movements passing up his arm into his body.

'What are you doing?'

'What do you think?' said Ivan.

'It must be very important,' Johnny said, 'if you have to do it now,' wriggling his fingers in under the hem of Ivan's vest.

'I'm writing my diary. It has to be done every day.'

Johnny worked his hand up over the silky warmth of his stomach, touched his soft right nipple. 'The day's not over yet.'

'If you don't write it down before you go to sleep you forget it,' said Ivan.

This didn't sound very flattering. 'So what are you saying about me?'

'Well, it's private, obviously.'

Johnny raised his head, watched him squint at the page in the lamp-light, amused or annoyed. He pushed himself up, kissed Ivan's neck and nuzzled under his chin, getting in the way. He let his hard-on make his case, pushing out at the waistband of his pants as he rolled half on top of him. 'Please . . . !' said Ivan, but he put the book aside, turned away for a moment for a drink of water, while Johnny in a trance of boldness groped in his pants, plump, semi-hard – then Ivan stretched up and switched off the lamp. 'That's better,' he said, snuggling back beside Johnny, who felt for him again, unaligned and with no idea in the sudden blackness of where Ivan was looking or what face he was making.

He woke early, 5.20 on his travel clock, the curtains light but the sun still behind the hills. Ivan was hunched away from him and also touching him, buttocks against his hip, a hard heel pressing his calf. Johnny shifted carefully, looked at what he could see of him in the dawn shadows, his shoulders, the back of his neck, the pale swoop of his vest. Rising on an elbow he took in the turned-away profile, soft but heavy in sleep, unwaking for minute after minute; the dark hair squashed up by the pillow where he'd pulled it round for comfort. Johnny dropped back, shifted so that only their bottoms touched, his boldly naked, Ivan at some unnoticed point back in his pants. He couldn't decide what had happened. He had spent the night with him, an achievement, nudging, turning and settling; but they hadn't had sex, not as Johnny thought of it and wanted it, and this was a failure – or it had the makings of one, after five months of waiting. Now the day after was beginning, and he felt tenuous, a stranger here, in the bedroom, the bed, of the copulating Goyles.

Ivan putting out the light – he felt it more than he should have done, like a small but lingering insult to his interest as a lover. Between their sighs and giggles, Ivan saying things, all the squirming round, big kisses sought and then half-avoided, he'd thought keenly of his hour in bed with Colin, its unstoppable, nearly speechless logic. Colin was totally a lights-on person, he loved seeing just what he was doing to you; and it was thinking of all that, in the teeming darkness, that had transformed him and made him fierce with Ivan, though he knew within seconds that he wasn't happy. 'Let's just play around a bit,' said Ivan, 'you know.' A few moments later he realized Ivan had come.

*

'The sea tumbling in harness,' said Ivan, very Welsh, looking out with the wind in his hair at the breakers rolling in far below.

'What's that?' said Johnny; he locked the car, and felt, by this second day, used to it, and even possessive.

'Oh, it's just a line from a Dylan Thomas poem,' said Ivan.

'Which one?' said Johnny. 'I love Dylan Thomas.'

Ivan gave him a quick doubting look. 'Let's go down,' he said.

The coast seemed to be all rocks and cliffs, except this one place tucked between two headlands, where a narrow white beach curved away for a sheltered quarter-mile. One other car was parked in the scooped-out parking place above; beyond it, a gap in the hedge and a rough path disappearing. A stream drained down through a little wood, the rocky path beside it, a stile at the bottom, and then the sand and breaking waves. The lone couple at the far end stared at the two boys – the woman had been swimming topless and wrapped a towel round herself as she came up to join the man, who lay reading on his front, half-hidden by a canvas bag, his hairy bottom naked to the sun. They were in their fifties perhaps, and to Johnny there was nothing exciting in the rare glimpse of nudity; though Ivan let out a disappointed 'Hmmm' when the man, who had ignored the woman's promptings, at last sat up and pulled on a pair of loose blue shorts.

'We should swim naked too,' said Johnny.

'Well, you can,' said Ivan.

'We'll have to,' said Johnny, 'we haven't got our things.'

'I mean I can't swim,' said Ivan; and it was clear from his faint smile at the horizon that he didn't like admitting this, and was hoping to suggest that swimming was a pointless activity anyway.

Johnny looked at him quizzically. 'So what would you do, if I swam out round those rocks and suddenly got into trouble? You'd just sit here and watch, I suppose.'

'Of course not,' said Ivan; and after a pause, 'I'd get that man over there involved' – and he glanced again along the beach to the plump figure treading down to the sea's edge, his chest hair all the whiter on his sun-browned body.

Ivan's joke was a kind of intimacy, though something within it was not. Johnny scuffed off his sandals, and pulled his shirt over his head, his hair falling on his bare shoulders. There was an image, lurking and folding in the tumble of the sea: the hour on a Cornish beach a long eight years ago, when Bastien held his eye and grinned and thought of someone else.

'Are you going in, then?' said Ivan.

Johnny said, 'I'll just soak up some rays,' and lay back on his elbows on the warm fine sand.

'OK . . . well . . .' – and Ivan had an odd expression, carrying on talking as he unbuttoned his shirt. 'I suppose Denis told you I'm a gerontophile, did he.'

'Oh, yes,' said Johnny, as if he didn't pay much heed to what Denis said.

'He tells most people.'

'Well,' Johnny glanced at the pale smooth torso he'd gripped, stroked, kissed here and there last night, but had hardly seen, 'do you mind?'

'Sometimes . . .' said Ivan, and sat back beside him. 'Do you know what it is?'

It was more delicacy towards Ivan than his own uncertainty that made him say, 'Sort of . . .'

'I tend to like older men, that's all.'

'Oh . . . I see,' said Johnny. Something clarified for him, a small sense of vindication mixed up with the bleaker meanings.

'I mean, I like young men too,' and he knocked his fist against him, as if Johnny had put him in the wrong.

'I can tell,' said Johnny chivalrously. 'Still, you like old men better?'

'Well . . .' Ivan smiled, the fist a finger now, running down Johnny's arm. 'Old-er. Not *really* old!'

So he had a new, serious and quite unexpected shortcoming, in Ivan's eyes: he was too young. It was wisdom turned on its head, but his immediate effort with all these disappointments was to be reasonable about it – it was frank, a confession, after all. 'I suppose there's more security, is there, with older men?'

Ivan twisted round and lay on his front, and to Johnny his round firm bottom seemed subtly different in the light of what he'd admitted. 'Perhaps that's it,' he said.

'Older people don't run off so much.'

'Oh, they can't believe their luck,' said Ivan, and had the grace to laugh at himself.

Johnny drew with a small stone in the gritty sand. 'And have you had . . . affairs?' – a note of irritation after all.

'Just this and that, you know. Nothing serious.'

'Right . . .'

'Not yet.'

'There are lots of old men out there,' said Johnny gamely.

'Oh, there are . . .'

'Just waiting for you.'

Ivan smiled at him and looked away. 'There's quite a lot of rivalry, you know, later on. You remember Jeff and Bradley.'

'Do I?'

'At the Solly.'

'The really fat old guy?'

Ivan raised his eyebrows. 'You say that, but Bradley's terrified Jeff will find someone even fatter and older, and run off with him instead.'

'Probably not run,' said Johnny.

The King's Arms was the hotel in the town, large and stony at the crest of the main street, and English in its bearing and its beers; Johnny couldn't decide if he was pleased or disappointed. There was nowhere else to get lunch, and he pushed open the glass-paned door into the hall with the apprehension of childhood holidays at the other end of Wales, the Sparsholt family torn between making do and walking out. 'It's all right,' said his father, his mother said, 'Mm, I don't know,' or it might be the other way round, Johnny prey to his own intuitions about the interest or dirt or smell of the place. Here there was a stale smell of beer and cigarette smoke, and as they looked into the lounge and then the bar something else under it, chilly, residual, the stink of cooked lamb. Johnny screwed up his nose, but Ivan didn't seem to notice. The waitress looked at them warily, and though the dining room was half-empty she gave them a table almost hidden by the swing door to the kitchen. Thick white cups inverted on saucers were part of the lunch setting, no tablecloth but blistered place mats with Lionel Edwards hunting scenes, just like his father and June now had, though neither of them took the least interest in hunting. The talk on the beach sank in, the odd shifting tension of pain and relief. He had got it all wrong. Ivan liked old men. All the hopes of the past few months were absurd. And yet here they were.

The lamb smell in the dining room was fresher, juicier, revived each day. Ivan ordered lamb, by unconscious suggestion, and Johnny had the chicken curry, written down carefully by the waitress, and clearly something of an experiment for the kitchen. There was a family at the table by the window, middle-aged couple, younger daughter and son of eighteen or so, towards the end of taking holidays with his parents, half-parental himself with his little sister. He sat back in a bored but uncomplaining way, made interventions, mocking, doctrinaire. His dark hair was parted in the middle, swept behind the ears. The barman came through with a tray, unloaded a Coke for the girl, a bitter lemon, two pints of shandy for the men. Johnny looked away, gently startled by his own absorption in the family, his sense of recall, the boy unreachable on the far side of the room. There was a glimpse under the table of blue shorts, brown legs. 'Well, don't make it too obvious,' said Ivan.

After lunch Ivan sat reading the obituaries in the *Telegraph*, and when the other man in the lounge went out he jumped up and seized his *Times* to compare the obituaries there. Johnny looked at the advertisements in *Country Life*. Did he prefer a magnificent Georgian house in Hampshire with ten bedrooms or a magnificent Elizabethan house in Cheshire with six acres and a staff cottage? To a guest at West Tarr they both looked rather overdone. He wrinkled his nose. He was struck by how he didn't get used to it, in fact the reverse, the smell pervaded the room, seemed to hang in the dusty pelmets and curtains and settle deep into the brown armchairs. He got up and wrestled for a minute with the unopening sash window. 'It's amazing,' Ivan said.

'What's that?'

'Percy Slater's died.'

'Oh, yeah . . . ?'

'The *Times* says, "He never married", and the *Telegraph* talks about his work with Hans Oder without even hinting that they were lovers for thirty years, though everyone knew.'

'Did they?' said Johnny.

'Well, almost everyone . . .' said Ivan, with a pert little smile.

Johnny banged at the window frame with his fist. He said, 'Not everyone wants every detail of their private lives in the paper.'

'Well,' said Ivan, 'you could argue . . .' – but he saw Johnny's point. 'I mean, do you know about Percy?'

Johnny turned, and went towards the door. 'Tell me later,' he said.

*

When they came back to the house, there was already, for Johnny, a ghostly sense of routine – Ivan getting out to undo the gate, the ruts and drops in the track remembered if not avoided, a more luminous pattern of two men passing their days together latent in the seizing of shopping bags, car doors nudged shut with a hip, the unlocking of the house, and the evidence on the kitchen table and the bedroom floor of the time they had spent here before they went out. Johnny stayed in the bedroom, pulled the curtains closed and lay down for an hour, feeling it just possible Ivan might join him. When he came back out at six o'clock he found him sitting at the little fold-down desk, writing in his diary.

Tonight Johnny was cooking, something else mastered last year at college, his best dish. Ivan, suddenly flirty, kissed him on the cheek as he poured him a drink and then leant against the sink to watch while he chopped onions. 'What is it exactly?' he said.

'I'm just doing fegato alla veneziana,' Johnny said.

'Oh, right . . . great,' said Ivan, looking thoughtfully at the ingredients on the table. 'By the way, we mustn't forget the postcards.'

'We must send one to my auntie, obviously.'

'Yes. And Iffy,' said Ivan. 'She'll want to know about the house.'

'And what about the girls?' All their friends seemed to have some sort of interest in their weekend.

'The girls definitely,' said Ivan. 'And I must send one to Evert.'

'Let's both send one, shall we?' said Johnny.

'Oh, OK – if you like,' said Ivan. 'And what about your friends? You must have friends from college?'

'Not really,' said Johnny.

Ivan smiled narrowly at him. 'Bit of a lone wolf, aren't you,

Jonathan.' He tilted his glass one way, then the other. 'And your parents?'

'Well, I could send one to Mum, I suppose.'

Ivan looked up almost slyly. 'What about your dad?'

'He's not really a postcard person.'

'It might be a nice surprise for him,' said Ivan.

Johnny drew the chopped onions into a neat line on the board. 'No, I'll send one to Mum and Barry, they'd like that.'

Ivan had the tactical smile of someone framing a new question; but all he said in the end was, 'I'll write Evert's card, anyway, shall I?'

'OK.' Johnny chuckled. 'You're quite close with old Evert, actually, aren't you?'

Ivan turned his brown eyes and large smile on him. 'Old Evert?' he said, 'Oh, I love him.' And as he went out through the door into the main room, 'Don't you?'

When he came back a minute later with the cards he said, 'I wonder what the girls are up to this weekend.'

'Yeah, I wonder.' They seemed far enough away to be talked about in a more exploratory light than in London.

'Probably going to that awful club.'

'Oh, I like it. The Solly, you mean.'

'It's all right,' said Ivan, flatly, the matter of their night there just under the surface.

'You'd think Fran and Una couldn't stand it, from what they say about it, but they seem to go there all the time.'

Ivan laughed and said, 'You know they want to have a baby.'

'Really?' Johnny stooped to light the gas, turned it up and edged it down. 'That might be a bit difficult!'

'There are ways, of course,' said Ivan.

'Adopting, you mean? – they wouldn't be allowed, would they?'

'No, silly, one of them would have a baby and they'd bring it up together.'

'Two mothers.'

'That's right.'

'Oh, OK . . . How would they . . . I mean how would it be done, physically?'

Ivan was a little obscure: 'They don't want to, you know, actually do it,' he said.

'No, right . . .' said Johnny, at sea once again in the radical imaginings of the lesbian world. 'So who do they want to be the father?'

'Well, they want someone they know,' said Ivan, and looked down rather sternly.

'I see . . . you mean they've asked you?' – Johnny laughed.

Again Ivan didn't quite answer. 'I wouldn't want to do it,' he said.

Johnny got on with moving the onions round in the hot pan – 'Oh, I don't know, I like small children.'

'First I've heard of that, my dear,' said Ivan. Johnny didn't answer either, but a few minutes later, as he dropped in the soft triangles of liver and the cold blood sizzled in the oil he thought two things: that there was a great deal about him Ivan had never heard of; and that after this week, perhaps even after today, he was never going to eat meat again.

He kept this to himself, and ten minutes later was forking down his dinner in a trancelike state, both eager and reluctant. He loved meat, he loved liver in particular, and while they went on chatting he found himself sighing and smiling at the imminent drama of change. It wasn't the taste but the intolerable meaning of food that came from slaughter that he wanted to excise from his life. The decision had been shaping inescapably for months, perhaps years, and even now he found he was keeping it, for a day or so longer, to himself. When they went to bed and Ivan snuggled up with his back to him, Johnny was happy just to lay an arm over him and hear him fall asleep. Long afterwards he turned on to his back and lay awake, his eyes reading more detail, and losing it, as the night darkened further, minute by minute, the shadowed rafters, the edge of the cupboard, the just paler stripe of the unlined curtain. The green darts of the hours on the square dial of his travel clock gleamed faintly, the luminous long hand hid the short hand for a minute at five past one, the little tick he'd heard muffled but amplified under his pillow at school for five years busied on uncomplainingly. He was excited, he turned and held Ivan again, his hard-on came and went, his hand lying, barely pressing, on the soft curved strip between his friend's rucked-up T-shirt and the waistband of his pants. He thought there were countless things he could do nothing about – being gay, and dyslexic, and in Ivan's eyes far too young. But this was a pure choice, it had the beauty of action, unlike the long compromise of being acted upon.

He woke again to a much brighter room, raised his head to see the clock, lay back, befuddled with late sleep and slow to understand, as the night's advances re-occupied his mind, that the pressure against his side was Ivan, sitting up next to him. He half-turned, looked quickly at him – he was on top of the covers, dressed already, in shirt and old grey flannels, leaning on his elbow to look down at him. 'You are a heavy sleeper,' he said. 'I've been watching you.'

'Oh have you . . .' said Johnny, huffing the sheet over himself, turning away, but then, with a slow yawning twist of his whole body rolling back to face Ivan. He had woken up hard as usual and wasn't sure if Ivan had noticed, or if he wanted him to notice. 'How did I look?'

'You must have been dreaming, you made little faces.'

'Well I dream a lot.' All his life he'd disliked being watched, but there was an unexpected sliver of pleasure in having been at Ivan's mercy. 'How long have you been up?'

'About an hour? I'm an early riser.' It was hard to work out the change of mood, Johnny looking up, wary but ready, into Ivan's eyes, with their glitter of promise and habitual reserve. Ivan reached out, the back of his hand for a moment against Johnny's cheek, fingertips tracing the line of his neck and running up, through his hair, holding him, his thumb just moving in tentative circles on the secret curve behind the ear. Johnny gasped softly, and with arms pinned under the bedclothes waited powerlessly for the kiss, not in the dark, after all, but in this thinly curtained daylight. He swallowed, closed his eyes, and felt Ivan pushing back his hair. 'It's amazing,' Ivan said.

Johnny laughed softly as he opened his eyes again. Ivan seemed to marvel at his face, his head, as if he had only just seen it, or seen what he ought to have found in it long before. 'Oh, yes?'

'Has anyone ever told you?'

Johnny looked solemn. 'I should get my hair cut.'

'No, silly.' In the new atmosphere Ivan himself hesitated. 'You look just like your dad when your hair's pulled back.'

'Ah . . .' This again. He turned his head slightly, stared past Ivan's shoulder. 'As far as I know, you've never met my dad.'

'No, but I know what he looks like, don't I.'

'Yeah,' said Johnny, 'I suppose so,' as if he didn't really mind, to get dad out of the way.

Ivan slid down more comfortably next to him, shrugged into his pillow, lay just smiling, his clothed knee above the covers pressing Johnny's naked one beneath. It was a long gaze, eyes questioning, avoiding and returning, and a doubt still in Johnny's mind as to what the question was. 'You poor thing . . .' said Ivan.

'I'm all right.' He braced himself, smiled slyly to show he was up for anything.

'It must have been so difficult for you,' said Ivan, and his hand still behind Johnny's ear made it hard for him to shift away. 'And, you know, finding out you were gay yourself.'

It was still strange to hear, in so many words, that he was. 'Well, it didn't help, I suppose,' said Johnny quietly. The point was, surely, here he was, with Ivan's soft breath in his face . . .

'Something so public . . .' Ivan raised his head slightly and leaning over him kissed him softly on the cheek, and then above his eye. 'I wish you'd tell me about it.'

The sense of years-long danger was mixed with a faint, never-faced uncertainty as to what the danger was. 'About what?'

'You know, when it happened.'

'It's all a bit of a blur . . . you know.'

Ivan's smile tightened for a second at this, then relaxed. 'I mean, did your dad ever talk to you about what went on?'

'No – of course not.'

'No, I suppose . . . .' Ivan laughed at himself. 'It would have been a bit odd!'

'That's right,' said Johnny, 'it would.'

'I just think it must have been so awful for you, with it on the news, everyone reading about it in the papers,' Ivan said.

'I didn't read the papers, Mum told me not to.' The bizarre idea that Ivan himself, at what? fifteen, had done so, came to him for the first time. 'Did you?'

'Oh, yes,' said Ivan, 'of course I did. Well, it was a big story, wasn't it, for a while. Money, power . . . gay shenanigans! It had everything.'

'Oh, yeah, it was perfect,' said Johnny.

Ivan lay back a little, still up against him, his hand drifted from his neck to the tight sheet over his shoulder, Johnny help-less in his hidden nakedness gazing close up at him. It had the fright of a new kind of excitement – to be in the power of some-one he was shiveringly keen to submit to entirely. 'And your poor dad at the centre of it. I mean how did he cope at first, you know, when he came out of prison?'

Johnny almost laughed, at his persistence, and at the coy

delay in whatever was starting to happen; he was making him work for it. 'He just carried on, really.'

'He must have picked himself up, somehow.'

'Dad always said, "Work's the thing,"' said Johnny. He thought no one had ever worked like his father, at whatever he did, and whether it was work or not.

'No, that's very good,' said Ivan responsibly. He stroked Johnny's shoulder before he went on: 'I mean, did you actually meet Clifford Haxby?' He made him sound like someone you might have wanted to meet, a film star.

After a moment Johnny said, 'Yes, I did.'

'I just remember that photo,' said Ivan, 'taken through a window.'

'Oh . . . yes.'

'I remember trying to work it out . . . you know . . . what was going on.'

'Well, I'm glad it turned you on,' said Johnny, pushing himself against him, as far as he could, with a little grunt.

'I mean, was Clifford in love with your dad, would you say?'

Johnny looked at him and at the question through the shimmer of his own early morning sensations. 'How would I know . . . ? Possibly?' – tender feelings had been nothing but sex, it seemed, in the glare of the case, and sex itself was a means to something else; but it was hard for him to think about, then or now. He shifted an inch or two, under the weight of Ivan's knee, drawn up a little further now, and holding him there.

'And what about your dad? Was he in love with him?'

'No!' said Johnny. 'Of course not.' He looked at Ivan, and his words took a strange weight and humour from the position he was in. 'Dad's not . . .' – he didn't know what was best – 'gay, not really.'

Ivan seemed slightly offended. 'Well, he must be bisexual, anyway, mustn't he.'

'No . . . well, I suppose he must have been, in a way. If he needed to be.' He met Ivan's smile with his own. 'You seem a bit obsessed with my dad.'

'Oh . . .' said Ivan.

'I can see I'm going to have to introduce you.'

Ivan laughed disparagingly, and they lay, not quite meeting each other's eye, in a tingling nearness that made Johnny gasp and twist with desire in his tight cocoon. Ivan leant in, gave him a soft kiss on the bridge of his nose, then swung round and stood up. He looked down at him for several seconds. 'When?' he said.

After breakfast Johnny said, 'I want to see what that building is.'

'Which building . . .?'

'Is it a barn – where the trees begin on the far side.'

'Oh, yes . . .' said Ivan. 'Well, let's have a walk before we go.'

Johnny's idea had been to go off by himself. 'If you feel like it.'

In five minutes they were ready. Johnny jumped off the edge of the platform and got stung on the arm by nettles for his bravado. 'You won't need a jacket,' he said as Ivan came round, having closed the windows, and locked the door. 'It's a boiling hot day.'

'Well, you never know,' he said.

'I can't tell what it is,' said Johnny. 'Have you been to it before?'

'I've never noticed it,' Ivan said, 'but let's see.'

They walked at first over the mown hayfields, already green with foggage. It was a lovely effect, the delicate first blades of grass among the silver stalks. Ivan was cheerful, but evasive, he went ahead, unusually alert for things to comment on; while Johnny was caught almost at once in the strange lulled swoon of each warm step to step: he saw how his footprint flattened the new growth and crunched the soft stubble inseparably. Ivan waited for him at the gate into the next field, nervous perhaps about the cows grazing a hundred yards off. He took Johnny's arm. 'Thank you for telling me all that, my dear, you know, earlier.'

Was he being sarcastic? 'Oh, well, it wasn't much.'

'No, no . . .'

'I never talk about it at all, normally, so you were lucky.'

Two or three of the cows noticed them, stared, unsure at first, and seemed to decide they were just about worth a closer look. Johnny wasn't frightened of cows; as a child he'd moved among them, on their friend Sam Peachey's farm; he slowed as he felt Ivan pull him forward: 'As long as you're all right,' squeezing his arm tighter for a second, as he looked round.

Johnny stopped, turned and waited, looked cheerfully into the brown face of the nearest cow, twenty yards off. 'I'm fine,' he said. 'I'm a Sparsholt, after all!', lowering his forehead and shaking his long hair, so that the cow stopped, puzzled a few moments, and cautiously dropped its head again to graze.

'And are *we* all right?' said Ivan, with a giggle.

'They're only cows, for Christ's sake,' said Johnny, as the others started coming forward, the whole herd following them for reasons of their own up to the next gate.

From here, when they climbed over and turned round, there was a clear view back across the valley to West Tarr, at an angle, glinting, and looking larger, among the crowding trees and bushes, than it did close-to. 'My word, it stands out,' said Ivan.

'Great, isn't it.'

'They'd never get away with it now, of course.'

'What year was it, before the War?'

'Nineteen thirty-nine,' said Ivan. 'It must have been easier then.'

From half a mile away the very notion of the glass box, the modernist ideal, seemed more principled, more foreign and more forlorn. Trees, grass, bleaching sun and rotting rain would undo any kind of house in time, but here these elements had been almost recklessly defied.

'It would be different in California or somewhere.'

'I suppose so . . .' Johnny saw that he was right – in England, in Wales, a building like this appeared a double self-assertion, against bad taste and bad weather. How much longer would it be there? As they walked in single file along the headland towards the ruined barn Johnny felt the pang of regret that came before leaving a place he would never see again. Ivan pressed on, while Johnny lingered and was brought almost to a stop. His father's word came from industrial relations – when they were out for a walk Johnny went on a 'go-slow': his parents got on with it while he hung back, unaccountably transfixed by the colour and the feeling of a field, a summer hedgerow, a church tower among trees. 'I don't know what you're gawping at, young man,' his father said, 'you look all gone out'; though his mother's impatience was different perhaps, a soft thwarted glance at the things she herself had once loved looking at and had been obliged to give up. In her smile there was a hint of hopeless allegiance. But not in Ivan's. He caught up with him, they walked to the next gate shoulder to shoulder, but it was a game of closeness, and Johnny, in the loneliness of his difference, felt something subtler than their failure in bed, but confirming it, that someone who shared so little of his mood could never share his life.

9

Fran said Johnny must do a picture of Una and herself together. The lesbian double portrait would be a novelty – at least she and Johnny couldn't think of any. Male lovers together were rare enough. There was the one from the 1940s where Benjamin Britten appeared oddly collaged on top of Peter Pears, and Johnny had cut out a picture from a magazine of a Hockney portrait of Isherwood and his boyfriend, sitting in chairs some way apart. But women together? They didn't discount the chance of there being some, but as Fran said it was the men who got all the attention. And now how were they going to be done? 'I've got a few thoughts about that,' she said.

The next Friday, after the shop had shut, Johnny walked down the street and round the corner into Cheyne Walk. He carried the black leather drawing case his mother and Barry had given him for his twenty-first, 'J. D. S.' stamped in gold across one corner. It was a bright early evening, the river at high tide, the throb and fume of traffic along the Embankment. He hadn't been asked to Sir George's house before, and he saw the visit as a nice step forward in his friendship with Fran, just shadowed by a feeling that he'd been called in, like some other workman, to do a job. He had an almost oppressive sense, as he pushed down the latch of the tall iron gate, which swung closed on a weighted string behind him, of being on her father's property, his flagged front path, in front of his tall red-brick house, a place where Fran and her friends would be kept in check by his sarcasm; and there was something further, intermittent but persistent, despite everything, the feeling of trailing a hint of scandal, in his makeup and in his very name, into places that would rather have done without it. Well, Sir George was away, 'In Frankfurt,' said Fran, as if that explained everything. Johnny stood a moment and looked at the beautiful old building. An ancient wistaria climbed up between the ground-floor windows and under the frail white balcony above, which it seemed to hold up while surely, over many slow decades, wrenching it away from the wall; mauve droplets of flowers showed still among the leaves. Two French windows gave on to the balcony, and one of them was open now, the narrow panes at an angle throwing back the sunlight.

Johnny spoke into the entryphone, but Una came down to let him in. In the gloom of the long narrow hall, closing the door and slipping past him to lead him upstairs, she was not just a friend but the inhabitant of Francesca's life, he felt it now – she went ahead of him, barefoot on the dark rugs and polished oak, with a kind of moody pride in the whole set-up, and a shy sense, when she showed him into the drawing room above, of admitting him to some new intimacy. But this, after all, was what he was here to capture. She stood and watched as he took in the room, the mild gleam from the river on plain oak panelling, the rich scent of polish, beeswax with a trace of turpentine, mixed up with the sweetness of white lilies in tall vases. He'd expected the place to be crammed with paintings, like Evert's house, but in this room at least there were only three, each glowing under its own brass picture-light: the Whistlers. He crossed to look at the smallest one, above the bureau opposite: a dusky horizontal with a boat and a man at the oar in silhouette against the grey water.

'This is amazing . . .'

'Do you like it,' said Una.

Then he had the dilemma of which to look at next. All three were Thames views, calmly hanging a few hundred yards from where they'd been painted. There was something worrying as well as wonderful about the narrow focus – it had the cool ruthlessness of Sir George himself, it was the soft-spoken proof of a complete success.

Francesca came in a moment later, kissed him on both cheeks and sat down before she'd really looked at him. She winced as she lit a cigarette, and snapped the lighter shut. 'You'd better take your shoes off, Johnny, with these priceless carpets.' He couldn't tell how much mockery, how much boredom at this house rule, was concealed by her hint of a smile. He

felt the more clumsy as he set down his drawing case and hopping forward undid his desert boots. She was wearing pointed
black heelless slippers, with tight black silk trousers and an
embroidered red chemise.

'Doesn't your father wear shoes in the house?' Johnny said,
placing the boots together by the door.

'What? – oh, Daddy does, yes, but *his* shoes never get dirty.'

He stood kneading the short silky pile of the carpet through
his old socks.

'Do you want a drink?' said Una. And though he did he
said,

'No, I'll wait till I've done the drawing, it's probably
best . . .' – wanting to be sober, and not wanting them drunk,
when he was working.

'We'll all wait,' said Francesca, and looked thoughtfully at
Una.

Johnny went to the window, stepped out, a bit testingly, on
to the thin strip of the balcony, with its delicate wrought-iron
fence. It was curious, the little altitude above the pavement, the
island of public garden with holly trees and benches, and then
the road, the balcony trembling when the lights changed to
amber and the juggernauts started their rumbling ascent
through the low gears. Beyond the traffic, between the plane
trees, lay the grey expanse of the river, the cold wellings and
streakings of its currents. And on the other side, an odd ruinous
nothing – which Whistler (when Johnny came back in and
looked again) seemed already to have noted in the three brown
brushstrokes whose mere accidents, the spread and flick of a
loose hair, the ghost of a bubble, the sticky split second as the
brush left the canvas, were also small miracles of observation, a
wall, a roof, a chimney rising through mist. Well, it was genius,
and he smiled round at the women, who were looking at each
other steadily through Fran's cigarette smoke.

Genius was inspiring, but Johnny felt he would rather not

draw them in here. 'Is there another room we can use?' he said.

'Another room?' said Fran.

'Somewhere a bit brighter?'

'Oh, I see,' she said, with a smile that showed she was only partly convinced.

'The kitchen,' said Una.

'Well, OK,' said Johnny.

'Or what about upstairs?' said Fran.

'OK,' said Una.

Fran stood up and carried her cigarette on to the balcony, from where she flicked it into the garden of the adjacent house. 'I've got this idea for the pose,' she said.

'Yes, I've got a few ideas,' said Johnny. He felt it was important to keep some control of the situation. He followed them upstairs, and along a passage, taking everything in slyly as they talked. And there, above a bowl of potpourri on a walnut chest, was *Late Summer, Dusk.* 'Aha!' he said.

Francesca turned, saw him smiling thinly at it. 'Oh, isn't it your picture, darling?'

'Yes, it is . . .' He was proud to find it here, ahead of him, but it was worrying too, after the pristine works downstairs. The retouches gleamed treacherously. He didn't like to look too closely, but surely Sir George must know?

It was something he wondered again as they shifted things round in the bedroom. If Fran and Una, pulling up the duvet, throwing clothes into a cupboard, were so in love and so inseparable, if they were even planning now to have a baby, Sir George must be aware of it all, and have accepted it, more or less. They occupied that large enlightened room he had not yet dared to enter with either of his own parents – Evert's room came the closest to the image in his mind.

There was a small French sofa whose curved back would bind the composition. 'Grimly uncomfortable,' Fran said, but they tried it out, the girls at an angle, both looking down, past each other, as if absorbed in the same thought. 'That's good,' said Johnny.

'You don't think we should touch more?'

'No, it's really good like that.' It had crept up on him, but this was really the first day of his professional career, he had to do it as if he knew how to do it, on his own – there was instinct, of course, and training, he had a Diploma, and memory of a hundred portraits, more a muddle than a help. And then when they were set he had to find his own angle on them, and his own distance. He looked round, shifted a chair, carefully moved the black bra that was on it, and sat down to draw.

He loved drawing, but it was a funny thing about portraits that you had an audience. Still, in a minute or two he settled, in the self-aware silence they all kept, just Una's breathing and the soft scratch of the chalk. 'You can put some music on if you like,' he said.

'Oh, let's not bother,' said Fran.

Their two heads were a contrast, and there was a question he hadn't thought out as to which of them should have more prominence, Una being bigger, but Fran the dominant partner, so it seemed to him. So there was tact in it.

'How are you getting on?' said Fran, slightly breaking the pose after five minutes to look across at him. Johnny smiled pleasantly as he worked with the edge of the chalk and stared across at them, not as conversationists but as subjects, whom he was free, and obliged, to stare at. 'Coming along?'

'Well, you know, I think so.' He was pleased by how little he now felt frightened of her.

'How long will it be, do you imagine?'

'Mm, don't be so impatient.'

She settled back, was silent for a minute, and then spoke with eyes dutifully averted. Only her blinking betrayed her tension. 'We were wondering if you might do a baby for us.'

He tried pretending to himself he didn't know what she

meant, his heart raced and the heat flooded his face; he took refuge in obtuseness. 'How big?'

'Well . . .' – the girls looked at each other.

'I mean, in oils, or a drawing like this?'

Una made one of her rare statements: 'We want your sperm, for god's sake.' He gasped, blushed deeper, shaded heavily with the chalk.

'Oh, I see!' he said.

'You see, we've rather set our hearts on having a baby,' said Fran.

'Right . . .'

'But we need, you know' – she glanced at Una – 'a donor.'

'We think you're quite nice,' said Una, in the tone of an unforeseen concession – she kept her pose, but there was something fleeting in her face now that Johnny would never capture.

'And reasonably good-looking,' said Fran. 'We don't want a hideous baby. And you're healthy, aren't you, darling.'

'Um . . . yes, I think so,' said Johnny.

'You mustn't do it for at least a week before,' said Una. 'You know, with anyone else.'

'That shouldn't be too much of a problem,' said Johnny, feeling they were getting ahead of themselves.

'Or indeed with yourself,' said Fran severely.

'Can I think about it?' said Johnny, though it sounded already as if he couldn't.

'Darling, of course you can,' said Fran, as if she too thought it merely a formality.

'I mean . . . who's going to be mother – if you don't mind me asking?'

'No, fair question,' said Fran. 'I am.'

'Well, we'll have one each, love,' said Una. 'We agreed on that.'

Johnny kept drawing, he worked up the back of the sofa between the near-blanks of the faces, glad of the task. He sensed the girls themselves, both a little flushed now, were glad of the pose – it made the whole strange conversation possible. But it wasn't so easy for the artist. He put his head on one side, and made showy marks like someone pretending he could draw. To be asked for your sperm seemed an outrageous compliment and then huge consequences, of a kind any young man might rather avoid, reared beyond it – the whole thing was a challenge, to his humour, his friendship and that untested thing his manhood. Had they really asked Ivan? If so, he had turned them down; and that in itself put pressure on him, even as it gave him an excuse, a precedent.

'You said you haven't got much money?' said Una.

'No, not really,' said Johnny, relieved for once, and not liking to ask how much they had. 'I get twenty-five pounds a week from Cyril; and my dad gives me ten pounds a month. I mean, we're not getting married, are we?' – finding he hadn't been paying attention to that large part of the conversation that hadn't yet happened, but that his friends must have been through ahead of him in great detail. He thought the lack of funds might be an invaluable get-out clause.

'You mean to both of us?' said Una, and smiled distantly at his silliness.

'Would the father be allowed to see the child?' said Johnny, taking shelter in a more abstract view; he supposed if they didn't get him they'd get someone else. He was surprisingly jealous of the idea, the ridiculous image, of Ivan with a baby.

'That could be part of it,' said Una, 'yes – if you like.'

'She'd have to take my name, though,' said Fran.

'Or he . . .' said Una, and Johnny, not quite in unison.

'Well, all right,' said Fran impatiently – whether at their simple-mindedness or at this undesirable alternative. Though it was other alternatives that occurred to Johnny – he felt his child was being taken away from him within seconds of its first being mentioned.

'I'll have to think about it,' he said absurdly and again.

'I want you to think about it very carefully,' Fran said.

He laughed at the redundancy of what he was saying – 'I mean, I've never done anything like this before.'

'No, nor have we,' said Una, very simply. Johnny saw it was a clever ploy. They had already planted the unthought-of possibility of being a father in his heart. He imagined for a moment telling his own father the news, the uncertain pride in this nearly heterosexual act, the unhoped-for vindication; and then he started thinking of all the richly ironic reasons he couldn't tell him.

'I can't do any more on this today,' he said with a surprising loud laugh, and flipped the cover of the pad back over the drawing. He felt things would be very different for all of them the next time they sat.

Fran sighed. 'Oh, thank god,' she said, quickly getting up. 'Let's have a drink.'

They went down to the kitchen and in a minute they all had cold glasses of rosé in their hands – 'It looks like a rather important one,' Fran said as she slipped it back into the fridge; but a strange mute fell over them, the felt lack of a toast, there being nothing, as yet, to celebrate. Johnny was glad of the drink, even so, whose effect he felt descending and spreading to mask the simultaneously spreading sense of everything that was entailed. Shouldn't he just say at once it was impossible? An odd diplomacy kept them off the subject, now it had been named. The girls sat down at the table side by side again, Johnny opposite them, with a sudden sense of his own yearning inadequacy, not having a partner of his own. 'Now, how was your romantic weekend in Wales?' said Fran.

'It was OK,' said Johnny.

'Oh . . . only OK?'

'The house was lovely.' He could smile at this at least.

'Did you really think so? You're too sweet about Grandpa's work.'

'Don't you like it?'

'I'm never totally sure. And I'm not sure Mummy is, either, to be absolutely honest.'

'All the stuff's still there, lots of Stanley's drawings.'

'Fascinating . . .' She lit a cigarette, snapped the lighter shut. 'And what about, you know . . . ?'

'What's that?' said Johnny.

'Sex,' said Una.

'Oh,' Johnny blushed yet again, 'a bit of that.'

'At last!' said Fran. 'Thank god.'

'Of course,' said Johnny, 'he's really a gerontophile.'

She took a long drag, exhaled. 'Well, you knew that, darling.'

'I got the feeling he's more in love with my dad than he is with me.' Fran looked at him oddly, but kindly. 'Yeah . . . and' – he didn't like to use the word cockteaser – 'yeah,' he said, and nodded, and emptied his glass.

It was cold when they went into the drawing room, and Fran closed the windows. The Whistlers glowed more richly in the slow dusk. It wasn't clear what was happening next. He was hungry, and it would be just as reasonable for them all to have supper together as it would be awkward. He picked up his boots by the door and followed the girls downstairs again, to the hall. The hall had been quite unknown when he arrived and now, with its console table and mirror and parked hall chairs, it was witness to the end of a visit – it was the same, but he saw it differently. Fran opened the door. 'Will you give me a ring, darling?' she said.

'Oh!' – he laughed – for a second he thought it was part of the compact, their not-quite wedding.

She didn't see it. 'I think you've got the number.'

*

Now Ivan found the planets were aligned. Yesterday, the painful row, flaring, three times, downstairs, the shocks of slammed doors passing up through the building, only a few phrases clear, shouted shamelessly, incredulously loud, among long silences; then new initiatives, guarded, expressionless at first; and at the third climax, Herta, splendid in her way, screaming out ultimata that nobody took any notice of. Denis had gone somewhere, his overnight bag, toothbrush, lubricant all missing when Ivan made his noiseless visit. Herta had indeed left too, though only, Evert said, for the weekend: Evert had coped as best he could, uncertain where things went, kitchen science tenuous from disuse. Ivan had helped him with the washing up, Evert in shirtsleeves and waistcoat drying, in a silent routine which to Ivan was a perilous vision, a quick trial run at happiness. Last night's plate, mug, wine glass, whisky glass; the morning's plate, bowl, spoon and cup and saucer: he turned them gently in the soapy water, rinsed each one under running water, before placing it on the rack or, once or twice, in Evert's hands. Evert went out to lunch, got back at seven, made phone calls. Ivan with his door left open heard the slick pop of a wine cork about eight; then from behind closed doors, orchestral music.

At nine, the daylight was fading in the attic room, and the moon, full, or one night shy of fullness, hung above the parapet and looked in, mild but implacable, over Ivan's table, his diary, the bundles of letters and cuttings, the rare Oxford photo of the Brasenose First Eight, Michaelmas Term 1940. He hardly saw it now, in his excitement, coming up from the third-floor bathroom, washed, baby-powdered, shaved and after-shaved. Johnny had told him his tight black jeans were sexy, and he pulled them on, over clean underpants; he felt bucked up by Johnny's compliments, steered by them. Tonight, if all went well, the girls were going to put their question to him. It would be another chapter, an amusing one, in the folder he had long been keeping, marked 'The Sparsholt Affair'. He chose a white Oxfam shirt, collarless, and left two buttons open, sleeves rolled up tight to the pale biceps. And no shoes. He would go down to Evert barefoot, caught in the act of dressing or undressing by his own desire. He would go down like a message from the brain to the pained heart and neglected body.

The old boards, the threadbare carpet on the landing, the last of the day through the skylight, the veil-like shadows on the upper stairs – he didn't turn the light on . . . The stairs creaked under him, as always, but his tread was the possessor's not the burglar's. A narrow strip of gold leaked out beneath the sitting-room door, and Ivan stood with his toes just touched by it, as if his nails were painted. The music came more freely, large, undomestic, far from what Ivan would have chosen, at a time of crisis (but he wasn't musical, Johnny said so, in a tone of odd stored-up resentment when they drove back from Wales). Evert *was*, he was terribly musical; well, they would work something out. He raised his knuckles to knock, his hand hovered in deep shadow then fell with a noiseless conviction to the round black doorknob, which he turned, and pushed the door open, the small squeak of the handle as it sprang back drowned miles deep by the howling brass of an enormous orchestra.

Evert was sprawled on the sofa in his shirtsleeves, and it was dark enough now for Ivan to see in the window the image of his face, head back, eyes closed, tie loosened – though his right hand rose and swept outwards beside him, inches from the carpet, in response and encouragement. He was conducting on his back. His unawareness of Ivan's presence in the room made it by moments more dreamlike and more problematic. To look at him unseen was a luxury Evert might resent if he opened his eyes. He tensed himself and cleared his throat, a small effect annulled by unrelenting horns and trombones. They ebbed away. 'Evert,' Ivan said. 'Hello, Evert.' And the old man started, twisted round as he half sat up and looked at him.

'Oh, hello, poppet. Gosh, you gave me a turn.'

'Sorry . . .'

'I didn't know anyone was here.' There was a glass too on the floor, empty. Evert groped for it as he swung his legs round and looked up at him. 'Is something wrong?'

'Oh . . . no, no,' said Ivan. He came forward, gently, to allay any fears, the carpet he'd often stood on in his brogues pleasingly rough under his bare feet. 'I just wondered if you were OK.'

'Ah . . . yes, sweet of you.'

The music had its own drama, and was clearly reaching for a climax it was hard to ignore politely – Evert was distracted by it still. 'Is it Mahler?' said Ivan.

'Mm, well done,' said Evert. They looked in each other's eyes, as if focusing together on the music, and to Ivan Evert seemed already captive.

'Can I get you another drink?'

'Oh, why not?' said Evert. 'The usual' – offering up the glass.

'I think I know what that is,' said Ivan, and went towards the tray, which was next to the stereo on the far side of the room. Evert said nothing more, sitting forward, arms loose between his thighs, under the spell not only of Mahler but of alcohol. The last rasp of the soda siphon barely diluted the dark two inches of Jameson's. 'Tell me if it's too strong,' Ivan said as he gave it him.

'Ooh,' Evert gasped, debated. 'No, it's lovely. What are you having?'

Ivan gave himself a long vodka and tonic. 'Can I get some ice?'

'Yes, of course' – Evert looked round – 'well, you know where it is.' And Ivan did. From the kitchen he heard the music end, with an almighty crash and falling off, and swung back in quickly just in case Evert put on something else. But the arm clicked back, the disc was still, just the red light and a brief reminding crackle through the speakers when the fridge started up next door. 'What have you been up to?'

'Oh, just writing,' said Ivan, and since Evert was sitting in the middle of the sofa, 'Budge up . . .' lifting and plumping a cushion as he sat down next to him.

'Cheers!'

'Cheers.' Ivan gripped Evert's forearm for a second, bracingly. Sitting beside him, facing the fireplace, Ivan's thoughts forming and flowing along the fronds and curls of the tapestried fire screen, running half-seeing across the line of postcards and invitations on the mantelpiece, beneath the brown frame of the biggest, the most valuable Ben Nicholson . . . He smiled, and it was as if Evert could sense him smiling.

'You still haven't told me,' he said, with a reproving pause, 'about your visit to West Tarr.'

'You had our card?'

'Yes, sweet of you, but it didn't tell me anything I wanted to know.'

'Oh . . . well, it was OK.'

'The house was all right?'

'Yes, not bad – a bit damp and dirty, but we made do.'

'Oh, good. I'd been wondering how you got on.'

'The two of us, you mean?'

'I've grown very fond of that boy.'

'Yes . . .'

'He's a good artist – good drawer, I don't know what his painting's like.'

Ivan didn't want too much of Johnny in the room. 'He sort of lives in a world of his own,' he said. 'I got him to open up a bit.'

Evert revolved his glass. 'He's quite smitten with you, I fancy.'

Ivan made a soft snuffle of disparagement.

'Did you . . . um?' – Evert seemed embarrassed. 'One knows so little about the young.'

'Oh, the young,' said Ivan and laughed.

'Though a certain young man knows far too much about this old one.'

'Really . . .?' said Ivan, pricked by the teasing, but turning his head to smile at Evert, who turned and smiled too.

Ivan didn't know how he would do it, but he knew it would happen. He savoured his own calm conviction, as they turned and faced forward again; something undeniable had been said in that smile. They leant lightly on each other, sliding down a little on the yielding cushions. Each held his glass in his right hand, and there was a moment's confusion as Ivan slid his fingers between Evert's – Evert lifted the glass in his other hand, took a swig from it as Ivan's hand took possession of his and they were clasped together. They sat, for ten strange exploratory seconds, small reciprocal pressures of fingers and palm, Evert's hand strong and hard with experience. 'I don't know if you want some music on,' he said. 'It doesn't have to be Mahler!'

Ivan grunted dismissively, leant forward to put his drink on the floor, fell back, shifted up and reached up to pull Evert's head towards him – in the mere moment of hesitation, Evert's eyes, dark, close-up, blurred by the buried arc of his bifocals, seemed to question, assess and then, as Ivan kissed him, to accept. He held his drink still in his left hand, and they had to disengage for a moment for him to seize another swig and set it down. His lips and tongue were whiskey, a tingle where his stubble grazed Ivan's soft lips and smooth jaw. They had their arms around each other, in the clumsy fervour of being still side by side. In a minute Ivan climbed on top of him, sat straddling his knees, Evert wincing, bracing himself as he took his weight. To Ivan there was something more stirring than their kisses in Evert's eyes, which had looked at lovers long before he was born, and now looked at him. He lifted his glasses off, leant aside to place them on the table, quick practicalities deepening the charm of the moment, the surrender to what had to happen. Evert blinked at him, his face naked for the first time, his bed-face – he groped Ivan, ran his hands up over his chest, 'I can't see a thing . . .' and down very confidently to rub and squeeze the hard ridge trapped at an angle in his jeans. It was as if with his glasses off he couldn't be seen: he coloured up not with shyness but with re-engaged appetite.

Ivan unbuttoned Evert's shirt, pushed his vest up, stroked him, went down on his knees between his legs to kiss his stomach, reached up to squeeze his small hard nipples. He saw that he'd once been quite fine, in the way that lean men are who never think about exercise; and then he'd been a soldier, wonderful in uniform, thirty years ago. Now he'd thickened sexily round the middle, his hairless chest had slid downwards and sideways by a creased half-inch, there were lovable creases of age under the arms. So one beauty melted in another, surviving youth and exquisite decline. To reveal him and look at him and touch his naked skin made Ivan's heart thump and his mouth go dry. He swiftly undid his own fly and pushed his jeans and pants down, tensed himself against the sickening chance of coming at once, his problem. He had really to think about something else, as he unbuttoned Evert's trousers at the waist and pulled the zip towards him, practical and blank-faced as a nurse.

FOUR

Losses

1

She sat on the hard wooden bench just in front of the portrait, and heard what members of the public were saying. Some strolled slowly past, others stood for ten seconds until the next picture, or the very bright one beyond it, caught their eye, and now and then a couple, or more often a man or woman with no one to talk to, gave the portrait their full attention for a minute or more, obstructing the sociable onward drift of the crowd. She herself felt proud of the picture, but bored by the long two hours of the occasion; she had her own sketchbook with her, which after initial uncertainty she got out of her bag, with the old cardboard packet of crayons, striped inside by the tips of the crayons when they slid in and out. It was hopeless drawing people when they kept moving, so she drew other things out of her head, or her memory, a house, and then a portrait of her mother; she would show it to her tomorrow, when she went home.

She was pleased if she heard someone praise the picture of Mary Harms, with her staring blue eyes among hundreds of red flowers (it was painted in a kind of conservatory), but took it philosophically if they said they didn't like it or made funny faces of their own in front of it; the people who strolled past talking about something else and not even looking were the ones she hated. It was a big painting, and a great deal of work (six months, on and off) had gone into it. She didn't know what she thought of it really, it was what her father did and had always been doing, and it was impossible for her to judge. An old lady, rather mad-looking, in a beret with a pewter badge on the side, spent five minutes studying the picture, getting so close an attendant asked her to stand back. She turned, and smiled sadly at Lucy, as if about to speak, as if she saw the connexion, but then moved on. The others closed in, curious for a moment as to what she had found in it – it wasn't clear if they found it too. Perhaps she *was* mad. The crowd at these Portrait Society events was certainly very mixed. 'Ah! I thought you were drawing a picture of a picture,' said a large man in a dark suit and a tie with elephants on it, looking over her shoulder.

'Oh . . . no,' said Lucy, and let him see what she was doing, since she thought it was quite good.

'Ah, yes, marvellous – you'll soon be showing here yourself, I should think.' Lucy smiled up at him. 'And what do you think of this portrait, tell me honestly.' It was almost as if he'd painted it, though she was pleased to know for sure that he hadn't.

'I don't know, really' – they both stared at it, beyond the intervening figures. She wanted to hear what he said before she explained. The people in her father's pictures often looked a little bit uncomfortable, as if something was being revealed about them that they'd rather have kept to themselves.

'It's my wife,' he said; and now she thought his stare had something else in it, he felt more exposed, in a way, than his wife, who'd been offered up to the public. People's comments wouldn't only be about it as a painting, they were also about the woman, Mrs Harms, and whether they liked the look of her. But before she could decide how to answer, Mr Harms had been called to by another man and with a little encouraging nod to her he drifted off.

Her father's own attitude was odd but she thought she understood it – he felt uncomfortable hanging round by his own work, so he just came past every few minutes, to check she was all right, and sometimes to introduce her to people, who could be surprised to find he had a daughter at all. Off he went again, not quite such a tramp as usual, he'd done what he thought of as dressing up for the occasion, though it was hardly what you'd call smart. '*You* may have to wear a uniform,' he said, 'but I don't.' He decided the day he left school he would always wear just what he wanted to wear; and anyway he was an artist. Now a rather drunk couple, the man in a pinstripe suit and bow tie, with gleaming black hair, the woman in a short red and black frock, were looking at Mary Harms's portrait.

'Sparsholt!' said the man, jutting his jaw as he peered at the signature. 'Hmmm, I don't think I'd advertise that.'

The woman said, 'Don't be silly, Henry, he can't help what he's called.'

'*Well* . . .' The man paused, as if trying to be fair. 'I mean you wouldn't want . . . I don't know . . . "Crippen" scrawled all over your portrait, would you?'

'There's no comparison, hardly. And anyway he's rather a good artist, don't you think? That could almost *be* Mary.'

'Mm, almost.'

'Oh, you're impossible,' said the woman and laughed at him happily.

The next couple were much nicer.

'It's quite contemporary, isn't it,' said the man.

'Oh, I like it,' said the woman.

The man smiled and stood back a little. 'I like it too, my love, in a gallery, but not to live with.'

'I wasn't thinking of buying it,' said the woman, taking his arm. 'Gosh, I thought that was Germaine Greer for a moment . . .'

'It is Germaine Greer,' said the man with a giggle as they moved on to the bright picture two along.

'Daddy, who's Crippen?' said Lucy, when her father came to get her at the end.

'Crippen?' he said, with a cautious laugh at the things she picked up. 'He was a man who murdered his wife.'

'He escaped on a ship with his girlfriend,' said Evert, 'but he was caught by a telegram.'

'Oh . . .' said Lucy. It was more mysterious now, and something told her not to go on with it.

'I don't know what you've been reading,' her father said.

She zipped up her bag. 'Oh, nothing.'

'Right, shall we get out of here. Pat will have supper ready – are you hungry, young lady?'

'Quite,' said Lucy, not sure she would like what Pat had cooked.

'You're probably rather tired,' said Evert. 'I am.' His face grew round as he hid a yawn; then he smiled goodbye at the portrait of Mrs Harms. 'You must be pleased, darling,' he said – but this was to her father. 'It's jolly good.'

'Oh, thanks, Evert,' said her father, placing his hand on the old man's shoulders as they steered out of the gallery.

'Daddy,' said Lucy, 'why does Evert call you darling?'

'I'm getting rather forgetful,' said Evert, turning and smiling at her, 'so I just call everyone darling – it's much easier.'

She thought about it. 'You remember my name,' she said.

Evert seemed almost shocked. 'Of course I remember *your* name, darling,' he said.

'Now, let's get our coats,' said her father.

In the taxi she sat squashed between Evert and Clover, and her father went on the seat facing backwards and hanging on to the handle; now and then he glanced over his shoulder. These journeys through the dusk, turning off at the lights beside road signs to unusual places, excited her, but were still slightly coloured by regret that she wasn't going to her real home, where most of her things were. Evert and her father were talking about art, with names she didn't know, and she peered out blankly on one side then the other, till Clover said, 'So how are you getting on at school, Lucy?', which was the most boring question one had to deal with.

'It's OK, thank you.'

'What do you like best?'

Lucy pretended to think. 'I'm top in English and art, but third in maths.'

'Well, third's not too bad,' said Clover.

Lucy looked out of the window with a strict little smile. They travelled on, her father now answering questions about money, which always made him uncomfortable – how much a picture had fetched, or would fetch.

'And how are Mummy and Una?' said Clover next.

'Una's got a cold, but Mummy's all right.'

Clover gazed for a moment at the passing shops. 'And how's your grandfather?'

'Which one?' said Lucy.

'Oh . . . !' said Clover – she hadn't thought. It was a funny thing about their family but Lucy had three grandfathers, Sir George, of course, Roy Davey, Una's father, and David Sparsholt who was her father's father, whom she seldom saw. In a way there were four, because her big brother Thomas had a different father from hers, who, like her father, lived with another man, and had a father of his own, who was a hopeless drunk and lived in Majorca. Lucy had a curious nature, but her questions about why things had worked out like this were never really answered. 'I meant Grandpa George,' Clover said.

'Oh, he's very well, thank you,' said Lucy. What all the grandfathers had was a kind of fierceness, not expressed directly to her but making things a bit tense when they were around.

'What's the latest on Freddie, Clo?' said her father suddenly, so that she felt ensconced in the middle of the adult talk. He used a tone of voice she knew, earnest and direct to cover up his guilt at not having asked about Freddie before.

'Mm . . .' – she wrinkled her nose as she said in her usual lethargic way, 'He should be out on Monday. They've taken out

the thing, you know, but there'll be masses of chemo to come.'
She put a heavy hand on Lucy's arm, so as not to frighten her.

'Is he in good spirits, though?' said Evert, as if that would
see him through.

'Oh, you know Freddie,' said Clover. 'He's propped up in
bed, reviewing Anita Brookner for the *New York Times*, and of
course getting hundreds more visitors than anyone else in the
ward.'

Her father's house was in Fulham, an area that lay in Lucy's
mind under a thin grey fog: Fullum they said, a dead footfall,
flour shaken in a Tupperware box (unlike sugar, with its quick
shoosh, which to her mind was the sound of Chelsea, where Sir
George lived, close by but a world away). In the Fulham Road
the numbers went up and up, what did they get to? – 600 – 700
– she kept a look out as they passed – and for miles it seemed
there was nothing but lamp-shops, window after window hung
from ceiling to floor with chandeliers. Then they turned off
into streets with no shops, which seemed twice as dark. When
they stopped outside the house she felt relief and a faint tension,
it was home of a kind, but something would have changed since
her last stay with her father. The house was semi-detached,
square, with a white porch, and frankly a bit decrepit. In the
hall there was always the chemical mystery of paint in the nos-
trils, and turpentine. Just visible through the sitting-room door
on the left was her own portrait, painted four years ago, and
life-size then, though not so now. She was always very curious
to see it, tacitly proud of it, but embarrassed by it too as she
grew older and the wide-eyed child in a blue smock remained
just the same. Two tall doors opened from the sitting room into
what should have been the dining room, but was now her
father's studio, facing north-east, and avoiding direct sunlight.
This meant they had to have meals in the kitchen – sometimes

whole evenings were spent in the kitchen. It was like watching TV, you followed Pat making ratatouille or a 'roast' of some kind from scratch, and if you were an adult you got drunk. This could take an hour or more. Then, when you were just about to die of hunger, he slammed the oven shut and said, 'Right! That should be done in forty-five minutes.' Often she shyly declined the strange food that was served while they waited, the horrible hummus Pat made in the blender, and tapenade, bitter and oily (it was meant to have anchovies in it, but no 'creatures' of course were allowed in the house).

Tonight as they came in, her father said, 'Dinner in ten minutes,' and she hurried upstairs to her room. The hall, stairs and landing were thick with his pictures, 'Sparsholt' or 'JS' all the way up, too many of them to look right; were they the treasures kept back or the ones no one wanted to buy? They were records of years of encounters in which she had played no part. The hang kept changing, and she noticed there were one or two new things staring out as she ran past; these looked like sketches for portraits, which were too good to throw away, and according to her father had more life in them sometimes than the finished article. Her own little room had a weird blue landscape over the bed, not by her father – it was a view she'd got used to, but with no warm feeling of knowing what or where it was. She carefully detached the picture of her mother from the grey glue binding of her sketch pad, and propped it up on the dressing table. The high bed with frilly pink pillow had the counterpane turned down but neither the comforting hump of a hot-water bottle nor the flex of an electric blanket was to be seen. Still, her row of books was on the mantelpiece, between two black elephants, there were frocks and a cardigan she'd half-forgotten in the wardrobe, and when she caught sight of herself in the wardrobe mirror she saw someone very nearly at home here. She went out to the bathroom (they didn't have a separate lavatory), which was the opposite of the bathroom at home – throwaway razors, not thrown away, but heaped up on the dirty glass shelf, two kinds of shaving soap, a laundry-basket full of smelly grey boxer shorts and vests. There was a shower with a mildewed curtain that hung over the bath, and dark bottles of body-washes, and an odd rough glove for washing with. When she had a bath or anything here she did it as quickly as possible. The towels were heaped thick on the heated rail, and even her clean one had a remote male smell.

There was a knock at the door and a 'Sorry!' when the handle was tried; she hurried to wash her hands. It was Evert, looking perplexed. 'I just awfully need to go,' he said, with a distant look on his face, sliding past her as she left and not locking the door behind him. She went back along the landing, and sitting at the little pine desk with her pencils, she coloured in a bit more of her mother's hair, in a much stronger yellow than the real colour, but it was all she had. The eyes too became a fiercely bright blue. In a minute there was another knock, and Evert looked round the door. 'Ah! Hello,' he said. 'It's you, um . . .'

'Hello . . .' she said, with the hint of reproach of any artist interrupted at work.

He came and stood over her. 'Ah, yes, now . . . who's this?'

'Don't you know?' she said.

He sucked in his breath. 'It's someone I know.'

'Yes!'

'It's . . . er . . . it's not, no . . . oh god.'

'Don't you know?' she said again, excited, and then sensing, when she looked up at him, a shallow breath of panic under his fixed smile. Maybe it wasn't only names he couldn't remember. 'It's . . . Francesca Skipton.'

'Ah, yes.'

'She's my mother, of course.'

'Well, I know that, darling! I've known your mother since the day she was born.' She held it up again and Evert craned forward, like the visitors in the gallery, and with his own private flinches, as an art expert too. 'You've only got those colours, I expect,' he said.

'Yes, I'm afraid so.'

'It's not a bad thing – you must make the most of what you have.'

'Do you think it looks like her?' said Lucy.

'It's hard to draw someone who's not in front of you,' he said. 'We remember things differently, you see, when we can't see them, especially faces, and so we make things up. You've made what I'd call a speculative portrait of your mother.'

'Oh . . . yes,' said Lucy. It was hard to tell if this increased or compromised its interest.

'I'll just sit quietly before dinner,' said Evert, 'if you don't mind, I get so terribly tired,' and moving the baby-sized doll from the little nursing chair where Lucy often sat to read, he lowered himself with a smile and a sharp grunt. She was surprised but didn't object to a visitor who sat quietly; she got on with her drawing, which had now become problematic in ways she felt powerless to solve. So in a minute she started a question, glanced round and saw his eyes were closed – but yes, he was still breathing, and her fright turned into a kind of amusement. She didn't want to look at him in case he opened his eyes and caught her. There were voices in the hall, Pat saying 'Is he all right?' in his competent way, footsteps on the stairs. There was a new tap at the door, and her father looked in, glanced from her to Evert in the armchair, chin down now in a snooze that looked thoughtful, the closed eyes of complete concentration – he pushed his chin forward a little as if grumpily accepting a point. Then he opened his eyes – stared at them both blankly for a second or two, and said, 'Is everyone here?'

'Yes, we're all ready,' said her father.

As they went downstairs she heard Clover saying to Pat, in the businesslike way of adults among themselves, 'How old is she now?' and Pat saying, 'Oh, God, seven, would she be?

I think she was two when we met.' Lucy was small for her age, and aware of the mild concern this was causing her parents. All she minded was being treated as more of a child than she was.

'I wonder what it will be,' Evert said to her as they sat down. He peered at Pat, his aproned bulk obscuring the hob where pans simmered on the flames.

'Mm, I wonder,' said Lucy.

'Do you eat creatures?' Evert said.

Lucy admitted she did.

'And so do I, I'm afraid. Which ones do you like eating best?'

Evert's tone obliged her to be childish too. 'I think lambs,' she said.

'Ah, yes!' said Evert.

Her father made a horrible face.

'Now here we are,' said Pat, turning round with a frown.

A dinner this late was a Fulham thing, not tolerated in Belsize Grove, and she did her practical best to live up to it. It was a thick soup like green porridge to start and they all tried to guess what was in it: she was the one who identified courgettes. She found herself over-active with excitement and determination not to let herself down. Pat said, 'Well done,' and she smiled and kept on tasting, almost giving the impression she liked courgettes.

'I'm sorry Ivan can't join us,' said Clover, in her usual tone of not minding very much.

'I know,' said Evert.

'But he's all right?' said Pat. With Lucy, on the few times they'd met, Ivan had been very awkward; she'd really had to make the conversational going herself. He was an old friend of her mother's, and he was one of the funny men who lived in the House of Horrors in Cranley Gardens.

'Yes, he's fine. He's been an angel to me, you know, with this recent thing. But I can still get about by myself!'

'Well, give him our love,' said her father. 'Clover, some more bread?'

'No, thanks . . . Perhaps some wine . . . So do you have anyone sitting for you?' she said, not taking her eye off the glass as it was filled.

Lucy's father looked at Evert as he said, 'I've just started on old George Chalmers, in fact.'

'Oh, you're doing him, are you?' said Evert.

'Well, thanks to your recommendation.'

'I'm glad it came off,' said Evert quietly; he looked at Clover, 'I don't expect you know George Chalmers. He used to hang around in Oxford when I was there, though he was still a schoolboy. He was a famous beauty, though rather hard to deal with.'

'No, I've met him, I think,' said Clover.

'Why was he?' said Lucy.

'Why was he what, darling?'

'Hard to deal with.'

Evert sighed as he looked for the answer, as though he'd gone into the junk room and didn't know what to bring out. 'I suppose really he was just terribly vain, you know . . .'

'No change there, then,' Lucy's father said.

'Ah, I'm sure . . . Does he come to you?'

'He does now. We started off down in Wiltshire – you know, I went for the weekend.'

'Was he all over you, I suppose?'

'Never came near me' – he grinned at Lucy, as if to sweep over the matter. 'A bit old for him, I think,' he said quietly.

'Well, you know of course my friend Peter Coyle and George . . .' said Evert.

'I don't think there's much Johnny doesn't know about George Chalmers's private life by now,' said Pat, who tended to get left out of these art talks; 'if you can even call it private.' He laughed, and kept smiling at Lucy too, with a hint of solidarity, as he stood to clear the soup bowls. Lucy smiled cautiously back, at this friend of her father with his unshaven face pink from cooking and drinking wine, and the soft dark eyes.

'Now how are you liking your lasagne?' Pat said to her five minutes later.

'Very nice, thank you,' said Lucy, with an almost reluctant awareness that she was quite enjoying it; there was something in it remarkably like mince. She thought she had better not mention it, in case Pat had made a terrible mistake, and they would have to go upstairs and make themselves sick, which had happened more than once, apparently, when they were in hotels abroad.

'Is it Quorn?' said Clover. 'I've read about it.'

'What do you think?' said Pat.

Lucy glanced at her father, who had his deaf-to-all-arguments vegetarian face on.

'Awfully good!' said Clover, picking out a tiny forkful, and so behind the others that she was bound, as usual, to leave almost everything on her plate. And yet she was enormous, bigger than Una, so perhaps like her a *snacker*. She lifted her empty glass – 'Could I?'

'Ah, yes' – Pat leant over to fill it with red wine, and she said,

'But what about your work, Pat?'

Did he sense, as Lucy did, the hint of helpless courtesy in the question? 'My work,' he said, 'is notoriously boring.'

'Really?' she said. 'I don't believe that.'

Pat shook his head happily at her. 'I don't mean I find it boring, not in the least, I love it, but it bores the socks off anyone I talk to about it.'

This was a challenge, and Clover, pushing her food about with her fork, said, 'I know it's organs.'

'Aha!' said Pat.

'Historical, though,' said Lucy's father.

'Restoration,' said Pat.

'Yes, of course, you restore organs.'

'No, Restoration organs.'

'Ah . . .'

'Organs built in the 1660s.'

'Oh, I see. So you do Restoration organ restoration!'

'I do,' Pat smiled politely.

'Goodness!' said Clover, and took a big swig of wine. 'I think that could be awfully interesting.'

'Well . . . So what are your plans, Evert?' said Pat.

'*Well*,' said Evert.

'You've got this trip, haven't you, Evert,' said Lucy's father.

'That's it, darling,' said Evert tactfully, as if unsure how many shared the secret.

'And where are you going to?' said Clover, almost teasing the poor man, Lucy thought.

'Well . . . !' – Evert sat back and smiled over their heads.

'Of course, you're going to Antwerp,' said Pat. 'Isn't that right?'

'That's it,' said Evert again, with a nod. Now it was out, and they could talk about it. Still, he seemed a little uneasy. He turned to Lucy. 'Do you know where Antwerp is, darling?'

'It's in Belgium,' said Lucy.

'Very good,' said Clover.

'It's a port.'

'Mm, that's right,' said Clover.

Evert had the whole thing now. 'I'm going to an Alternative Book Fair,' he said. 'They've invited me, to talk about A. V. – you know, he's coming out in Dutch.'

315

'You mean you're coming out in Dutch,' said Lucy's father.

'Yes – well, he's in Dutch already, he always has been,' said Evert. 'You know, I get a cheque every year for sixty guilders or something, and it's the royalties.'

'It'll be more now,' said Pat.

'Will it?'

'With your book!'

'Oh, well, let's hope.'

They sat for a long time over their plates, forgetting Lucy. Pudding was still to come, but to her it was almost too late. Her appetite itself was falling asleep. Her father caught her eye now and then, in an irksome way. But the talk by this stage had moved into a baffling square dance of first names, combining and recombining, Evert and Pat themselves at cross-purposes, and the Olivia, whom she followed hopefully at first, urging her on with smiles of recognition, turned out to be a quite different Olivia from the one who was a friend of her mother's. Well, she'd known it would happen, the obvious truth of the night was that the adults had their own endless things to talk about, and the wine they were knocking back made them all speak more freely and with less and less thought for her. She was aware of the light burden it put on any adult seated next to her, to keep one ear on the real conversation while they turned to make small talk with her. Now her father was mentioning his mother, who'd been in hospital, but of course was not a celebrity patient like Freddie.

'Do you know my granny,' Lucy asked Evert, 'Granny Connie, I mean?'

'Well,' Evert stared at the table, 'I knew her, let me see, it's 1994, fifty-four years ago.'

'It's not,' said Lucy, 'it's 1995.'

'Ah, well, in that case even longer. It was when she was engaged to your grandpa, during the War.'

'Did you know Grandpa David then?'

'David . . . oh, yes, I knew him awfully well,' said Evert. 'We used to do things together . . . sometimes, you know . . .'

These two sentences sounded a little inconsistent. Lucy saw he was being polite, or perhaps couldn't really remember. She smiled understandingly, but it was too long ago to be interesting now, and a stronger wave of sleep swept through her, she yawned before she could help it. In a minute she was standing and waving them goodnight, pulled in by Clover for an approximate kiss, and then, at a nod from her father, she went off upstairs.

2

A bleak scene, lasting less than half an hour, was enacted some weeks later at the Mortlake Crematorium. Ivan went with Evert, who made a point of wearing a pink scarf with his black overcoat, and sat biting his cheek and pursing his lips so that Ivan couldn't tell what he was feeling or thinking. Above all he seemed impatient. He had insisted, as an old friend, on sitting at the front; Ivan had to come out of the pew to let someone else get by, and stood looking frankly across the half-empty rows behind, nodding and giving rueful smiles to Brian Savory and Sally, and old Dorothy Denham; he was surprised to see Dorothy here, and when he sat down again jotted her name on the back of the order of service; he wasn't sure if they had anything on her or not. He had been to a good few funerals, of Evert's friends and of others he took an interest in, but it was his first time at Mortlake – sunlight through a cloud seemed to pick out the dormant first syllable of the name. They spoke of this room as a chapel, though Christian symbols had been carefully omitted from its design – and seemed none the less to lurk, for those who craved them, in the arrangement of the room, the coloured glass and the woodwork of the pews, with their narrow prayer-book ledge. Where the altar would have been was the automated bier, looking more than anything like a four-poster bed, with pillars and a canopy.

On the printed card there was a recent photo of Jill, in colour, caught at a party in a genial mood. Seeing it, Ivan heard her, telling him what to do or, more probably, what he should have done, with the dogged irony that was her disappointing means of engaging with all comers. Over the loudspeakers came, mildly distorted, a tune Ivan had heard before, the 'Dance of the Blessed Spirits' by C. W. Gluck, a flute solo ushering onstage an incongruous new Jill, liberated, light-footed, welcomed into the next world, which she had perhaps thought of herself in pagan more than Christian terms. An unprompted silence fell over the congregation. 'Ah, here's the party,' said Evert – they stood and half-turned to check as Jill was borne in. Her friends were too old for it, and she frightened the young, so the pall-bearers were the men from the undertakers', one of them wall-eyed, another, put at the back, with a surgical boot. The V&A had sent a coldly artistic wreath of white lilies, which bobbed its way along at head height on top of the coffin towards its brief stay at the front.

And Jill had chosen hymns; she was a pagan but she wanted them to enjoy themselves, and singing was the only enjoyable part of a funeral, as a rule. She had sung herself, in one of the London choirs in the fifties, and referred just occasionally to Sir Adrian Boult as one might to a long-ago fling. It must be a woman from a choir now, a row or two behind them, an old but unembarrassed soprano with throbbing vibrato. Either the others were encouraged by her or they gave up altogether. Ivan glanced across the aisle at the military-looking man on the end of the row, looking forward, lips parted, an occasional drop of the jaw intended to convey the act of singing.

Afterwards Jill's godson, a doctor from Taunton whom none of them knew, invited everyone back to Jill's flat for sandwiches and a drink; the word went round that he was called Adrian. Had any of them been there before? Evert said once, thirty years ago, he'd got into the hall, but no further. The woman called Margaret, from the V&A, who had given the address, claimed to have had lunch there, but when pressed admitted it was 'quite some while ago'. 'Oh, what was it like?' said Ivan. 'Well, you'll see,' she said; 'she had some nice things.' 'Oh, she was quite a collector,' said Adrian, who it turned out was also her sole heir.

The flat was in a large Georgian house in Kew that had been subdivided; they went up to the second floor, Evert taking Ivan's arm, in one of his cosy pretences of infirmity. The door stood open by the time they reached the landing, and they had a view in through the dark little lobby to a brighter room beyond. Curiosity about the flat seemed keener than grief among the mourners – as well as Brian and Sally, there were Freddie and Clover, Iffy, friends who only saw Jill at Cranley Gardens, and a woman called Arabella, who lived on the floor below, and had clearly being dying to get past the door for years. Evert stood in the hall looking up and down at three Piranesis hung one above the other – not familiar views but recondite studies of funerary fragments, broken tiles and inscriptions. 'Fascinating,' he said, which Ivan took for a joke.

They went into a small room at the side, with a single bed, where they heaped up their coats. The unvisited feel of any spare bedroom was redoubled in this unvisited flat. Behind them Brian shuffled in with his stick and Sally set about tugging his coat off, pulling it down one arm, then the other, while he examined the books in the bookcase as if nothing was happening. 'Well, well, I hadn't got old Jill down as a Wodehouse reader,' he said. 'Nor Tolkien, come to that.'

'Well, she knew him at Oxford, of course,' said Ivan.

'Though none of them read very recently, by the look of it,' said Brian, stooping to get *Summer Lightning*, which slid out like a slice of cake with its own thick layer of dust on top.

The unused room and its neglected clues to the dead woman's past appealed to Ivan. Above the bookcase was a framed poster for a Picasso exhibition in New York which again was unlikely, faded over thirty-five summers into palest beiges and blues. Ivan wedged his briefcase in a small armchair with a tear in the cane backing – the welcome to overnight guests (the godson perhaps on occasion) seemed made with all the rejected goods from the rest of the owner's life.

'Oh, lord . . .' said Sally, tucking Brian's scarf into his coat sleeve, and staring at the chest of drawers between the bed and the window.

'Sally, darling,' said Clover, coming in behind them, and unpinning her black hat. Sally was belittled by her friends, and famous (among half a dozen people) for getting the wrong end of the stick, and the attention they gave her now was both delayed and momentary. She shook her head.

'No . . . I just thought. Oh, never mind.' But she kept a canny eye on the chest, and the odd group of items on top of it, for a moment longer, while the others trailed out of the room.

The proceedings got under way, with the desire to have a normal chat curbed for the first few minutes at least by the propriety of the occasion – the spirit of where they had come from still lingered in dark suits and a quiet postponing manner, until, with a glass of wine down, people turned away in sudden conversation towards the window or the sofa and the unselfconscious life of the party, which after all was life itself, began. Ivan watched as a small wavy-haired man in his sixties, with large glasses and a boyish smile, approached the majestic Margaret. 'Margaret, it's Gordon!' he said.

'How are you?' said Margaret, smiling down at him in untroubled vagueness before moving to the table for a refill. Gordon filled his glass too. A minute later he went up to the old man on the far side of Evert.

'It's Gordon!' he said. He seemed to hope to identify himself not just as Gordon, but as that especial Gordon who had brightened their lives long ago.

'Who is that man?' said Evert.

'I don't know,' said Ivan; 'he says his name's Gordon.' Ivan noticed that no one greeted Gordon, and quick individual decisions that they needn't bother with him took the semblance, in ten minutes, of a general intention to ignore him. Still, he came round, small and bright-eyed as he looked up at them. 'It's Gordon!' he said.

'I know who it is,' said Clover sharply, as if his main purpose had been not eager friendship but reproach.

Ivan heard candid questions asked by people who were as close as friends ever were to Jill. 'I wish I'd known her better. She was very private, wasn't she.'

'Of course sometimes, with the very private ones, you go to the funeral and find the most astonishing people – they'd just compartmentalized their lives, and you had no idea. Here, though, I have the feeling I've known everyone for years.'

'Did she ever read anything to the Memo Club?'

'Well, yes, years ago . . . perhaps you weren't there? A rather surprising thing about her sister, who was killed when she was a child. And the alcoholic mother. Tragic, really. I remember it was very short, and she looked as if she wished she hadn't written it – or hadn't read it out, anyway.'

'Really she just liked seeing other people exposing themselves.'

'And correcting them afterwards.' They laughed. 'Poor Jill.'

*

Ivan talked for a while to Freddie, asked a few straight questions about his health, and then turned, he hoped reassuringly, to other things, such as travels, and what he was writing, which all tended to curve magnetically to the fact he was avoiding, that Freddie wasn't going to be writing or travelling much longer. After the operation and the chemo, he was shockingly bald and gaunt. The slight improbable pot he had got in his late sixties had gone, and the eccentric mixture of clashing clothes that had long been his trademark hung large on him as if he had dressed himself from a charity shop on the way here. There had been something almost sexy about him, in Ivan's eyes, when they'd first met, more than twenty years ago – the sexiness of cleverness, of labyrinthine knowledge and the charm that focused on you like a seduction. It was an appeal that Freddie's appearance made all the more confusing and authentic.

As always a small group formed round him, with a shared understanding now that they wouldn't often do so again. 'Was there ever anyone?' said Margaret.

'An affair, you mean?' said Sally.

'Someone in the War she once mentioned?'

Clover peered at Freddie in an archly ingenuous fashion, a raised eyebrow, a pert smile. Freddie took a moment to say, 'Oh, they don't want to hear about all that,' with a look he had when quickly calculating whether and how to hold court.

'I'm not sure you're right,' said Clover, in the friendly but uncertain silence that had fallen.

'It seems unlikely now, somehow.'

'What's that?' said Sally.

'Evert could explain it very well,' Freddie said more loudly, his voice hoarse, looking quite pleased with himself, in his emaciated way.

'What's that?' said Evert, turning from talking to Brian.

'We're going back to Oxford days,' said Clover.

'Let me tell it, darling,' said Freddie, holding his wine glass in both hands, rather like a microphone. 'It seems proper to record,' he said drolly, 'that Jill Darrow in her youth cut quite a figure.'

'Oh, gosh,' said Sally.

'You know, she was actually quite magnificent,' said Freddie. 'The truth is I adored her – she was so big and so virginal, and beautiful in her way. She was really my first love.' He grinned at them, self-mocking, self-entranced.

'Goodness, Freddie!' – no one could say what they thought as they looked at him now.

'So you had a romance . . .' said Margaret, with rather dry enthusiasm.

Freddie looked at her. 'Romance was never exactly Jill's thing,' he said. 'But I pursued her for over a year. I don't think I was ever asked into her rooms. It was just like later on, I suppose. None of us ever came here.'

'Well, Freddie, you dark horse,' said Gordon, in the flirty tone of a nurse to a childish old man; though Freddie didn't disown the compliment. And there was a sense, as he took another swig from his glass, lurched slightly and caught Clover's arm, that the matter should now be dropped.

After this unexpected testimony from a sick man to a dead woman scant further light was shed on the intervening half-century. She went – unrevealed – into a space like the hall of her flat, no windows, fragments of epitaphs on the wall, a door open still on to the sitting room behind her, and the door beyond now open too, on to the common parts, and the shadowy downward stairs. The godson seemed unprepared for the curiosity of her friends and colleagues, who he surely supposed knew her better than he did. He explained what he could, that his parents had met Jill in Berlin after the War; that she'd been a proper postal-order sort of godmother, with a pipe of port when he was twenty-one, and meetings once a year or so since then. He went along with them a certain way, looking from face to face, but drew back at the hints of comedy, something unseemly. She was preserved for him in tender and unquestioned sentiment they seemed not to share. Besides, she had left him everything she had, a flat which Ivan supposed was worth quarter of a million, and her large miscellaneous collection of porcelain, silver and pictures. Ivan, by himself for a moment at the window, was looking at a row of china figures on the sill. He thought, because of Evert having some, that they were Chelsea, but he didn't know (what he knew you had to know) the marks. The figure he picked up and turned over had a small golden anchor, but his feeling that this was a good sign coexisted with a sense of half-forgotten warnings about rivals and imitations. The fact was he didn't care – about the things themselves; though as objects of Evert's interest, or of Jill's, they were worth knowing just enough about.

There was a small regrouping of the party, and Sally came across and stood by him, looking at the room over her glass. 'I find it all so sad.'

'I know . . .' Ivan found it gloomy, intriguing, but as it happened not sad.

'Are you doing her?'

'We've got someone, yes,' he said. 'We didn't have her ready.'

'Oh, I'd have thought . . . but perhaps she wasn't quite . . . I don't know.'

'No, no, definitely something,' he assured her.

'Not very long, I suppose?'

'Shortish, I think,' said Ivan, with a businesslike smile. He made an absolute point of not saying who wrote the obituaries. For Jill he'd asked Evert to do it, since he'd known her for more than fifty years, but it was a joint effort, Ivan splicing in details he'd been gathering himself for nearly half that time. Like most of the members of the now vestigial gang, she had a pocket of her own in his concertina files.

Sally laughed nervously, and said, 'I don't want to make a fuss, but I've just found something rather odd.'

'Oh . . . ?' said Ivan, and felt a hand on his shoulder.

'Cup of tea?' said Adrian.

'Oh . . .' – Ivan looked around, at the already dishevelled and surprisingly noisy little group. Evert had had two or three glasses of Adrian's red wine, and seemed to be enjoying himself more than he should have been. 'Probably a good idea . . . Do you want a hand?'

'I'll tell you later,' said Sally.

Ivan went with Adrian into the small old-fashioned kitchen – blue cupboards, old cooker with eye-level grill, net curtain on a string halfway up the window, which looked on to the car park and the road. Oval plates of sandwiches, ham or egg, still waited under clingfilm, enough for a much larger or hungrier party. Adrian started taking down cups and saucers from a cupboard. 'How many are we?' he said. A tray was quickly covered with a much-laundered cloth, the best teapot warmed from the boiling kettle. Then Freddie came in, he had to take his pills, and wanted a glass of water. He knocked them back, burped, and leant against the sink, and his eyes settled on the tray, the six smart tea cups augmented by others stacked for a moment in tilting pairs, relics of tea sets long gone, or just things Jill had picked up, and his lips, thin and dry, spread into what seemed, on his gaunt head, a smile of sickly tenderness.

'How funny. She told me fifty years ago that I didn't understand her. Naturally I thought she was wrong, but now I'm not so sure.'

Ivan smiled uncertainly. 'It seems you knew her quite well, Freddie.'

'I wonder if you'd do me a favour,' Freddie said to Adrian, and when he raised his eyebrows: 'When the tea's made will you give that cup there to Evert Dax?'

'This fancy one . . .'

'The Meissen one,' said Freddie. 'I want to see what he says.'

Ivan doubted he'd say very much. He picked it up himself, wondering if there was something obviously funny about it – he thought it was just the sort of thing, with its rippling gilt rim and tiny pictures of pink shepherds on blue hills, that any old lady might have.

He went to find the loo, which was locked, and as he waited in the hallway there was a knock at the open front door and Johnny looked in. 'You're a bit late, my dear,' Ivan said.

'Yeah, I know,' said Johnny, 'I've had Lucy . . .'

'Ah, yes.' Ivan had never got on with Lucy, for reasons he smoothly avoided thinking about. 'You couldn't bring her?'

'She was quite keen, actually, she's been longing to go to somebody's funeral, but her mother was against it.'

'Ah well, she'll have plenty more chances. How are you?'

'Fine!' said Johnny, coming in now, and kissing him quickly as he peered past into the room. 'How did it go?'

Ivan smiled at him and shrugged. 'Oh, you know. About twenty people, I suppose.'

'Poor old Jill.'

'Actually, the V&A woman gave a good address.'

'Oh, OK.'

Ivan thought Johnny had made some fractional effort – he was wearing an old pinstripe jacket over his roll-neck jersey, and a pair of black boots like a policeman's.

'How's Pat?'

'He's very well, thank you,' said Johnny, with a straight-faced stare at him, even after twenty years – not that Ivan supposed Johnny fancied him any longer, it was something more subtle, the feeling a pretence should be made of still very distantly minding that things hadn't worked out between them. 'He was sorry you couldn't come a few weeks back . . . you know.' They were both looking in through the door of the sitting room. 'How is Evert?'

'Well, there he is,' said Ivan. There was a small rather animated group at the window now, some with tea cups, others holding the Chelsea figures and turning them over, like experts in a shop. 'Go and say hello.' He was aware of a slight tendency among their friends to avoid Evert since his stroke, odd instinctual counterpart to the genuine desire to help.

'I will,' said Johnny.

When he came back from the loo, Ivan smiled at the others but he had the stupid feeling of having missed something – they were already adjusting to what had happened, the formulas of surprise passed round, repeated but diminishing, half-phrases. He looked from one to another, as if the joke might yet be on him. 'What is it . . . ?' Evert was holding the Chelsea figure Ivan had been looking at earlier, Dorothy Denham clutched a small silver box, Freddie himself held up the fancy cup and saucer:

'You must remember,' he said, 'I had a whole set from my mother.'

Evert didn't seem sure; he said, 'I remember this all right.'

'What is it?' said Ivan again.

'Well, it's too extraordinary,' said Arabella.

Sally came in behind them, holding aloft, like something everyone had been looking for, a painted china girl, in apron and bonnet, on a round white base. 'This is what I mean,' she said, 'do you remember, Brian?'; and when she'd shown it him she placed it, after a brief hesitation, in Adrian's hands.

'Well, I don't know!' said Adrian, turning it over, reasonable but defensive.

Margaret didn't speak at first. Then she said, 'This is actually rather serious, you know.' On the table beside her, among wine glasses and discarded paper napkins, were ten small objects, typical of the impersonal clutter of the room. 'We're going to have to have a long hard think about this.'

'Are you absolutely sure?' said Gordon, who didn't seem to be holding anything.

'It was actually reported missing,' Margaret said, 'well, of course it was, it's a very rare object. Jill was interviewed by the police about it herself.' And she cleared a space round a bowl on the table – it looked Chinese, and even to Ivan had the dull gleam of importance and no doubt value.

'Well, she's dead now,' said Clover, perhaps too straightfor-wardly.

But Sally in her worry saw the really delicate problem. 'Oh, Adrian, I'm so sorry,' she said.

When they left they all agreed their things should remain in the flat, until Margaret had spoken to her colleagues at the museum, and a plan was worked out. It seemed Jill had even had the nerve to nick something from Arabella downstairs, on one of her unreturned visits. 'Well, it all makes sense,' Arabella said – though in the minicab going home Ivan didn't know quite what it meant. Evert was sleepy with the drink, and seemed already to have forgotten about it. 'No, extraordinary,' he agreed, when Ivan brought the subject up.

Evert's stroke had had two main consequences – his short-term memory was impaired, leaving him sometimes at sea in the midst of a conversation started with a clear sense of purpose and subject. He said he saw soft white squares, where facts in the form of images, or images of words, should be, pale blanks that floated on his mind's eye like the shape of a bright window. The other effect, somehow doubly surprising, was release from worry – not only the worry that pervaded decisions and plans, but the worry that was caused by not being able to remember. This felt like a blessing, but was also, Ivan felt, a bit worrying in itself.

There was a rather oppressive need to keep him focused – on day-to-day matters, and on the looming plans for the house. Victor was tidied up now, really for good. And all the things that had been put off until he was tidied up loomed much larger. The advance for the biography was £10,000, a much smaller figure when the book was delivered than it had been when the contract was signed. The work on the house might cost ten times as much. Besides which, Evert needed a new project. A proper memoir was the obvious idea; but it could be another art book, portraits of artists he had known over fifty years. Otherwise he was going to spend every day forgetting what he'd gone out for and picking up strangers in Marks and Spencer's.

Ivan had forced him to make an inventory of all the pictures, which had been like getting a child to do his homework; he wriggled out of it, or else, going through the contents of a print chest on the top landing, fell under the spell of forgotten images and their suddenly woken associations. There were also the various items on loan, to museums and so forth. A certain ruthlessness was called for here, if the sale was to realize the best figure. Ivan felt everything should be looked at, and the threat of ending the loans, if it seemed worth it, put into play.

A few months ago Evert had been invited to a Feast at his old College, and Ivan had gone with him. He wanted to see the portrait of Victor by George Lambert which Evert was sure he'd given them, but which Ivan discovered on a look through some old files was merely on loan. At the drinks before, in a room that was virtually panelled in old portraits, Ivan brought up the question with one of the dons, who it turned out had never heard of the sitter, let alone the portrait. But he introduced him to a Dr Fraser, who ran the College art collection, and Ivan said again he thought they had it. 'In*deed* we do . . . !' said Dr Fraser: 'I'll ask Mr Tarlow to show it to you after dinner.' 'It's not in here, then,' said Ivan. 'We *don't* keep it in here,' said Dr Fraser, with no further explanation, but conveying a sense that wherever it was was the best place for it. He himself had promptly forgotten his promise, but Ivan pressed him again later on, and after dessert he and Evert were taken out by Mr Tarlow across the quad, through an archway and into another quad, then into a staircase next to the kitchens, into a range of old buildings lately adapted for graduate accommodation, where up two flights of stairs were two guest rooms for overnight visitors. They unlocked the first and looked in, but it wasn't there, so they tried the second, Mr Tarlow emitting a hearty 'Aha!' as he stood back and let them have a look. The room contained almost nothing – a single bed, a completely empty bookcase, and a refrigerator. And on the wall above the refrigerator hung *Arnold Victor Dax (1880–1954)* by George Lambert (1873–1930), in a heavily ornate gilt frame missing a cusp at one corner. It was further described, on the small label on the frame, as on 'permanent loan' from Evert Dax, 1939 – the year, of course, of his matriculation. Ivan found himself wondering what on earth the guests made of it, with its wary gleam and villainous moustache. 'We like to keep as much of the collection on view as we can,' said Mr Tarlow warmly, stumbling on the tail of his gown as he stepped back across the squawking floorboards. 'Well, no one could say it brightened up the room,' said Evert, which left Mr Tarlow a little at a loss as they all trooped out again.

When they got home Evert went to lie down, and Ivan dealt with the mail that had come that morning. The main item was from the Dean of Humanities at Lichfield University, at first glance just a brochure about their development programme, but with a covering letter that concealed towards the end a rather delicate piece of news. The enhanced facilities, the expanded library, the new Gottfried Wenk International Business School, were described in Utopian detail, or lack of it. It was all going to be marvellous, and the one possibly regrettable consequence of the works was the demolition of the old 1960s Arts Building, whose much-loved but now sadly outdated amenities included of course the A. V. Dax Theatre. 'It is hoped', the Dean wrote, 'that the memory of your father will be preserved in some other way in the department. I believe Professor Bishop will be in touch with you soon about the digitisation of the A. V. Dax Archive.' This sounded like a good thing, though Ivan couldn't help wondering if the actual manuscripts, once digitally preserved, would still be thought necessary. He saw a van arriving at Cranley Gardens with the forty boxes which Evert had so cleverly got rid of twenty-five years earlier.

He kept it till they were going to bed, and the two or three minutes when Evert, in his pyjama bottoms, sat on a stool in the bedroom while Ivan, standing behind him, worked Deep Heat into his stiff neck and left shoulder. It was a moment when he had him captive, and with his gently kneading thumbs and fingers could coax and comfort and half-hypnotize him. He smiled at him in the mirror: 'You had a funny letter today from the man at Lichfield.'

'Oh!' said Evert, fluttering his eyelashes at the appearance of something so remote from his present thoughts. 'I'd forgotten about them.'

'Just as well, perhaps,' said Ivan. Evert's skin was warm now and soft, the springy little grey hairs on his shoulders were smoothed flat by the ointment; then curled up again. The fumes of menthol and eucalyptus, the trace of turpentine, offered their old-fashioned reassurance. Ivan told him about the Theatre. He didn't present it as something bad, and had little idea, after all these years, how Evert would take it.

'Oh, lord,' he said.

'It's a shame, isn't it,' Ivan said.

'You've never seen it, have you,' said Evert. 'It wasn't a very nice theatre.'

'No, you said.'

'I mean it wasn't a theatre, it was a lecture room.'

331

'And at least it's going to be demolished,' said Ivan. 'They're not renaming it after someone else.'

'Someone with more money usually.'

'That would be an insult. Still, it's rather awful,' said Ivan, slipping his arms round Evert's neck and resting his chin on the crown of his head. They examined themselves in the mirror.

'Yes, it's awful,' said Evert, looking down as if he might be about to cry, or was just possibly stifling a laugh. Ivan had a sense he minded it more than Evert did. If the memorial itself was destroyed, then what remained? 'Thanks,' Evert said, and rolled his shoulders as he stood up. 'Mm, that's much better.' He put on his pyjama jacket and buttoned it as he went off to clean his teeth.

Ivan got undressed too. He had a responsible feeling of surviving, tonight, of carrying on in the world when a friend had left it for ever. He imagined Jill's godson Adrian, a kindly hard-working man of about his own age, clearing up after the strangers had gone and turning out the lights on the prospects of a small, entirely unforeseen scandal. Margaret would do her best to control it, but all organizations were leaky, the V&A literally so, crumbling and underfunded, with staff laid off – Ivan knew about it, and saw he must press for the obituary to appear before the story broke.

They usually read for ten minutes or so in bed, but tonight Ivan, halfway through Chips Channon's *Diaries*, felt tired and switched off his light after a page or so. Evert had been livelier in bed since his stroke, which was nice, but made Ivan himself a bit cautious, out of worry he might have another stroke from the exertion. They now had their once-a-monthers about three times a week. Ivan heard him coming back from the bathroom, his quiet, random, spaced-out remarks. Evert, who'd been half of a couple for the past forty years, now talked to himself like someone who lived alone. He had always spoken in his sleep, odd phrases that turned over as if in bed themselves and settled some unheard argument ('which of course was why . . .' 'so you see he couldn't . . .'); now he talked in his sleep when he was awake, made passing observations, wistful or sly, and often surely sexual, wandering in a field of reminiscence peopled by men other and earlier than Ivan. He smiled contentedly as he came into the room, set down his glass of water, and slipped into bed. 'Good night,' said Ivan with a vocal sort of yawn, pulling up the covers.

Evert pushed up beside him. 'Because he was always passive, you know, in bed,' he said, cosily but conclusively.

Ivan's voice was toneless, a last dim formality before sleep as he turned away from Evert and shrugged into the pillow. 'Who was that, Evert?'

'Mm, never you mind,' said Evert, raising a knee and breathing a kiss on to his neck; and it soon became clear Ivan wasn't going to get off that lightly.

3

George Chalmers hung his coat up in the hall, folded his silk scarf and laid his gloves on top of it on the table. He had chosen to be painted in a crimson velvet smoking jacket, and cut a quaint figure at ten in the morning in the cold studio. The portrait, it turned out, was his present to himself for his seventieth birthday, though he said he'd been urged by any number of old friends to have it done. It stood now, a pale sketched ghost with a staring pink face, on the big easel, still so far from the desired effect that he walked past without looking at it; he stepped up with a short grunt on to the low rostrum and took his place in the high-backed chair. Johnny had picked up the chair for £10 at an auction – fake Venetian, oak and shabby velvet not quite the same colour as George's jacket, and fixed with rows of brass studs. George sat upright, crossed his legs, and laid his hands along the down-curling arms of the throne.

So the new sitting, the fifth, began, Johnny passing in a minute or two through social self-consciousness into the familiar absorption of work. He preferred to have music playing, but because George was deaf it made talk even harder, so he dabbed and darted and pondered to the soundtrack of his subject's monologues. Sometimes talk in the studio formed mysterious counterpoints to the actions of painting, sometimes it distracted and interfered. George Chalmers was a good subject, but an unsympathetic person. He preserved into old age something starkly coquettish, an unrelinquished belief in his own naughtiness and appeal. His stories about himself at Oxford, and in the Navy, and in Egypt and Italy after the War, were both savage and sentimental. He'd been madly in love, his heart had been broken; but Peter Coyle and Willy Fitchet and Jack Ducane were all shits and he'd seen through them and outlived them all – Peter of course by half a century. Outliving his lovers, a mere accident, seemed to suit his competitive view of life. Johnny's compliant smiles and absent murmurs of 'Oh!' and 'Really . . . ?' flattered him at first, but offered not enough resistance. Pressed for anecdotes about his own love life, Johnny felt like an unadventurous simpleton. 'Yes, well I once met this really nice Irish guy . . .' Chalmers anyway didn't seem to take in what he said, he wasn't looking for any parity between the younger man's fumblings and his own legendary adventures; though occasionally, from fatigue and good manners, he showed a distant interest, a weak unexpectant encouragement. Because of the deafness Johnny had to say his little stories loudly, as if addressing and failing to amuse a whole roomful of people.

Johnny's strength, from the social point of view, was knowing Evert, who had encouraged George to commission the portrait; but Johnny had never had the gift of anecdote, and things he said about Freddie, or Iffy Skipton, or the goings-on at the Royal Soc of Portrait Painters, stories which had tickled Pat, and Evert himself, made little impression on Chalmers. He expected the old man to come round at some point to the Sparsholt Affair, but he never did, perhaps simply because it didn't involve him or anyone he knew personally, and was, besides, a hideous balls-up, of the kind that Chalmers himself, for all his much wilder adventures, had been far too clever to get caught up in. Johnny felt his father's term at Oxford might have overlapped with George's time there, but it seemed most unlikely they would have met.

It was people with a different kind of fame that he talked about as he sat. 'Of course I'll never forget when I was in Florence for a few months in 1947, picked up this amazing young kid, who wanted to get into the theatre. I say kid, he was probably only a year or so younger than me. He was already working for Visconti, whom I knew reasonably well, of course. I had the clap at the time, can't remember if it was in the arse or the cock, both probably, what? so I had to let that one pass. Then a few years later he turned up in London and gave me a ring – he was directing *Tosca* at Covent Garden! Of course you realize who it was.'

'Daddy?'

Johnny didn't turn, but he gasped at the thought of what she might have heard. 'What is it, sweetheart?' And now there was the creak of the floorboards behind him.

'When are we going out?'

'Not till after lunch, I'm working this morning, as you can see.'

'Oh . . .' He was aware of her, at the edge of his vision, standing.

'Good morning,' said George crisply.

'George, this is my daughter Lucy – this is Mr Chalmers, I told you about.'

'Good morning,' said Lucy, with a momentary lowering of the voice and (he knew) the eyes. He pictured her view of the studio, the opaque adult world of the process, the talk, the canvas taller than she was. Once she had sat for him herself, or wriggled and slumped and slept for him, and he knew he must paint her again, on one of their weeks together. It was a long time since he'd done anything more than a sketch for love, not money.

On the Wednesday afternoon, Timothy Gorley-Whittaker, a superbly polite little boy, sanctioned even by Francesca, came round for the second time to see Lucy. Although it was half-term he arrived with his satchel, 'T. G.-W.' stamped on the flap. They were up in her room for over an hour, and as on his previous visit no sound of voices or footsteps could be heard in the studio below. At four Johnny went upstairs to tell them tea was ready and stood for a moment outside the door – there was continuous but rather strained, even argumentative, conversation. He tapped and went in a little anxiously to find Lucy seated on the bed and Timothy leaning against the mantelpiece, which for him was at shoulder height. They each held a small open book, and they stared at him with a mixture of impatience and embarrassment. 'Tea's up!' said Johnny.

'OK,' said Lucy, glancing at Timothy.

'May we just finish this scene, sir?' Timothy said.

Johnny smiled dimly at the phrase before he saw that of course they were reading a play – he ducked his head and withdrew. Timothy's gentlemanly treble went on. 'Fanny, let us keep it to ourselves.'

'Oh . . . sorry . . . um, um,' said Lucy.

Johnny put his head round the door again and said quite

loudly, 'You don't have to call me sir, you know.' Then he went downstairs. His own father had liked Johnny's schoolfriends to call him sir, which they either resented or overdid, both things mortifying to Johnny himself.

On the kitchen table he had set out a plate of Jaffa Cakes, a glisteningly dense but fat-free fruit cake that Pat had made, and a nice trimmed stack of banana and peanut-butter sandwiches he had made himself, eating one impulsively with a spasm of nostalgia at the peanut paste parching his throat. After tea it would be dark enough for some indoor fireworks that had caught his eye at the corner shop, the red packet like a box of combustible biscuits, volcanoes, Roman candles and five sparklers each. The children came down a minute later. 'May I wash my hands, sir?' said Timothy.

Johnny let it pass. 'Both wash your hands,' he said, and peeped at his own, which as usual were scabbed with paint, and the nails black. Lucy washed her hands first, and passed the towel apologetically to Timothy. 'So what have you two been up to?' Johnny said.

Timothy sat on the chair Lucy indicated. 'We're reading *Mary Rose*,' he said.

'Oh, yes,' said Johnny: 'what's that?'

Timothy looked bewildered for a second, but decided it wasn't a joke and smiled reassuringly: 'Oh – it's by J. M. Barrie . . . you know.'

'Ah, yes,' said Johnny.

'It's very amusing, actually.'

'Have something to eat, have a sandwich.'

'Thank you, Mr Sparsholt.'

'There's quite a lot of writing in it,' said Lucy.

Timothy glanced at her tenderly. 'Yes, all the stage directions.'

'Oh, yes,' said Johnny.

337

'I read those out as well, it's almost like reading a book, you know.'

'We have to be several people at once,' explained Lucy, as if this were both exciting and rather a drawback.

'Well, I hope it's suitable,' said Johnny, just a little bit as a joke; he thought it was all rather rum. Lucy looked as if she'd like to make a further comment, but her own politeness prevented her. Timothy was protractedly chewing a mouthful of bread and peanut butter, but his eyebrows signalled a desire to speak.

'Oh, completely suitable, sir,' he said at length.

'Good lad,' said Johnny, and wondered again at the language that his own part, the bluff but caring parent, was written in.

After tea he went into the studio and came back with the box of indoor fireworks. 'I thought these might be fun,' he said.

There was a trace of anxiety on Lucy's face, but Timothy smiled. 'I used to love them when I was small,' he said.

'Hmm, so did I,' said Johnny. 'Shall we go in the other room, we can make it darker in there.'

They went out through the hall, and into the sitting room; the doors into the studio were closed, and the street light outside the gate threw autumnal gleams among the shadowy sofas and armchairs. Johnny switched just one lamp on, before he pulled the heavy curtains across. A saucer on the marble hearth – and the children to stand back, while he lit the little tabs of blue paper. He saw, when he opened the box and peered at the contents, that they were not only few in number but poor quality – in the shop he hadn't noticed the brand, which evidently wasn't English: 'Putt in Earth or flower-pots' it said on the Roman candle. He did just that, in the pot of an old cactus, lit the fuse and quickly turned off the lamp. In the dark the tiny burning dot twitched slightly and after a wavering ten seconds appeared to expire. 'Daddy ...' warned Lucy as he went towards it, and at just that moment there was a pop and a low fountain of blue sparks began to play from the top, much more on the right than the left, where it sputtered and seemed blocked. The mouth of the fireplace and the brown Minton tiles around it were lit up, and in the mantelpiece mirror Johnny saw the youngsters' faces, ghostly against the dark, Lucy biting her cheek.

When she agreed it was safe to go in, he turned on the lamp again. 'This one should be a bit more thrilling,' he said, tipping the debris into the grate and setting a small black cone on the saucer. 'These used to be my favourites.' He crouched down and struck a match. 'Your granny used to get them for me as a special treat, darling.'

'Yes,' said Lucy.

'They can be really pretty.' He touched the match to the tip of the cone which caught and smoked at once. The paper peeled back, and before he'd turned the light off the softly fizzling volcano spewed out purple worms for four seconds and then went out – dormant or extinct it was hard to say, though they stood back in case of some further eruption, even a titchy one, in the flat half-minute that followed. An unpleasant nitrous smell hung in the air. It was her mother that Johnny heard in Lucy's voice from the darkness: 'That was *really* pathetic!' At which, disappointingly, Timothy giggled.

Well, there were still the sparklers. 'Let's play with fire,' said Johnny, and saw Timothy's uncertain smile. The harmlessness of sparklers was their magic, as much as the danger of other fireworks – the sparks showered where they would, on chairs and carpets, and left no trace. At the centre, though, the wand of incandescence, fading at the tip as the sparks crept fizzing towards the hand, must surely be hot. These particular sparklers were made of very thin and bendy wire. 'Be careful now . . .' And with the lamp switched off again, Johnny lit a Vesta, the children dipped their two tips into the flame, they were slow to catch, then seemed to fuse for a second in the glare

339

before they lifted them away and Johnny shook out the match that was suddenly burning his fingers. The sparklers cast only a short-range light, there was a dreamy weakness of effect. Timothy drew decorous circles in the air with his, Lucy was a bit more arabesque, the portrait of herself glimmering in its varnish as she waved in front of it. Then the three of them were in the dark again. 'Great, well there are four more each!' said Johnny.

They grew more adventurous with the next two goes, they shuffled round the room, writing vanishing letters on the air in front of them, Lucy made fairy swoops, and Timothy was a plane, with cautious sound effects, coming quickly, even so, to the limits of sparklers and what you could do with them. When they had got through three of them, Lucy said, 'Daddy, why don't you have a go?'

'Yes, do, Mr Sparsholt,' said Timothy.

'No, no, I bought them for you,' said Johnny, with a laugh at his cut-price benevolence.

'Well, we've had a go,' said Lucy; and when he still demurred, 'In fact we've had three goes.'

So he took one, as instructed, and let Lucy light it, her face intent and to him very beautiful. The thing spat and crackled, and then it was going. He stood, with the advantage of height, and not a clue what to do with it, he was conducting in the air above their heads, it seemed to be the Tragic Overture, then he waited staring with a patient smile at the sparks hissing down over his raised hand into the shadows.

At six o'clock Annabel Gorley-Whittaker arrived to pick up her son, just as Pat was getting home from work. He pushed open the door with a flourish, but she showed an odd reluctance to come into the house. She advanced as far as the coat stand and tried to carry off the difficult feat of not actually looking at any of the two dozen pictures on the walls. 'Ah,

Timothy, there you are,' she said, as if kept waiting for hours, when he appeared at the head of the stairs.

'He's been no trouble,' said Johnny, amazed to find himself, as a parent, in relations with this woman.

She looked at him keenly for a second – whatever she had imagined was surely the other way round. Her politeness, like her son's, was excessive – for two or three seconds her face became a mask of intimate understanding and apology. 'It's been awfully good of you to have him,' she said.

The following day was set aside for an outing. There was an expectation of outings and also a slight resistance to them. Lucy could take an interest in houses and pictures, he flattered her and got her on his side by saying he knew she liked art – but he knew too that the liking was finite and fatiguable. A place with a lot of gilding and drapery excited her for fifteen or twenty minutes, as an ideal setting for herself, but then the monotony of history made her eyes restless and her feet on the tourists' drugget would drag in mutiny or her hand jerk him hopefully forward and round the corner. Now and then he would see their passing image in the depth of an old mirror hung between windows, an ill-assorted pair, scruffy man with his thick, too-long hair, and neat, restless, critical child.

Coming at it another way, he once stopped her without explanation in the Bayswater backstreet where the great Peter Orban had fitted a cool Corbusian house (his first in London) into the long shabby terrace. 'Isn't it beautiful,' he said. For a moment she gave him credit for a joke – of the forced paternal kind – and she seemed to think it an unfair trick when he told her her own great-grandfather had built it. She cocked her head as she looked at it afresh; but it wasn't going to wash. Better gilding and drapes than that.

'Why couldn't he make it the same as all the other houses?' she said.

'Well, sometimes, darling,' said Johnny, holding her there just a little bit longer, 'there's a point in being completely different and new.'

'Well, I think it's nasty,' she said quietly, and turned her head to carry on down the street.

'A bomb knocked down the old house, you see, in the War,' said Johnny, now rather on his mettle to defend the building. But talk of the War, which had coloured and conditioned so much of his own childhood, was meaningless to her.

Today's outing was to Dulwich, to see the picture gallery. She had been there, unrememberingly, before, when she was small enough to ride in a backpack, little ranee on a jogging elephant, her view of the paintings relieved by the back of her father's neck. Though he said, 'Look!' from time to time they had gone there wholly for his own pleasure. She had combed his hair with her fingers, produced tiny ditties and operatic shrieks, and by the room of the Poussins was emitting a powerful smell. It was one of his favourite places, and today's return was threatened from the start by the way he talked it up to her. Like her mother, she disliked being told what to think, or feel – 'great art in a great building, sweetheart', he said, and saw the small frown of incipient resistance. Off they went in the Volvo, with its muddle of Pat's things and Johnny's things, and an unignorable smell of its own. The safety net was the Fairmile sculpture garden, a short drive further on, where they'd been last summer, when Lucy had said it was 'lovely' and 'enormous fun'; though she was capable of hair-raising changes of mind.

Well, the gallery wasn't a success, and not, somehow, for itself, but because of what he'd said, all the greatness of it. Greatness didn't excite her yet – it had if anything the opposite effect. 'What do you think, then?' he said, holding her to him parentally in her red coat with black velvet collar. She shrugged him off to look round, as if the question hadn't crossed her mind in the previous half-hour.

'It's OK,' she said.

'Oh, well that's good!' said Johnny, wounded of course but knowing enough now not to press her and harden her further. 'We'll just look at one more room, shall we.'

'Daddy, when can we see the sculpture garden?' She looked up at him, she could be charming.

'You want to go there now, do you?'

'Yes, please.'

'Just one more room?'

She thought it through. 'OK.' And he took her hand again and strolled with her into the cross-gallery at the end, where twenty little Dutch pictures hung, small oils, full of interest and even comedy of a kind.

'Gosh, look . . .' said Johnny. 'What do you think that lady's doing?' It was the wrong tone, baby-talk nearly.

She pulled him away, apparently towards another picture, as if anything would be better than the one they were looking at already. She twirled round, a kaleidoscope of cows, trees, boats and rivers. 'Daddy . . . ?'

'Yes, Lucy?'

She stared up at him, almost pitying. 'This is *really* boring!'

It was a clearer statement than the dismal disaffected, 'It's OK,' and he laughed and gave in. He saw what she meant, in a way. And now she was happy, good sense had prevailed, she seemed to feel she'd saved them both from an experience not only trying but unnecessary. 'So not even a drink,' he said, 'or an ice cream?'

This time she smiled as she said it, as if he'd done enough: 'It's OK.'

'Sure?'

'I'm sure,' she said. 'Sure, sure, sure . . .'

She'd won, he felt it too much, as they went back, past the Van Dycks and Reynoldses, other canvases skyed high above all adults, let alone children. And then a kind of puzzlement settled in him that he should be so vulnerable to his own child. Too much was focused on these visits, these outings, with their inbuilt obstacles to success.

Fifteen minutes later they had left the car and chosen not the looping accessible path but the steep romantic steps down through the trees. In the late afternoon light the wooded dell with its fifteen looming inhabitants (a couple kinetic, and turning on their axes now and then to catch the wind, and thus the light) had the otherworldly mood of a Symbolist painting; autumn leaves were fluttering down and the passers-through thinned out and only one or two voices could be heard, from the planted maze at the top corner of the site. To Lucy it was a playground of choices, of sequence, she had her favourites, and climbed first into the broad curl of a Caro, her little boots striking echoes from the iron; then she was off. As she saw more she remembered more, the sculptures hid from one another among bushes and round corners, and she wanted to give each piece its due; though as she ran on she looked round for Johnny, moving at a fatherly pace along the path. She came back to him, with a breathless report or plan, then was off again, leaving him with an odd emptiness in the air beside him: the phantom adult, not exactly her mother, whose talk, as they ambled, would have risen, each time Lucy ran up to them, into brief shows of interest and encouragement, before dropping back, when she ran off, into the mysterious monotone of grown-up affairs.

He was relieved she was happy with a place he liked well enough himself, but he sensed that something else about the garden unnerved her. She took his hand as they went up the path on the far side, where the tall silver mobile creaked as it swivelled towards them. Their previous visit had been on a summer Sunday, other children in possession of certain sculptures, engaging her, abruptly, or doubtingly, in games and challenges. Now, in the last thirty minutes before November closing time, it issued a subtle challenge of its own. They pressed on, arms swinging.

What they both called the maze, the tapering half-acre where the garden ran up to the junction of two neighbouring properties, was really a pattern of joining and dividing paths between high-hedged circles, three of them, with sculptures in each. The big gardens of the houses beyond, with their dense firs and laurels, made you think that the maze was much bigger, until, pushing through a clump of young hazels, you came up against the high black fence. To a child, of course, the place had a scale that Johnny, looking through and over the hedges, brown beech and dark green yew, could see beyond. In the three clearings people liked to dawdle, or sit on the curved benches, ambiguously sculptures in themselves, carved from the branches of a fallen oak. Now the sun was nearly horizontal, the paths and circles were filled with shadow, and Johnny felt a faint nervousness, not only on Lucy's behalf, pressed on him through her cool tight hand, but of his own. The voices, two men talking quietly, inconstantly, as if engaged in some task, the gardeners perhaps, seemed already to have claimed the place – they spoke quietly, but with no thought of being overheard, in the rhythms and pauses of unselfconscious speech. 'I think you like this one, don't you?' Johnny said, somehow shy to be overheard himself.

'Yes, I do,' said Lucy, as they stood in front of the bronze Diana with a bow, on her cusp of moon, a figure rescued from some Deco fountain and quite different from the assorted abstractions in the garden below. She enjoyed the closeness with him now. 'It's different, isn't it.'

'It is,' he said, aware as they got closer and walked right round Diana, of a pause in the nearby talk, and then a brisk continuation which showed the men were aware of the newcomers.

The sunlight, in its odd scattered piercings of the foliage, fell on litter far under the hedge, torn squares of black and silver foil. But the idea moved slowly in Johnny's head. 'Do you want to see the others, or shall we go back now?'

'Let's *see*,' she said, and shook her head, a completist when she wanted to be.

They went on, round the corner, and saw a man coming towards them, jeans and denim jacket, bald, muscular, about Johnny's age, and looking at him sharply for a moment, as if spotting and then doubting something and showing, with a grunt of acknowledgement, he had got it wrong. He walked quickly past them, and after a pace or two Lucy glanced back, frowning still. 'Daddy, do you know that man?' she said.

'What? Good lord no,' said Johnny; and was suddenly more apprehensive about the other, unseen, stranger. He smiled and peered ahead, imperceptibly restraining Lucy as she led him forward. But in the small third circle there was no sign of anyone else, and the tapering steel shaft, by some Japanese disciple of Brancusi, didn't keep them there long. So the other man had left along the further path. But the atmosphere of what they had surely been doing quickened Johnny's pulse and seemed to haunt the deepening shadows under the trees. He found he wanted to see what the other man was like, and looked out for him while talking emptily about something else. He might still be lurking somewhere – it was almost a relief to hear the hand-bell ringing, from the gate by the car park. 'Ah, time to head back,' Johnny said, and Lucy again agreed.

She had no sense of direction, his was a rarely faulted instinct, and her doubts about it were forgotten in the moment of escaping the maze. A path along the top led more directly to the exit, across lawns half-hidden in fallen leaves and screened by sombre clumps of rhododendrons. They swung their linked hands. 'Daddy, where are we going for supper?' Lucy said.

'Oh, Lucy . . .' – her demands had their own economy, one

treat triggered the need for another one. Would Francesca give in, was this how decisions were made at Belsize Grove? Or was he being tested? He said, 'Well, we'll see,' and from a gap in the bushes to the left of them a man emerged, hands in pockets, scuffing the leaves with his boots.

'Daddy . . .' she said, warningly, though against what he couldn't tell.

'We'll see,' he said again. He could tell she was glad of his protection, though she scorned any sign of timidity, and stared at the stranger. She would have spun herself a story, a mere thread of rationale, for the man's presence here, though to a small girl a looming giant in black was a creature of a different order from the potent beauty Johnny saw, hands in pockets of a short leather jacket pulled tight across the top of his bum. They nodded curtly but pleasantly as he came down to the path, there was a moment's uncertainty if he would wait, but he cut in in front of them, jogged a pace or two, looking back with a quick tut of thanks, and after a few paces looking back again, with the little doubting smile of recognition.

'It *is* you,' he said, so that Johnny seemed to see himself, and wondered if it was.

'Hi . . .'

'You don't remember. Well, I am hurt!' – his voice big, saucy, capable.

Johnny knew a face, it was his calling and career, but something in him delayed a second longer the emergence from the past of this brown-eyed humorous mask, changed inexorably by the journey, but settling and clarifying now, the lips sharper, the curly hair thinner and cropped short, the big powerful frame itself heavier, with the lumbering ease of continuous training. 'It's Mark . . .' said Johnny, in the awkward pleasure of finding the stranger was a friend all along.

'Well, how are you!'

'I'm very well . . .' They had stopped, Johnny stuck out his hand to prevent a hug or a kiss, and Mark shook it and winked, squaring his shoulders.

'Johnny Sparsholt . . . How amazing.'

'I know . . .' – Johnny watched Mark turn his seductive smile on the red-coated child beside him. 'This is Lucy,' he said firmly, and not to say more.

'Hello, Lucy! I'm Mark' – stooping to her but sensing no handshake was forthcoming.

'Hello,' said Lucy, suddenly younger, turning on her heel in boredom or unease while she held her father's hand. She felt for the currents of adult talk, hints of reserve, of real or merely pretended warmth, but she made her own immediate judgements on people too, not easy to shift.

'It must be fifteen years,' said Johnny.

'Yeah,' said Mark tolerantly. 'What have you been up to? Still painting?'

'I certainly am.'

'Going well?'

'Yeah, I think so . . .'

The bell rang again from the gate, some sad echo of school in the darkening afternoon. 'Daddy . . .' said Lucy.

Johnny touched Mark's upper arm and they moved on together.

'So things have changed a bit for you,' said Mark, 'by the look of it.'

'Yes – a lot of things, actually.'

Mark looked at him in friendly calculation. 'So you're married . . .'

'Married . . . ? Oh, I see. No – well, Lucy here is my daughter, but I'm not married, no' – as she scuffed the leaves and yanked on his hand.

'Hmm . . .' said Mark.

'And what about you? Still in Camberwell?'

'God, it was that long ago . . .'

'I remember the house,' said Johnny – it was a glimpse, as if he'd pulled open the front of a doll's house, of a dozen different lives going on on five floors, a cooperative, with its meetings and parties in bright-coloured rooms and the danger, all the time, of a small group of members seizing control.

'We were kicked out of there in the end,' Mark said. 'We had some good times, though.'

'Yes,' said Johnny, 'indeed,' not sure if he meant the times he had there with him in particular. Good times were a basic requirement for Mark – dazzling, exhausting all-nighters. He must have had a job, but Johnny, then as now, never quite took in what people did. 'And what are you doing these days?'

'Ooh, I keep pretty busy,' said Mark, 'if you know what I mean!' The patter, it had always been a thing about Mark, everything bounced into a joke of a kind, innuendo so endless you checked what you were about to say, with a longing, after days of it, for talk as dull and unequivocal as could be. Still, feeling the tug of his presence now, hands pouched in jacket pockets, the faint raw smell of the leather, Johnny was amazed to think someone so handsome, active and unthinking had spent a whole month of nights with him, drinking, dancing and in bed.

They came up towards the big Henry Moore by the gate, only two cars beyond in the further hedged maze of the small car park. 'I must nip off for a sec,' said Mark with a grin, 'but great to have seen you.'

'And you!' said Johnny, not sure what he meant by nip off – but it seemed he needed a piss.

'Run into you again, maybe' —and now a quick hug, Mark's warm breath at Johnny's ear. He walked off fast, with a minute to spare, as the attendant came back with the key tied to a short red baton.

'He's just coming,' said Johnny, and as Lucy ran out by herself towards the Volvo he turned and watched him for a moment through the gap in the Henry Moore – a two-piece reclining figure which from most points of view overlapped and combined as if one but from this narrow vantage was revealed as two separate weathered hunks.

Lucy sat up in the car, in the dignity and disadvantage of a small person, as they made their way through thickening traffic on to the South Circular. The ebbing of enthusiasm in a child was upsetting to Johnny in part because he understood it – it was like a judgement on himself. His own dawdles and go-slows, the beauty-struck trances of childhood and adolescence, had been lonely at the time, understood by none of the other boys. Why should Lucy share this peculiar, faintly disabling gift? 'Daddy,' she said, 'did you ever want to get married?'

'Oh, darling . . . it never really seemed likely.' He slid a glance at her. 'Why do you ask?'

'I wish you'd marry Mummy,' she said.

'Sweetheart . . .' – the wish was too poignant to sound quite believable; but something had unsettled her this afternoon. 'I don't think we'd have got on very well, do you?'

'Lots of people's parents don't get on,' Lucy said.

'Well, that's very true. But then what happens? Think of Granny and Grandpa.'

'Hmm. Which ones?'

'Well, I meant my parents – but Mummy's too, come to that. Your mother and I are very different sorts of people. I'm sure you'd agree.'

She stared out at the cars and vans which seemed to close in, to slow and set firm all round them as they waited for a light a hundred yards ahead. 'Timothy's asked me to marry him,' she said.

Important not to laugh – and not to take it too seriously,

which would soon sound like mockery. 'I see. When did this happen?'

'When we went upstairs after the fireworks.'

'The excitement must have got to him.'

'Daddy,' said Lucy.

'And what did you say?'

She perhaps thought him unworthy of this confidence after all. 'I said I'd think about it.'

'Quite right.' The lights changed, the slow release of inertia passed backwards through the crowd of cars. 'What he needs to do, of course, is come and ask me for your hand in marriage.'

'Hm.'

'That's the proper thing.'

'OK.'

'I mean it would have to be quite a long engagement, wouldn't it.'

'I know,' said Lucy: 'I just don't know what I'll feel when the time comes.'

'And nor does he, sweetheart, remember that.'

The journey home took much longer than the easy drive down. Sidelights, headlights, were on, the long line of street-lights stretched ahead as the road turned to night, and high above, even so, the sky whitened and gleamed clear, long strands of purple-black cloud sinking over the housetops. Once or twice he sensed she was asleep, but she moved irritably when he peeped at her to check. He thought about what they would do later, ideally something with Pat, a game of Cluedo, which she loved, or Monopoly, with its different kind of killings, which she naturally expected to win; and he thought of Mark, strolling towards him so suddenly out of the past, and then jogging off under the trees, surely never to be seen again.

4

Freddie's funeral was held at Kensal Green, and Lucy was taken to it, at her own insistence. She was aware of the disagreements about whether she should go, her father's wishes more or less clear from her mother's response to them on the phone. When the day arrived she got up in a thoughtful variant of her dark school uniform and went into her mother and Una's room to look in the big mirror; she was to travel to the crematorium with the Skipton family, but would come away from the 'wake' that followed with her father. In the evening she would go on with him, wearing something nicer, but still, she imagined, with a lingering gravity, to the Musson Gallery for the private view of Evert's pictures. 'It's unfortunate,' said her mother, 'having the two things on the same day.' But Lucy, adjusting her hat and looking for her in the mirror, disagreed. 'After all the sadness,' she said, 'I think it will be a blessed relief.'

What she forgot, because it had no purchase on her yet, and she hoped never would, was the drink. Clover put on a party with waiters, back at the house, and it was just as noisy and successful as the party that Lucy had been to a year ago there, when Freddie was alive. Granny Iffy became, as she herself said, 'Granny Squiffy', Clover was 'half-cut' (according to Evert) before they started, and Evert himself got so sloshed he kissed one of the waiters. 'It was what he wanted,' said Clover, angling her glass for a refill: 'he wanted to go out with a bang'; and to Lucy, standing at first by the door to the kitchen, the pop of champagne corks was the defining noise. Well, perhaps wakes were like this – it took a little getting used to, like the funeral itself, and she wasn't going to show surprise. The solemn feeling that had silenced and upset her in the crematorium was not really to do with Freddie, whom she'd hardly known, and whose smile at her had always been a general one, of tolerance for all the confusing children of his friends' children. The sight of the coffin, and the thought of him inside it, just a few feet away – this must have been what her mother wanted to protect her from, and what her father thought she was old enough now to see. She felt somehow both grateful and indignant.

She arrived at Clover's with her mother and Una, and didn't join up with her father and Pat again till later on, when the room was full, and ten or twelve people, in spite of the damp, grey weather, had gone into the garden. 'There's your father outside with Clover,' said her mother: 'run and talk to them.' Lucy went through the French windows at the tactful pace which mixed eagerness to see one parent with reluctance to leave the other. A waiter had just come up to their little group.

'Now I've asked them for things you can eat!' said Clover, as her father shook his head at a tray of something wrapped in bacon. 'I mentioned it specifically.'

'Don't worry,' he said, 'you've got enough to think about.'

'You've made something vegetarian, haven't you,' she said to the waiter, 'specifically?'

'I'll certainly ask, madam,' said the waiter.

'They've taken over the kitchen,' said Clover, 'it's out of my hands.' She looked down and smiled dimly at Lucy. Her father, in an old striped suit, pulled her to him and kissed her, and Pat stooped too, eyes narrowed in concern.

'Are you all right now, Lucy?' he said.

'Yes, thank you,' said Lucy, though his tenderness threatened to upset her again.

'And have you got a drink?' said Clover.

The waiter came back a minute later with a special plate of food for Lucy and condescending flourishes, smiled on by the adults: 'There you are, young lady, you'll enjoy that,' patting her on the head as he went away. The vegetarians were going to have to wait rather longer.

Lucy had a sense of people being very nice to Clover, considering what they said about her normally, behind her back. She was suddenly a closer friend than she'd been before. This was partly because they were all being nice about Freddie – remarkable tributes were paid to him, now he was gone, and more than once Lucy heard someone say, 'Well, he was a great man!' and look away as if overcome with strong feeling.

'Actually, you know, Clover, love,' a tall drunk woman said, shaking her head in helpless frankness, 'he was a *bloody* good writer!'

'Well, he was, wasn't he,' said Clover mildly. 'He understood people so well' – this drew a thoughtful murmur from the others.

'I was wondering if we were going to have another instalment of the famous diary,' said a man with a slightly anxious laugh.

Clover reflected. 'I mean there's masses there. He wrote every day of his life, almost to the last. I said something about it to Ivan Goyle, you know – I thought he might make another selection. Or even two.'

'Oh, wonderful . . .' said the drunk woman.

'The absolute truth is the last one caused such a fuss I'm not sure I can take it.'

'Well not yet anyway perhaps, love.'

'Look, do you want to go inside?' said Clover.

'No, it's fine, Clo,' said her father. He looked round. 'It's hardly raining at all.'

Lucy took her cue from this, and turned her back to the drizzle as she chewed her sausage roll.

'It is quite nice to be out, isn't it,' said Clover, a fine mist glistening on the stitch of her shawl.

'Oh, it's nothing much,' said Pat, looking up reassuringly at the blurred grey sky above the rooftops. Clover stood, smiling dimly, miles away. And a minute later, as the rain turned unignorable, 'You know, it is rather wet' – and with a sudden collective coming to their senses everyone in the garden walked, almost ran, back into the house.

A little later Lucy went and stood near Grandpa George, who was in a corner of the crowded room with a tall white-haired man – she knew he hated people barging in when he was talking. After a minute, though, the older man nodded pleasantly at her and said, 'And this must be your granddaughter, George?'

He looked down to check. 'Yes . . . yes, it is' – with a momentary smile at her, as if confirming he hadn't lost his car keys.

'And where is her beautiful mother?'

'Oh, she's about somewhere . . .'

'It'll be nice to see her again. They're still in . . . Belsize Park?'

'The last I heard, yes,' said George, with quick facetiousness, since, as Lucy knew, the question meant was she still living with Una?

'I thought I saw her friend earlier.'

'I expect,' said George.

'I couldn't remember her name.'

'Oh, it's Una.'

'Una, that's right. A nice name.'

'Yes. Quite easy to remember.'

'If you can remember anything . . .' said the man, rather self-admiringly. 'She does something, doesn't she.'

Sir George smiled more pleasantly. 'She sells completely useless items that she calls Essentials. Rather a clever idea – I believe she's doing very well.'

Lucy slipped away.

She half remembered the house, with its hundreds, its thousands of books, but it was interesting in a new way to see where

Freddie had lived and worked – until two weeks ago. Una said the move to Blenheim Crescent had been paid for by the film he wrote about the Cambridge Spies (Communists and homosexuals, whom Lucy imagined peering through binoculars from one college into the next). There were pictures of Freddie all over the house; in the large gloomy study, which she went into, hesitantly, after the lavatory, there was a photo of him getting married to someone who wasn't Clover, long ago obviously, when he had dark hair and was a foot taller. Other photographs hung in the hall, and if you read the small twiddly writing you could find him in a school photo, which hung in the lavatory itself. Then there was the portrait her father had painted last year, which loomed over the drinks tray in the drawing room, and was smiled at today with respect and regret. Freddie had already been ill when it was done, very gaunt, she remembered her father talking about it, the problems of being truthful but kind. She took in this difficulty, it seemed to her an excellent picture, though not one she would want to have herself. Then she thought of Freddie, gaunter still, in the coffin, perhaps still in that striped jacket and red bow tie – she must remember he would just be ashes now, awful but a relief. (But then, what happened to the ashes? Where were they?)

She went through the hall, checked up on the visitors' book, open on the table for the mourners to write their names: her own now two pages back, before her father's, whose big S swung up and circled Pat's B on the line above – Patrick Browning. She heard voices and went past the open door of the dining room . . . her father, but with Ivan, sitting with their backs to the door. 'It's been worked on recently, but it probably dates from 1967 or 8,' Ivan was saying, 'when your dad was in the news again. It may have been meant for the Memos, but I'm pretty sure he never read it there. A bit near the knuckle, perhaps.'

'I thought that was the point of the Memos,' her father said. He laughed oddly, and laid his hand on a stack of paper on the table. 'Do I have to read it?' He lifted the top sheet, up to head height – it was a printout, the pages a long concertina, the strip of punch-holes down the side so pleasing to tear off; then he let it drop, with a momentary rippling noise. 'Why don't you just tell me what it says?'

'No, I think you should read it yourself. Of course, I don't know how accurate it is, I haven't seen the diary for that period, and we all know Freddie could enhance things a certain amount, but . . . it's good,' said Ivan. 'I don't want to spoil it for you.'

Her father sighed. 'Has Evert seen it?'

'I thought it best not to upset him.'

'What about me?'

Ivan put a hand on his shoulder, then took it away. 'I don't think you will find it upsetting.'

'It's just more stuff about Dad . . .'

'Well . . . yes,' said Ivan, 'it's about an affair, you know – another one . . . I must say it came as a surprise to me.'

'Daddy,' said Lucy.

'Oh, hello!' said Ivan. Both the men glanced round, alarmed for a second – then not alarmed at all. 'Well, I'll leave it with you' – Ivan stood up and smiling remotely at Lucy, patting his pockets as if remembering what was next on his list, he went past her and into the hall. She came forward. Her father's right hand, alien and familiar, large, big-knuckled, scrubbed up for the occasion, lay on the document. With his left he pulled her in.

'Are Mummy and Una still here?'

She said they were. She stood and read the beginning, 'The evening when we first heard', and later bits, between his fingers . . . 'Evert Dax' . . . 'secretary'; her father watched her for a moment, then read too, shifting his hand to cover the rest of the page – but she was faster than he was. 'Is it about you, Daddy?'

'Oh, I don't think so, no; it's something Freddie wrote about your grandpa.'

'Grandpa David,' she said.

'That's right.' He picked it up, rolled it as best he could, tried to push it into his jacket pocket; it was quite thick. She'd become aware, mainly from something Timothy's mother had said, of some sort of problem about this particular grandfather, and his getting divorced from Granny Connie.

'Is it nice?'

'I'm sure it is – it's about when they were at Oxford, you know, in the War.'

'Freddie and Grandpa were?'

'Yup.'

'Oh,' said Lucy, 'I didn't know that' – the War again, the great dreary fog that old people conjured up and disappeared into whenever they had a chance.

Her father frowned at her. 'Do you want to go?'

'I don't mind.'

'You're supposed to say yes, then I'll have to take you.'

'Oh, well, yes, then,' she said, 'of course.'

About the evening, and the sale of Evert's pictures, she felt she knew more than most. Her mother had had the whole story from Ivan, and explained it to her crossly: 'He needs the money, Lucy, and that's that.' Her father was more sympathetic: 'It's all very sad really – it's that great big house, it'll fall down if he can't find some extra cash.'

'The House of Horrors?'

He allowed the name, but he didn't much like it. 'You've never been there, have you?'

'Mummy said when I was very small.'

'I mean not to remember.'

She agreed she hadn't; though in her mind she had visited it, and in a taxi once she was told they'd just gone past it – she'd twisted and stared back, at the tall bleak terrace of identical houses, grey brick, white porches, with numbers on the pillars, she didn't know which number it was. Now that real grey house had to coexist, rather feebly, with the more enduring one she'd imagined before.

'Well, we'll go and see, shall we?'

'Before it falls down?' She looked narrowly at him.

And so it was that two months ago, on a cold Sunday morning, they had taken a huge walk up the Fulham Road, turning into Cranley Gardens at last about eleven o'clock. She saw now which house it was, though several were shabby and neglected, with dead brown plants on the balconies and weeds round the area railings; Evert's house had a piece of tarpaulin suspended above the top-floor windows. 'It's just to catch anything if it drops off,' her father said. They darted in under the porch. There was a muddle of doorbells, several not working, new ones fixed with makeshift wiring. He let her work it out: DAX / GOYLE: she pressed it, smiling forbearingly. As they waited he explained: Mrs Lenska, the Polish widow, had the ground floor ('Please, Press Hard, Twice!') and Parfitt, a banker no one ever saw, the first floor. The basement was empty, because of the damp. The smart new entryphone, more permanent-looking than the rest, had the label DRURY.

'Hello, it's Lucy!' she said, and after a moment's uncertainty they were in.

On the table in the hall she noticed many unopened letters. They climbed the stairs, Lucy just behind her father, peering at the antiquated lift that ran up the centre in a cage. 'Evert's father had that put in,' he said. 'You know, having only one leg.'

It was just the sort of thing she'd been expecting. 'Oh, dear!' she said.

'I'm afraid it hasn't worked for years.' She assumed he meant the lift.

There was a tall window on each turn of the stair, throwing dirty light across the carpet, which was worn through to the floorboards in places. As they climbed they passed large dim oblongs, huge hooks, black drapery of cobwebs where pictures must have hung for a very long time. When they reached the landing they saw them stacked against the wall, in their heavy gilt frames, trying to stay dignified while peering nervously over each other's shoulders. The pictures left hanging, perhaps not worth selling, looked hopeless without them. Lucy was intrigued to be walking upstairs in someone else's house and looking at things. On the second-floor landing there was a nasty sweet reek that went to the back of the nose – she wasn't sure what it was, though she'd smelt it once or twice at home, when friends of Una's had been round. A lock snapped, a door opened and two men came out, in jeans and T-shirts, no shoes – it was rather odd because it was a lavatory. She said nothing but as they went into the room in front they must have heard her, and her father. 'Oh, my god!' said one of them, and the other turned too and said, 'Ooh, hello . . . !' They were young men, in their twenties, and the first one had extraordinary big eyes swimming in his face. She didn't think they could be workmen.

Her father put his arm round her shoulders. 'Is Evert around?' he said.

They both laughed. 'Which one's he?'

'Is he the old guy?'

'You're in his house,' her father said.

'Oh, are we!' The one with huge eyes giggled and gripped the other round the arm. 'We're just friends of Denis's,' he said. They went into the big room beyond, still laughing, their arms round each other. The sense that something wasn't right made Lucy stick close by her father – she followed him into what seemed to be a pleasant drawing room, but the curtains were still closed, and with only a couple of lamps on it was hard to tell. In the odd daytime gloom she made out Denis Drury, lying on the sofa, looking away from them.

'Put some more music on,' he said. There was a stereo on

the far side of the room, and a heap of records out of their sleeves. Her father seemed angry, but it wasn't his house – he waved his hand as if to clear the smell and said,

'Hello, Denis, I've come to see Evert.'

Denis tensed, then turned his head slowly, and smiled at them. His cheeks in the lamplight were red, and his flat shiny hair stood up in spikes here and there; his black eyes were bulging too. '*Mister* Sparsholt!' he said, and half sitting up – 'and *Miss* Sparsholt, my goodness me . . .'

Lucy didn't correct him, there were bigger things to worry about.

'Have you got anything a bit more, like, modern?' said the man by the record player, giving up on the pile of discs and looking round. The large-eyed one had sat on the floor and was making a giant cigarette by pulling apart several other cigarettes and heaping up the contents. Denis looked very carefully at his watch and said,

'Have you come for lunch? I'm afraid you're rather early if so.'

'I told Evert we'd come this morning and help him with the pictures. Musson's coming at twelve.'

Denis thought, and said quietly, 'Oh, she's not, is she?' He clearly wasn't himself, the change itself was alarming, and yet there was something nicer about him than usual – he gave them an almost friendly look. 'This is Kevin and Gogo,' he said. 'Jonathan and Lucy.'

'Hello, Lucy,' said Kevin.

'George,' said Gogo, grinning at her over the tobacco. It was spread on a record box – she construed the word 'Resurrection', and when he lifted the giant cigarette to lick the paper she saw a picture of an old man in glasses smoking a pipe.

'Is this Evert your boyfriend then?' said Kevin.

'Oh, no . . .' said Lucy, then looked anxiously around.

Denis lay there with a strange smile. 'Years and years ago,' he said, 'I was his *amanuensis*.'

'Ooh, what's that?' said Gogo, and watched Denis raising his hand and wiggling his fingers as if pulling on a rubber glove.

'I'm going to find Ivan,' her father said, and they went back out on to the landing, just as Ivan came downstairs. His sleeves were rolled up and he was wearing an apron.

'Hello,' he said, 'hello,' going past them, really too busy to talk. They drifted back after him into the room. 'Can we have this room clear, please?' he said.

'Oh, my god, it's the housemaid!' said Denis, falling back on the sofa. 'Boys, meet Ivy.' Lucy's mother and Una sometimes spoke of him as Ivy, but she held her breath to hear him called it to his face. He stood, small and plump, in front of the fireplace, with his hands on his hips.

'We've got Hughie Musson coming round any minute.'

'Is he cute?' said Gogo.

'You wouldn't say cute, would you, Ivy?' said Denis. 'Or perhaps you would . . .'

'Hugh Musson is a very important man. So I need you all out of here, please.' Denis rolled his head moodily. 'You can all go and play in Denis's room.'

'Sounds good,' said Gogo.

'I'm too exhausted to move,' said Denis. 'How long were we in that club? Eight hours? In that hell-hole of debauchery?'

But Ivan crossed the room and tugged back the curtains, and the cold lunchtime light seemed enough to push them upstairs, blinking and lazily protesting.

Lucy helped, and in ten minutes the room was straight, the carpet hoovered, and the records put hastily into sleeves – she knew some of them were in the wrong ones. The window was left open to clear the air, and it got quite chilly. Probably it had been a lovely room once, but it was all a bit shabby and sagging now, the walls covered with pictures like a junk shop. In

Grandpa George's drawing room there were just three pictures, each worth fifty thousand pounds. In Evert's there were (she nodded as she turned from wall to wall) thirty-seven – how much *they* were worth remained to be seen. They went into the kitchen, and Ivan took off his apron.

'Where's Herta, when you need her?' said her father.

'Who's Herta, Daddy?' Lucy said.

Ivan set about making coffee with a paper cone and a glass jug. 'Poor Herta,' he said. 'We went to see her last week.'

'She was Evert's housekeeper for years and years,' her father said.

'She was his father's housekeeper,' said Ivan.

'You mean the man with one leg?' said Lucy.

'A. V. Dax,' said Ivan, 'the novelist.'

Evert came in, looked at them, waved a kiss at them with his fingers. 'Is Denis about?' he said.

'He's gone upstairs,' said Ivan, 'he's got some young friends round.'

'I thought I heard something,' said Evert.

When the coffee was made, and Lucy given the Pepsi Ivan said she would prefer, they went off for a preliminary look at the pictures. 'Let's go to Johnny's room,' Evert said. They entered a small bedroom, opposite the lavatory, where perhaps a dozen paintings stood propped against the chest of drawers.

'Why do you call it Johnny's room?' said Lucy.

'It's so sweet of you,' said her father.

'Your dear papa lived in this room, darling, long ago,' said Evert. 'Twenty years ago?'

'That's right, 1975, wasn't it, my early London period . . .'

'A good year or more, I should think,' Evert said.

'Just about,' said her father.

'About ten months,' said Ivan.

Evert hoisted up a medium-sized brown painting. Lucy imagined her father then, with his awful long hair, coming into this room each day, sleeping on this hard bed, which now had a big folder of drawings lying on it. She'd never thought of him not having a house of his own.

'These are Victor's pictures, then?' he said.

'That's right. I think I'll probably sell most of them.'

'I've not seen this before, I don't think' – her father peered forward at it.

'It's Witsen, Rotterdam Harbour. It's a bit dirty, but it's meant to be more or less that colour.'

Ivan made a deeply unimpressed face. 'We're aiming for a much sparer hang, Johnny,' he said. 'Get rid of a lot of junk.'

'Oh, I like it,' said her father. 'But yes, I guess . . .'

'I remember it very well when I was a boy,' said Evert. 'It used to hang in the dining room downstairs. My father knew Willem Witsen, I think he bought it off him; it may even have been given to him, since Witsen was rich, and very generous. Do you know about him?'

Lucy shook her head. 'Not really,' said her father.

'Oh, a fascinating figure – also a very good photographer, wealthy, but extremely bohemian. I always wanted to put on a little show somewhere, you know, at a small gallery, but—'

'We just can't keep getting into all these reminiscences all the time,' said Ivan, 'darling – or we'll never get anywhere.'

'Well . . .' said Evert.

'OK . . .' said Lucy's father, with an embarrassed laugh.

'In or out?' said Ivan.

Evert looked at him, obediently, but with a last hint of resistance. 'Do you mean in or out of the house, or in or out of the sale?'

Ivan smiled tightly. 'Out of the house,' he said.

'In that case . . . out, I suppose.'

Lucy thought she'd never seen anyone look so sad.

*

First of all Hughie Musson looked at the pictures on the landing. 'Your father thought big, didn't he.'

'Oh, always,' said Evert.

Hughie glanced down the cavernous stairwell. 'He had a lot
of walls to cover, of course, I can see that . . .' He himself was
big, he'd wheezed his way up to the second floor with several
pauses to peer at the unworking lift. 'Quite a period piece,' he
said.

'It was the same in his own work,' Evert went on, 'he felt
space was there to be used.'

'It's awful,' said Hughie with a grin, 'I've *hardly* read him.'

'He had no time for what he called *minchers*,' Evert said.

'Ah, yes . . . ! Well, no . . .' said Musson; and businesslike
after all, 'Well, I don't think any of these, I'm afraid, for our
show.'

'I'm sure you're right,' said Evert, and smiled. 'We'd better
look at the things in the drawing room.'

'I want to see the Sutherland,' said Hughie. 'Modern British
art: after you . . .' and as they went through: 'I've got an idea
about who could write something – you know, for the catalogue.'

'Oh, have you . . .' said Evert.

'This is marvellous,' said Hughie, surveying the mad jumble.
'I'd forgotten just how good it was.'

Evert turned round, and nodded slowly, as though seeing it
all again for the first time – and also, Lucy thought but didn't
say, for the last. If she didn't like much of it herself, she was
impressed that Hughie did. He was in his element. He took
things down, reaching higher than Ivan, who was helping him;
she was entrusted with a small picture herself, which she carried
across the room and propped on the sofa for them all to stare
at. 'You're thinking of an exhibition, of course,' her father said.
'I'm trying to remember the space.' It was the exercise of a skill
that couldn't be explained.

'The big Ben Nicholson, obviously,' said Hughie.

'Ah . . . yes,' said Evert.

'The two little Nicholsons,' said Ivan.

'Well, they're marvellous. One I think not in good nick.' This turned out to be Lucy's picture.

'Really?'

'Well, have a look at it,' said Hughie. Lucy peered at it, propped on the cushions, and thought it looked very rough indeed, the paint in a thick brown corner actually chipped off.

'Oh, and what about the Chagall?' Ivan said.

Hughie was charming but brisk. 'I think just paintings, don't you? I mean, it would probably sell, but it wouldn't fit.'

'Which one's that?' Lucy asked her father. He showed her – a lovely, rather funny, picture of a red man, a green woman and a blue cow flying overhead. She read in the corner, 'À mon ami Dax'.

'It's just a print, you see, Lucy.'

'Oh . . . yes, I see,' she said. He'd explained prints before.

'There's a lot of prints,' said Ivan, with a frown at this unexpected objection. She sensed it was something he was going to come back to.

'Now there are half a dozen Goyles,' said Evert.

'That may be too many,' said Hughie.

Lucy peered at Ivan: was he a painter? Her impression was that Ivan didn't like art, was bothered by it somehow, as he was by children.

'I remember that one,' her father said, as a little painting, green, white and black, was unhooked from above the bureau.

'Of course, beside the Nicholsons . . .' Hughie said, with a sharp breath. 'I know he's a favourite of yours, Evert!'

'I do think he was good,' Evert said mildly.

'What do you think, I wonder, Jonathan,' said Hughie, 'as a painter?'

'Oh . . .' – as if he'd never thought about it. 'No, he's got something, hasn't he . . .'

'I mean he's far from contemptible,' Hughie said, 'obviously' – though contempt, now he'd mentioned it, seemed to steal into the room, like the draught from the window. He grinned. 'There's something rather brilliant, in a way, about the *total* lack of intellectual interest.'

'Oh, dear!' said Ivan. 'Poor old Uncle Stanley!'

The other thing Hughie said he very much hoped they would have was the sculpture by Barbara Hepworth. The others looked down on it on its table in front of the mirror, while Lucy had it at eye level, the back of it reflected, smooth as a bowl, when she moved her head to right or left. It was hollowed out, the rim polished, the rougher inside painted white. Or it had been white once; now she peered into a tilted cup that was yellowish at the top and at the bottom almost grey, as if water had stood in it. The painted surface had fine cracks over it, and she noticed that one of the strings across the gap had been replaced – it had a bigger knot underneath the rim, which only she perhaps could see. 'Simply stunning,' said Hughie. 'Nineteen-fifty or so, I imagine.'

'I expect you're right. I bought it after my father died, which was 1952. Ivan will correct me if I'm wrong. I've always loved it.'

'I'd have thought, what . . . thirty thousand?' said Hughie.

Lucy gave it a stern look, as if haggling the price down. She thought it was nice, as a little thing to have, but £30,000 made her want to laugh in protest.

'Well . . .' said Evert, who seemed rather thrown by the price himself, 'I'm glad you like it' – he turned away suddenly to look for something in the bureau.

To see the Sutherland they had to go to a bedroom along a short passage also lined with pictures. Lucy glanced at them in a carefully expressionless way; they seemed to be drawings and photographs mainly. But her father stopped and, a little short-sighted now, looked at one of them, a red drawing of a naked man, obviously, but with no head and cut off above the knee; there was a funny squiggle where his tool, as Thomas called it, should have been. 'You're keeping this, I hope?' he said.

'What?' Evert turned back. 'You've always had a soft spot for that one, haven't you. I think I'll have to leave it you when I die.'

'Ah! Thank you,' said her father, and touched Evert's sleeve: 'Though I can wait! It's by . . . remind me . . . ?'

'It's by Peter Coyle,' said Evert, 'you know . . .'

'Oh, that's a Coyle,' her father said. 'Coyle not Goyle!'

'Oh, very much not Goyle,' Evert agreed. They stood pondering it for a moment, it must have been some body-builder, a bit grotesque, frankly. Ivan said,

'What would that be worth, I wonder?'

Hughie came back. He made a humorous show of giving it his consideration. 'Coyle?' he said. 'His time has yet to come. Who can say, he may enjoy a revival.'

'I knew him, of course,' said Evert. 'You know he went into camouflage in the War – painting whole ships. It satisfied his sense of scale.'

'He thought big, like your father,' said Hughie.

'Well, there you are,' said Evert.

'He was killed, I believe, in 1942,' said Ivan.

'Alas,' said Evert.

'A certain problem of scale here, too, I think, don't you?' said Hughie with a laugh. 'Or do you imagine the model really looked like that?'

'Hah – I wonder,' said Evert; he smiled for a moment at Lucy, then leaning on her father's arm he led them into the bedroom.

Therefore, when she arrived at Hughie's gallery for the Private View Lucy knew most of the pictures, and the main interest lay in seeing them uprooted, divorced, regrouped, and sometimes repaired; her little Ben Nicholson had been very cleverly patched up – even in the bright spotlight you could only tell if you already knew. It struck her it all became a Collection, with a beautiful book about it, just at the moment it was being dispersed. She felt the pictures were like . . . not friends really, but acquaintances – like those adults in the room who had met you before but now boomed at each other over your head. She stood for a while by the desk at the front, reading the backwards writing on the window: 'Modern British Art The Evert Dax Collection'. Even after she'd worked it out it remained to be solved. Evert was standing in the middle of it all, red in the face, with Ivan helping him, and Hughie saying, 'Evert, you remember Georgia Screamer,' (or something like that) as people came up. She went back through the room. She was the only child there, glimpsed, greeted, disregarded, and the onset of boredom was mixed with a larger disappointment, a sadness she felt hanging, lurking in the heat and noise of the party. No one paid much attention to the pictures, and soon the gallery was so crowded you couldn't have looked at them properly even if you'd wanted to. For the guests it was really a private view of each other.

She went to her father, who was on the edge of a group of people who'd been at the funeral earlier and had the unstuck look that came with drinking all day.

'I know . . . I found myself thinking, what did it all add up to, really?' a tall red-faced man said.

'Well, it wasn't a bad life, was it?' – this was the woman called Sally.

'No, no, I wouldn't say bad. Funerals always throw me.'

'If it wasn't exactly a good life, it was one that Freddie himself thoroughly enjoyed,' said a small amusing man.

'He enjoyed being Freddie, I suppose. I don't think I'd have liked it, but it quite suited him.'

Lucy looked up and her father took her hand. All the reverence of earlier seemed to have vanished, the tributes she'd heard spoken over the coffin, and in the garden afterwards; she felt for the first time that she'd been quite fond of Freddie.

'A shame he never had children,' said Sally.

'Probably a good thing,' said the tall man, and after a second gave a crinkly smile at Lucy.

'I sometimes wondered,' said the short man, 'if he wasn't really queer, you know, deep down.'

'Oh . . .' – Sally gave a worried laugh, and also a quick glance at Lucy, and then her father. 'I think you'd have to ask Clover that!'

'Mm, perhaps later,' the man said, and they laughed and turned with their glasses out in barely concealed rivalry as the pretty girl with the bottle of champagne came alongside.

Lucy tugged her father's hand, and they went round together, sidling, pushing, rubbing backs with these fickle drinkers. There was the Barbara Hepworth, put on a special plinth. She jumped protectively as a large man, making way for the waitress, backed into it, it jolted but didn't fall. 'Oops . . . must be more careful,' he said, glanced down at Lucy, the witness, with a moment's rough calculation, then turned and went on shouting at the woman beyond him.

5

Pat stood up, sweaty, burly, and stooped to find his jeans in the tangle of clothes on the chair. In the bleak dissociation after sex there was something touching still in seeing him move naked around their room – soft light through the curtains on his broad back and hairy thighs and long fat member, retiring now after a hard half-hour's work. There was the noise, like a rough breath, of the drawer pulled open for socks and pants, the surprised little squeak of the wardrobe and the flick of hangers as he chose a shirt. Everything businesslike about him seemed to Johnny a guarantee of everything else. He stood at the foot of the bed with his clothes in his hands and looked down on him. 'What time are you meeting David?'

'Oh, Christ,' said Johnny, and pulled the duvet back up to his chin.

'You hadn't forgotten?'

Johnny closed his eyes. 'Twelve forty-five.'

'Well, give him my best.'

'I will,' said Johnny.

'Make sure you do,' said Pat, and went off to the bathroom.

It was one of those sad things they had to live with: his father wouldn't come to Fulham. There was a bit of puffing about it being too far, a sly access of elderly exhaustion at the prospect. He had visited them once, the year they'd moved in, and given them a lot of advice about the garden. The arrangements in the house itself – the studio, the big bedroom the men shared – were stubborn evidence of the way Johnny lived his life: the puzzle and worry of his being an artist, the subtler problem of no one, in David's world, having heard of him, and hiding behind these convenient concerns ('You'll be working, I don't want to disturb you') the irreducible fact that Johnny was doing openly what for David had been a matter of secrecy and then of very public shame.

Johnny dozed and woke and dozed, nursed the afterglow, the slight invalidish luxury of having been had, while Pat was shaving and showering and pushing on, yet again, with the day. The day could be held off a little longer, in the stale refuge of the bed, while the parent, up as always at six, was already inexorably in motion; a hundred teenage mornings were huddled in the heap of the duvet. His father's habit was to be early for everything; June would drive him to the station, he would wait, noticed probably but speaking to no one, and when the signal changed he would stroll to the end of the platform, where the first-class carriage was due to halt. His figure, tall, lean, muscled to an abnormal degree for a man in his seventies, was ghosted now, in Johnny's mind, by the boyish figure of Freddie's chapters, Dad in training, exploring his strength and a latent power he had over others – he wasn't sure Ivan was right to make him read it, it was something entirely unsuspected that he needn't have known, and he saw the knowledge burning in his face when he met his father in four hours' time.

After Pat had left, Johnny went down, made coffee, and worked on the curtains in the Chalmers job, then applied himself to the round brass studs of the doge's chair, each carried off with a quick curled highlight, dimmed almost to nothing in the shadow of George's knee. Important of course not to let the interest of the background distract from the beauty of the sitter . . . In a further background, Johnny's thoughts took shape from the work of the three brushes, in delicate dashes, quick circlings, inexplicable fusings of his actions with his remote and shifting ideas. His practised hand brought some order to his unruly and incompetently managed feelings about his father – the wan dutiful optimism as each visit loomed, the magnetic conflicts of the visits themselves, when a longing for harmony was always frustrated by deep-set habits of rejection. The thought that he should really go home and paint his father's portrait hung in the air today. Was that portrait a palpable absence, a gesture David hoped for but could never ask for? Johnny could bring it up at lunch, if the mood seemed right, and if, seated in the old man's strong personal atmosphere, he felt they could stand the much longer hours of mutual scrutiny. His plan for later in the afternoon had been agreed to in a cheerily unreflecting tone, but it might be unwise to press any harder.

In London David was away from June, and so notionally more pliable; though invitations to bend often made him more vertical still.

The fact was that David had his own London, so long established that it was now in part imaginary. From Euston he took a cab to the RAF Club in Piccadilly. From there he might pay calls on a shirt-maker in Queen Victoria Street, and, early in the evening, an expensive Chinese restaurant at the narrow top end of Kensington High Street. There were better shirt-shops and restaurants of all kinds far closer to the Club, but the journeys by black cab between his places were as much a part of his knowing London as the places themselves. He had a number of contacts, and in the old days had had lunch at the Club, every March, with his stockbroker, 'old Veezey', but Veezey had retired three years ago, his firm absorbed into a huge conglomerate, and the one attempt to have lunch with his successor had led to a casual rebuff. After that he had shifted his business to a broker in Birmingham. And then he had sold out to a huge conglomerate himself. The Works, DDS Engineering, which for decades had welcomed arrivals on that side of the town with its high brick wall and chimney, was now someone else's: a good business move, the money in the bank a salve perhaps for his suddenly purposeless days.

His father never said so, but Johnny believed that in his keen, unpoetical mind a feeling endured that he had helped save London and everything it once represented. He must have known it first in the War, when large parts of it were already in rubble. Even twenty years later, when Johnny was first brought here by his parents, grass-grown ruins still flanked Ludgate Hill. A disgrace, his father said, but gratifying proof, even so, of the scale of the crisis he'd played his part in. Johnny remembered their arrival that day – he was seven or eight, with every reason, coming down from the Midlands, with the noisy street ahead of them, to take his mother's hand. He pulled her round, to look up at it – the Euston Arch, the height and the mass of the pillars so frightening and compelling that a shiver of sub-mission went through him. His father's feelings seemed divided – he was proud of it, part of railway history, the entry to London, to which he'd brought his wife and son; but he was pleased too, in his progressive way, that it was going to be pulled down, and a brand new station built. Somehow, in the sway of his confidence, they ignored the taxi rank, and he led them on, till he stood by the Euston Road in his trilby, his rain-coat over one arm, the other arm raised as a dozen cabs ran past with passengers already in them, smoking, reading the paper and leaning forward to joke with the driver. It was a first glimpse of his father's fallibility, just when he'd intended to impress.

'Squadron Leader Sparsholt . . .'

The young woman in a dark suit looked at him over the desk as if she thought this unlikely. 'Oh, yes . . . ?'

Johnny stared, then laughed. 'Oh, not me! No, I'm his son. He said to meet him in the lounge.'

She smiled calmly at his muddle. 'You should go up to the first floor.'

Sloping across the hall Johnny saw himself in a big mirror, something mutinous in his lumpy shirt collar, the tie twisted probably under it. His hair, plastered down after his shower, had jumped to life again. But the trim and blazered old men coming past him on the stairs or, at the top, holding the door for him, seemed less conscious of his oddity, brown boots worn with a baggy black suit, than he did himself. He said thank you, held the door in turn for a man in uniform – four stripes, group captain – and though he saw at once his father wasn't there made his way with a mild searching frown to the far end of the busy room. A party of three got up, Johnny hovered and bagged the table, sat down in the low armchair looking blankly at their sudded half-pint mugs and the glass beaker of tooth-picks.

Did his father even notice the things that sank on Johnny's spirits here? – perhaps, yes: at a level beneath thought, he was reassured by the clusters of maroon armchairs and sofas, the thin Georgian pretensions of the pastel-coloured panelling, the table lamps, the fake mahogany desk; was cheered by the tied-back chintz curtains and brightly lit portrait of the Queen. It wasn't a posh club, the RAF, it was united by something other than class and money, woven into Johnny's life so early on that his rebellion against it was matched by a helpless under-standing and even sympathy for it. It wasn't White's, thank god, or Boodle's, to which George Chalmers kept making it clear he wasn't going to invite him. Still, it required a surrender, to meeting-room monotony, bare institutional comfort, the knowledge that no one here saw anything wrong with it. In a way, what Johnny liked best were the paintings of aeroplanes on the stairs – a subject even more resistant to art than the Queen, and not much depicted anywhere else.

It was unlike David to be late, but very slight debilities and lapses were entering his behaviour, which to Johnny felt almost a relief. He looked down the long room to the door, told the waitress who cleared and wiped the table he would hang on till he arrived. For ten years or more his father had avoided the Club, after the crisis, till some time in the late 70s Terry Bark-worth had asked him in for a game of squash, which led on to the braving of the bar, and dinner – David had done a lot of braving by then, but it must have been stiff, at the RAF Club, even for a former squadron leader, DFC. There were members who didn't speak to him still, and it was that sense of courted rejection that Johnny found more painful than anything else about meeting him here – silly snobberies about the furniture were a buffer for that other barely visible thing.

Ah, there he was, looming in pieces through the bevelled panes of the door, pushing into the room, strolling past the seated groups almost as if disguising his destination – though Johnny raised an arm, grinned and half stood up. But he had seen someone, stopped by his table, was introduced to the woman with him, the name Sparsholt said clearly, the woman's smile and tilt of the head at the touch of fame and at her own skill in greeting and absorbing it. Johnny thought no one in person was the person you expected, and pictured, wrote to or spoke to on the phone; and his father especially seemed at each appearance to be more strangely and sharply himself. Each phase of his life suited him, he was startlingly handsome in old age, in his old-fashioned way, the small moustache darker than his hair, and with the upright bearing of a man quite as fit as his son, who was thirty years younger. All this would have charmed the woman too. David in himself wasn't charming, and had no way with words, but a power glanced off him; so that when he moved on at last with a smile and a nod towards Johnny in the far corner the whole story of Evert's love for him fifty years earlier made unanswerable sense, in a way that it hadn't for Johnny when toiling through Freddie's peculiar memoir.

David sat down, the waitress took their order and left, and he and Johnny looked at each other and at the table, intimates or strangers, neither of them seemed sure. Johnny heard that the journey had been eventless, that his health was good, and that he'd mowed the lawn for the last time this year. He got it out of the way as smoothly as he could: 'And June's all right?'

'Oh, she's fine . . . you know, she's got this neck problem, trapped nerve, gives her a bit of grief' – his own sympathy vague, or as if sparing Johnny.

'Ah, well, give her my love.'

His father smiled quickly at him, in gratitude or doubt, and sat back as the drinks arrived – his perpetual sherry and a glass of white wine for Johnny. 'Ah, good . . .' It was all settled in, and had been for years, not ideal and not easy to change – the way they got on, the way June and his father lived. 'She makes me happy,' his father said to him once, not in answer to a question, but from a pondered need to make it clear. It was amazing to think anyone as perennially dissatisfied as June could bring happiness to another person's life, but it seemed she'd done it. She was so unlike Connie as to suggest a radical correction, a try at something bracingly different, but perhaps always needed and missed. And presumably she loved him, she'd guarded his door and typed his letters for years; the sheer force of her forbearance in marrying him, knowing what she did, must have come as a great blessing to him.

'Well, cheers!'

'Cheers. And how about you, old lad? Keeping busy?' – as if Johnny was a pensioner too.

'Yes, Dad, I'm always busy! I've got a big portrait nearly done – old chap who must have been at Oxford the same time as you, though he says he didn't know you.'

David raised his eyebrows – 'I was hardly there.'

'George Chalmers.' To someone else he might have said Chalmers was an awful old queen; today it felt daring just to mention Oxford.

His father said, quite modestly, 'I don't really count myself as having been to Oxford – you know, I could have gone back after the War, but I chose not to.'

'I know.'

'What did it add up to, really? – just a few weeks. I can barely remember it, if I'm honest.'

'Well,' said Johnny as he lifted his glass, 'it will be interesting for you to see Evert again'; and found he was blushing, while his father grunted and said,

'Yes, I wonder what gave him that idea?'

'Mmm, he just mentioned he'd like to see you.'

'I hope he won't want to talk about art.'

Johnny laughed forgivingly and said, 'I expect he'll want to talk about the past.'

But his father gave nothing on that. 'He was in the Army, wasn't he?' – that was what the past meant above all.

'Yes, he's never said much about it – to me at least.'

'Ah,' said his father, and set down his glass, already empty. 'We might as well go down,' with a note of welcome routine.

'Steady on, Dad . . .' Johnny took a moment to knock back his wine, then stood up and said, 'Oh, Pat sends his best, by the way.'

'Ah . . . yes,' his father smiled, accepted it, but didn't ask him to send his to Pat.

In the noisy dining room, they were led to a small table at the back; white napkins stood lop-eared in the wine glasses. The head waiter pushed in David's chair as they sat, and laid the wine list beside him. 'Well now . . .': they both needed more drink to have lunch together, and in a minute David said as usual, 'Merlot all right?' while Johnny worked his way through the verbiage of the menu towards equally inevitable questions. In a minute or two another waiter came, sleekly handsome, in white shirt and tight black trousers, and so young that the battles commemorated all around must have been mere remote and random hearsay to him. Johnny sent him off again to check about ingredients. 'They'll see you right,' said David. That his son was a vegetarian was something he fully accepted, he took a practical interest in it, and complained about menus and kitchens as sternly as if he'd been one of that troublesome minority himself. 'For God's sake,' he said, when the waiter returned to confirm there was chicken stock in the soup. Johnny bent the waiter to his will, with a slow smile that he saw wake some other recognition in the boy, quickly repressed, but then coming out again in a sly smile of his own as he said he was sure the chef would do something special for him. Johnny raised his hand as his father started to say it was the least they could do – 'It's OK, Dad' – watching the waiter move off, and the old irresolvable thing in the air, of not knowing what the old man picked up on or blocked out.

Over the soup (green salad for Johnny) they talked about the Works, and what the new people were making of it. It was a difficult subject, charged with the regrets of an active man who had made a decision to give up something he loved. 'Well, they've taken the sign down,' he said.

'DDS?'

His father nodded. 'Not that it matters, but they left it for six months, you know, out of respect.'

Johnny wondered if that was the reason. 'What is it now?'

'Stella. In huge bloody letters, hideous.'

'Stella . . . It must look like a brewery.'

His father perhaps didn't get the allusion. 'They're Chinese,' he said, 'of course,' and it was that that made him almost laugh.

'Are they laying people off?'

He dabbed at his moustache with his napkin. 'I see Stewart Dibden at the Lions, he keeps me in the picture. He says they're planning to expand.'

'Well, that's good, isn't it?'

'No, excellent.' In his gloomy look across the table some suggestion, not aired for twenty years, seemed still to be remembered: that Johnny might have taken an interest in the firm himself.

'I think you were quite right to get out when you did, Dad,' he said.

Johnny had a view, beyond his father's head, of a portrait of an airman in flying suit, goggles raised, very simple: the tall square-jawed figure against a tan-coloured background. Well, he couldn't do him like that, and the question of just how he might do him was a hard one – how much of the glorious past to convey without irony or sentiment. He'd had enough to drink, when his pasta arrived, to say, 'Dad, have you ever had your portrait done?'

Was there something bashful in his father's tone: 'No, not really.'

'Not really?' Johnny smiled at him. 'Not in the RAF?'

'Well, there was a chap who did a picture of me, yes, a portrait.'

'Oh?'

'I've no idea what became of it. He was killed, lost at sea, so I heard.' He raised his eyebrows as he lifted his fork: 'A very talented artist.'

It was a phrase he had never heard his father utter. 'What was his name?'

'Well, you'll probably have heard of him. He was called Coyle.'

'Peter Coyle, do you mean?' – Johnny hopeless at dissembling, though his father, eating, briefly contemplative, didn't notice anything odd. 'Well, yes, I have heard of him. Didn't he go into camouflage in the War?'

'He may well have done. All this was before I signed up – at Oxford.'

'So you do remember Oxford!'

'A few things, obviously,' with the hint of a scowl at any clever contradiction. 'I don't suppose the picture still exists.'

'Well, I bet someone's got it. Just a sketch, probably, was it?'

He seemed doubtful for a moment, but not of his facts: 'I'm not sure what you mean. I wouldn't say a sketch, it was a big oil painting, of me in rowing kit. It took weeks – he kept asking for more time. Of course I was very tied up with other things then.'

'I can imagine.' Johnny sat back, then remembered his food, and got on with it. What his father had said, for the very first time, seemed to fix and authenticate the whole story Freddie had told – though the claim about the large oil painting showed in a salutary way that Freddie didn't know everything. David himself seemed unaware of the value of what he had let drop.

'So what are your holiday plans, old lad?' he said. 'Italy again?'

'Dad, the thing is, I wondered if you'd sit for me?'

The slightly technical way of putting it delayed the reaction by a further second or two. Then, 'Ooh, you don't want to be bothered with that.'

'It wouldn't be a bother, Dad.'

'No, no.' He cut at the thick lump of lamb on his plate. 'I'm not the right . . . subject for you.'

'Well, I don't agree with that at all. It's ridiculous I've never painted you before.'

'You're too busy,' said his father, and in his quick look down and away Johnny knew he had glimpsed a long-established habit of making excuses for him, and for his failure, as a prize-winning portrait painter, to turn his gaze on his own father. It was as touching as it was annoying.

'In fact I've got a fairly empty period coming up, so that's not a problem.'

'Anyway, where would we do it?'

'I could come up and stay for a week, if you like; we could have a sitting each day.'

The prospect was so unusual it seemed almost to alarm him. 'Too much bother,' he said again, chasing the lamb down with a swig of wine; though something in his eyes suggested he was moved too by the thought of the visit. The bother, Johnny thought, would really be with June.

'Well, think about it, will you?'

He didn't promise to do so, but a moment later said, 'You must have drawn me dozens of times when you were a lad.'

'I certainly did.'

'Yes. You were always bloody good at capturing people.'

'You never told me that before!'

'Of course I did.'

Johnny weighed up the situation. 'Well, it's good to come back to someone years later. They've changed, and so have you.'

'God knows,' said his father, and after a second looked straight at him.

When their cab came down the Old Brompton Road, David, vigilant for reference points, Tube stations, street names, saw Cranley Gardens, and said, 'A good part of town.' Though when he saw the house itself, the flaking porch and high-hanging swag of tarpaulin, he seemed to take in, with a little flinch and then a setting of his features, that the visit might require unexpected tact. Johnny rang the bell, they were let in and went upstairs. His father, peering up and down, tongue on lip, examined the antique apparatus of the lift. 'They ought to get this going,' he said. The house, quite new and strange to him, appeared in an odd light to Johnny too, pictures reshuffled on the landing, and the glimpse through the door of 'his' room of different things hanging on the stained and bleached wallpaper: the room seemed a cell, a shrine almost, of the precious life he had led wholly without his father's knowledge or participation.

David hung back on the landing to look at the Chagall print – he had the air of someone humorously suppressing his prejudices, and with a hint of nerves too as a new arrival in this long-established household: 'À mon ami Dax . . .' Johnny went into the sitting room, where Evert was standing by the fire.

'Hi, Evert – I've just brought my dad in to see you.'

Evert looked up, and across towards the door, with a hint of alarm, not knowing whom to expect – the entrance delayed by a few seconds. Then, 'Oh, hello, David . . .' as if he came round all the time, and was even a bit of a nuisance; but it was probably shyness. He walked away from him and then turned. 'You're looking very well.'

'You know me,' said David; and then, obliged to reply: 'So are you, Evert. You've hardly changed.'

'I must have been a bloody wreck before, then!' said Evert, and laughed cheerfully. 'Have a seat.' There was a faint sense still that he didn't know exactly who his visitor was. And Johnny couldn't tell for a minute or two if they needed him there, or if nothing much could happen or be said until he'd gone. What would two long-ago lovers be likely to feel, one of them twice-married, the other losing his memory?

'I'll make you some tea, shall I?' he said.

'Oh, thank you, darling,' said Evert.

'Well!' said David, sitting down and looking round keenly. 'So this is the famous house.'

'Ah,' said Evert, 'you'll have heard about it, I expect.'

'Well, from Jonathan, of course. And a long time ago, Evert, from you!'

'Oh, really, yes,' said Evert.

'Your father was still alive then, of course – in the War.' He smiled at him. 'I remember you saying what a monster he was.'

'Oh, did I?'

'I'll never forget that.'

Evert looked at Johnny, hovering. 'Do you want a hand?'

'No, no, it's fine,' said Johnny, and went out to the kitchen, where in a minute the roar of the kettle covered all that could be heard of their talk.

When he came back with the tray his father had stood up again and was going round looking up and down at the pictures, and then, on rather surer ground, out of the window. Evert sat watching him, with a host's patience and some other calculation under it. He was taking him in. Johnny, confused by his own feelings and expectations, said, 'Shall I be Herta?'

'Mm?' said his father.

'Oh, do,' said Evert.

Johnny took him a cup first. Then, 'Dad, I'll put yours here.'

'Oh, thanks, old lad,' his father coming over and sitting on the other side of the hearth, in Ivan's chair, with the double stack of books, biographies, memoirs, on the floor beside it.

'And I found these eclairs in the fridge.' They were his father's favourite, odd tea-room predilection from Johnny's childhood, bought fresh then from Pinnock's in Abbey Street – now, packaged, the chocolate sweating slightly, from Waitrose in the King's Road.

'My one vice,' said David, taking the little plate, with its cusped cake fork and folded napkin, and setting it on the table beside him.

Johnny stood back, surveyed the two men, wondering quite what he'd done. 'Well, I'll leave you to it,' he said.

'You won't stay and have a cup, lovie?' said Evert.

'I'll be back in a couple of hours. I've got to pick up Lucy from one party and take her to another – it's Thomas's birthday, you see' – he just came out with it, and let his father handle it as he would. In fact it was Evert who seized on it, with relief but a certain vagueness.

'Ah, *Thomas*, yes . . . how is he?'

'I think he's all right.' Johnny didn't much care for this boy, whom Lucy called her brother though as Una's child he was no blood relation at all – and could hardly have been more unlike her. 'It's his eighteenth today.'

'I always forget how much older he is than . . . er . . . your little girl.'

'Than Lucy . . . yes.'

'That's right.' And there they were – David rarely mentioned Lucy, and found the whole thing tricky when his friends went on about their grandchildren and the like. He sat there

384

now as if the subject had never been mentioned. Evert looked at him. 'Johnny took quite a while to decide to be a father.'

Miraculously, David, with a narrow smile, as if doubting this strange opportunity to shine, said, 'Well, so did I, Evert, come to that!'

They all laughed, though for Johnny the strangeness lay in his saying something so personal: it was promising. It was only as he went out and down the stairs, past large pale shadows where pictures had hung, that he realized what he'd done for Evert and his father was just what Freddie had done for them, fifty-five years ago. He'd set them up together. It wasn't clear what Freddie had hoped for from the meeting, and he'd acted himself on a conviction he couldn't explain.

He left Lucy back at Belsize Grove, and when he was let into Evert's house again and went upstairs he found his mood of mild anxiety about his daughter's social life carried over to his father's – had he had a nice time? had they got on? did they play games? He looked round the door of the drawing room not knowing if he was their saviour or if he was spoiling the fun at a critical moment. They were sitting just where they had been, Evert with an excited but unfocused expression, David, saying something in desultory agreement, with a look of unusual and virtuous patience. They had drunk their tea, and the little chocolate and cream-smeared plates lay on the tables beside them. Johnny as Herta cleared them away, not asking questions. 'Well, I suppose I'd better be going, Evert,' his father said, in a tone of polite regret unusual to him.

The odd moment came when they stood and said goodbye. Johnny worried, wondered, hoped for a moment that Evert was about to kiss his father. He watched him come close to him, in front of the fire, perhaps uncertain what to say, not looking him in the eye; then he raised his right hand and abstractedly but tenderly fingered the Fighter Command badge in David's buttonhole – a small gesture of quizzical familiarity that struck Johnny as quite outside the repertoire of his father's life, or of what he knew of it. Then David patted Evert on the shoulder – it was half an embrace. 'Do come again!' Evert said, and left it to Johnny to lead him out of the room.

He'd just opened the door when the light on the stairs came on, and in a second or two the noise from far down of someone climbing, determined and unseen. Johnny and his father waited a moment at the top and Ivan appeared at the turn below, looked up and saw them, saw he had arrived only just in time. '*Hello!*' he said, beaming at David, rich in his sense of the moment, which to David of course meant nothing – he'd never heard of Ivan. 'I'm so glad I caught you.'

'Dad, this is Ivan, old friend of mine, and Evert's.'

His father, courteous, nodded, said, 'David Sparsholt,' pleasantly and with an indissoluble grain of awareness of all the name had meant.

And now what would Ivan say? *I've heard so much about you . . .* ? His strange randy feeling for old men, and handsome well-preserved ones especially, seemed to Johnny to glow in his smiling face as he got his breath back – he must have left work early, rushed home. 'It's a great pleasure to meet you – at last.'

'Well,' said David, unaware of just how long that had been.

'Johnny and I've been friends for twenty-one years, so I feel I know you already.'

Their position at the top of the downward flight, David's hand already on the knob of the banister, didn't promise a long chat. 'Well, Evert's just been telling me all about you,' he said, wrong-footing Johnny; and Ivan said,

'Oh, dear!'

David gave a smile Johnny hadn't seen since childhood, cautiously teasing, entering a game, though at seventy-three he made a bigger effect with it. 'His saviour, he called you' – and

386

the smile played on Ivan as if surprised at the fact, but obliged, and even pleased, to accept it, in this house full of gay men.

'Oh, well . . .' said Ivan, with a little slump, as though under the weight of those duties. Then he beamed again: 'Do you have to go? Stay and have a drink, it will mean so much to Evert, seeing you again after all this time.'

The old man's smile narrowed a little, but he was still genial as he went down the first step. 'He did write to me, at least twice, and I'm ashamed to say I didn't reply.' This really wasn't for discussion, and he was almost at the turn of the stair when he looked back and said, 'I've never been much of a letter-writer'; he waved his hand in the air as he went on down and was hidden by the cage of the lift.

It was only when they were in the hall, Johnny picking up the second post from the floor, greeting but not introducing Mrs Lenska on the doorstep, that he saw, with his father beside him, how filial his feelings for Evert had become. Had his father himself sensed this, and been touched by it – wounded, per-haps, though possibly reassured? And if so, had he admitted the irony, or anyway oddity, of these two father-figures having long ago been friends, and then, astonishingly, lovers? They walked quickly away from the house, towards the Old Brompton Road – to Johnny the very pavement, the area gates, the numbered pillars of the porches, familiar to him for twenty years, seemed proof of his belonging, and of his father's transience, a rare and wary visitor. As they turned the corner into the brighter street, David's face seemed to show the uneasy relief of another kind of visitor, leaving a hospital when the time is up. 'Poor old Evvie,' he said – it wasn't a diminutive any of his real friends used, and seemed a clumsy claim on intimacy, and sympathy. Though might it, just possibly, have been what he called him at Oxford?

'You were very close once, weren't you?' Johnny said – and

then to lessen the pressure of implication: 'I mean, fifty years ago!'

His father glanced with habitual interest at a parked Bentley, S-series, his own sliding reflection in its windows and body-work. He said, 'I suppose he was pretty keen on me then. You know, looking back.'

'Mm, and what did you feel about him?' It was almost as if in the chill and change of the dusk, in the ambiguous minutes when streetlights came on under a high pink sky, a new freedom was possible. That strange 'Evvie', like a girl's name, with its touch of pathos and nostalgia, seemed to hint at a desire for it. Things had happened, not quite named before; why not name them now? His father looked at him, with a pinch of a smile, as if at a much cleverer cross-examiner.

'Things were very different then, old lad. But no, you're right, we were good mates for a while.'

'Oh, Dad, well that's lovely.'

There was a pause before he said, 'Just for a moment' – explaining but not subtracting from what he'd said. They walked on, Johnny looking around, with only a quick con-cealed peek at his father. There was a wine bar just opening – could the new mood carry them across the street and into the red glow of its doorway? He sensed his father's restlessness, and it came out oddly for all the inner rehearsal:

'I didn't know before that you'd been in trouble with the authorities.'

'What's that!' – the shadows of a later trouble were as tall as the houses.

'You know, at Oxford, about having Mum in your room.' Any mention of Mum to his father had a hint of reproach, an unwelcome persistence, though it could hardly be avoided. But now he seemed almost pleased, he had the set smile of someone making a good-natured effort to think back, even if pretty sure what he was going to find. It was candour that cost him nothing, and he shook his head amiably—

'No, no, old lad, there was never any trouble like that.'

'Oh,' said Johnny, 'I'd heard you were fined twenty pounds by the College!'

His father laughed briefly at this further absurdity. 'Have you got a clue how much that was then? No, no . . .' Though as they walked on he seemed to see some charm in the idea. 'I won't deny we got up to no good, but I wasn't so stupid as to get caught.'

'Right,' said Johnny, not knowing how to proceed, but knowing of course his father's ingrained habit of denial. 'I heard Evert lent you the money.'

'Is this what old Evvie says? You can't really believe him, not these days, he was talking all kinds of nonsense just now.' And then again, more freely and more considerately, 'Not that I care a damn. It just didn't happen.'

They never knew how to say goodbye, his father sensed and avoided any impulse of Johnny's to hug him or kiss him, and his parting words were said over his shoulder as he strode suddenly into the road: 'I must get to Euston!' – hand raised, a grin of clarified affection and relief. The taxi signalled and slowed to a stop fifty yards down the street. Johnny watched his father as he went towards it, silver hair and turned-up collar of the sheepskin jacket, the suggestion, even now, of an impulse to march subdued to the civilian briskness of his walk. He said two words to the driver and got into the cab without glancing back. The new intimacy had been just for a moment too.

FIVE

Consolations

1

Bella Miserden was a friend of Una's, famous from makeover TV, and married to Alan Miserden, who'd got out of rightnow.com with eight million a mere two days before it folded in 1999. At a corporate party held in the NPG, Bella had been trapped for ten minutes in a side room showing new accessions, which included Johnny's portrait of Freddie Green, bequeathed by his widow. Bella captured the label displaying these facts on her iPhone: *Jonathan Sparsholt (b 1952)* – so, sixty years old, and fairly experienced, but, since she'd never heard of him, perhaps not too expensive. She'd barely heard of Freddie Green either – *1920–1995 . . . Writer and broadcaster . . .* a scrawny old thing though possibly attractive to women – but she felt, as she stared at him over her empty champagne glass, that Jonathan Sparsholt had 'got' him. All this she relayed by chance to Una, who said, 'God Bella it was Johnny that did the sperm for Lucy,' and after a rather breathless two minutes had offered to put them in touch.

At the meeting it had been unnervingly (for Bella) as if she were asking for sperm for herself – she couldn't get the idea out of her mind. She knew he was gay, but he wasn't like other sixty-year-old gays Bella knew, who tended to fine suits, directorships and much younger boyfriends not everyone got to meet. He was handsome, with a thick shock of grey hair, and clothes – suede boots, thick jeans, a sort of waistcoat worn over a roll-neck sweater – that spoke of a dogged adherence to a style he had settled on decades before. There was nothing you could do for someone like that. Of course he had recently lost his husband (how Alan had snorted when she'd used that word, quite smoothly, over breakfast), and this made him seem almost touchingly ditched, all alone, into a modern world whose styles had long ago moved on. He had a large brown album with photos of earlier commissions; there was nothing swaggering or presumptuous about him, and she felt he might almost be rather simple – simple anyway to push around, and get what she wanted. She wanted a 'conversation piece', all the family, six feet wide. She saw herself changing her will, and leaving the picture to the National Portrait Gallery; it would save the kids from bickering about who should keep it. Alan said if he was called Sparsholt he might well be the son of a man who'd been in some sort of scandal – before either of them were born; she'd googled it, and confirmed it, didn't really take it in, and didn't mention it at all, of course, at that first meeting; she planned to work tactfully round to it during the sittings, when they would each be at the other's mercy.

Soon Johnny was driving down in the Volvo to the Miserdens' would-be-Georgian mansion in Virginia Water for the first of a wearisome sequence of sittings: with the vain but restless Alan, with the amusing bitch Bella, and with Samuel (16), Alfie (12) and Tallulah (7). Work was the thing, and there was something oddly bracing, in his new solitude, about examining a couple and their offspring still locked in their furious collective life. Upstairs at the NPG, Bella had also admired the portrait of George V and family by Lavery, which she thought might work as a model for the Miserdens. Johnny never contradicted his sitters, but hoped it would be enough to use a sofa, as Lavery had done. There would doubtless be squabbles, the first day, about who was going to sit on it; and as only two of George V's children appeared in the original, the violent economy of musical chairs seemed to haunt the arrangements.

In the first week he had driven to and fro three times, M40 and M25, the vast blue signs to Heathrow Airport looming and dropping behind, plunging reminders of travels with Pat that were over for ever. Could he imagine flying anywhere again, whom would he fly with, who share his tastes and urges so unspeakingly? These stifled traipses through commuter traffic, tailbacks, closed lanes and contraflows, were his ambit now. There was muddy grass, red buses, but England had descended already into driver's grey, grey road, grey sky, grey buildings and leafless trees between, the cars all grey to match. The old red Vulva, so useful and depended-on, dear and derided, was smelly, dented and rusted, its windows rimmed in a delicate moss that had itself now died. Bella, coming out on to the circular drive of her house, had hovered between mocking and tactfully ignoring the car; then suggested he drive it round to the back, into the paved yard where their Range Rovers and Porsches glinted from the shadows of six garages.

On that first day, he'd got them all together, old party conjuror, the moment of novelty, the sitters' uncertainty and readiness for surprise. The setting for the portrait was the drawing room, with its shiny simulacra of country-house style: white marble fireplace, low squashy sofas, books by celebrities and media tie-ins stacked on a round table, a large number of lamps clashing with the battery of ceiling spots trained on the nondescript pictures on the walls. It was a funny thing about working on location that you might have to paint other people's pictures in the background – they were part of the portrait too. He tried a number of groupings, Alan sitting down, Bella sitting down, Alan and Bella standing and the children sitting down. 'I thought, you, know, George the Fifth . . .' said Bella. 'Well, quite,' said Johnny. Samuel was red-haired, skinny, taller than both his parents, his face a tragi-comedy of spots. His mother wanted him to stand behind. Alan was neat, handsome, silky-haired and oddly devoid of sex appeal; Bella, heightened and hardened by being so much seen, was sharply pretty, a business-like blonde with a good figure. The room near the back door with weights and an exercise bike was clearly much used, though not perhaps by fat little Alfie, in his Arsenal strip: he hoped to be painted holding a ball. Tallulah was self-possessed, gracious, and sitting for her picture from the moment she entered the room.

Johnny made quick sketches, rearranged the grouping, tapped what excitement there was among the boys, staved off cleverly the boredom that threatened after half an hour when he saw a slight resentment setting in that the picture wasn't finished already. They were glimpsing the enormity of the thing – the dawn of an appalled understanding that painting a portrait took time. The trick then was to make the very length of the process intriguing to them. They would all want to keep look-ing, and there was an art to that too – the managing of their vanity, curiosity and impatience. 'You could just take a photo-graph, and be done with it,' said Alan amiably. 'Darling . . . !' said Bella, disgraced by this remark but redeemed by it too perhaps, as the artistic member of the family, the one with an eye.

Johnny perched on a stool, at the same height he would be when standing at the easel. This first day he wanted one work-able sketch of the whole group – much smaller in scale than the planned picture. 'Sort of a dress rehearsal,' said Bella, for whom the whole thing had a flavour of showbiz. But then – it was hard to bring it up, but how *were* they going to dress? It was like giving notes to a cast of slightly truculent amateurs. 'Now remember,' Johnny called out, as they all got up and started talking, 'whatever you wear when you come for your first sitting you'll have to wear all the way through.' He raised his eyebrows at Alfie, humorously, but the boy seemed alarmed.

Surely Bella didn't want him captured for all time in football shorts and a red top.

Then Johnny packed up and left them and set off home, became part of the eternal evening traffic, bored, protesting at one delay after another, but hardly wanting to be back. The house he was returning to held nothing that he craved, and he neglected it. In the garden unchecked summer growth fell under rains and frosts into leafless dereliction. Yet he dreaded the time when he would tend it again carefully, resigned to the facts. He unlocked the door, stooped for the mail, one uncertain post a day now, and the envelopes impersonal, thrown unopened on the hall table. His own pictures, with their evident merits and flaws, crowded up the stairs, witness to his years of painting while Pat was at his office or out for days on end at churches in Hertfordshire, Bedfordshire, Lincolnshire – the slow solitude of those weeks passing in the confidence of his coming back, and of the talk when he did. Each person if he was lucky found the place where he could shine, and the person to shine on. At Cranley Gardens Johnny had been audience, to Evert, to Ivan, to the whole clever, memoir-swapping gang. But with Pat he was a closely attended performer – he was funny, almost articulate, and rich in things worth saying.

He always needed a lot of sittings, and the Miserden job, which he would have liked to do quickly, looked set to take an especially long time. Because of school terms and the parents' crowded diaries the visits were oddly spaced out. Johnny went to bed and turned out the light on to a special shade of darkness when he knew he was going to Virginia Water next day – what he saw in his mind's eye was the journey, the grey road in the rain. He set the alarm, and woke before it went off. Waking alone had a different darkness from sleeping alone, singleness reasserted and unremitting. But later in the day he would find himself there, and the work would pick up and go on and he was glad to be out of his own house, and with other people, even with people like this.

He seemed to see them, as they sat individually, with a new clarity – he felt more than ever his power to expose them lurking like under-drawing to the flattery, the diplomacy of the commissioned portrait. Alan, fit and sleek in tight jeans, with no apparent genitals, had the overall smoothness of features that expects good fortune but never attracts much personal devotion. He seemed to Johnny a child conditioned by success that had never failed him yet. To paint a man so uninteresting to look at became a challenge. Samuel was in the Sixth Form at Harrow, and was set on a more formal style than his parents – an awful tweed hacking jacket doubling the colours of his face and hair. Tallulah showed an unworldly neglect of her appearance, as if she believed not only in the artist but in her own innate interest to make the thing a masterpiece. She just came in and sat, and Johnny, feeling he'd met his match, made a bright infanta of her, in school uniform.

But how strange the chat between artist and sitter became in the long shadow of Pat's death, he couldn't describe it, it seemed a molecular change in the material of life itself. He knew his role so well, thirty years in the business, part servant, part entertainer, the visiting artisan with his humble superiority, his gift, and now and then the air of inspiration with which he pleased them, reassured them, and kept his distance. He followed the familiar pattern of talk, nothing serious or sequential; he agreed, made brief distracted demurrals, eyes focused on detail; he kept things away from himself, an inveterate habit with new force. Everything in *their* talk was somehow of having (however fretful and spoilt and blind), as if having was their right, and unending. They hadn't started to imagine his condition, where everything was crystallized in the aching cold of having lost.

Johnny liked to have Radio 3 on and brought in from the car, with his easel, paintboxes and groundsheet, the spattered old ghetto-blaster with its yard-long aerial, and its cassette deck, which dropped open sleepily, as if surprised to be still in use. 'Composer of the Week' first of all was Haydn, a happy one to work to. Alfie was learning the violin but had no more interest in classical music than the others – Tallulah, something saccharine about her, said she really liked this bit or that bit, but Johnny saw this as social training, instilled early. There was some vacant buck-passing between Alan and Bella, who in their separate sittings both claimed that their spouse's lack of interest in music had sadly prevented them from going to concerts and so forth. Johnny was in charge of the music, and more than ever it was a screen. Sometimes of course he'd had sitters who were musical, and the music itself formed a medium of agreement, sustaining them both in the strange social intercourse of the sessions. But these days fewer and fewer people knew music, they couldn't be expected to, there was no shame to Alan in talking all through the slow movement of the Lark Quartet about the relative performance of equities and gilts.

Something further emerged, in the careful process of building up their two figures, which also meant breaking them down. It was like those brief raw glimpses, in adolescence, of the private life of his parents – moments of lust or animosity, frighteningly unlike the normal banter of home. The summer, the autumn when everything went wrong, had been full of them, tones overheard from another room, of muttered violence or dead calm, the hard 'I'm sorry?' of a couple not wanting to hear one another: a cold irritated question, rising to hold off the downward truth, apology and regret, 'I'm sorry,' 'No, *I'm* sorry.' Now he was watching two adults younger than himself hiding, and hinting at, their mutual dissatisfaction. It struck him the portrait was like a late child, produced to lend new purpose to a marriage – all Bella's idea, of course.

Both Alan and Bella asked him, 'How am I doing?' – he with a grin of impatience, as if saying 'How am I doing for time?' Bella was more anxious to feel she was getting it right and giving of her best, as if 1.5 million viewers were watching. The way with any impatient subject, anyone who couldn't attain the right kind of passive alertness, was to tell them what good sitters they were. Alan was briefly convinced by this; though a suspicion it was just the ruse of an underling, and a slight discontent with himself for having swallowed it, showed in his tight hint of a smile after a further ten minutes. Such physical inspection was unusual for him, beyond the sanitized codes of the barber's or dentist's half-hour. But to Bella, who lived in, and lived off, the world of appearances, any sacrifice was reasonable, and she entered into it wholeheartedly. Johnny found himself giving her tart unsentimental features small spiritual touches – unsure as he did so if they were flattery or divination.

Bella, he knew, would want Johnny to talk, like an indiscreet cleaner, about other people he'd done, a famous cricketer, a famous dancer, and Sophie Wessex, of course. Royalty was approached with a mixture of irony and raw fascination. 'You're awfully discreet,' Bella said. 'Well, I hope you're reassured by that,' said Johnny, very smoothly, as his glance went back and forth between her left eyebrow and its image on the canvas. The fact was, of course, he knew no one who would be interested in Bella's ratings rivalries and feuds with producers. She asked him a bit about himself, perkily at first, anticipating no resistance – he felt a heightened risk in disclosure, in colouring the sitting with his own emotions, his history, his artist's escape from worlds like this.

He was forced, by the nature of the thing, to show the children as their children. No doubt the picture would go in to the Royal Soc of Portrait Painters' annual show, and be seen then, if never again, by strangers. They would recognize Bella, and look from face to face, and at the room with its flashes of crimson and gilt, for a glimpse of her life, much as she had given them glimpses, in fact terrible glaring analyses, of the homes of others. They would look at smug, impatient little Alan, at wide-eyed Tallulah, Alfie posing with his ball, and Samuel, lazily fomenting all that was worst in his parents' world. He kept Samuel's sittings to a minimum, which suited both of them, since he was a fidget, casually mutinous, full of dismissive gossip about people in his mother's world whom he was none the less proud to know. He was always hard to find, when the time for his sitting came, and took his position ten minutes late with an air of disdain for the process, but a moody concern with the result. On Johnny's fourth visit to Virginia Water he was kept waiting for nearly half an hour. The door into the hall was ajar, and at last he heard voices.

'For fuck's sake, Mummy,' Samuel was saying, 'I've sat for him already for hundreds of hours.'

'Yes, well, real proper art takes a bit of time you know, sweetie.'

'Well, he's hardly Sir John Lavvy, is he?' said Samuel, snorting in spite of himself; 'not, I hasten to add, that I'm that familiar with Lavatory's work.'

'Jonathan Sparsholt just happens to be a first-rate painter – he's painted royalty, you know.'

'Mother, royalty have their portraits painted twice a week, there's nothing special about it, in fact they're usually a load of wank.'

'None the less, my darling,' said Bella grimly, 'they sit, they damn well have to. Now get in there.' Clearly, by the inexplicable physics of motherhood, she was winning, despite having (even Johnny felt) the worse arguments. Samuel was whinily yielding as he said,

'And he's such an awful old pervert, I don't like him peering at me all day long.' But here a dull whack of something, half missing its target, sent the boy with a laugh and a shout of 'All right!' into the room.

'Good afternoon,' said Johnny.

'*Hi*, Jonathan – sorry I'm late!' said Samuel: 'got held up by the great nattering mother-bird.'

'Right, let's get on,' said Johnny, with a snap of a smile. He peered, reluctantly, at the boy, whose physical repulsiveness he'd previously felt bound to disguise; but over the following hour (he kept him fixed on the hard stool a long twenty minutes more than was needed) he gave himself with a kind of sour enthusiasm to telling the truth.

'Oh, Christ,' said Samuel, when he stood up at last and came round to see the work, 'I'm covered in shag-spots.' Johnny had brought up two or three of them, tiny flushed confections of impasto in the hot translucency of teenage skin. 'God, you awful man, you're going to have to take those out. I mean, I can't go in the National Portrait Gallery looking like that.'

'Well, it's a risk you take,' said Johnny, with a rueful shake of the head, 'when you have your portrait painted.'

The boy thought about it. 'I'm going to tell my mother not to bloody well pay you,' he said.

Of course, by the time she came next day, half-amused, to see for herself, Johnny had applied the Clearasil of art, he'd smoothed him out, and taken something else out too, his character, such as it was. Now he was any spoilt teenaged brat.

Before his next visit, Bella suggested he stay the night – they were going to Mexico for Christmas and it would be a chance to get ahead first. They had dinner in the kitchen, cooked and served by Briony, a local woman with a fatuous confidence in her own opinions – she ate with the family too. She'd been to Mexico herself, and had nothing good to say for the place. 'Don't touch the food, Bella, that's my advice. God, was I ill.'

'How will we live then?' said Samuel, insolent but curious.

'I'm sure we'll eat splendidly,' said Alan.

Briony looked at him, with a pretence of a huff as she opened the lower oven: 'Of course the sort of place you're staying I'm sure everything will be very nice.'

'You've been to Mexico?' Alan said.

'Yes – yes, we went about ten years ago,' said Johnny – lost coupledom trailed and inviting questions. 'We both loved it.'

Briony set a plate in front of him, baked pasta in a thick cream gloop, under cheesy breadcrumbs. 'I'll have you know I've gone to a good deal of trouble over this,' she said.

'Thanks very much,' said Johnny. Vegetarians often gave their hosts a new sense of their own virtue.

'You're missing out on a lovely bit of veal, though I say it myself,' she said, turning back to the range. Well, they weren't always as brutal as that.

Alan glanced at him and said, 'I was wondering if your old man was still alive? He must be getting on a bit if so.'

'Dad? – oh, yes, he's fighting fit,' said Johnny. 'He'll be ninety next year' – startled by the subject, and Alan's belief it was all right to talk about it. He lifted his fork, sheared the stacked plateful to let it cool and saw with a familiar sinking of the heart a dozen small pink flakes in the sauce. He pressed one discreetly between two tines of the fork: salmon.

'Gosh, marvellous . . .' – Alan blinked at him and smiled. 'Because that must have been quite a business, back in the 60s.'

'Oh, yes,' said Bella, with a wince of sympathy, 'I heard something about that.'

'Well, it was very famous, darling,' said Alan. 'I'm sure Jonathan won't mind me saying.'

'What was it?' said Samuel.

'I'm not sure . . .' said Bella, looking at Tallulah.

'Well, there are books about it, aren't there.'

'Something very sad,' said Bella primly, but then looked at

Johnny as if half-hoping he would speak. None of them even imagined his quandary, but he knew how it would be once he started to explain – 'I'm sorry . . .' 'No, I'm sorry,' and Briony's fury when she took the plate away and offered him the salad they were all due to have later.

Alan said, 'It reminded me of the Poulson business, in a way.'

'Well, people sometimes say that,' said Johnny.

'All the planning carry-on. But of course with the addition of er' – he looked shrewdly at his daughter – 'the other business.'

'Sounds interesting,' said Samuel, sitting back as his veal was put in front of him, and smiling meanly at Johnny – who saw that he still held the cards, he could honour or refuse their claim on him, or, as he usually did, dodge sideways.

Alan was reasonable. 'I suppose if it had happened a year or two later, the affair with . . . what was he called?'

Johnny stared. 'Clifford Haxby?'

'Yes, that's right – would have been quite legal. Damn bad luck that.'

'It wasn't exactly an affair,' said Johnny.

'And wasn't there some terrifically dodgy MP involved?'

'Yes, there was.'

'I don't know what you're talking about,' said Briony, tucking her chin in, 'but it sounds very fishy to me.'

'But your mother's still alive?' Alan said, with a note of sympathy for her.

'No. No, she died, some time ago now. In 19 . . . 98,' said Johnny.

'Right . . .' – Alan nodding, thrown momentarily off-course. 'But they . . .'

'Oh, they didn't stay together. No, Dad remarried, more than forty years ago now . . . what? . . . his secretary, yes,' said Johnny – so Alan knew, but wanted, for some primitive reason, to have confirmation from the closest and most reluctant source.

'Ooh, wonderful,' said Alan, unaccommodating as he surveyed his plate.

'I hope you don't mind us eating meat,' Bella said.

'Oh! . . . no . . .' said Johnny. 'Though, um . . .'

'Poor veals,' said Tallulah tentatively.

'They're not bloody veals,' said Samuel, in grinning disgust at her.

'Actually, that's just what they are, isn't it,' said Bella, receiving her fillet in its nearly black sauce. 'I often think I could easily become a vegetarian.'

'Mum, do I have to have courgettes?' said Alfie.

'I mean, I virtually am already. I hardly ever have red meat.'

'For Christ's sake,' said Samuel.

'Samuel,' said Alan, but laughed rather drily at the idea himself.

Johnny ran back over what he had said to Bella – he was quite sure, no creatures. He smiled at her. 'Is something wrong?' she said.

After dinner they went through to a sort of family room, beyond the kitchen, with big soft sofas flanking a wood-burning stove, a TV screen about the same size as the portrait he was working on, a table with a jigsaw that Bella and Tallulah were doing, Picasso's *Three Musicians*, in 1,687 pieces. Tallulah had told him about it earlier, as she sat – the special problems with modern art, which she seemed determined to solve. 'Mummy brought it back from New York for me,' she said. 'I love art.' Johnny declined a brandy, which he knew would give him a headache, but yielded to a further glass of wine, which Alan poured for him with a small disparaging smile. 'You were going to look up Jonathan's website, darling,' Bella said.

'Oh, yes,' said Alan, sitting down equably beside Johnny and opening the MacBook left on the sofa, which lit up for a second on the Wikipedia page about the Sparsholt Affair – he slumped backwards, pulled it towards him and typed in Johnny's name instead, seeming unbothered. 'You've got quite an individual style,' he said, a minute later, nodding slowly as if taking the measure of what he was in for.

'Well, I've been doing it for well over thirty years,' said Johnny, 'so I'm sure I have my bad habits as well as some good ones.'

'I like your style,' said Bella, making no bones about it. 'Your painting style.'

'Ah, I see you painted Freddie Green,' Alan said.

'Yes, I did.'

'Must have been right at the end of his life, from the look of him.'

Johnny thought, about the question and about what it implied. 'Yes, he was very ill. I think his wife wanted to get him on canvas before anything worse happened.'

'Mm . . . terrific,' said Alan.

'You knew him, then?'

'Oh, I met him a couple of times,' said Alan.

'I didn't know that,' said Bella.

'There's one of his books around the house somewhere . . . Now, *Nudes*, I'm not sure I ought to look at those.'

Johnny saw him do so, sat in the mild inanity of anyone having their work looked at.

'I hope you're not still hungry,' said Bella.

'I'm fine,' said Johnny. Soon he would ask if he could go to bed.

'Golly,' said Alan. 'I'm glad my wife didn't see these before she took you on.'

'Of course I saw them,' said Bella.

'Can you see me in that sort of pose, darling?' – Alan turning the screen to show them one of Johnny's pictures of Svend, the tall Danish model he'd painted several times ten years ago.

'Well . . .' she said, loyalty tested.

'Extraordinary,' said Alan, turning the screen back. Johnny saw that he thought himself rather broad-minded in employing him, and if put on the spot would explain it as his wife's doing. Women were often quite thick with the gays, they prided themselves on knowing them, just as Alan took care to keep his distance. 'Now . . .' he said, '*Families*,' peering down like some old buffer, one of David Sparsholt's friends: 'That's more like it!'

2

Waiting while Michael unlocked the front door, he wasn't sure if he was going to meet his parents, or what to say to them if he did; he imagined them, smart, wealthy, busy, and ten years younger than himself. It was hard to ask about them without sounding anxious. 'So what does your dad do?' he said.

The door swung open on to a long empty entrance hall, floored in grey and white marble. 'Oh . . . all kinds of stuff!' said Michael.

'Right.'

'He's in LA right now.'

'Oh, OK.'

Michael seemed to be both English and American. 'Well, this is it' – he locked the door behind them, and there was something about him, haunted or haunting, touching buttons on a lit panel, going on down the hall with his coat on, the young man in the absent father's house: it was a drawing charged with inexplicable emotion, a dozen quick strokes converging on a line and a shape.

'Wow . . .' – on the left a vast rectangular stairwell rose into shadow, and Johnny walked into the centre of it and stared upwards at the glimmering skylight four floors above. 'That's amazing' – with an echo, subtle index of true Georgian grandeur. 'These are Adam houses, aren't they?'

'Yeah, it's Adam,' said Michael, coming back.

'You'll have to show me.' He felt it lent glamour to the frictionless unfolding of the date; he would have the house to remember at least. He put out an arm and found himself holding Michael's cool hand. Then he turned, bent his head and kissed him on the mouth.

'Hey . . .' said Michael.

A door under the cantilever of the stairs opened and a woman, Chinese perhaps, in a dark skirt and blouse appeared. She stood smiling, not quite in greeting, but in readiness. 'Hey, Lin,' said Michael. Johnny smiled back, wondering for a moment what unrehearsed fiction would explain his presence, and was still standing there as Michael started up the stairs – he nodded and turned and went up after him.

On the first floor were two large interconnecting rooms, and Johnny hardly knew what to say about the pictures, while Michael switched on lamps, closed the shutters on the two tall windows to the street, activated the TV, volume low, on some unknown channel, music videos, edited like distraction itself, near-naked black women lip-synching from six different angles. High above, the drawing-room ceiling, with its graceful light roundels and quadrants of stucco, its lovely repeating formulae of fans, bows and garlands, had been painted all over a heavy brassy gold, shiny enough to reflect the lamps below. It was such a glaring disaster that it made you wonder, almost, if it mightn't be rather a triumph. Michael opened a door and a light came on in a mirrored cupboard. 'Do you want a drink?'

Johnny asked for a whisky with ice, watched Michael's reflection, sleek, attractive, pale, as he took down glasses, clinked
among bottles, triggered the short clatter of an ice machine. It
was Jack Daniel's he gave him, they tipped glasses, the whole
focus of the date, imagined by Johnny as hungry and immediate, blurred again as Michael went out of the room for a minute.
Johnny hovered, looking at the expensive contemporary furniture, all of it very low, in steel, black glass, white leather, and
barely impinging on the tall expanses of wall given over to the
paintings. These were two or three times larger than anything
he himself had painted, or felt the least urge to paint, and must
have been difficult to get into the house; they seemed to him
monstrous, garish, trophies of international art-fairs made for
fashionable buyers with a great deal of money. He sat down and
slithered forward in involuntary mimicry of a laidback person
on a low pony-skin sofa, staring up at a huge pink and black
daub. And again a little bleakness of uncertainty crept in, that
these were in fact brilliant works of art, which he was too old,
too stubborn, or too ill-informed, to like or value. The contemporary had left him behind.

The soft burn of the drink was a comfort, as he watched
Michael come back, carefully close the door, set down laptop,
iPad, a small lacquered box on the low table. Johnny moved
up to make room, but he sat cross-legged on the floor. His
movements and conversation made no allusion at all to these
surroundings, he seemed not to see them, and it was hard to
know if to him they were a glorious given modestly ignored or
an obvious eyesore tactfully disowned. With his laminated student card he squashed and chopped a lump of what Johnny
assumed was coke on the glass tabletop, drew it out into four
stubby lines. He rolled a twenty-pound note and held it up to
Johnny, and smiled – he had a beautiful smile that Johnny
thought, as he crouched forward, blocked one nostril and
snorted through the other, would be interesting but hard to

capture, innocent and sceptical. The snort was a thought, an unexpected zip back eight or nine years, to when he last did it with Pat, and Lucy came in early from a party and caught them at it.

Things sped up a bit then, Johnny happy but wary, his strange eloquence heard at moments as if he were someone else. Michael nodded, grinned and chatted too, they had another drink, the completely talentless half-sung songs pulsed on in the background, glances now and then at the crouching and strutting figures, explosions, odd banal details, a car, a bed, in teeming succession on the screen. A man older than himself whom Johnny had sat next to at dinner last week had told him dating apps were tickets to instant sex, and had shown him two that he used, scores of men a mere hundred yards away, always ready. 'Not for me,' said Johnny; and three days later found himself downloading one, which meant inescapably setting up a profile, a sort of self-portrait – his old holiday snap had its undertow of lost happiness, and he sighed as he tried to define what his interests were. But then it had all happened, quite quickly and naturally, in this wholly new way; and now here he was as if on a date forty years ago, having a drink and a chat about Michael's course. Michael had three modules to do. '*Three* modules,' said Johnny, 'right.'

'Yeah, I've got till the end of this month to complete my Subjectivity module.'

Johnny said, 'What is that, exactly?' and leant forward to take Michael's hand again, but just as the phone chirped, and he picked it up and dealt with the message and another one that followed.

'Are you on WhatsApp?' Michael said.

'Not yet,' said Johnny.

'You should do it! We can WhatsApp each other.'

'We've sort of got each other anyway, haven't we,' said Johnny.

Then Michael seemed to have finished all his phoning and texting. He sat back, grinned at Johnny in anticipation, and said, 'So, hey, enough about my dad, what did your dad do?'

'My dad?' said Johnny briskly. 'He was a manufacturer – you know, he made machine parts, engines, generators.'

'Oh cool,' said Michael, his eye distracted at once by the small coloured screen.

'I mean he's still alive. He's nearly ninety now, he's sold the business.'

'Right . . .' It all probably seemed small beer to Michael, picking up his phone, with a quick chuckle over the message he'd just got. Why did Johnny say this, when for decades he'd done all he could to avoid and deflect the subject: 'You've probably heard of the Sparsholt Affair?'

Michael smiled, almost tenderly, at his screen, murmured, 'No, bitch . . .' and thumbed in a quick answer. He glanced at Johnny. 'Sorry, what was it called? A movie, right?'

'Well, not yet,' said Johnny. 'No, it was . . . oh, it doesn't matter.'

'Oh, OK . . .' said Michael, with a little doubting look. 'Is it a book?'

Johnny lay back, relieved and remotely indignant, dry-mouthed, communicative, waiting to hear himself go on. 'Well, there have been a couple of books about it, someone called Ivan Goyle wrote one, and there's one by a *Sunday Times* journalist.'

'Yeah, I don't have much time for reading,' Michael said.

He had another line of coke (Johnny, still buzzing, not) and fetched them both fresh drinks; then he showed Johnny the profiles of three or four people on Grindr he fancied, and one or two he'd hooked up with. Johnny felt put out by this but agreed magnanimously that they were hot or cute. Michael sent messages to a couple of them and laughed at the replies. There was another app too that he hadn't heard of, for older men and their admirers. Some of these looked so geriatric as to be beyond sex, even with modern aids. Johnny went out to the lavatory, tall and bright, and when he came back he bent over Michael and ruffled his dark hair. But it seemed that for Michael a half-dozen birds in the bush were worth one in the hand, the shimmer of potential sex was more alluring than the fact of it, here in the gold-ceilinged drawing room. 'I'm attracted to older men,' said Michael, as he peered into the screen of his phone.

'Oh, good . . .' said Johnny, sitting down again, and starting to wonder if perhaps he just wasn't old enough.

Michael went upstairs for a bit and left Johnny to swipe through the photos on his phone, endless selfies against backgrounds in Paris, Cape Town or New York, Michael among friends, party-goers, the phone held high so that they looked up from the crowd with arms round each other and always more clown-like expressions than Michael, who seemed fixed, as though by some botched cosmetic surgery, in a rictus of glamour. Here he was last month in a packed London club, among shirtless young beauties, their arms and chests badged, swirled and enlaced in tattoos: Johnny prised the picture wide to read the details. His old friend Graham had said they should go out, the two of them – the idea of joining a crowd like this was both enchanting and absurd. Going out, dancing, not just getting drunk as he had in his twenties, but taking powerful drugs, as he had a few times in his forties, ranked among the high pleasures of his life, free of all inhibition and doubt. Odd, then, that he'd surrendered it, he'd denied himself such nights for ten years or more. It seemed to him part of the tact of age.

Michael came back with his laptop and sat pressing lightly against Johnny on the low sofa. 'You've got to look at this,' he said, dopy but manic with the coke, clicking on a link that opened a new window, the tall portrait shape of an iPhone video. He smiled at the entertainment Johnny was about to have. 'It's my friend Snapstud,' he seemed to say.

'That's an unusual name,' said Johnny, leaning in, putting an

arm round him. 'Who is he?' He saw a naked young man wanking and staring at the camera while sliding a translucent blue
dildo in and out of his arse. 'Good grief . . . !' It wasn't remotely
the sort of thing he was used to looking at, and he was giddy
for a moment at the sequence of casual revelations, that people
did this, and that they filmed it, and that others watched it.
It was like a first teenage glimpse of a hard-core mag, but in its
matter-of-fact way not like pornography at all.

'Do you love him? He's so cute,' said Michael.

'Mm,' said Johnny, blushing and frowning down at the
screen. Snapstud had dirty blond hair, and a left arm sleeved to
the neck in multi-coloured tattoos. 'How do you get this?'

'What's that . . . ?' said Michael, with a slow shake of his
head as he watched, 'It's just on his Tumblr. Go, Snappy!' in his
hazed mid-Atlantic voice, as Snappy sent up an astonishing
plume of semen, a quick sequence of plumes that could be
heard very faintly pattering on to a surface out of view. Then
he winked and raised a thumb in self-approval as the image
froze.

'Can anybody look at these?' said Johnny.

'Yeah, they're just like on his page . . .' and Michael clicked
back and scrolled through the 'archive', where dozens of such
videos of himself, alone or having sex with other men, were
thumbnailed.

'What does he do, your friend?'

'What . . . ? I don't know, I've never met him,' said Michael.
'I think he like works in a bank?' He took Johnny's confusion
for excitement, and selected another, which it took a moment
to work out showed Snappy with his knees behind his head
fellating himself.

'Well, well,' said Johnny, and sat forward and closed the
laptop as he took it out of Michael's hands – it was a small not
quite friendly struggle.

'I thought you were into young guys,' said Michael.

Johnny set the machine carefully on the table. Hearing his preference defined, as plainly as Michael had stated his own taste for older men, he felt there was something amiss with it, a quick desire to exonerate himself that ran ahead of a more puzzled feeling: that young guys weren't what he particularly wanted. But he said bluffly, 'That's why I'm here, isn't it,' and after some brief wriggling and dodging on Michael's part they started kissing.

Johnny stayed for most of the night. It wasn't a great success, but belonged even so to a private sub-category in his life, the miss that was an achievement in another way. Michael was twenty-three and it was twenty-three years since Johnny had slept with anyone new. The boy's body retained something ideal, and he visited it with faintly amused respect, with several admiring intakes of breath at its smoothness and beauty, and some looser but larger dissatisfaction, that it seemed to know nothing. His cock had more character than he did, tight-skinned and curving to the left. Johnny marvelled at it, amazed to think cocks were still going on, all over the place, when for years he'd rarely seen anyone's but his own and Pat's. Michael's made its own undoubting bid for attention; and received it. But it was all very quick when it came to it. 'Oh, is that it?' Johnny thought. 'Well, what did you expect?'

'So do you have a partner?' said Michael, a few minutes later, curling up with his head on Johnny's chest, in a cautious late start at showing a personal interest in him – all his gadgets were elsewhere and Johnny feared doing anything that might alert him to their absence. He pulled him closer against him.

'Did have,' he said. 'He died a few months ago.'

Michael seemed to make, in the blurred close focus, a pouting face. He might have been respectfully absorbing the news – he didn't say he was sorry to hear it. 'What did he die of?' he asked, with a flutter of eyelashes, a silent whirr of scanning the previous half-hour for any possible risk.

'He had prostate cancer.'

'Oh, right. That's bad, isn't it?'

'It's . . . yes, it is.'

'Must make sex a bit difficult, so I've heard.'

'Oh, our sex life was buggered,' said Johnny, which was Pat's joke. 'Though it didn't seem so important, you know, compared with life itself.'

'No . . .'

'Sex doesn't matter that much when you're my age.'

Michael twisted his head round to smile at him. 'That's not the impression I got just now,' he said, as if referring to a rather greater triumph than they'd had ten minutes before.

'What about you?' said Johnny. 'Any long-term affairs?'

'Yeah, I have a boyfriend,' said Michael.

'Hmm, what's his name?'

'Oh, Robert.'

'Is he in London?'

'He's in LA right now.'

'What, with your father?'

Michael laughed rather grimly. 'Absolutely no way!' He got out of bed, put on a dressing gown and went into the next room – soon Johnny heard him on the phone, it seemed he'd put an idea into his head, he was talking to Robert, in the early LA afternoon. 'Yeah? . . . Oh, cool, no . . . Well, I hope you get it, you deserve it! What? . . . Oh, no . . . nothing much going on here, just having a night in by myself . . . You can tell? Yeah, I guess I'm a bit high.' For a moment Johnny enjoyed the deceit, then suspected its cooler reverse – he wasn't worth mentioning to Robert.

'What was your partner called?' said Michael when he came back into the bedroom.

'Patrick,' said Johnny. 'How was Robert?'

'Oh, fine,' said Michael, slipping out of his dressing gown. They snuggled up together again. 'Did you have rows?'

'Mm, of course we did,' said Johnny. 'They never mattered much – you know, I wasn't afraid of him. We always said what we liked.' Though he'd been astonished, as a row-avoider, a conciliator all his life, at Pat's sudden and furious naming of his faults, new ones he'd never guessed and old ones unforgotten, such as being too conciliatory, and not wanting a good row. Johnny always sat waiting for the humour that crept up through the shouting, and was fatal to it. 'Why, do you have rows with Robert?'

'No, no,' said Michael, as if already thinking of something else.

Johnny ran his hand over the boy's buttocks and pressed in a middle finger, a forgotten luxury. 'Could he tell you had someone here?'

Michael didn't answer, and what he did next made it hard for him to do so coherently.

When they turned off the light Johnny reached a fraternal arm around Michael, who laid his head on it, and shifted every thirty seconds. Johnny had an old idea of his own looming discomfort, the numbness of the well-intentioned embrace when to move the arm is to wake the man sleeping on it; but there was something nostalgic in it too – a trace of forty years ago, when all such embraces were experiments. Still, he detached himself, turned again and lay flat on his back, a thin slip of light above the curtains defining the near zone of the ceiling. He knew now that the coke would keep him awake. That, and Michael snoring, half-waking himself, shifting, and wrapping himself round Johnny in a muttering convulsion, arguments of a dream.

Still, Johnny slept; and in the early winter light, about seven o'clock, found himself awake, eased himself free (Michael turned as if in a huff to the far side of the bed), and went through into the bathroom. He was looking forward to going home. The faint distracting throb grew slowly louder, overlaid after a minute with a higher mechanical whine. He parted the curtain as the busy green bug of the street-cleaning truck roared into view in the mews below, busy but slow-moving, its circular brushes almost beautifully missing the seven or eight bits of rubbish on the cobbles and leaving a wet dirty smear as it circled, turned, and disappeared the way it had come. He watched a little longer, as the swirled pattern started to dry and fade, like a canvas in a dream whose erasure began the moment the brush had made its marks.

The next week Johnny found Michael back in his mind, not the sex, or really his smoothly undeveloped features, but the feel of a warm young person moving in his arms – it wasn't just making up for Pat, it was something he'd never thought to have again. Better perhaps not to have met Michael, but once met he set off a painful yearning. Johnny decided to write him an email, finding the tone hard to get, not to be clumsily courtly or offputtingly brisk, unsure how much to use their thirty-year difference in age. He heard back from him next day, a cool, almost contentless paragraph, 'You're right, I am working on my Subjectivity module. You have a good memory Johnny.' And signed off disconcertingly, 'Thanks for reaching out, MX'. The phrase disturbed him, and went on doing so. There was a euphemistic kindness to it, a hint of surprise at his worthy but absurd attempt to see Michael again. He had an image of a hand stretching out through the bars of a cell – he might have reached out, but he hadn't, by some distance, reached what he wanted; and Michael, it was clear, was unlikely to reach back.

3

At the end of January he was rung up again by his old friend, originally Pat's friend, Graham, who'd been keeping an eye on him post-bereavement. Graham was five or six years younger than Johnny and had never had a long-term partner himself: he was someone for whom 'settling down' represented a terrifying rejection of choice; even so, there was a hint of changed valency in the call, from one single man to another. Johnny pictured him as he spoke: bald, black-eyed, still fit, in a way he himself had never bothered to be, with the look, in his jeans and blue-checked short-sleeved shirt, of a schoolmaster spotted in the private depths of the holidays. He used the old language, over the phone, 'Yeah, I got some good gear, wanna go out?' – always parody, and said now with a sweet sense of absurdity half-masking his excitement. He was a civil servant doing some-thing that Johnny had never grasped, a set of abstract terms; in the very moment he told you his job description you found yourself helplessly forgetting it. For twenty years he'd been a distant but a good friend, whose pleasure was in seeing you, with no hint of blame on either side for the time you hadn't been in touch. It was a kind of trust, and Johnny knew, if he was going to do anything so silly, so much in defiance of his own loneliness, that Graham was the person to do it with.

They met for dinner in a noisy Clerkenwell eatery, cocktails first and then a bottle of Shiraz. Graham had forgotten Johnny was vegetarian, or perhaps thought, now Pat was gone, he would revert to common sense, or taste; Johnny made do with two starters, the drink going straight to his head. They talked about Pat for a while, but Johnny saw Graham looking beyond him now, with an amiable waning of patience; he talked instead about the Brazilian boy behind the bar, and a dazzling young couple two tables away who they worked out were going on to the club as well. One of them, late thirties perhaps, had the gay voice that survived through generations, the illusionless adenoidal whine and drag, just a far-off hint of Australia in the colour of the vowels. Why did he mind it now, when he'd heard it, been thinly amused and reassured by it, all his adult life? He felt somehow troubled by their beautiful necks and biceps and hair.

Graham leant forward, charming, demonic in the uplight of the candle, covered Johnny's hand at the table and left in it the almost insensible presence of a twist of film, small (when he peeped at it) as the blue twisted paper of salt in a childhood packet of crisps. 'Good stuff,' said Graham: 'well, put it away' – perhaps unprepared for his innocence.

'In my day,' said Johnny, 'it was pills.'

Graham looked for the waiter. 'Yeah, this is better. Don't take it all at once, for god's sake. You've got seven or eight hits there.'

'OK,' said Johnny, 'thanks very much.' The sense of his trusting incompetence spread and he thought, when they'd paid the bill and got outside, he might just give the wrap back to Graham and put up his arm for a passing taxi. Graham would understand.

They walked for five minutes to the club, which wasn't a building, just a roped-off doorway giving on to a lobby and a deep descending staircase. 'You have no idea,' said Graham, 'what that doorway leads to.' 'Well, I have a bit,' said Johnny. In the queue the mood was unexpectedly exciting, and Johnny didn't mind waiting, adapting himself with a kind of shy watchfulness to the attitudes of the much younger men jiggling in front and massing, very quickly, behind. He caught their own reflections in the dark shop window beside them, two other people they were surprisingly connected to, Graham in his bomber-jacket, Johnny his old greatcoat, the collar turned up. He remembered the inexorable routine, new arrivals striding up or stepping out of taxis, squeals and kisses. Some of the men were sombre and subdued, saving themselves for a long and demanding night: it seemed something almost grim they put themselves through. He and Graham kept chatting quietly, but he felt a tightening in his gut, and was glad to be drunk already when the queue started moving forward. In the lobby a door opened and they heard the music from far inside stripped down by distance to a rapid menacing thump. They paid at a little window, £12, Johnny peering anxiously at the young ticket-seller, who smiled back and seemed unconcerned by his age; or was the smile too insistent, a hint of concern and amusement shown to the elderly? Immediately the ticket was taken from him and the back of his hand was stamped in black ink with an illegible emblem.

On the huge square stairway going down the banging of the music grew louder and louder like a boring threat, the noise of other people's pleasure. When they opened the door into the bar it came at them hard, the bright ping-ponging happiness of a tune on top, all warmed up, geared up, and bouncing fast, while he still had his coat on and wondered as they joined the queue for the coat check if he wanted to bounce at all. The medium of the club, three floors below ground, was an absolute darkness, on which multicoloured light played and darted incessantly, over the naked shoulders and handsome faces of the milling and gathering men. Johnny's fear here was the sixteen-year-old's again, that he would lose Graham, that his friend would make out with someone else, leaving him more lonely than ever in an alien crowd. He thought, for god's sake, I'm a father, I'm on the committee of the Royal Society of Portrait Painters, I own a large house in Fulham. He handed in his coat and scarf and big jersey and came away with his ticket and a little shiver past the huge ducted air-conditioning. And the truth was he had made a puzzled private attempt, back home, at looking sexy, a raid on his youthful self, old jeans shabby and tight, a faded T-shirt he'd screen-printed himself – a deniable effort but perhaps an appealing one. The two beautiful men from the restaurant came past and looked at them in the split-second misapprehension of their knowing each other, the twitch of a smile sliding at once to some worthier object – the smile deniable too. Graham marched him into the bar.

It was in the toilet stall, with his bottle of Corona and his twist of crystalline powder, that he saw himself most starkly, as if in a security camera, risky, ridiculous: what if he collapsed on the dance floor, and died? What would his father say, what would he tell his friends when the news appeared in the *Telegraph*? For a moment, above the narrow, black-walled cubicle, his father hovered like a genie. He wetted a finger, dipped it and licked it again, tiny granules bitter and authentic as he washed them down with two swigs of beer. He unbolted the door with unexpected firmness and relief, and went back to the bar.

He found Graham talking with a huge shirtless blond, formidable torso a swirl of tattoos, cogs and blades, Celtic but industrial, a legend on his chest in a font so fancy you had to work it out . . . *If You Want You Can Do It*: ah, well, thought Johnny. They were at different stages, Graham standing with his drink, a man at a party, the blond chewing, eyes dilated, touching him and stroking him. 'Johnny, this is Billy,' Graham said – Johnny found himself pulled in, kissed, held under Billy's fondly protective left arm, his skin silky and warm, Johnny's hand round his waist in lightly adhesive contact as he rocked to the music. 'Having a good time?' said Billy. 'I'm starting to,' said Johnny. Billy kissed him again and squeezed him – then shouted, reached out over Johnny's head to another massive beauty going past, and in a moment he was off, pulled away by the other man, but leaning back to kiss Graham too – 'Catch you later!' before he was taken into the surge that was moving and building towards the dance floor beyond. 'How do you know Billy?' said Johnny. Graham smiled and shrugged – 'Never seen him before,' he said.

He felt tired as they waited, the music, which all the others seemed to know and love, demanding something impossible of him, and someone was looking at him over Graham's shoulder, could it be a man he knew, a friend's child? A friend's grand-child . . . ? Not a sitter, he was sure of that. He went on past, turned and squinted at Johnny, said something to the boy with him, and hung around before coming back: 'Hello, Mr Spar-sholt!' Johnny looked narrowly at him, skinny, posh boy, dark, borderline pretty, eyes chemically engorged. 'It's Tim! – you remember, I was going to marry Lucy . . .' 'Oh, *Tim* . . .' said Johnny, then worked it out, as the boy shook his hand and kissed him on both cheeks. 'It's Mr Sparsholt!' Tim said to his friend. It was what he had called him in the days when Johnny took Lucy to play with him, or he came round to the house to play with her. At the age of eight he proposed to Lucy, but at some point in the twenty years since then had clearly thought better of it. Now he had nothing on but shorts and trainers and was hand in hand with this restless young man already tugging him on towards the dance floor, who also had something tat-tooed on his chest like a necklace, in flowing script: *Never A Failure Always A Lesson* – well, that was great too. Johnny followed them with his eyes, explained to Graham who he was, and felt his feet slyly shifting and rocking, an effortless energy pulsing up his legs, his head nodding, right arm rising on invis-ible currents to part the air in time to the music. He knew he was a lightweight, when they'd gone out in the old days he'd danced all night on half a pill. This was much quicker than a pill, he felt it lift him and stagger him at the same time. But it was lovely, absurdly lovely, too lovely for the mere materials at hand, and so with its own fine filament of regret, though he couldn't stop smiling. 'Shall we dance?' he said, and they threaded their way through to the edge of the floor, Graham shifting his shoulders, looking round, not up yet himself, but playing up to Johnny's sudden bold gestures. It was fabulous to move without thinking, among all the others, accepted. Graham touched his arm, gave him chewing gum, a swig of his water. 'That stuff's all right, then!' The big tune they all knew came back, held back, waited for, a countdown, open faces of the crowd turned towards the DJ in his booth, Johnny laughed and shook his head and his hand pointed skywards when it came.

Later he was watching a man dancing with friends, the rightness and beauty of him first of all, the strain of his neck, the face tighter but longer from baldness, but yes it must be Mark, he beamed at him, and Mark saw him too, and came over smiling – shirt tucked in his belt, leather bands tight round his biceps, all the handsome maintained muscled of a fifty-year-old, and the single small tattoo of thirty years before on the left arm, just below the shoulder, a rose: Johnny rubbed it with his fingers, with the ball of his thumb, magical, testing it. It was more touching, and more pleasing, than he could say, and Mark, who had probably half-forgotten it himself, rolled his shoulder to peer at it, and peered at Johnny with his funny saucy smile. He pulled him in, Johnny glanced back for Graham, who nodded happily at him, Mark took both his hands and they were dancing together.

There were questions Johnny dropped before bothering to ask, had Mark stayed on the scene, needing it, loving it, these past twenty years, or was this a rare nostalgic venture for him too? Johnny knew the answer, Mark gripping his shoulder and making happy incoherent remarks: flashes of memory and facts about the people he was with and what he'd been doing earlier in the evening all mixed up without connexion: he was very high. And Johnny got the drift, he was touched and charmed by the rubbish Mark was saying. They danced with a third man,

Max, in a leather harness, their arms round each other's shoulders and waists, Max losing the rhythm as he got out his phone and tried to make sense of a text, and struggled for a minute or two, jaw working and pupils like dark pools, to send a reply – the phone was fertile with predictions as he thumbed the wrong keys. Johnny offered to help him, which was a joke in itself, but they got it off just as the friend he was texting, a tall black man clutching bottles of water and Lucozade, squeezed his way through the crowd beside them: *Smirnofg and redbBull*, it said. The black man was called Arnold, and made droll conversation with Johnny before someone else claimed him. All around them in the fluent glancing colours of the lights men half their age danced, shoulders rolling, hands rising and pointing; among them Johnny spotted here and there the bald and grizzled pillars of his own generation, and was troubled by them for a second, and then as quickly grateful that some looked older than him. After a bit, Mark pulled him into the amorous headlock that signalled a wish to speak, and said again, 'Who are you with?' Johnny looked back, said, 'Well, I came with Graham' – and wondered as Mark's fingers slid down his arm and interlocked with his own in a warm strong grasp if there was more to this question, some faint enduring thread through the great perspective of time that seemed to open up under the glittering archway of the club. He danced for a while with his hands on Mark's shoulders, Mark holding him lightly round the waist with one arm, and smiling, at him, and over his head at Arnold, whom he reached out to with his other hand to bring him into the circle. Arnold kept his shirt on and had a nice ironical slant on the place and the people – it was hard to say if he was high himself or not. 'How long have you known Mark?' he said. 'Thirty years!' said Johnny. 'Mm, I'll have to ask him all about you,' said Arnold. Johnny said, 'How about you?' nodding at Mark, who was smiling from far away in the tunnel of pleasure, though his hand was squeezing Johnny's neck. Arnold raised three fingers, and then with one of his gracious ironical gestures lifted Mark's other hand and showed their matching gold bands side by side.

Johnny needed the toilets, asked several people, he passed Graham in the bar talking to two other men – 'Aren't you dancing?' – Graham hugged him and said, 'We'll join you in five!' In the mirror as he queued he saw himself, astonished wide-eyed figure, pink-faced, grey thatch rustic among the sharp cuts and shaven heads of the young people sliding and barging past behind him, but there was nothing he could do about it now and giving himself a sexy smile which got an 'All right?' from the friendly Chinese boy pressing in beside him, he went to a place at the trough. A few minutes later he set off again at a strange wading swagger to find his friends.

He thought he knew the way through the dense crowd that had taken over the bar and made intimate shouting colonies in every bay and niche of the underground space. There it was, for a long minute, the feared and lurking strain of loneliness – high as a lark and with no one to hold or even to talk to. It was like an ache in his arms. He waited and bought himself water, at the bar, no sign now of Graham. At the edge of the dance floor again he was moving with the music, peering casually round at people showing in flashes and shadows, as if in flowing water, barely noticing him. He couldn't see Graham or Mark at all, just overlapping bald-headed men who in the recurrent split seconds of light proved not to be them. Now a dark-haired young man was pressed against him, saying something in his ear, and they moved hand in hand into the dancing crowd, the young man stepping back to protect a space for them and make a cute little act of dancing with Johnny – he thought for a moment he was teasing him. He was lean and large-eyed, with a long nose, and a smile which only faded as he lost himself in his trance, then came back as he looked at Johnny, and hugged up close with him as they danced. The music wasn't so fast now, and around them other couples rubbed and bobbed, smiled out like nodding dogs at each other and their neighbours, all bathed in the same absurd ongoing surge of feeling. 'What's your name?' his friend said – Johnny told him and saw it slide past him like a pulse of the lights. He came back to him, hesitated as before some difficult question, and said in his ear what sounded like, 'I'm Zay,' nodding at the fact and at the music as he stepped back, holding both Johnny's hands. 'Zay . . .' said Johnny, grinning at his warmth and his grip. The boy came in close again, to clarify, paused, and said exactly what he'd said before – now he pulled Johnny's forearm out straight and wrote with his finger 'Z', trailing back down his arm till they were holding hands again. 'Z!' One or two of the people around them seemed to know Z, and made remarks to him he laughed at if he heard them or not, or they merely squeezed his arm or neck with an outreached hand and told Johnny their names and squeezed and kissed him too. 'What's your name?' – Johnny told them and saw Z listen to make sure. When they danced up close Johnny took unthinking possession of his body, in its damp black tank top, arms loose round the boy's waist, fingertips tucked in the waistband of his jeans. It was beautiful in the thick of the dance floor to feel the silky hairs in the warm cleft of his arse, and of course though Z had a phone in one front pocket and a plastic bottle in the other he felt his half-excited sideways bulge rubbing and bumping against him, though nothing sexy was said or any suggestion even made that Z was aware of his own excitement; while Johnny was too full of E and perhaps, could it be?, too old to answer him so instinctually. He wanted to kiss Z but felt even here a delicacy, a decorum, in the crowds of people he didn't know and Z did. Now the strong hand on his neck was Mark's, with Arnold, still smart in his shirt, behind him, smiling slyly and raising an eyebrow – they were still here, it was all going on, this was how they did things, there wasn't any question of anyone leaving.

Johnny pulled Z to him, he didn't want to lose him, and they all said hello, Mark moving the whole time, heavy and handsome, as he drew them in close to him and dabbed a little finger in a sachet he had, and stuck it in Johnny's smiling mouth – he was only faintly concerned to ask what it was, so bitter that he screwed up his face and Z laughed and administered water. Arnold leaned in to Johnny and said, 'Well, you're all right then!' and rocked back and carried on his minimal slightly parody dancing as Mark grinned and made up and down gestures with both hands as if fanning himself – he plucked at the bottom of Johnny's T-shirt and twitched it up over his belly, while Johnny stared at him, wriggled and resisted and found in a moment he was bare-chested, arms up, hair tugged back, and then tucking his shirt with Z's help into the belt of his jeans. The air of the fan wafting over him and the nudging oneness with all the other half-naked men was entrancing, a rebirth, he saw one or two glances drop over him curiously and peeped down at himself, not sure what he'd see, while Mark laid a strong absolving palm on his stomach. Still, Z wanted him more to himself, he didn't care so much for these new friends who were much older friends than he was – Johnny made a comic mime of being yanked away, looked back over his shoulder, and it wasn't goodbye, everyone was happy.

They were going somewhere, Z leading him off through an arch into an area he hadn't seen before . . . was this another dance floor? . . . different music, different crowd . . . he was completely at sea among the bargers and blockers, Z's hot strong hand threaded tight with his own, and squeezing tighter, a spasm of protection, he wasn't letting him go. In this room there were structures like beds laid out and though there wasn't a space Z got them in there, against the wall, where they half sat, half lay with their arms round each other. Z was saying, 'You been here before, right?' and Johnny shook his head. 'So where are you from?' he said. 'Me? Brazil!' said Z, and looked round, 'All these guys from Brazil!' 'Ah, yes . . .' said Johnny; it was great to have gone underground into another country, a Little Brazil . . . 'You been in Brazil?' Johnny shook his head again, shifted and interlocked with him more closely: 'Never been to South America.' 'You come,' said Z, 'you come with me.' 'Thank you,' said Johnny, and laughed, which perhaps offended Z – he looked serious. 'I think this guy know you,' he said, and it took Johnny a minute to understand Graham was there – 'I'm off!' he said, kneeling and leaning in to kiss him and saying in his ear, 'You're all right then!' and grasping Z's right hand with his left. Johnny had a little twinge, even so: was *Graham* all right? – the old trouper going already – there was a hint that he'd lost his friend to Z, but a much stronger hint that this was exactly what he wanted. Johnny felt the bearable embarrassment of someone who's been benignly looked after, his need acknowledged in being met. He watched Graham take the hand of a tall black man and melt with him into the shadow of the shuffling parade, and happy after all that his friend had made out Johnny curled up sideways, with Z's right leg between his own. He was having a heavenly night, and only now thought of the things that had been stopping him, and in the twinge of last year's grief, more a reflex or echo here than the thing itself, he snuggled in closer with Z and smiled into his foreign face in the inexplicable knowledge that he was his.

Z had his hand on Johnny's neck, stared almost painfully: '*I love your hair.*' 'Oh, thank you . . .' said Johnny, still allowing for teasing. He didn't know Z at all, or what he thought was funny. Z pushed his hands through it, gently but greedily – 'I *love* grey hair.' He marvelled at it, he asked with his lips to his ear: 'Is it natural?' Johnny promised him it was. He closed his eyes as they kissed, holding each other tight, lips working together with a passion that he knew in another cool but painless moment he'd rarely known the like of with Pat (the rapturous possession of the lover's mouth which the blind tongue described to the seeing mind) – perhaps he never had. When he dropped back and looked up he saw the other men round them, some watching with the tranced but unintrusive stares of the drugged at something private which flourished unexpectedly in this public place with complete security. He had his hand round Z under his little tank top and the feel of his warm skin was exquisite but still somehow not sexual. He felt he might stay in this heaven of perpetual foreplay, when Z lifted Johnny's hand and pressed it instead between his legs. 'You want to go in the toilets?'

'I'm fine, thanks,' said Johnny, stroking his neck, his thumb circling on the little rise behind his ear. But Z rubbed the captive hand against himself till Johnny with a certain bashful good manners as well as a marvellous surrender to the currents of the night scrambled up after him and they went off, a bit unsteadily at first among the crushed plastic bottles on the floor, to do some undisclosed thing in the lavs.

There was a queue, which Z cut in near the front of, behind some other Brazilians he knew, and stood introducing Johnny to the boys who were too off their faces to be much surprised or interested by him. They gabbled away in their own language. In a little defensive reflex, another passing few seconds of shyness, Johnny took out his phone, which was a puzzle to get into in his own addled state, with the mad old black queen who ran the room trailing up and down shouting, 'Hurry up! Hurry up! No fuckin in the toilets!' and banging on the closed doors, lively with voices on the other side, which opened here and there, now and then, to let two people out and another two or three in. He had two shots at entering his passcode. 'Here we go!' said Z, and Johnny went in with him, and felt a buzz in his palm – he had voicemail, and then he saw messages, which, chewing and grinning, he felt were both charming and ungraspably remote. Ivan . . . Pete G . . . Lucy had all texted him. Z pulled him forward and bolted the door against another man who was pressing to come in. Lucy had texted at 12.27, an unnoticed three hours ago. The letters were swollen and sugary and he had a sense of a joke and its warmth, though he didn't quite get it . . . David who?

'What is?' said Z, angling his head.

The weirdly cushioned shock; the unstoppable chemicals dancing and smiling in his brain as his throat closed on the need to make a decision.

'Bad news,' Johnny said, but still in the intimate, confidential way, mouth to ear, of their earlier nonsense, his hand again unthinkingly round Z's warm waist. He let Z take the phone and look at it. 'Dad SOOOOO sorry about David XXXX Thinking of u.' 'My father,' said Johnny. 'I don't know . . .' Z noticed the voicemail, put the phone up to Johnny's ear. It was a woman, and he could hear her with strange clarity, intimate but impersonal, with the roar of voices outside, the club music booming beyond and the mad old queen shouting, 'Move along! Move along! No jiggy-jiggy in the toilets!': 'Hello Jonathan. Your father's died. He was eighty-nine. I'm very sorry. I'll try you again' – a little finishing clatter, then, 'It's June, as you probably realized.' He reached out for Pat, who was leaning in an archway beyond and a little above the wild crowd of strangers; but Pat had *gone before*, he felt the phrase, a further room of the club, far deeper and darker, an infinitude of people, with only those on the near edge, just over the threshold, fleetingly distinct before they merged into the mass.

They went back into the bar, Z a little preoccupied now; but he was unexpectedly wonderful. As they waited at the coat check Johnny squinted at the other texts, Pete Grey remote good news about an exhibition, Ivan on to it as if by telepathy, *V sorry about your old man. Will call tomorrow IXX* – of course, he would be writing the *Telegraph* obituary . . . and the thought that his father would be in the papers again seemed to heighten the crisis, which he saw massing and approaching, like a squadron of planes still lightless and soundless in the depth of the night. Surely no one else knew about it yet. Then he listened to June's message again, hearing the hard reproof in it, and a sense of the future, which she, unlike Johnny, had long been giving thought to. They stumbled upstairs towards the entrance, the music from below in wafts here, through opened and closing doors, people coming in still, others going, going on, in the artificial madness of the night. From the outer doors, in front of them, the January night air, four in the morning, balm for a moment, then, as they stood confusedly, too cold for them, in their heightened warmth. The security, in black, stood around.

Z came out with him to where the taxis were. 'You like I come?' – and of course he was still off his face, he hadn't had bad news himself, and all the energy and love of the drug still filled and absorbed him. 'Oh, no – it's all right.' Z stood shivering in his T-shirt with an arm round Johnny under the greatcoat in which he stood hot and reeling and incapable as Z spoke to the security man and then the driver, not letting go of him. Then he said, 'I come with,' and went back in, while the security grew impatient and Johnny stood and watched for Z, unable to explain. In the back of the car they each had a sense of the crisis; Z sat looking ahead but holding Johnny's hand. It was the hot unhesitating grip of the night, the unconscious oneness of feeling, floating very strangely for Johnny over the knowledge that something momentous and terrible was still waiting to be felt. He felt acutely thirsty, and the driver gave him a bottle of water – an old black man whose view of the wrecks he picked up all the time from the exits of clubs was hidden by dark glasses and laconic humour. 'Had a good night, have we?' Z didn't treat the driver with much respect, and Johnny as a sixty-year-old very rarely in this world tried to show himself sober, while all Z's kindness was kept for him. 'Yeah, we get you home, yeah,' said Z.

'What a night,' said Johnny, holding Z's hand. 'Thank you.'

And there they were, fifty quid later, in the kitchen, Z wandering into the studio. And why were they here? There was nothing to do, for four or five hours, till he could talk to people. Z came back, hugged him and put his head on his shoulder and then started kissing him. But they had a cup of tea, and then a Pepsi, which Z thought helped bring you down, and then just a toke on a tiny little joint Z had in his wallet. 'I've got to go to Nuneaton tomorrow . . . today.' It was a sentence lofted weakly against the dark north light of the studio. 'My father's died,' said Johnny.

'Yeah . . . is very sad,' said Z, taking his hand. 'Sad for you.'

Johnny stared at him, sadly enough. He said, 'I'm going to have a shower,' and went up to the bathroom not sure if he wanted Z to follow him. He was very glad when he did, he pulled the curtain round, Z stepped into his arms under the wide pan of the jet, Johnny gasping as he held him in the falling water.

4

The next afternoon Johnny made the old train journey from Euston to Nuneaton, an hour and ten minutes with half a century packed into it. For years his rare visits had been made by car, but now he was in no state, sleepless, bog-eyed, ears still distantly ringing, to drive. It was like when he'd first lived in London, long before the red Cortina or the Vulva, going home by train for Christmas in Warwickshire one year, Somerset the next. Now suddenly, at last, he was an orphan; he was ambushed again by the loss of his mother, felt the hard downward drag, too familiar now, of a death close at hand, of things irrefusibly to be done. He slid down in his seat, saw his own face weary and apprehensive in the black screen of his laptop before he turned it on, the chunky positive chord, the photo of himself and Pat in Granada, framed in ripples of white stucco – another life: unknown to these hikers with backpacks on the seat, the couple who'd been up to town for a show, students plugged into smartphones, parents with kids sallying to and from the bar, none of them aware that among them was a man whose father had died last night.

He looked at new emails, no news yet, in a Google search, the story still slept, on a winter Sunday. He looked out of the window, travelling fast towards childhood, a hundred half-forgotten sights in their half-remembered sequence reeling him in, warehouse, sewage farm, rusty barn, the brick tower of an edge-of-town Tesco. And other odd evidence, exposed in the winter woods – a round pond fenced off, two blue tents, a long shed of unguessable purpose, its roof under moss and dead leaves, the tone of dead leaves over all.

He googled again, and now the *Coventry Telegraph* had it, he felt the clutch of alarm at his father's name in a headline, and scrolled in long jerks down the article, a crude cut-and-paste of all the old lumpy quotes and blown-up photos, 'David Sparsholt at the time of his trial' – it was a local story first and last. His own name appeared at the end, 'an artist, who lives in London' – he was paranoid today, but he felt the thrust of that plain provincial phrase. David and Connie's divorce was mentioned, and Johnny again had a nearly palpable sense of her presence. She'd got away, of course. She'd had a perfectly good thirty years with Barry in Bridgwater, after her life had been publicly ruined by David. She was Connie Jefferies, a new person in a way her ex-husband could never quite be, for all his industry.

And now the overgrown slagheaps had appeared, like the

steep tufted hills of a Caribbean island, exotic markers of home, and Nuneaton was announced as the next station stop.

He took a taxi from the station to the house, the driver a cheerful young Sikh whose talk at first was so beside the point of anything Johnny was doing or feeling that he entered into it gratefully and cheerfully himself. 'No, I grew up here,' he admitted; so did he have family in Nuneaton? Johnny smiled wistfully at the young man's softly bearded profile, then found he was being talked to in the mirror – their eyes met. But you couldn't land all that on a boy merely doing his job. 'My step-mother still lives here,' he said, tactful to both of them, and felt the thing close at his throat again for a moment. They turned into Weddington Avenue. 'Very good area,' said the driver. 'The last house on the left,' Johnny said, his horror of meeting June abruptly darker when he saw the firs, the brick gateposts, the light on in the sitting room. They came in at a respectful speed over the deep gravel, with a sound as if the car drew its own wash.

Did he still have a key to the house? – certainly not on him. It was the place even June called 'home' when she spoke of his coming here; but he stood with his bag in the porch and after the driver had gone he rang the bell.

June opened the door, small, perfect, no thought of smiling – he stepped in, dropped his bag, found he'd kissed her on the cheek. 'I'm so sorry,' he said. They stood and spoke stiffly in the hall, which he was keenly aware of today as hers. He sensed at once that he mustn't look at anything with curiosity or even affection, which she might misread, as irony or possessiveness. The primary impact of the drugs had long worn off, but he was still largely attuned, he saw through things and round things with intuitive speed and feeling; perhaps he saw too much. Nothing, as yet, had been said, but he assumed all this had been left to her.

The house held the strangely unexpected evidence of his father's most recent life. In the downstairs cloakroom there were rails flanking the loo, in the sitting room a hideous adjustable armchair, outsize intruder among the oak and chintz; on the coffee table a square magnifying glass. 'I've put a few bits and pieces away,' June said. A year or more's history was elided in those first tactful glances as he talked to her, and tried to find out how she was taking things. How he was taking them himself came as a rough shock, five minutes later, when he found himself staring at the photos on the windowsill: his father in uniform, the invulnerable smile of early success, not a man Johnny remembered, an ideal one, and next to him at an angle, in a silver frame, Johnny himself, in the Sixth Form, soft-faced, wary in front of the camera – he felt a pain like a thump in the throat, the corners of his mouth pulled down as fiercely as a tragic mask: he couldn't help it, though to June it perhaps looked unmanly, theatrical. She rested her fingers briefly on his forearm, then the touch was a push: 'I'll make some tea.'

Johnny stayed, recovered himself, snorted again in a bewildering access of grief, went for decency into the sunroom at the back, where he stood at the window, looking out across the lawn but seeing a brief jerky loop of his father, a momentary montage, walking, turning, smiling at him as he climbed into the parked Jensen.

June made a noise in the sitting room with the tray, and he went back to her. She looked at him with guarded curiosity, as a fellow griever who was taking it in his own way. He sat holding his cup in both hands with a sense of it as symbolic, although he was thirsty, while June ran quietly over just what had happened the day before, the shout, the fall, the ambulance. 'Do you want to see him?' she said – and it was almost like years ago, when she'd welcomed or discouraged the callers at his father's office.

It was a question, a decision, Johnny had dreaded, but he said yes straight away. 'I'll take you,' she said, 'in a minute. I won't see him again myself.' He finished his tea quickly then, and put on his coat while she got out the Golf. In six minutes they were at the hospital. She waited in the car, it wasn't expected to be a long visit. He went in, explained, was led down long hallways to a door and shown into a room that he entered as considerately as if his father were still alive. Then he was alone with him. There was a sort of calm distinction in the completely immobile face with its eyes closed. Johnny saw the formal sadness of the moment, all its cues for feeling and reflection, but felt almost nothing – it was his father's absence that had dealt him the primitive shock. This was just a dead man's face, which the light of scandal might play over as readily as that of acclaim. He thought the convention was to kiss the dead parent on the brow, but a sense that that wasn't his father's style deterred him, and he felt he wouldn't regret not having done so. He took out his pocketbook, moved the visitor's chair to the head of the bed and sat down and drew him, a rapid but careful and observant sketch, five minutes' intent work. He thought, this is what we get to do. He couldn't remember for the life of him what colour his father's eyes had been.

They both had a large drink at six, June a brandy and ginger ale which she took into the kitchen with her, to get on. Johnny carried his Scotch and soda upstairs, a new carpet on the landing, the bathroom re-decorated, a new walk-in shower installed. The return to the house was an oddly clear lesson in the history of his parents' taste, long ago, of June's restless alterations and improvements, and, still detectable, of his own taste. In his room there were pictures he'd done at school, the drawing of the Abbey which had won second prize in the Warwickshire Schools Junior Art Competition nearly half a century before.

Was he taking all this away – now, or after the funeral perhaps? Did either of them suppose he would come back to see her, or that she would want him to? 'I'm sorry, Jonathan,' June had said, on the way back from the hospital, 'I feel you'll be without an anchor' – which was a kind remark, perhaps, or a reproachful one, since he had been there so rarely. He was touched by an uncomfortable sense of duty towards her, the woman who had made his father happy, and who had always dreaded the talk among their friends coming round to what her stepson was doing – *he has a daughter, doing very well – you know he painted the Countess of Wessex – Sophie, yes – charming, apparently . . . no he's not married . . .* oh, it all came back to Dad, and the much huger embarrassment she'd shouldered already, in her blind decisive youth, in a long-sustained feat of denial: fending off reporters, pretending the wounding articles and later the books about her husband didn't exist. They'd lived together for forty-five years, and had known each other for two or three years before the crisis and divorce. She had come to dinner sometimes, when his mother was away. What he'd hated from the start, far more than the corruption case, which he'd never fully grasped, or the intimate shame of the Haxby business, was David's sequence of betrayals of Connie, begun more than seventy years ago now, with poor besotted Evert. It was in his power, it was how he got his way.

Johnny pulled out the four drawers of the chest, the bottom one had the Christmas decorations in it, but in the others he found a roll-neck jersey and folded shirts he hadn't worn since the 80s, but had left for some reason in the limbo of neglect and just possible resurrection. On the shelf above the bed there were school books, his James Bond Aston Martin with bulletproof shield and ejector seat (the ejected figure long lost), a brown-glazed pot he'd made at Hoole: things the long steady continuum of his father's life had robbed him of any desire to take away. He opened the wardrobe, a jangle of hangers, and on the top shelf among a heap of teenage daubs found a worn old sketchbook that he knew but could barely place. He sat on the bed with it, slipped off the perished elastic strap. Scrawny studies of roots, a vase of snowdrops, schoolboy stuff, a woman in a hat whom he didn't recognize. What on earth was it? Who was that . . . ? The almost forgotten holiday, in Cornwall. And there, oh god, thick, overworked, a little bulging mannequin: Bastien! Bastien, Bastien, again and again. With almost a sixth sense he knew the drawings, but the occasions when he'd made them had gone completely. They were childishly stiff, with a stroke here and there of something like talent, a mannered dash forwards. At the time they had been private triumphs, acts of magic over thwarted desire.

June made them cauliflower cheese, a supper out of the past which Johnny, his stomach shrunken and his palate dead from a night of drugs, ate what he could of. In the welcome reprieve, the sweet second chance, of the whisky and wine he saw a bright poignancy in the objects June took pride in, the glass and china, the small silver pheasants on the sideboard and the glinting silver labels round the necks of the decanters. 'Gosh, this takes me back,' he said, with a smile across the glooming mahogany of the table, where she had laid their places face to face.

'It's the best I can do in the circumstances,' June said; which might still have been awkward modesty, and not just her nose for a slight in any compliment. Later she went to the hatch and brought through two stemmed bowls of gooseberry fool, each with a brandy snap.

'Mm, lovely!' said Johnny.

June ate with a rather compromised air. 'I had the gooseberries in the freezer,' she said.

*

He yawned and signalled readiness for bed at a childish hour. 'You look tired,' said June.

'Yes – I didn't sleep very well last night.'

She looked quickly at him – 'No . . . well, an awful shock for you.'

When he got into bed he found he filled it, or it had shrunk under him, and might even shrink more. He seemed to hang on the edge of the mattress, in a kind of headlong reverse – condemned to sleep alone since Pat had died, and now to squash back into adolescence. He really was tired, he hadn't slept at all with Z, they had lain together in a sweaty parched fatigue, the news and its gravity clarifying in his mind, and the need for sex inexplicably, compellingly strong. He'd popped one of Pat's blue pills, with a new half-spooky half-comical sense of drawing on his strength whom he missed more than ever at this moment; but after a good hour of trying he'd been unable to come, though the need to do so drove him on till all pleasurable sensation had gone. Z suffered none of these senior setbacks, and came like a dream after five or six minutes. Johnny had to keep getting up to piss, and saw himself in the bathroom mirror, a grizzled old figure with the swollen belly and implacable erection of a satyr.

Now he turned on his back, and resignedly took in the late noises of the house; after London, with its endless roar just this side of silence, the stillness of the suburb was unsparing. It threw the creaks of cooling radiators, the little whine and click of the immersion heater going off, into clearer relief. The bed still made the quick nagging noise it had always made when you turned in it; the moment you thought of having a wank the news was announced to the rest of the house. The room in which June too was lying alone after decades of coupledom was far enough away for him to risk it. He wondered about Zé, which was really his name, José, and if he would see him again – he felt he would never have noticed him himself, but Zé seemed crazy about Johnny, and it was a stroke of amazing luck to have got off with someone half his age who was simply so kind. He was the opposite of Michael. Johnny reached for his phone by the bedside and thumbed in a message which magically corrected itself: *I'm in bed and thinking of you X*, and sent it with a beating heart and forgotten sense of daring. In a second the perky arpeggio, the bright screen, how could he have written so much so quickly? – *thinking of you 2 all day!! sleep well my darlin Wish I was there with u!! Cum back soon!!! XXXXZ*. The words were abnormally vivid to him, a caress and above all a promise, and he switched off the lamp, turned on his side and dropped gaping into sleep as if under a spell.

He was woken after seven by June moving about, the noise of doors downstairs, never thought of, never forgotten. A bit later he swung out of bed, and parted the curtains. In the grey dusk of the garden only frail winter jasmine made a sign of the world of colour and light. He hadn't said how long he was staying – he knew June didn't want him hanging around, but thought she might resent it if he left. The date of the funeral was yet to be fixed, and he longed to be back in London, but there was something bleak and illusionless in going away, a first clear admission they didn't need each other.

After breakfast he went out for a walk through the town, and there were things June said she needed him to get. He felt flat, colourless himself today, but lurkingly conspicuous, a returning son, who had known these streets, walls, crossroads, gable ends in the 1950s. But no one knew him, even though in Walsh's he stared smiling at the little man who slipped the loaf into the bag and twizzled the ends as he had forty years ago, but in plastic gloves now and a hairnet, the stay-at-home son turning into his old mother. Walsh's at least was there, with its yellow linoleum, its doughnuts and cream horns, and the opaque glass dish like an ashtray, where they put your change. Three or four other shops were empty, and stripped bare. Some were chain stores, burger joints, places Johnny might have hung about in, if he'd been a teenager now, looking at men. In Pinnock's tea rooms the cheap cups and saucers, CDs and high heels of a charity shop were lined up in the window, for the time being. Johnny stared in, remembering, the string curtain in the kitchen door, the steep narrow staircase to the first-floor lavatory, and Gordon Pinnock himself, one of the certain homosexuals of his own childhood, another man who'd once been in love with David Sparsholt. Gordon had retired to Madeira, twenty years ago, with one of his waiters. Johnny strolled on, with an uncanny sense of knowing this town in a thousand details, the past showing through the present, and of being on the brink of saying goodbye to it for ever.

Not wanting to go back yet he cut down Coton Road, over the Ringway and into Riversley Park – here nothing had changed but the seasons, the beds of salvias and geraniums in front of the Museum dug over for winter, but, happy and strange, the soldier back, with his startled look, gun in one hand, eyes lifted under his soft-brimmed hat: a memorial to the Boer War, stolen years ago, a local outrage, and now lovingly recast, when the Boer War was beyond memory. Johnny strolled along the landscaped curve of the river-bank. It felt a moment to think alone about time, loss and change, and the path by the water seemed a fitting invitation, with the bare scraped minimum of poetry to it . . . It had rained in the night, and there was a sheen of damp still on the tarmac, an untraceable sad glimpse out of childhood in this very spot. Fifty yards ahead of him a couple in their twenties were dawdling just where he wanted to be, the man much taller, but their arms round each other, tightly but not quite containing their energy, which broke out in quick wriggles and tuggings apart, mock fights, as if they were ten years younger. Now the man ran away a few yards, struck a pose, she drifted scornfully then rushed at him with a shriek and jumped on him and kissed him. Johnny felt a weary resentment of them, their happiness, claiming the full heterosexual allowance to carry on in public. He fell behind, and in doing so seemed more consciously to be following them. He thought about holding and kissing Zé, and Zé fucking him, and wondered if this could be it – the question turning, as he walked under the bare willows, from a warm but doubtful one about taking things further with him into a much colder one about a future without love, sex, the repeatedly chased and in his case rarely captured affair. The couple ahead were hard to get away from because they kept stopping. Johnny stopped too, with a sudden weird thought they were just like his parents sixty years ago – even, for a moment, tall good-looking man, short lively woman, that they were them. Twice she looked over her shoulder at Johnny, then said something to the man, who glanced round too. He laughed as he saw he was spoiling it for them, just as they were spoiling it for him.

When he got back to the house, June was putting her coat on and said she was going to top up the bird feeder, but Johnny insisted on doing it for her. He went out through the cold utility room, with its square pot sink where his father had washed his hands after work of all kinds, the cracked white bar of soap marbled with his dirt. When he opened the connecting door into the garage and turned on the light, there was the sleek superannuated Jaguar, heavy and silent, a dead man's car; and beyond it June's blue Golf GTi. 'I've done something I never thought I'd do,' his father had said, 'I've bought a bloody German car.' Johnny took in the remote chilled smell of oil and wood shavings from the workbench at the back where David had tinkered away his retirement mornings. On the floor in the corner, heavy, as if magnetized and movable by no one else, his large black barbell rested, and, delicately cobwebbed, the hand-weights with their stack of iron discs, used all his adult life, in staring daily sessions, until work on his arms and chest became a threat to his heart.

Johnny found a bag of birdseed on a shelf and went out through the back door. The absolute confirming greyness of the winter sky, in every direction . . . the lawn dark green with the wet, and the shaped clumps of conifers, severe and cemetery-like today, blocking off the view from the flanking houses. The bark-covered beds, the roses pruned down hard. He unhooked the green tube of the feeder, a cage within a cage, with its squirrel-proof outer guard, jiggled out its little chained lid and poured the pretty particoloured seed in a pleasing flow over the small bars which half-obstructed the entrance. The seed fell as if through time, threshed corn streaming from its chute between timbers and into the dryer at Peachey's farm. But in a moment it was full, overfull, and he tipped some out and flung it on the grass, where the squirrels could eat it to their heart's content. Then he hung the feeder back on the rustic frame his father had made and erected, with every structural safeguard, outside the kitchen window, where June could watch it and occasionally, for some rare visitor or a great congregation of coal tits or sparrows, call him through to have a look. Through he would come, just too late, and to a scowl from June that suggested his own thoughtless movements had frightened them off.

'We must talk about the funeral,' she said, when Johnny joined her again in the sitting room. She had got out three possible photos for the order of service, which might have been captioned 'War Hero', 'Criminal', 'Old Gent'.

'Did Dad say anything about it?'

It seemed that he hadn't. 'He wasn't religious, as you know,' said June.

'It's a cremation, anyway, I hope.'

443

'I'm afraid,' said June, 'he wanted to be buried' – and looked away at the sudden rush of agreement between them. 'It's in his will.'

Johnny stared at the airman photo and wished very much that the square-jawed squadron leader had given the order, when it finally came to it, for incineration. 'Well, if that's what he wants, I mean wanted.'

'And with his own father, of course.'

'Well, I suppose.' He got up and gazed out of the window at the empty quadrant of the drive. It was a strength to him to know that Pat was (illicitly, nocturnally) scattered on Eel Brook Common – even if he felt a literal-minded reluctance to walk there in the months that followed, when the frost on the grass or the wind-blown grit on the paths might hold microscopic parts of him. He still wondered, when he saw the damp chevrons of his boot soles on the floor of the porch, if in fact he wasn't treading Pat back into the house. But Dad was going down, in an armour-plated box, into the red Warwickshire earth, and would lie there stubbornly, immaculately dressed, until long after everyone who remembered him alive was dead too.

5

There seemed to be no more to do on the Miserden job, and he was keen to be shot of it; still, something kept him dabbing away. His preliminary sketches, lively and rhythmical, were pinned up in the studio, and the five individual oil studies painted at the house stood propped in their clearer and narrower promise along the wall. And there, across two easels, was the almost finished canvas. Large, expert, pointless, it seemed to Johnny, when he stood back from it. Certain passages still had the interest of his remembered work on them, but this would soon fade; the room was evoked with all the skill of a lifetime, suggestive but precise, the figures were cleverly grouped in their odd open knot as a family, with shades of doubt and humour to set off their staring self-importance. Yet the joy of construction, the magic of depiction, the bright run up the keyboard that told you suddenly it was done, all eluded him.

He suggested to Bella she might like to come by herself to take a look. And she did like that idea, with its hint of secrecy and the glamour of a studio visit. Johnny himself felt apologetic, exposed, in the place where he padded about all day; it was just the old dining room, with a dais made of pallets and a dingy velvet throne. But Bella was in TV, she knew about illusion, and there was something underlying their contract, that it was a meeting of illusionists. She came on a Sunday afternoon, about three o'clock: a white Range Rover Evoque outside, the bang of the knocker, Bella in the hall in tight jeans and trainers and a short coat of thick golden fur that Johnny peered at in a quandary of confirmation as he followed her through. In the studio the painting had its back to them, facing the window, and he watched her go round, acting just a little, for her first encounter. He tried to imagine seeing it for the first time himself, and the inescapable pressure to say, as she did, 'It's brilliant, Jonathan' – as a first position, while her eyes kept running over it into more specialized kinds of reaction, harder to know how to put into words. He knew she would want to like it, wouldn't want to let herself down, as a person with an eye, and hoped she would take its small critical notes as compliments to her intelligence, if not to her pride. He came round and joined her, as if to find out if he deserved her praise, and also to help her, and lead her interpretation of it.

'God, you've got both my boys, to the life!' Bella said.

'Oh . . . good!' said Johnny.

'And little Tallulah, look at her . . .'

She hung back about the two adults. 'Alan's jolly hard to get, I must say,' said Johnny.

'Oh . . .' said Bella, going close, perhaps sensing a chance to say *Tell me about it!* but in fact saying, 'Oh, no, I know that look very well.'

Now Johnny stood back, against the window. 'He didn't like sitting, that was the thing.'

'Well, he can't always do what he likes, can he.' She turned and looked at him. 'Oh, it's marvellous, Jonathan,' she said and ran over and gave him a kiss on the cheek and a hard fluffy hug in which he felt all sorts of other hopes and worries were buried.

'People often don't like their portrait when they see it first,' he said; 'because it's not how they see themselves, or the idea they have from photos, or just looking in the mirror.'

'Well, I like it,' said Bella, with affected stubbornness. And then, more slyly, 'I can't wait to see what the kids say.'

'Can I get you something?'

'Oh . . .' She winced, denying herself. 'Perhaps a herbal?'

Johnny listed them, till she grew confused, ginger, ginkgo, ginseng . . . 'Shall I come?' she said. But he wanted to leave her for a minute or two by herself with the portrait, in case something settled after all, some little objection.

When he came back she was standing looking out into the garden. He gave her the mug with the fluttering tag. 'I'm sorry it's taken so long,' he said.

'Oh . . .'

'The whole business of Dad's death put me out by a few weeks.'

'Oh . . . darling, of course it did,' said Bella. 'And are you all right?'

'I'm all right about him dying, really, yes.'

'Hmmm. All the other stuff, though . . . I must say I felt for you, when I saw all that.'

'I ought to be used to it by now, but it was all so long ago I'd got used to it being forgotten – and young people of course had never heard of it.'

'Well, I hardly had, you know, myself . . .' – not knowing how to place herself.

'Anyway, everyone knows now.' Bella wasn't someone to confide in, but her fame and energy drew something from him, a desire for validation. Not, of course, that he'd ever heard of her till she asked him to paint her.

'Funny, though,' she said, 'having an affair named after you.'

'It's not quite the honour it may seem,' said Johnny, not for the first time. 'It's not like a TV show, say . . .'

Bella hesitated. 'I shouldn't tell you this, it's what my Samuel calls the picture – our portrait, I mean. *The Sparsholt Affair.*'

'Oh . . . yes . . . hah.' Again this wasn't original of Samuel.

'Seriously, though,' said Bella, 'I suppose with something like that, it could colour your whole life, if you let it.'

'Well . . . I dare say everyone's whole life is coloured by something.' Given the chance, he forgot it for months on end, but could never be wholly free from requests to explain, and have feelings about it, though his cautious patter was now nearly meaningless with repetition. 'I do remember how terrible it was when it all blew up, I'd just started a new school, and I think I told you I always had problems reading.'

'You were dyslexic, darling.'

'Yeah, *thick* was the word in those days. The other kids read about it in the papers – they knew more about what Dad had been up to than I did.'

Bella nursed her mug. 'Think what they'd know now,' she said.

'Well, I suppose.'

'It scares me, what my kids can see online. Porn, and – oh

447

god, I shouldn't tell you this, I found Samuel has one of these dating apps on his phone.'

'Oh, lord!' said Johnny, and went over and looked closely at Alan Miserden's gleaming left loafer.

'It must feel strange,' said Bella a bit later, 'when you finish a big piece like this. I know I feel awful when we've wrapped a new series.'

'I always have something else on the go,' Johnny said. 'I'm never not doing a job. That's something really positive I get from my dad.'

'You're a worker,' said Bella, 'like me.' And she went off a few steps round the back of her own picture to see what else might be going on. 'Anything interesting?'

'Oh . . . well, I've been painting my daughter – I told you she's getting married next month, so I want to do it first.'

'Before you lose her – aah, darling,' said Bella.

'I hope not.'

'Can I see . . . ?'

'Well, it's not nearly finished . . .' It wasn't a good idea to show sitters other work in progress – it gave them unhelpful ideas, retrospective doubts. Yet he wanted Bella to admire this one – the sitter as much as the picture, eyes, nose, mouth worked on with extraordinary care amid the loose swirls of hair and curve of her collar. He went over to where it was propped up, not touched for a week, and covered with a cloth – he lifted it out, and she followed him to the light.

'Oh, she's a beauty, isn't she.'

'Her dad's not the best judge of that,' said Johnny.

Bella glanced at him. 'I can see her mother in her, but she's more like you.'

'Really?' This pleased him, as the picture itself did; the patient re-creation of his own daughter lent the work on the portrait a challenge and a charge of emotion quite lacking in the Miserden job.

'And you like the husband – husband-to-be?'

'Yeah, he's OK,' said Johnny, and grinned – neither of them quite knew what he meant.

'Well, thank you for sharing,' said Bella, watching as he took the canvas away. 'And what's this?' There was a danger of her getting into her stride, and Johnny said absent-mindedly,

'Which one's that . . . ? Ah, no, that's not by me.' He came over and they looked at the drawing hanging by the door into the hall, Bella with eyes narrowed, as if preparing to speak. 'It was left to me by an old friend who died a few years ago – Evert Dax?'

She half-nodded, then made a little moue: 'I don't think . . .'

'Fran knew him – in fact I first met her in his house, long ago.'

'Ah . . . yes.'

'It's by an artist called Peter Coyle, who was killed in the War, very young. I've only ever seen one other thing by him.'

'Well, it's very striking,' said Bella. 'I mean, marvellous drawing . . .' There was a little teeter on the boundary between them, what could be said about so much muscular male flesh.

'I'd been looking at this picture for years at Evert's house without guessing what it was.'

'And that is?'

Johnny paused respectfully, 'It's my father.'

Bella's head went back. 'My word, Jonathan.'

'Done when he was a student, early in the War.'

She leaned in more closely. 'No wonder he had affairs!'

Johnny didn't mind this. 'He was a handsome man,' he said.

'But he didn't want his head in the picture.'

'I suppose not – who knows?'

'You never asked him?'

Johnny's eyes ran over the ridged abdomen and sleek pectorals, familiar in chalk, in reality known differently, and remotely. 'We never talked about things like that.'

'No . . . perhaps . . . And you never painted him yourself?'
– Bella turning her gaze on him now.

'Sadly, no. We had a first sitting for a portrait about twenty years ago, but then we had a terrible row, it was impossible.'

'That's a real shame.'

'We never really knew each other,' said Johnny, 'what with everything.'

It wasn't clear from Bella's thoughtful stare if she was absorbing wisdom or about to dispense it.

When she had gone Johnny drifted back almost reluctantly into the studio, and looked at the family portrait again. The afternoon was darkening, and he switched on the big lamp – the colours leapt into gallery brilliance, and the handling seemed more exposed and temperamental. He knew Bella felt it could all have been glossier, goldener, while part of his own regret was that he hadn't been blacker and sharper. He had failed as both eulogist and satirist: it was the compromise of his trade, though at best, of course, the truth. Then the sweep of harp strings in his pocket, the upward run after all, Johnny read the words carefully and smiled.

A week later a boy came to take the Miserden family away and enshrine them in the massive gilt frame that Bella had ordered, twenty times the weight of the canvas itself – which was so long, on its light pine stretcher, that it wobbled and twisted slightly as they lifted it. He was called Eduard, a Catalan, yes from Barcelona, lean, long-faced, clear-skinned, with short dark hair that was roughed up into a sort of quiff at the front, and at his nape, as he bent forwards, tapered and graded so delicately to the neck it seemed more like nature than barbering. His white teeth and his short dark beard were together something Johnny wanted to paint, so that he was smilingly distracted in the way he looked at him doing his work. Eduard wore green boxer shorts whose rear waistband, and a crescent of brown back, were shown every time he squatted down or leant across the package once he'd laid it flat. Johnny studied the waistband for ten seconds, the word overlapping itself nonsensically at the join.

Eduard smiled and nodded at the portrait before he half-hid it, as if underwater, in bubble-wrap, then hid it wholly in a second glistening layer: 'Is Bella' – his recognition not for the work of art but for its subject, a celebrity. Millions were on first-name terms with this woman they'd never met. Johnny had a mental glimpse of the hundreds and hundreds of pictures Eduard spent his days wrapping and packing, taping and boxing, with the professional pride and personal indifference of a security guard. Well, sometimes perhaps he liked one picture more than another, but Johnny's instincts towards him were so tender and disproportionate he kept off the subject of art. It killed his interest if a man said something stupid about a picture. In a minute they angled the package out together, with quick clenches and grunts, giver and receiver, to the van. Johnny signed the manifest, and was handed the third pink under-copy, barely legible, his signature not visible at all. And then Eduard was gone, Johnny went back indoors, and stood holding and folding the piece of paper, in a room that was doubly empty, of the large expensive portrait and the priceless warm young man.

Lucy came at lunchtime, her keen-eyed commitment to keeping her engagement made clearer by the number of other things she was evidently holding off – she dealt with a string of intrusive texts, saying, 'Sorry, Daddy . . .' but sounding nearly annoyed with him for putting her in this position, on a busy day in a hectic week. 'I'm going to turn the thing off,' she said, as they went through into the studio.

'OK,' said Johnny mildly.

She sat in the chair, shook her shoulders, shutting things out. 'You don't know what it's like,' she said.

He smiled, raised his eyebrows. 'I got married once, you know.'

'True,' she said, straightening herself, her mother's prompt distance from her own careless remarks. 'You did. But not in York Minster, I think.'

Johnny squeezed out the third of the colours that made up her hair, a little duck-shit squirt on the palette. 'You're right, Chelsea Town Hall was good enough for us.'

'I think Ollie would be happy with that too,' said Lucy.

'And what about you?'

'Oh, I've come round to doing it in the grand style.'

'Indeed . . .' said Johnny, quickly abstracted as she settled, and to help her negotiate the first invisible fence of a face-to-face sitting, the unsocial staring at one another. Within a minute or two she would transmute into a subject, while to her he would be something more ambiguous, a quietly busy peeper and gazer licensed by work and practice. It was the third time he'd painted her, and the lessons for both of them changed.

'Talking of style,' she said a little later.

'Oh, yes . . . ?'

'Mummy said to ask if you've got your suit ordered.'

Johnny peered, tongue on lip, as he brought up the gilt swerve of the hair behind her right ear. She had very well looked-after hair. 'You don't want old man Steptoe marching you up the aisle.'

'Mm?'

'Or rather up the nave.'

'Aisle? – well, you would know,' she said. 'But you are going to make an extra effort, aren't you.'

'I am.'

'Top hats too.'

He clenched his jaw. 'I don't know about top hats.'

'Oh, Daddy.'

'Well, I will if your mother does.'

She laughed semi-humorously. To Johnny the hunger for a wedding, a 'society' wedding, was a mystery, people of all ages decked up in beaming submission and acclaim of a union between two young people they barely knew, everyone in disguise, though something loutish broke out now and then among the ushers and the uncles. At Chelsea he and Pat had had ten guests, both groom and groom were in their fifties, and the event was no less heartfelt for the element of irony and surprise that ran all through it.

He heard the key in the front door, and saw Lucy absorb his lack of concern, as footsteps passed down the hall and then a noise of running water came from the kitchen. 'Your cleaner,' she said.

Johnny smiled but said nothing, waited to hear what would happen next; the footsteps came back, there was a tap at the door – 'Hi' as he came in.

'Sorry . . .'

'No, come in, Zé. Zé, this is my daughter Lucy.'

'Hello,' said Lucy firmly, with a little break of her pose, and a sense of her own pleasantness in talking socially to staff. 'Zé?'

'Zé – José. How you do?'

'Well, as you can see . . .' said Lucy.

'I heard a lot about you.'

'Oh, really?'

'Johnny talk about you. You getting married.'

'Yes, that's absolutely right,' said Lucy.

Johnny looked across from the canvas at him: could he see him as Lucy saw him, without intimacy, without interest? He smiled and Zé came close for a moment, examined the picture and the sitter in rapid comparison (always a tease to the sitter), then kissed Johnny on the cheek, out of pride it seemed.

*

453

Johnny thought they might all have lunch, but she only had the ninety minutes for him today. 'Well, nice to meet you,' said Zé, going upstairs, he must have thought tactfully, to leave father and daughter alone in the hall.

'Thanks so much, dear Daddy,' said Lucy. 'See you in York!'

'Oh, darling . . .' He hugged her, lovely scent of this creature known in a way, but at once with the reasserted push of independence. They heard the door close above.

'And, you know . . . if you want to bring . . . *José.*'

Johnny nodded. 'Well, I'm sure he'd love it' – more, probably, than he would love it himself. He smiled at her.

'Let me know, you know, for the seating.' She looked him in the face, differently now, with no easel between them. 'He's rather a find.'

'Ah,' said Johnny. 'Yes, you could say that.'

He saw her off at the door, and when he looked out five minutes later she was still there, sitting in the car, talking on the phone to someone he almost certainly didn't know. Now and then she ran her hand through her hair, a gesture of self-assertion, of controlled impatience not seen but felt perhaps at the other end of the line. When she turned her head suddenly he wasn't sure if she saw him watching. He went back into the studio, capped the paint-tubes and peered with familiar yearning and dissatisfaction at the portrait, the eyes the blue-grey (he saw it at last) of her dead grandfather's, the lips, redone, still wet and workable.